Rancher's Arms

JANICE MAYNARD
CA............N

ide

Library Learning Information

To renew this item call:

0333 370 4700

(Local rate call)

or visit
www.ideastore.co.uk

Created and managed by Tower Hamlets Council

WITHDRAWN

MILLS
BOON

All rights reserved including the right of reproduction in whole or in part in any form. This edition is published by arrangement with Harlequin Books S.A.

This is a work of fiction. Names, characters, places, locations and incidents are purely fictional and bear no relationship to any real life individuals, living or dead, or to any actual places, business establishments, locations, events or incidents. Any resemblance is entirely coincidental.

This book is sold subject to the condition that it shall not, by way of trade or otherwise, be lent, resold, hired out or otherwise circulated without the prior consent of the publisher in any form of binding or cover other than that in which it is published and without a similar condition including this condition being imposed on the subsequent purchaser.

® and ™ are trademarks owned and used by the trademark owner and/or its licensee. Trademarks marked with ® are registered with the United Kingdom Patent Office and/or the Office for Harmonisation in the Internal Market and in other countries.

First Published in Great Britain 2016
By Mills & Boon, an imprint of HarperCollins*Publishers*
1 London Bridge Street, London, SE1 9GF

SAFE IN THE RANCHER'S ARMS © 2016 Harlequin Books S. A.

Stranded with the Rancher, *Sheltered by the Millionaire* and *Pregnant by the Texan* were first published in Great Britain by Harlequin (UK) Limited.

Stranded with the Rancher, © 2014 Harlequin Books S. A.
Sheltered by the Millionaire © 2014 Harlequin Books S. A.
Pregnant by the Texan © 2014 Harlequin Books S. A.

Special thanks and acknowledgement are given to Janice Maynard, Catherine Mann and Sara Orwig for their contributions to the *Safe in the Rancher's Arms* series

ISBN: 978-0-263-92094-9

05-1216

Our policy is to use papers that are natural, renewable and recyclable products and made from wood grown in sustainable forests. The logging and manufacturing processes conform to the legal environmental regulations of the country of origin.

Printed and bound in Spain
by CPI, Barcelona

STRANDED WITH THE RANCHER

BY
JANICE MAYNARD

Tower Hamlets Libraries	
91000008011551	
Askews & Holts	
AF	
THISWH	TH16001084/0012

Janice Maynard is a *USA TODAY* bestselling author who lives in beautiful East Tennessee with her husband. She holds a BA from Emory and Henry College and an MA from East Tennessee State University. In 2002 Janice left a fifteen-year career as an elementary school teacher to pursue writing full-time. Now her first love is creating sexy, character-driven, contemporary romance stories.

Janice loves to travel and enjoys using those experiences as settings for books. Hearing from readers is one of the best perks of the job!

Visit her website, www.janicemaynard.com, and follow her on Facebook and Twitter.

To police, fire and rescue personnel who rush
in during times of chaos to keep us all safe…
Thank you for what you do…

One

Drew Farrell glanced at the sky. Storm clouds roiled and twisted, setting his mood on edge. He shoved the truck's gearshift into park, jammed his Stetson on his head and strode across the road. Dust billowed with each angry step, coating his hand-tooled cowboy boots.

Deliberately, he crossed the line that separated his property from his neighbor's. Beth Andrews. His beautiful, long-legged, sexy-as-hell neighbor. After two years of butting heads with her at regular intervals, you'd think he would be immune to her considerable physical appeal.

But no. Her naturally curly blond hair and green eyes hit his libido at a weak spot. Sadly, there was no twelve-step program for men wanting women who drove them nuts.

He approached Beth's organic produce stand and ground his teeth when he saw she had multiple customers waiting. Cooling his heels, jaw clenched, he courted patience. But he wanted to lambast her with righteous indignation while his temper was hot.

Like every day recently, at least a dozen cars had parked haphazardly up and down the private lane, causing congestion and spooking Drew's prize-winning thoroughbreds in the adjoining pasture. This morning, his men had been forced to move seven horses to a grassy field on the opposite side of his property, for no other reason than because Beth had started selling pumpkins.

Pumpkins, for God's sake. The traffic she had created during the summer—selling squash and tomatoes and a dozen other vegetables—had increased tenfold since she'd put up signs all over Royal advertising fall harvest decorations. At least during the summer months the crowd was spread out. But come October first, it was as if everyone within a fifty-mile radius of Drew's ranch had decided they *had* to buy one of Beth's fat, healthy pumpkins for their porches.

As Drew waited impatiently, several of the patrons loaded up their purchases and drove away. Finally, only one woman remained—a young blonde. Very pregnant. From what Drew could tell, she had picked out the largest pumpkin she could find. Beth and the customer squatted to lift the pumpkin from its perch on a bale of hay. The big, orange orb slipped out of their hands, nearly rolling onto their feet.

Oh, good grief. Snapping out of his funk, Drew strode forward, determined to stop them before somebody got hurt. The thing must weigh forty pounds.

"Let me do that," he said, elbowing them out of the way. "One of you has a baby to consider and you, Ms. Andrews, ought to know better." The spark of surprise and irritation in Beth's eyes made him want to grin despite his surly mood. The pregnant woman's car sat only a few feet away in the handicapped parking spot. For Halloween, Beth had designated the space beside the shed with a sign and a skeleton holding a crutch. She was creative—he'd give her that.

Hefting the pumpkin with ease, he set it gently in the trunk. Fortunately, the base of the thing was pretty flat.

Given its weight, there was little chance it would roll over unless the driver made a reckless turn.

The customer smiled at him. "Thanks for your help." Unlike Beth's sunshiny curls, this woman's straight blond hair was so fair it was almost white. Her skin was pale as well. Despite her advanced pregnancy, she was thin, almost frail.

He dusted his hands on his pants. "No problem. Get someone to help you lift that thing when you get home."

"I will." She paused, one handing resting protectively on her rounded abdomen. "I always loved Halloween as a kid. I thought it would be fun this year to carve a jack-o'-lantern for my daughter and put pictures of it in her baby book."

Beth glanced at the woman's belly. "Are you due that soon?"

"No. I have another eight or nine weeks to go. But she's already a person to me. I talk to her all the time. I guess that sounds crazy."

"Not at all."

Beth's smile struck Drew as wistful. Maybe if her biological clock ticked loud enough, she'd meet some guy and move away. Then Drew could buy the land she had stolen from him. Oddly, that notion was not as appealing as it should have been.

Beth spoke up again. "Who's your master carver? The baby's dad?"

A flash of anguish darkened the woman's eyes, but it was gone so quickly Drew thought he might have imagined it. "*I'm* going to do it. I'm trained in graphic design, so this is right up my alley. I should go," she said, as if suddenly realizing that the weather was going downhill fast. "Don't want to get caught in the rain."

Drew stood shoulder to shoulder with Beth as they

watched the car disappear into the distance. "Did she look familiar to you?" he asked, frowning.

"Maybe. Why?"

"I don't know. Just an odd feeling that I might have seen her before."

At that moment, a strong gust of wind snatched the plastic banner and ripped it off the top of Beth's produce stand. The bright green lettering spelled out GREEN ACRES. Drew seldom had time to watch TV, but even *he* got the reference to the old sitcom where the wealthy Manhattan couple moved to the country and bought a farm. It was easy to imagine Beth wearing an evening gown and heels. She was tall for a woman, at least five seven. But Drew had half a dozen inches or more on her.

He helped her capture the surprisingly heavy sign and roll it up. "You might as well put it away for now," he said. "The wind is not going to die down anytime soon."

When they had stashed the sign beneath a plywood counter, Beth shook her head and stared at him. "I'd be happy to sell you a pumpkin, Drew, but somehow, I don't think that's why you're here."

The derision in her voice made it sound as if he were the most boring guy on the planet. "I decorate the ranch for fall," he said, wincing inwardly when he heard the defensive note in his voice.

"Correction. You have *people* who do that for you. It's not the same thing at all, Drew."

He'd grown accustomed to her barbs. In fact, if he were honest, he occasionally enjoyed their heated spats. Beth gave as good as she got. He liked that in a woman. Now, when he didn't shoot back immediately with a retort, she watched him with a wary gaze, her arms wrapped around her waist in a cautious posture.

The tint of her green eyes was nothing as simple as

grass or emerald. They were an unusual mix of shades, shot through with tinges of amber and gold. The color reminded him of a prize marble he'd had as a kid. He still kept the little ball of glass as a good luck charm in his dresser. Perhaps that was why he had so much trouble getting Beth out of his head. Every day when he reached in the drawer to grab a pair of socks, he saw that beautiful marble.

"Earth to Drew. If you're not buying anything, please leave."

Every time she pursed her lips in that disapproving schoolmarm fashion, he wanted to kiss her. Even when he was mad as hell. Today was no different. But today he was determined to get a few things ironed out.

Glaring at her with his best intimidating frown, he spoke firmly. "You have to relocate your produce stand. The traffic jams spook my horses, block the road and besides...." He pulled up short, about to voice something best left unsaid.

Beth's shoulder-length hair danced in the breeze, the curls swirling and tangling. It gave her a just-out-of-bed look that was not helping him in his determination to be businesslike and resolute.

"Besides what?" she asked sharply. "Spit it out."

He hesitated. But what the hell... He and Beth shared the road. She might as well know where he was coming from. "My clientele is high-end. When they come to Willowbrook Farms to drop several million dollars on a thoroughbred that might have a shot at the Triple Crown, your little set-up here gives the wrong impression. It's like having a lemonade stand on the steps of a major banking institution. Your business is frivolous, mine is not."

Beth absorbed his words with a pang of regret. Virtually everybody in town liked Drew Farrell and thought of him as a decent down-to-earth guy. He was an important member of the Texas Cattleman's Club. Membership in the TCC—an elite enclave where the wealthy ranchers of Royal met to broker deals, kick back, relax and count their millions—was a privilege and a lifelong commitment. Not that Beth really knew what went on behind those hallowed doors, but she could imagine. Which meant that Beth, who saw Drew as arrogant and self-important, was out of step with the rest of the county. For whatever reason, she and Drew were the proverbial oil and water.

But he'd just exposed the root of the matter. His lineage was impeccable. He was blue-blooded old money, while she came from near-poverty, part of a family line that was crooked on its best days.

"If the traffic is such a big deal to you, put a road in somewhere else."

"There *is* nowhere else," he said, his jaw carved in stone. "My plan two years ago was to buy this land we're standing on and put a beautiful white fence along both sides of the road. A Kentucky horse farm look, minus the bluegrass. But you stole it out from under me."

"I didn't steal anything," she said patiently, hiding her glee that for once in her life she had staged a coup. "You lowballed the guy because you thought nobody else wanted it. I merely had the good sense to make a reasonable offer. He accepted. End of story. I might point out that you're trespassing."

The wind had really kicked up now. Even so, the heat was oppressive. The sky changed colors in rapid succession…one moment angry gray, the next a sickly green.

Beth glanced toward Drew's property, feeling her skin tighten with unease. "Have you listened to a weather forecast?" she asked. It wasn't a deliberate attempt to change the subject. She was concerned. Normally, she would keep the shed open until four-thirty at least, but today she wanted to batten down the hatches and be tucked up in her cozy two-bedroom bungalow before the first raindrop fell.

In the time since she purchased the farm, she had updated the inside of the cute little house and made it her own. If Drew had bought the property, he probably would have bulldozed the place. The farmhouse was old, but Beth loved it. Not only was it a wonderful home, it was concrete proof that she had made something of her life.

She had a knack for growing things. The Texas soil was rich and fertile. She wasn't going to let a self-important billionaire push her around. Drew had been born into money, but his horse breeding enterprise had added to the coffers substantially.

Now Drew's gaze scanned the sky as well. "The radio said we have a tornado watch, but I doubt it will be too bad. We're a little bit out of the usual path for storms like that. Haven't had one in years. Even when we do, the ones that do the damage tend to happen in the spring, not the fall. I don't think you have anything to worry about."

"I hope not."

"So back to my original point," he said. "Your little enterprise here is adversely affecting my business. If we can't come to some kind of amicable solution, I'll have to involve the county planning board."

"Are you actually threatening me?" She looked at him askance.

His wording made her heart race. In some perverse way, she got a charge out of their frequent heated arguments. Despite his suborn refusal to acknowledge her right to operate her produce stand as she saw fit, she was secretly attracted to him, much against her better judgment.

Although most days she would be more than happy to wring Drew Farrell's wealthy, entitled neck, she couldn't discount the fact that he was 100 percent grade A prime beef. That probably wasn't a politically correct description, but seriously, the man was incredibly handsome. He wore his dark brown hair a little on the shaggy side. The untamed look suited him, though. And his bright blue eyes had probably been getting females into trouble since he graduated from kindergarten.

She knew he had been engaged once in his mid-twenties. Something happened to break it off, so Drew had been a free agent for the last six or seven years. He was a mover and shaker in Royal, Texas. In short, everything Beth was not.

She didn't have a chip on her shoulder about her upbringing. More like a large splinter, really. But it didn't take a genius to see that she and Drew were not at all suited. Still, it was difficult to ignore his physical appeal.

His eyes narrowed. "It's not a threat, Beth. But I'll do whatever I have to in order to protect my investments. It's worth it to me to restore peace and quiet to this road, to my life for that matter."

"So mature and staid," she mocked.

"I'm only four years older than you," he snapped.

His knowledge surprised her. "Be reasonable, Drew. I have as much right to be here as you do. True, I may be David to your Goliath. But if you remember your Sunday school lessons, that didn't end well for the giant."

"Now who's threatening whom?"

For the first time, a nuance of humor lightened his expression. But it was gone so quickly it was possible she imagined it. He was definitely spoiling for a fight. If it weren't for her splitting headache caused by the change in weather, she would be more inclined to oblige him.

She really did understand his frustration. As a horse breeder, Drew's reputation was world-renowned. He sold beautiful, competitive animals to movie stars, sheikhs, and many other eccentric wealthy patrons. Her modest organic farming operation must drive him berserk.

But why should *she* have to suffer? Her small house and a few acres of land were all she had in the world. She'd worked hard to get them.

"Plant some trees," she said. "Fast-growing ones. You really should quit harassing me. I might have to get a restraining order or something."

She was kidding, of course. But her humor fell flat. Drew was not amused. "I don't think you understand how serious I am about this. There's a road on the far side of your place. Why can't customers come to the produce stand that way?"

Hands on hips, she glared at him. "It's a cattle path, not a road. It would take thousands of dollars to improve it, and in case you haven't noticed, I'm not the one with the silver spoon in my mouth."

His gaze was stormy. "Why did you want this particular piece of land anyway?"

She shrugged, unable to fully explain the emotions that had overtaken her when she realized she could finally afford a place of her own. "It was the right size and the right price. And I fell in love with it."

"You can't run a serious business based on feelings."

"Wanna bet?" His patronizing attitude began to get on her nerves. "Why don't you tell your elite clients that I'm a sharecropper, and you're doing your good deed for the year?"

"That's not funny."

Earlier, she had picked up an inkling of humor from him. Now he looked like he would sooner murder her in her sleep than make a joke.

"I have two whole fields of pumpkins ready to sell,"

she said. "And a third bunch not far behind. I'll make enough money this month to keep my books in the black during the winter. Lucky for you, a horse is still a horse in the middle of January. But my farm will be cold and dead until spring."

"You're fighting a losing battle. In this economy, you can't hope to survive long term. And in the meantime, you're creating enormous problems for me."

Fury tightened her throat. She had struggled her entire life to make something of herself, against pretty long odds. To have Drew dismiss the fruits of her labor with such careless male superiority told her he had no clue who she really was.

"Maybe I'll fail," she said, her tone as dispassionate as she could make it. "And maybe I won't. But I'm like Scarlett O'Hara in *Gone With the Wind*. I read the book when I was thirteen. Even then, I understood what her father told her. Land is what's important. Land is the only thing that lasts."

Drew rubbed his eyes with the heels of his hands, probably to keep from strangling her. "That makes perfect sense," he said quietly, "*if* this had been in your family's possession for generations. But it's *not* Andrews land. And I freely admit that it's *not* Farrell land either. It does, however, adjoin my property, Beth."

"If you were so hell bent on having it, you should have outbid me." They squabbled frequently about her supposed infractions of the "neighbor" code, but this was the first time he'd been so visibly angry. She knew that at the heart of the matter was his desire to buy her out, though he hadn't mentioned it today. The last time he'd tried, she'd accused him of harassment.

"I'm merely asking you to see reason."

His implication that she was *un*reasonable made her

grind her teeth. "I think we'll have to agree to disagree on this one."

"Will you at least consider selling your produce somewhere in town? If you think about it, the central location could increase your customer base and it would keep the traffic off this road."

Darn him, he had a point. But she wasn't willing to cede the field yet. Her involuntary mental pun might have made her laugh if she hadn't been in the midst of a heated argument with her macho, gorgeous neighbor. "Part of the experience of coming to Green Acres is for tourists and locals to *see* the pumpkins in the field. They can take pictures to their heart's content and post them on Facebook. If they want to, they can traipse around the lot and choose their own prize. The ambience would be totally different in town."

Drew knew when to back off strategically. He had given her something to think about. For the moment. But he wasn't going to give up. Horse breeding was a long-term venture. Patience and planning and persistence made the difference. Of course, a little dollop of luck now and then didn't hurt either.

Beth was stubborn and passionate. He could respect that. "I tell you what," he said. "If you think about my suggestion and decide you could sell in bigger quantities in town, my guys will help you get set up, including all the logistics of hauling your stuff. Does that sound fair?" He paused. "You can have as much time as you need to think about it."

She tugged at a strand of hair the wind had whipped into her mouth. He couldn't help noticing her lips. They were pink and perfect. Eminently kissable. He wondered if her lip gloss was flavored. The random thought caught him off guard. He was in the midst of a serious conflict, not an intimate proposition. Though the latter had definite appeal.

Beth stared at him, her expression hard to fathom. "Do you always get what you want?" she asked quietly.

Guilt pinched hard. His life had been golden up until this point. He had a hunch Beth's had not. "It's not a sin to go after what you want," he muttered.

"Exactly," she said. "And that's what I did when I bought my home. You had a chance, but you made a poor business decision. You can't blame me for that."

Drew noticed in some unoccupied corner of his mind that the wind was no longer as wild. The air was thick and moist. Sweat trickled down his back. Beth, however, looked cool and comfortable in a navy tank top that hugged her breasts and khaki shorts that showcased her stunning legs.

What stuck in his craw was that she was right on one point. It *was* his fault that he had lost this property. If he had wanted it so badly, he should have made a generous offer and sealed the deal. Unfortunately, Drew had been in Dubai at the moment the land came on the market. His business manager, a smart, well-intentioned employee, had taken the initiative and made an offer on Drew's behalf.

No one had imagined that the small farm would attract any buyers, hence the lowball offer. Drew had been as surprised as anyone to hear he'd been outbid.

Beth touched his arm. "Look at that," she said, pointing.

He tried to ignore the spark of heat where her fingers made contact with his skin. But it was immediately replaced by a chilling sensation as he glanced upward. The clouds had settled into an ominous pattern. It looked as if someone had taken a black marker and drawn a line across the sky—parallel to the ground—about halfway between heaven and earth. Below the line everything seemed normal. But in that unusual formation above, menace lurked.

"It's a wall cloud," he said, feeling the hair on his arms stand up. "I saw one as a kid. We have to take shelter. All hell is about to break loose."

As the words left his mouth, two things happened almost simultaneously. Warning sirens far in the distance sounded their eerie wail. And a dark, perfectly-shaped funnel dropped out of the cloud.

Beth gasped. "Oh, God, Drew."

He grabbed her arm. "The storm cellar. Hurry." He didn't bother asking where it was. Everyone in this part of the country had a shelter as close as possible to an exit from their home, so that if things happened in the middle of the night, everyone could make it to safety.

They ran as if all the hounds of hell were after them. He thought about picking her up, but Beth was in great shape, and her long legs ate up the distance. Her house was a quarter of a mile away. If necessary, they could hit the ground and cover their heads, but he had a bad feeling about this storm.

Beth panted, her face red from exertion. "Are we going to make it?"

He glanced over his shoulder, nearly tripping over a root. "It's headed our way...but at an angle. We *have* to make it. Run, Beth. Faster."

The rain hit when they were still a hundred yards from the house. They were drenched to the bone instantly. It was as if some unseen hand had opened a zipper and emptied the sky. Unfortunately, the rain was the least of their worries. A roar in the distance grew louder, the sound chilling in volume.

They vaulted across the remaining distance, their feet barely touching the ground.

In tandem, they yanked at the cellar doors. The furious wind snatched Beth's side out of her hand, flinging it outward.

"Inside," Drew yelled.

Beth took one last look at the monster bearing down on them, her wide-eyed gaze panicked. But she ducked into the cellar immediately. Drew wrestled one door shut, slid partway down the ladder, and dragged the final side with him, ramming home the board that served as an anchor, threading it through two metal plates.

On the bottom was a large handle. He knew what it was for and wished he didn't. If the winds of the tornado were strong enough, the simple cellar doors would be put to the test.

The dark was menacing for a moment, but gradually his eyes adjusted. Tiny cracks let in slivers of daylight. He turned and found Beth huddled against a cinder block wall. "Come sit down," he said, taking one of her hands in his and drawing her toward the two metal folding chairs. Her fingers were icy as she resisted him.

"I don't want to sit. What are we going to do?"

The storm's fury grew louder minute by minute. He had a sick feeling that Beth's property was going to take a direct hit. Given the angle of the storm's path, it was possible that his place was in danger, too. The most he could do was pray. His crew was trained for emergencies. They would protect human life first, but they would also do everything they could to save the horses.

He ran his hands up and down Beth's arms. She was wet and cold and terrified. Not that she voiced the latter. "Take my shirt, Beth. Here." When he wrapped it around her and she didn't protest, he knew she was seriously rattled. "I'm scared, too," he said, with blunt honesty. "But we'll be okay."

The violent tornado mocked him. Debris began hitting the cellar doors. Beth cried out at one particularly loud blow. She stuffed her fist against her mouth. He put his arms around her and tucked her head against his shoulder.

For the first time, he understood the old life-flashing-before-your-eyes thing. It couldn't end like this. But he had no illusions about the security of their shelter. It was old and not very well built.

How ironic that he was trapped with the one woman who evoked such a confusing mix of emotions. Though he knew her to be tough and independent, in his arms she felt fragile and in need of his protection. He held her tightly, drawing comfort from the human contact.

Regrets choked him as he inhaled the scent of her hair. If they were going to die, he should have kissed her first.

Two

Beth clung to Drew unashamedly. He was her anchor in the storm. The very arrogance that irritated her on an almost daily basis was a plus in this situation. Drew said they were going to be okay. She chose to believe him.

Beneath her cheek she felt the steady, reassuring beat of his heart. His bare skin, lightly dusted with hair, was as warm as hers was cool. If anyone had told her twenty-four hours before that she would be standing in a dark room wrapped in Drew Farrell's arms, she would have laughed her head off. Now, she couldn't imagine letting go.

Above their heads, the winds howled and shrieked like banshees delivering a portent of doom. Time slowed down. Perhaps she should have been making contingency plans for what came next, but the only thing that seemed at all real in this horrifying nightmare was Drew's big warm body sheltering hers.

The small space was claustrophobic. It was dank and dark and smelled of raw dirt. But no matter how lacking in ambience, it felt more like a haven than a grave. At least as long as she had Drew. She couldn't bear to think about what it would have been like to survive this storm alone. For one thing, she wasn't sure she could have closed the cellar doors by herself given the strength of the winds.

How long did a tornado last?

The sound began to fill her head. Just when she thought it couldn't get any louder, it did. She was stunned when Drew released her. He shouted something at her. It took him three tries to make her understand.

"The hinges," he yelled. "They're old. I don't think they're going to hold. Put your arms around my waist and hang on to my belt." She stumbled toward him as he grabbed the handle on the base of the cellar doors and prepared to battle the mighty winds. The thought of Drew getting sucked away from her was more terrifying than the tornado itself. She flung herself against his back, circling his waist with her arms and wrapping her fingers around his belt.

She could actually feel the winds pulling at him. Closing her eyes, she prayed.

Drew was not going to let this son of a bitch win. He'd deal with whatever aftermath they had to sift through. But he and Beth were going to make it. The vicious noise was no longer merely above them. It raged and swelled and battered itself into their small shelter. Beth pressed against him, adding her weight to his.

His fingers were numb already. His grip on the handle weakened as his arms strained to hold on. The pain in his shoulders radiated through his torso into his gut, leaving him breathless. For a split second, one mighty gust ripped at the fragile barrier, actually lifting his feet a couple of inches off the ground.

Despair shredded his determination. His grip was slipping. Life couldn't end like this. If the storm won they would be sucked into oblivion.

It was Beth who saved him, Beth who shored up his will. Even without speaking, she was with him. Fighting. He focused on the sensation of her warm body wrapped around his. Blocking his mind to the pain, he concentrated on her and only her. She held him like a lover. A woman who never wanted to let go.

An enormous crash sent tiny bits of debris filtering through the cracks above them. He heard Beth cry out. The fury of the wind was terrifying. Like some apocalyptic beast locked in struggle with a foe, the tornado did its mad dance.

In a second wave of terror, hail pelted their hiding place. The sound echoed like a million gunshots. He couldn't have heard Beth's voice now even if she *tried* to speak. Pieces of ice big enough to make such a racket would decimate her crops and ruin roofs and property.

The storm crescendoed for long, agonizing minutes. Hail changed to the steadier, quieter deluge of rain. And then it was over. The pressure on the cellar door vanished abruptly, causing him to stagger.

Beth's finger's dug into his waist. In the growing silence as the storm moved away, he could hear her rapid breathing. His own pulse racketed at an alarming rate, helped along by the surge of adrenaline that had stayed with him when he needed it.

He flexed his fingers, forcing them to uncurl. Dropping his arms to his sides, he groaned. "Are you okay?"

He had to *make* her release him. Holding her shoulders, he shook her gently. "It's over, Beth. We made it."

For some reason, it was darker now. Virtually no light found its way into their bolt-hole. He could barely make out her face. "We have supplies," she said, her voice shaky but clear. "I saw a metal box on the floor when we climbed down."

Releasing her reluctantly, he felt around in the darkness until he found the chest. It wasn't locked. Lifting the lid, he located flashlights and handed her one. The illumination they provided enabled him to see her expression. She appeared stunned, perhaps in shock. He didn't feel too steady, himself, for that matter.

Grabbing a couple of water bottles, he pulled her toward the chairs and sat beside her. "Take a minute," he said. "Breathe."

"How do we know it's safe to go out? What if there's another one?"

"I'll check the radar." He pulled his phone from his pocket, touched a couple of icons, and cursed.

"What's wrong?"

"The cell towers must be out. No service at all. We'll give it a few minutes and then see what things are like up top. If we hear the sirens again, we can always come back down here."

"What time is it?"

It was oddly surreal to be asked that question. He honestly had no idea how long they had been in the cellar. It felt like hours. When he checked the illuminated dial of his watch, he shook his head. "It's only four thirty."

"That can't be right."

"Drink some water. Let's catch our breath." Honest to God, he was in no real hurry to survey the damage. He'd seen enough news footage in the past to know what a monster tornado could do. Tuscaloosa, Alabama, Moore, Oklahoma, small towns in Tennessee. Hopefully, Royal's storm hadn't been that bad.

He wasn't counting on it, though. The winds they had heard and *felt* carried the force of destruction. Which meant lots of structural damage, but hopefully, no loss of life.

Beth set her bottle on the floor. She had barely drained an inch. "I can't stay down here anymore. I want to know what happened."

"You realize this isn't going to be a walk in the park." They stood facing each other. He took her hands in his. "We'll deal with whatever it is. We're neighbors. Neighbors help each other."

"Thank you, Drew." She squeezed his fingers and released them. "I can handle it. But not knowing is worse."

"Fair enough. Let's get out of here."

Surviving a ferocious tornado was the most terrifying experience of Beth's life. Right up until the moment she realized they were trapped in an eight by eight storm cellar. Her skin crawled at the thought of being buried alive.

Drew had managed to remove the piece of wood that served as a locking mechanism for the cellar doors, but they wouldn't budge. Something heavy lay against them. Shining a beam of light on her cell mate, she saw the muscles in his arms and torso flex and strain as he tried to dislodge whatever was blocking their escape route.

She turned off the flashlight despite the false sense of security it afforded. Drew was balanced on a step, the awkward position making his job even harder. "Can I help push?" she asked, proud of the calm she projected. The fact that it was entirely false seemed immaterial.

"I don't know if we can both fit on the step, but sure. It can't hurt."

He extended his arm and helped her balance beside him. Bracing themselves, they shoved in tandem against the unforgiving wood. Beth's foot slipped, and she nearly tumbled backward. "Sorry," she muttered.

Drew beat his fist against the doors. "Damn it, this is pointless. It won't budge. Whatever is up there has us pinned down for good. I'm sorry, Beth."

She could do one of two things—indulge in a full-blown panic attack...or convince Drew that she was a calm, rational, capable woman. "No apologies necessary. I'm sure someone will find us. Eventually." *When the roads are cleared and when at least one person remembers that Drew came to Green Acres this afternoon.* She cleared her throat. "Did you happen to mention to anyone at the ranch that you were coming over here to read me the riot act?" *Please say yes, please say yes, please say yes.*

"No." He helped her down to the floor and began to pace. It wasn't much of an exercise since his long legs ate up the space in two strides. "Will your family check up on you?"

"We're not close," she said, choosing not to go into detail. No need for him to see the seedy underbelly of her upbringing. Despite Drew's cell phone experience, she pulled hers out of the pocket of her shorts and tried to make a call. No bars…not even one.

Drew saw what she was doing. "Try a text," he said. "Sometimes those will go through even with no signal."

She stared at the screen glumly, holding up the phone so he could see. "It says *not delivered.*"

"Well, hell."

Her sentiments exactly. "I wish I had eaten lunch."

"Concentrate on something else," he urged. "We don't want to dig into the food supply unless it's absolutely necessary."

What he *wasn't* saying was that they could be trapped for days.

Beth refused to contemplate the implications. The storm cellar was equipped with a small, portable hospital commode tucked in the far corner. Things would have to get pretty bad before she could imagine using the john in front of Drew Farrell. *Oh, Lordy.*

Now all she could think about was waterfalls and babbling brooks and the state of her bladder.

Drew sat down beside her. They had both extinguished their flashlights to save the batteries. She gazed at her phone, feeling its solid weight in her hand as a lifeline. "I suppose we should turn these off."

"Yeah. We need to preserve as much charge as we can. We'll check one or the other on the hour in case service is restored."

"But you don't think it's likely."

"No."

In the semidarkness, soon to get even more inky black when the sun went down, she couldn't see much of him at all. But their chairs were close. She was certain she could feel the heat radiating from his body. "I feel so helpless," she said, unable to mask the quiver in her voice.

"So do I." The tone in his voice was weary, but resigned. It must be unusual for a man who was the undisputed boss of his domain to be bested by an act of nature.

"At least we know someone at the ranch will realize you're missing," she said. "You're an important man."

"I don't know about that, but my brother, Jed, is visiting from Dallas. He'll be looking for me."

She wanted to touch him, to feel that tangible reassurance that she was not alone. But she and Drew did not have that kind of relationship. Even without the filter of social convention, they were simply two people trapped in an untenable situation.

His voice rumbled in her ear. "Why don't we call a truce? Until we get rescued. I've lost the urge to yell at you for the moment."

"Please don't be nice to me now," she begged, her anxiety level rising.

"Why not?"

"Because it means you think we're going to die entombed in the ground."

He shifted on his chair, making the metal creak. "Of course we're not going to die. At the very worst we might have to spend a week or more in here. In which case we'd run out of food and water. We'd be miserable, but we wouldn't die."

"Don't sugarcoat it, Farrell." His analytical summation of their predicament was in no way reassuring.

The dark began to close in on her. Even with Drew at her side, her stomach jumped and pitched with nerves. "I need a distraction," she blurted out. "Tell me an embarrassing story about your past that no one knows."

"That sounds dangerous."

"Not at all. What happens in the storm cellar stays in the storm cellar. You can trust me."

His muffled snort of laughter comforted her in some odd way. She enjoyed this softer side of him. When he stood to pace again, she missed his closeness. His scent clung to the shirt he had given her, so she pulled it more tightly around her in the absence of its owner and waited for him to speak.

Drew was worried. Really worried. Not about his and Beth's situation. He'd leveled with her on that score. But what had his stomach in knots was the bigger picture. He should be out there helping with recovery efforts. To sit idly by—while who knows what tragedy unfolded in Royal and the surrounding environs—made him antsy. He was not a man accustomed to waiting.

He made things happen. *He* controlled his destiny. It was humbling to realize that one random roll of the dice, weather-wise, had completely upended his natural behavior. All he could do at the moment was to reassure Beth and to make sure she was okay. Not that he regarded such responsibility as insignificant. He felt a visceral need to protect her. But he also realized that Beth was a strong woman. If they ever got out of here, she would be right by his side helping where she could. He knew her at least that well.

Her random request was not a bad way to pass the time. He cast back through his memories, knowing there was at least one painful spot worth sharing. The anonymity of the dark made it seem easier.

"I was engaged once," he said.

"Good grief, Drew. I know that. Everyone knows that."

"Okay. Then how about the time I took my dad's car out for a joyride when I was ten years old, smoked a cigar and got sick all over his cream leather upholstery?"

"And you lived to tell the tale?"

"Nobody ever knew. My brother helped me clean up the mess, and I put the car back in its spot before Mom and Dad woke up."

"Are your parents still living?"

"Yes. Why?" he asked, suddenly suspicious. "Are you going to complain to them about their hard-assed son?"

"Don't tempt me. And for the record, my secret is not nearly as colorful. One day when I was nine years old I took money out of my mother's billfold and bought a loaf of bread so I could fix lunch to take to school."

"Seriously?" he asked, wondering if she was deliberately trying to tug at his heartstrings.

Without answering, she stood and went to the ladder, peering up at their prison door. "I don't hear anything at all," she said. "What if we have to spend the night here? I don't want to sleep on the concrete floor. And I'm hungry, dammit."

He heard the moment she cracked. Her quiet sobs raked him with guilt. He'd upset her with his snide comment, and now he had to fix things. Jumping to his feet, he took her in his arms and shushed her. "I'm sorry. I was being a jerk. Tell me the rest."

"No. I don't want to. All I want is to get out of this stupid hole in the ground." Residual fear and tension made her implode.

He let her cry it out, surmising that the tears were healthy. This afternoon had been scary as hell, and to make things worse, they had no clue if help was on the way and no means of communication.

Beth felt good in his arms. Though he usually had the urge to argue with her, this was better. Her hair was still wet, the natural curls alive and thick with vitality. Though he had felt the pull of sexual attraction between them before, he had never acted on it. Now, trapped in the dark with nothing to do, he wondered what would happen if he kissed her.

Wondering led to fantasizing which led to action. Tangling his fingers in the hair at her nape, he tugged back her head and looked at her, wishing he could see her expression. "Better now?" The crying was over except for the occasional hitching breath.

"Yes." He felt her nod.

"I want to kiss you, Beth. But you can say no."

She lifted her shoulders and let them fall. "You saved my life. I suppose a kiss is in order."

He frowned. "We saved *each other's* lives," he said firmly. "I'm not interested in kisses as legal tender."

"Oh, just do it," she said, the words sharp instead of romantic. "We've both thought about this over the last two years. Don't deny it."

He brushed the pad of his thumb over her lower lip. "I wasn't planning to."

When their lips touched, something spectacular happened. Not the pageantry and flourish of fireworks, but something sweeter, softer, infinitely more beautiful. Time stood still. Not as it had in the frantic fury of the storm, but with a hushed anticipation that made him hard as his heart bounced in his chest.

Beth put her arms around his neck and kissed him back. Never in his wildest dreams had he imagined connecting with her at this level in the midst of a dark, dismal, cellar. Women deserved soft sheets and candlelight and sophisticated wooing.

There was, however, something to be said for primeval bonding in life-and-death situations. He was so damned glad he had been with her. In truth, he didn't know if she could have managed to lock herself in the cellar on her own. And if the hinges hadn't held…. It made him ill to think of what might have happened to her.

"Beth?"

"Hmm?" The tone in her voice made him hungry for something that was definitely not on the menu at this moment.

"We need to stop."

"Why? I enjoy kissing you. Who knew?"

He swallowed against a tight throat. "You're doing something to me that won't be entirely comfortable given our situation." Gently pushing his hips against hers, he let her feel the extent of his arousal.

Beth jerked out of his arms so quickly it was a wonder they didn't both end up on the floor. Her voice escalated an octave. "You don't even like me."

Three

Beth was mortified…and aroused…and exhausted from their ordeal. And aroused. Did she say that out loud? Fantasizing about kissing Drew Farrell was nothing like the real deal. For one thing, he was far gentler with her than she'd imagined he'd be. Almost as if he expected her to be afraid of him. Fat chance. She'd been dreaming about this moment for months.

But why did it have to happen in such incredibly drab and dreadful surroundings? As truly thankful and grateful as she was to be alive, getting out of this cheerless hole was fast becoming a necessity. She was pretty tough. Not only that, she had beaten some pretty tough odds to make it as far in life as she had. But claustrophobia and fear of the dark were gaining the upper hand. Even hanky-panky with Drew was not quite enough to steady her nerves when she felt the walls closing in.

She decided to ignore his *situation*. He'd been right to call a halt to their exploratory madness. Such impulsive actions would only embarrass them both after they were rescued.

When she sat down again, her legs weak, Drew resumed his pacing. If sexual energy had an aura, she was pretty sure the two of them could have lit up their confined cell without ever using a flashlight.

Silence reigned after that. With her phone turned off, she had no way to check the time. She didn't want to ask Drew. So she sat.

The chair grew harder. The air grew damper. Far in the distance, she thought she heard the wail of sirens. Not another tornado alarm, but a medical vehicle this time. Now, she could no longer pretend that she and Drew were a couple enjoying an innocent kiss. What waited for them above was terrifying. She had no clue what to expect, and she was pretty sure she didn't want to know.

After a half hour passed in dead quiet, she heard him sigh heavily. He reclaimed his spot beside her, scooting his chair a few inches away from hers. She didn't waste time being offended. It was survival of the fittest at this moment. Sexual insanity would only exacerbate matters.

When he finally spoke, she jumped.

"Did you really steal money to buy bread?"

Drew wasn't sure why he wanted to know. But he did.

After a very long pause, Beth finally spoke. "Yes. My mother was not very responsible when it came to things like that. I often had to fake her signature on permission slips for my brother and me. Most kids learn to count money in kindergarten and first grade because it's part of the curriculum. I learned out of necessity."

Drew sat in silence absorbing the spare details of Beth's story. Contrasting her early life with the way he had grown up made him wince at his good fortune.

He knew instinctively that she wouldn't want his sympathy. So instead, he focused on that kiss. Beth had been eager and responsive and fully in the moment. He adjusted his jeans, groaning inwardly. The last thing he needed right now was to acknowledge an attraction that had been growing for two years. Beth was beautiful and smart and capable. Of course, he was drawn to her. But that didn't mean he had to be stupid. His sole focus at the moment needed to be making sure he and Beth could manage until help arrived.

Her quiet voice startled him. "Will you check the time, please? And see if cell service is back up."

"Sure." He hit the dial on his watch. "Nine o'clock." He turned on his phone, waited, and winced when he saw the battery at sixty-eight percent. "Still nothing."

Sitting was no longer an option. His muscles twitched with the need to do something…anything. He went to the cellar doors and tried again to push upward. Whatever was holding them in place might as well have been an elephant. He and Beth were never going to be able to get out on their own.

Leaning his hip against the ladder, he admitted the truth. "We might as well accept the fact that we're going to be here overnight. It's dark up top. There are probably power lines down and roads that are blocked. Search and rescue will have a wide area to cover, and they may not get to us until morning."

"If then."

He let that one pass. "I think it's time to eat something." Rummaging in the footlocker, he found a small metal tin full of beef jerky. He removed a couple pieces and handed one to Beth. *"Bon appétit."*

She didn't say anything, but he heard the rustle of plastic packaging as she opened the snack.

There were two more box-shaped flashlights in the footlocker. If he wanted to, he could turn on one of the smaller ones they were already using to illuminate their living space—until the juice ran out. But on the off chance their incarceration lasted longer than twenty-four hours or more, it made sense to preserve the batteries.

He rummaged a second time and handed Beth a bottle of water. "Drink only half if you can. We need to hope for the best and plan for the worst."

"If we ever get out of here, I'll put that on a T-shirt for you. *The wisdom of Drew Farrell*."

"Are you making fun of me?"

"Not at all. Merely trying to stave off feminine hysteria."

He grinned in the darkness, chewing the jerky and swallowing it with a grimace. "You're about the least hysterical woman I've ever met."

"I have my moments."

"Not that I've seen. I admire you, Beth, despite my grousing."

"There you go again…being nice. It creeps me out."

"That's because you've only seen one side of me. I can actually be quite a gentleman when I choose. Case in point, I promise not to have my wicked way with you while we sleep tonight."

She laughed out loud. "I don't think I can get down on this floor unless we turn on a light and check for spiders and other nasty stuff."

The husky feminine amusement in her voice made him happy. At least he'd distracted her for a moment. "That's doable. I came across one of those reflective silver space blankets in the trunk. I thought we could spread that on the ground. It won't make us any more comfortable, but at least it will be clean. I'll sit up and lean against the wall. You can put your head in my lap for a pillow."

"You can't sleep sitting up. Either we both lie down, or we perch on these folding chairs until we fall over."

"Stubborn woman."

"Definitely the pot calling the kettle black."

"Are you tired?"

"I don't really know. All my synapses are fried. Sheer terror will do that to you."

She was right. The adrenaline had flowed hot and heavy this afternoon. "I'm betting if we keep still long enough we might be able to sleep. We'll need rest to handle whatever happens tomorrow."

He heard rather than saw her stand up. When her hand touched his arm, he realized that she had come to him…. one human seeking comfort from another. "It's going to be bad, isn't it?"

He nodded, squeezing her hand briefly. "Yeah. Wind strong enough to lift whatever is on top of us will have done a hell of a lot of damage."

Her sigh was audible. "Let's get settled for the night, then. The sooner we sleep, the sooner morning will come."

Beth wanted to weep with joy when Drew turned on one of the flashlights so they could construct their makeshift bed. Being able to see his face gave her a shot of confidence and relief. Everything in Royal might have changed, but Drew was still Drew. His features were drawn and tired, though. She could only imagine what *she* looked like. It was probably a good thing she didn't have a mirror. Her hair felt like a rat's nest.

Thankfully, the cellar was not as bad as she'd imagined. Drew checked every corner and cranny, killing a couple of spiders, but nothing major. By the time they had spread the silver blanket on the floor, she was more than ready to close her eyes.

But first, she had to deal with something that couldn't wait. "Drew…I…." Her face flamed.

He was quick on the uptake. "We'll both use the facilities." He went to the ladder and stood with his back to her, beaming the flashlight toward the cellar doors, diffusing the illumination so that she could see but not feel exposed.

Beth did what had to be done and swapped places with him. In hindsight, it was not nearly as embarrassing as she had expected. She and Drew were survivors in a bad situation. No point in being prissy or overly modest.

At last, they were ready to court sleep. She knelt awkwardly, wincing when the concrete floor abraded her knees through the thin barrier that was their only comfort. She curled onto her side, facing the wall.

Drew joined her, facing the same direction, but leaving a safe distance between them. "All set?" he asked.

"Yes. But I should give you your shirt. You'll get cold."

"I'm fine." He sighed, a deep, ragged exhale that could have meant anything. "I'm turning off the light now."

Her stomach clenched. "Okay."

This time the darkness was even worse after she'd been able to see for the last half hour. Her eyes stung with tears she would not let fall. She was okay. Drew was okay. That was all that mattered.

Her heart thundered too rapidly for sleep. And she couldn't regulate her breathing. She trembled all over—delayed reaction probably.

Drew's arms came around her, dragging her against him, his hands settling below her breasts. "Relax, Beth. Things will look better in the morning."

The feel of his warm chest against her back kept her sane—that and his careful embrace. Her head rested on his arm. It must have been painful for him, but he didn't voice a single complaint.

"Thank you," she whispered.

"Go to sleep."

For Drew, the night was a million hours long. He barely slept—and then only in snatches. His gritty eyes and aching body reminded him that he wasn't a kid anymore. But even a teenager would have trouble relaxing on a bare cement floor. To take his mind off the physical discomfort, he concentrated on Beth.

It took her a half hour to fall asleep. He knew, because he kept sneaking peeks at his watch. Her body had been tense in his embrace, either from the miserable sleeping arrangements, or because she was uneasy about their inescapable physical intimacy. Or perhaps both.

Either way, she finally succumbed to exhaustion.

He liked holding her. As he tucked a swath of hair behind her ear, he inhaled the faint scent of her shampoo. Apple maybe…or some other fruity smell. In the dark, his senses were magnified. The curl he wrapped around his finger was soft and springy and damp. He allowed himself for one indulgent moment to imagine Beth's beautiful hair tumbling across his chest as they made love.

The image took his breath away. All these months of verbal sparring had hidden a disturbing truth. He was hungry for Beth Andrews—totally captivated by her spunky charm—and physically drawn to her sexy body.

If he hadn't been in pain, and if every one of his muscles weren't drained from battling a tornado, he would have been more than a little aroused. As it was, his body reacted. But only for a short moment. He closed his eyes and prayed for oblivion.

Beth woke up with a sensation of doom she couldn't shake. It was only after she opened her eyes that she remembered why. Her concrete prison was still intact with no way out.

Despite the circumstances, it wasn't the worst *morning after* she'd ever experienced. Far from it. Drew's right arm lay heavy across her waist. His right hand cupped her breast. Even though his gentle snore reassured her that he was still asleep, she blushed from her toes to her hairline. Until yesterday, Drew Farrell had been nothing more than her annoying, arrogant neighbor.

Except for the fact that he was incredibly gorgeous, masculine and sexy, she had been able to ignore him and his continuing dissatisfaction with her thriving business. But now, in one brief stormy adventure, they had been thrust together in a pressure cooker. No longer were they merely bickering acquaintances.

For better or for worse, they were comrades in arms. Friends.

It was difficult to sleep with someone, even fully clothed, and not experience a sense of intimacy. Not necessarily sexual intimacy, though that was certainly a real possibility when it came to her feelings for Drew.

But they shared another equally real type of closeness. They had stared death in the face.

Even now the words sounded too dramatic. But when she remembered looking over her shoulder and seeing the monster storm barreling toward them with ferocity, something inside her shivered with dread. Disaster had come close enough to breathe down their necks. They had escaped with their lives, but they weren't out of the woods yet.

It was probably still early. Whatever landed on them during the tornado had darkened most of the tiny holes in the cellar doors that let in light. But the few that were left filtered the faint glow of dawn.

She felt no real urgency to move. Though her hip ached where it had spent the better part of the night battling with the unforgiving floor, she was surprisingly content. Being held close in Drew's warm, comforting embrace was better than a tranquilizer. His big body was hard and muscular, reminding her without words that she was under the protection of a confident, capable male.

There was something to be said for primitive responses. Though Beth could hold her own in most situations, the fact remained that Drew was larger and stronger and more equipped to deal with the physical challenges of their crisis.

She let her mind wander. How badly had her farm been damaged? What about Drew's horses? And the town of Royal? Had it avoided a direct hit? Thankfully, the storm had struck late enough in the day that most children would have already been home from school. But businesses in town would still have been open.

The not knowing drove her crazy. Even so, worrying accomplished nothing. She had no other choice but to live in the moment.

Closing her eyes, she savored the unfamiliar sensation of her cheek resting on Drew's arm. The light covering of masculine hair tickled her nose. His scent was so familiar to her now that she could pick him out of a crowd in a dark room.

He must be very uncomfortable. But there was no reason to wake him. Had he thought it odd to hold her like this?

They had been adversaries from the beginning. It seemed he was always rubbing his good fortune in her face. Though perhaps she was too sensitive on that score, because most people thought he was a great guy. In fact, the only person she knew in Maverick County who ever got crossways with the owner of Willowbrook Farms was Beth Andrews.

Their feud had gone on a long time, probably because they were too much alike. Both stubborn. Both sure they were right.

He muttered in his sleep, tightening his grasp, his fingers brushing her nipple though three thin layers: his shirt, her tank top, and a lacy bra. Was he dreaming about a woman?

Unbidden, arousal stirred in Beth's veins. It was sweet and yearning and ultimately for naught. Nothing was going to happen. The time and place were wrong. More importantly, she and Drew had to hope that rescue was on the way and that whatever they discovered above ground was not going to be too terrible.

She felt his steady breathing ruffle the hair at her nape. Had he thought about kissing her there? Or had he been too wiped out to even notice she was a woman? How sad that their first opportunity to really get to know each other was fraught with difficulty and struggle.

Being Drew's neighbor had been a pain in the ass until today. His repeated bluster about the problems her business caused his had added to the stress of getting the farm up and running. In the midst of his frequent complaints, she had been busy tending to her fledgling crops, learning new things she needed to know and trying to keep the checkbook in the black.

Now, there would be no going back. What would this new awareness mean to their ongoing battle?

Sometime later she realized that she must have dozed off again. One of her legs was trapped between Drew's thighs. It was as if his body was trying to stake a claim. She knew she should wake him, if only to let him move his arm. But this moment was pleasurable despite the context.

Once they were officially awake and alert, they would have to face things like a tiny water supply, dwindling stores of food, and the reality that no one knew where they were. All the harsh realities that defined them at the moment.

Given that truth, she closed her eyes and drifted back to sleep.

* * *

When Drew woke up, he stifled a groan. His body was one big throbbing toothache, and he wasn't at all sure he would be able to stand. But having Beth tucked up against him was a bonus. Carefully, he eased his arm out from under her head, wincing as the blood returned. Beth muttered and frowned when her cheek came to rest on the unsympathetic ground.

He checked his watch. Seven thirty. Surely late enough for police and rescue personnel to begin going house to house. Rolling to his feet, he tried to ignore the sudden craving for eggs and bacon and hot coffee. Sadly, beef jerky was on the menu again. But not until Beth joined him.

Standing on the ladder, he turned on his phone and held it as close as he could to the cellar doors, praying for a signal. Still nothing…not that he really expected an overnight miracle. The storm had probably destroyed numerous cell towers.

He heard Beth sit up. "Any change?" she asked.

He wanted to be able to give her good news, but there was none. "No. You okay?" She was nothing more than a dim outline in the gloom.

"I've been better."

"We have to eat and drink something. If this drags on, we'll need to keep our energy up." He hopped down from his perch and located more beef jerky and water. "Welcome to breakfast, *Survivor*-style."

"Thanks. I think."

He joined her on the floor, their knees touching as they sat cross-legged on the crinkly blanket. "Somehow, during all those years in the Boy Scouts, I never imagined this scenario."

"Did you make it all the way to Eagle?"

"Yeah. My dad was a stickler for never giving up on anything."

"Ah, now I get it," she said. "That's why you continue to browbeat me."

"Eat your breakfast, woman."

If he had to be trapped in a hole in the ground, Beth was the perfect companion. She hadn't whined. She hadn't panicked. Her sense of humor had survived the tornado intact even though she had to know, as he did, that things would probably get worse before they got better.

Holding her as they slept last night tapped into more than his human need to cheat death. With all the societal expectations stripped away, he discovered something deeper than physical attraction. Beth Andrews had edged her way into his heart.

That information was sensitive—need-to-know basis only. But it was something to be tucked away and savored at a later date.

"Seriously, Drew. What are we going to do to pass the time? If we can't use our flashlights, our options are seriously limited."

Several inappropriate suggestions came to mind immediately. But he squelched the impulse to voice them. "We can try lifting the doors again."

"And that will take all of ten minutes."

"Sarcasm, Beth? I thought we'd reached a détente."

A faint noise from above interrupted her answer. He put a hand on her knee. "Shh…did you hear that?"

Four

They both froze, their ears straining in the darkness. Next came the screech of metal, followed by a muffled shout. "Anybody down there?"

Drew leapt to his feet, dragging Beth with him. "Yes," he shouted. "Yes."

Beth was trembling. Hell, he probably was, too. He wrapped his arm around her narrow waist and she curled her arms around him. Together, they faced the specter of uncertainty.

They waited for what seemed like forever but might only have been a minute or two. Thumps and curses rained down on them, along with dust particles that made them cough. The voice came again, louder this time. "Hang on."

Beth leaned into him. "What's taking so long?"

"I think they're trying to move whatever has the doors stuck. It must be big."

She murmured something under her breath.

"What?" he asked, still straining to hear what was going on up top.

"I hope the doors don't break and whatever that is doesn't fall and crush us in this pit."

He chuckled, despite the tension gripping him. "An active imagination can be a curse at times."

"Tell me about it."

They fell silent again. All the commotion above them had ceased. Surely the rescue team had heard him shout.

Beth voiced his concern. "What if they didn't hear you? What if they went away?"

"I don't think they would give up without making sure no one is down here…even if they *didn't* hear me."

But doubt began to creep in. Why was nothing happening?

Beth burrowed her face into his chest. He held her close. "Don't freak out. If they left, they'll come back." *God, I hope so.*

He checked his watch. "It's almost nine."

"What time did we hear the first shout?" The words were muffled.

"I'm not sure. Maybe ten minutes ago? Fifteen?"

The return of absolute silence was infinitely more difficult than if they had never received a ray of hope.

Beth was shaking.

He rubbed her back. "Hang on. We've made it this far."

Suddenly, the loud racket returned, a shrill high-pitched noise that might have been a winch. Then a dreadful dragging scrape, and finally a human shout.

Seconds later the cellar doors were flung wide. The brilliant sunlight, after hours of captivity, blinded them.

A figure crouched at the opening. "Ms. Andrews? Are you down there?"

Drew shielded his eyes with his arm. "She is. And me, too. Is that you, Jed?"

The minutes that followed were chaos. Drew boosted Beth up the ladder, passing her up to helping hands, and then followed her. He grabbed his brother in a bear hug. "God, I'm so glad to see you."

Jed's face was grim. "You scared the hell out of me. No one had any idea where you were." Two EMTs muscled in, checking Drew's and Beth's blood pressure, firing off questions, taking care of business. Drew gave a terse summation of the events that had stranded them below ground.

It was easy to see why he and Beth had been trapped. Her small car, now a mangled mess of metal, had been snatched up and dumped...right on top of the cellar.

When the immediate furor died, he searched for Beth. She had walked several hundred feet away and stood gazing at what was left of her fall pumpkin crop. Virtually nothing. The tornado had ripped across her land, decimating everything in its path.

The front left portion of her bungalow was sheared off, but two-thirds of the house remained intact.

He stood by her side. "I'll help you with repairs."

She turned to face him, her expression lost. "I appreciate the offer. But unless you know how to grow a pumpkin overnight, my revenue stream just vanished until June at the earliest." She searched his face. "What did he tell you about *your* place?"

The day was already heating up. Beth slipped off his shirt and handed it to him. He slid his arms into it and fastened a few buttons. "I was very lucky. We lost a lot of fencing...and one outbuilding. But the staff and the horses are all safe."

"Your house?"

"Minor stuff."

Jed joined them. "Let's get you two back to Willowbrook. You can shower and have a decent meal."

Beth glanced at Drew's brother, her eyes haunted. "Tell us about Royal. How bad is it?"

Jed hesitated.

Drew squeezed Beth's hand. "Tell us, Jed. We've been imagining the worst."

Jed's shoulders slumped. He bent his head and stared

at the ground before looking up with a grim-faced stare. "Mass destruction. The storm was an EF4. A quarter-mile wide and on the ground for twenty-two miles. The center of the storm missed Willowbrook, but it turned and traveled straight over Beth's place and on east."

"God help us," Drew said. Nothing so tragic had ever touched the town of Royal. "How many dead?"

"As of this morning, the count stood at thirteen. A family of four…tourists. They took shelter beneath an overpass, but you know how dangerous that is. A young couple in a mobile home."

Beth put her hand to her mouth, tears spilling down her cheeks. "And the other seven?"

Jed's jaw worked as if couldn't form the words. "The town hall was destroyed."

"Jesus." Drew's stomach pitched. Beth sobbed openly now.

Jed shook his head, grief on his face. "The deputy mayor is dead. Also, Craig Richardson, who owned the Double R. Plus five others who were in the building at the time."

"And the mayor? Richard Vance?" Drew knew the man by sight and respected him.

"Life threatening injuries. But stable. I don't have a clue about the total number injured. The hospital is overloaded but managing."

Beth put her hand on Jed's arm briefly, claiming his attention. "A pregnant woman. She stopped by my produce stand just before the storm hit. Do you know anything about her?"

"I'm afraid I do. We found her car late last night when we were searching for the two of you. The tornado flipped her vehicle. She has severe head injuries, so they've put her in a medically induced coma."

Beth had stopped crying and now visibly pulled herself together. "And the baby?"

"Delivered by emergency C-section. Last I heard, they think she will make it."

Drew remembered the odd feeling that he knew the woman. "Do you know the mother's name?"

"They've listed her for now as a *Jane Doe*. Her car was destroyed. Cell phone and purse missing, probably in someone's backyard five miles away."

Jed motioned toward his car. "We need to go. Drew, after you've had a few minutes to rest, I know they could use the two of us in town."

Beth still stared at her forlorn house. "You guys go on. I'll stay here. There's plenty to do."

Drew realized then that Beth was definitely in shock. He put his arm around her shoulders, steering her toward the car. It disturbed him that her skin was icy cold. "We can bring some tarps over this evening, but you can't stay here. I know you don't want to enter the enemy camp, but I'll promise you good food, a hot shower and a bed for as long as you need it."

Beth allowed Drew to take charge because it was in her best interests and because she was too disheartened to deal with anything but basic needs at the moment.

The road between her house and the magnificent entrance to Willowbrook Farms was two miles long. Ninety-nine percent of the time when Beth departed her property, she turned left out of her driveway. So it felt odd to be deliberately closing the gap between her home and Drew's. She had only been out this way once or twice, more out of curiosity than anything else. Both times she had been struck by the pristine appearance of Drew's ranch. It was an enormous, well-cared-for equine operation.

As they drove along—slowly because of the debris littering the road—it was far too easy to see the storm's path. The twister had clipped a section of Drew's acreage, veered toward the private road and traveled along it until deciding to thunder across Beth's once thriving farm. She knew in her heart she was lucky her house was still standing. There were almost surely others in far more dire straits.

"I should have gotten clean clothes," she cried, realizing her omission.

Drew shook his head vehemently. "You can't go inside your house until an expert checks for structural damage. Not unless you want to chance spending another night beneath a pile of rubble."

"Low blow, Farrell," she muttered. "What am I supposed to wear? I have plans to burn this current outfit."

"I have seven women on my staff. I'm sure between them they can come up with a solution."

By the time they finally pulled up in front of Drew's classic two-story farmhouse, she was so tired her eyes had trouble focusing. He helped her out of the car. Jed followed them inside.

Drew took her arm, steering her toward the back of the house. "Food first."

"And a bathroom."

That made him grin. "Of course."

Jed smiled as well. "If you would like me to, while the two of you are eating, I can round up some necessities for Ms. Andrews and have the housekeeper put them in a guest room."

"That would be wonderful. Thank you. And please call me Beth. I'm pretty sure that rescuing me from a storm cellar puts us on a first name basis."

She was surprised when Drew spoke up, his face a mix of emotions. "Thanks, Jed. That would be great. Get a couple of the women in the front office to help you. But I'll pick out a bedroom."

The brothers exchanged an odd glance that Beth was unable to decipher.

In the kitchen, the housekeeper was waiting. Evidently, she had been on standby since Jed called to say he thought Drew and Beth had been found.

The size of the breakfast was overwhelming, but Beth did her best to try some of everything. Biscuits, ham, fresh peaches and eggs so light and fluffy they almost floated off the plate. Beth hated eating in her grubby clothes, but her stomach held sway, demanding to be fed. The coffee was something exotic and imported. Nothing at all like the stuff she drank at home.

She and Drew exchanged barely a dozen words as they ate. The housekeeper had excused herself, leaving them to their meal in private. Surrounded by windows, the cozy breakfast nook overlooked a small pond.

Drew touched the back of her hand briefly. "Promise me you'll take a nap. You've been through a lot in the last twenty-four hours."

Her eyes teared up again. She hated feeling so emotional, but the enormity of what had happened was almost impossible to comprehend. And she hadn't even seen the damage elsewhere.

"You were right there with me. How can Jed expect you to go into town when you're exhausted?"

"I'll be fine. My house wasn't torn apart. You've had a terrible shock. Give yourself time to get back on your feet."

"I'll nap," she said, knowing that he was right. "But after that I want to do something to help out in the community."

His bright blue eyes warmed her to the bone. "Fair

enough. And I swear to you that we'll take care of securing your house before dark."

"Thanks." She felt shy suddenly, sitting beside him in this brightly lit room. All of the appliances looked like something out of a catalog. Compared to her small, antiquated kitchen, this room was worthy of a palace.

That impression only increased as Drew ushered her down a hallway and into a large guest suite. Throughout the house, she saw beautiful, gleaming hardwood floors, accented by Oriental rugs that were probably more expensive than her car. Or what used to be her car. Panic encroached as she contemplated everything she needed to do in the aftermath of the storm. In addition to handling details about insurance claims and repairs, she wasn't sure she had enough cash flow to wait for checks to arrive.

Drew interrupted her internal meltdown. "I thought you would like this side of the house. It gets the morning sun and you can spot the last of the hummingbirds stopping by our feeders on the way south."

He stood with his hands in his pockets as if he didn't know what to do with them. His obvious unease was so unusual she was taken aback. "Something's bothering you," she said quietly.

"Not bothering me," he said quickly. "But I do have something important I want to say to you."

"What is it?" Her stomach quivered. She couldn't imagine what they had to discuss at this moment.

"I want you to live here at Willowbrook…until the repairs on your house are completed. No hidden agenda, I swear. I know we don't see eye to eye, but we need to table our disagreement in the short term while things are in chaos."

Her stomach fell to her knees. He was entirely serious. Though it seemed he was trying to be nice, suspicion reared its ugly head. "We don't even know each other," she said faintly.

Drew leaned against a post of the giant rice-carved bed and gave her a crooked smile. "I'm not sure you can say that anymore. We've lived a lifetime in the last twenty-four hours, don't you think? I have plenty of room, and you would have online access and fax machines to deal with your insurance claims. You wouldn't have to worry about grocery shopping or cooking or anything else. You could concentrate on getting Green Acres back in shape."

What he offered was infinitely tempting. Her world was in tatters. But she was a mature woman. Would taking Drew's help be too needy?

"I'll think about it," she said. "Thank you for the invitation."

"Accepting help doesn't mean you're weak, Beth."

"What, you're a mind reader now?"

He crossed to where she stood by the window. "I'm grateful that my house is still standing. But if it weren't, I would gladly accept a helping hand from my neighbor."

"Horse hockey," she said, laughing in spite of herself.

"It's true. So please swallow your pride and let me do this for you."

He liked the notion of being her savior. She could tell. It was a guy thing. Looking around the sumptuous, exquisitely decorated bedroom, she grimaced inwardly. This was a far cry from the roach-infested apartments where she had grown up. It was difficult to admit, even to herself, how much she wanted to stay.

On a normal day, she might have summoned the strength to turn him down. But after the tornado and last night's ordeal, she was working from a final store of reserves. "I suppose I'd be a fool to say no."

"I happen to know you're a very smart woman."

She couldn't allow herself to depend on him indefinitely. This gilded world of wealth and privilege was not hers. The life she had carved out for herself was a good one, but it wasn't this.

Even so, surely it couldn't hurt to pretend for a while. "Okay," she sighed. "You win. But only because I'm at a low point. And because I'm guessing that bathroom over there has a jetted tub."

"You are and it does."

Something happened then—something she couldn't explain. The attraction that neither of them had acknowledged over the last months and days was tangible now. Fired in the crucible of the tornado's fury, it had proven to be far more real than she could ever have imagined.

Desire hovered between them...around them. Drew's expression was serious now. His warm gaze seeped into her bones, rejuvenating her. Did his interest in her have an ulterior motive? Did he think if they were intimate, he could manipulate her more easily? "I know what you're thinking," she said.

Hunger flashed in his eyes. "Not the half of it," he muttered.

His mouth settled over hers in slow motion. Their lips met, clung. Strong arms circled her waist, pulling her up against his big, hard frame.

Dimly, in some far recess of her subconscious, she understood that this was a really bad idea. Living in Drew's house...accepting his help. *Playing with fire.*

When his tongue slid between her lips, stroking inside her mouth intimately, a curl of desire, sweet and hot, made her legs tremble. She clung to him, flashing back to their terrifying dash to the storm cellar. Would she have made it in time without him? Awash with emotions that ran the gamut from gratitude to sheer need, she kissed him back.

Drew said she was a smart woman. But here, locked in his arms, with his mouth hot and demanding on hers, she knew that she was not. Despite every obstacle standing in their way, both past and present, she wanted to share his bed.

The town they both loved had been ripped apart. Lives were lost. Her own home was in shambles.

Perhaps it was the very existence of disaster that made her reach for what she wanted. Life was short. Life was precious. Even without a happy ending, she could have Drew. It wasn't vanity to think so. She saw it in his eyes, felt it in the restless caress of his hands.

Deliberately, she nipped his bottom lip with her teeth. "You have things to do. But I'll be here when you're ready."

Five

I'll be here when you're ready. Drew replayed that sentence in his head a thousand times as he made his way from stall to stall checking on his horses. He relied on top-notch employees. But he wanted to see for himself that the horses were safe. These beautiful animals were more than dollar signs to him. They were noble steeds with bloodlines that went further back than his own.

He spoke softly to each one, smiling when a whinny of recognition greeted him. They were muscle and sinew and most of all—heart. Ever since he was a boy, he had loved the sights and sounds and smells of the horse barn. As an adult, he was fortunate to make his living working with these creatures. Though he would be reluctant to admit it, he grieved each time one of his prized stallions left the ranch.

An hour later, walking shoulder to shoulder with Jed down the streets of Royal—or what was left of them—he forgot all about Willowbrook. The random pattern of the destruction was hard to fathom. On one block, houses had been razed to the ground, no more than piles of rubble. But one road over, dwellings were untouched.

The west side of town was hardest hit; almost all of the businesses there a total loss. Smaller tornadoes had touched down across the county.

Drew had seen TV coverage of bad tornadoes. In his lifetime he'd personally witnessed a few storms that ripped up trees and tore off roofs. But nothing like this. Ever. The governor and his entourage had helicoptered in at daybreak and assessed the damage in preparation for a news conference. Faces from national news stations and The Weather Channel popped up everywhere. That, more than anything else, brought home the enormity of the disaster.

Royal was about to become famous for all the wrong reasons.

Earlier in the day, Jed had made contact with the point man for search and rescue. Now, he and Drew and a half dozen other members of the Texas Cattleman's Club joined a team with canine support going from house to house looking for survivors. Thankfully, almost everyone had been accounted for by this point. While Drew and Beth had been trapped in the cellar the afternoon and evening before, the immediate rush to find missing and dead had been urgent and thorough.

Today was about making sure nothing was overlooked. Sometimes the elderly had no one to raise a red flag if they went missing. And they might be too weak to cry out for help. Hence, the careful attention of a half dozen teams working a grid system across the town.

Drew squatted in a sea of pink insulation and crumpled Sheetrock to pick up a lavender teddy bear, probably some little girl's prized possession. He set it in a prominent place, hoping someone would find it.

Families were beginning the grim and heartbreaking task of sifting through what was left of their homes in an effort to reclaim valuables. National Guard units patrolled the hardest hit neighborhoods, discouraging looting.

Royal was a great place to live and raise a family, but

in situations of chaos, the occasional vermin crawled out to prey on others' misfortune.

By the time the sun hung low in the sky, Drew was beat. He and Jed grabbed a burger at a restaurant offering free dinners to rescue personnel. They stood outside to eat, in full view of what was left of Town Hall. Almost all of the three-story building had been leveled. Only a portion of the clock tower still stood, the hands of time perpetually frozen at 4:14.

Drew's stomach knotted. He tossed the last half of his meal in a trash receptacle and stared at the eerie scene. It was painful remembering where he and Beth had been at the moment they heard the sirens. Why had they been spared when others had not?

It was one of those questions with no answer.

He turned his back on the tragic scene and rubbed the heels of his hands over his eyes. Jed's light touch on his shoulder startled him.

"You doin' okay, big brother?"

Drew nodded automatically, but inside he wondered if anything would ever be okay again. "Yeah."

Jed rolled his neck. "A bunch of the TCC guys and gals are going to meet at the club first thing in the morning for another follow-up meeting."

"Good idea." Jed lived in Dallas and was a part of that branch of the Texas Cattleman's Club. He was only visiting Royal for the moment, but he knew most of the same people Jed knew. Unfortunately, he'd picked a hell of a time to come. Drew was glad to have him around.

"I ran into Gil Addison while you were talking to the fire chief. Gil has been coordinating the whole thing. He wants to ensure that we're pooling resources and maximizing relief efforts."

"Makes sense." Gil owned a thriving ranch south of

town and had been TCC president for two years. Drew checked his watch. "I promised Beth we'd get her house secure before tonight. We'd better head back."

"Suits me. There's going to be plenty to do tomorrow."

Beth couldn't wait to see Drew again. When he wandered into the kitchen, she could see from his expression that the work today had been heartbreaking and difficult.

"Have you eaten?" she asked.

"Jed and I got a burger in town."

"You want some dessert? Mrs. Simmons made apple pie."

"Maybe later. We need to get out to your place."

She nodded. "Your foreman has been so kind. He's already loaded everything we'll need into the back of your truck."

"Jed's going to help me. You don't have to go. It might be dangerous."

She frowned. "It's my house."

"Fine," he said, his tone resigned. "Be out front in five minutes."

Beth grabbed a jacket and a flashlight. Despite what Drew had said that morning, she planned to recover a few valuables. She lived out in the country, but even so, she didn't like the idea of her home being vulnerable to anyone who chose to intrude. Drew was used to being obeyed. That much was clear. But he would have to get over it. Accepting his help did *not* mean letting him boss her around.

He climbed behind the wheel of his huge truck, leaving Beth and Jed to enter from the other side. Beth found herself sandwiched between two handsome Farrell males. Both men carried an air of exhaustion. She decided then and there not to deliberately provoke Drew.

He had been out working, while *she* had enjoyed the

luxury of a wonderful nap tucked beneath a fluffy comforter, resting on sheets soft as a whisper. The bed Drew had chosen for her was huge and comfy and decadent. Did he have any thought of sharing it with his guest at some point in the future?

Her focus changed entirely as they traveled the relatively short distance between the two properties. Not a word was spoken in the cab of the truck as they witnessed the storm's track. It had effectively ripped a trail along the private road, turning abruptly to power over Beth's property and head toward town.

As they parked in front of her house and got out, the memories of the tornado came rushing back. *It's over,* she told herself repeatedly, but still her knees knocked and her stomach pitched.

She touched Drew's arm, her gaze beseeching. "I'd like to get my computer and pack a few clothes. If I go in through the side that's not damaged, I'm sure it will be fine."

He glanced back at Jed. "I'll stay with her. Do you mind sorting out the supplies? We'll do the tarps in a few minutes."

Jed nodded. "No problem."

Beth's house was small, but even so, it was almost unbelievable to see what was damaged and what was not. The back of the house was relatively unscathed. One broken window…a few shingles missing. The bedrooms were habitable. At the front of the house, the small living room wasn't in bad shape except where a piece of lumber had punctured the vinyl siding. But the kitchen was a mess. The tornado had ripped apart one quarter of the house, shattering crockery and literally plucking off the roof and twisting it into an unrecognizable mess.

Standing in what used to be the doorway to her kitchen,

Beth lifted her shoulders and let them fall. "Well," she said, forcing words from a tight throat. "I needed new appliances anyway."

Drew took her hand and tugged her backward to a safer part of the house. "Don't go in there, please. Anything could fall on your head. And Beth...." He trailed off, his expression troubled.

"What?"

"Just because the rest of the home *seems* intact doesn't mean that it is. It's entirely possible that the house was momentarily lifted off its foundation. Which means you may have structural damage that could result in leaks or other problems. I don't want to upset you, but it's better to assume the worst and then be happy if it turns out not to be as bad as we think."

He was right, of course. But hearing it laid out logically did nothing to lessen the impact of what had happened. She had worked so hard for this house. It was more than four walls and a roof. It was a symbol of all she had overcome. Seeing it in shambles broke her heart.

With Drew hovering, she quickly packed a bag with as many clothes as she could grab. Other than her computer and some pieces of jewelry, the only things worth stealing were her television and Blu-ray player. She sincerely doubted anyone would go to the trouble to drive out here and take electronics, so she left the living room as it was. As she handed off her small suitcase to Drew, it occurred to her that theft might be the least of her worries. What was going to happen when it rained? The tarps were surely a short-term solution.

Clearly, she wasn't doing a very good job of hiding her jangled emotions. Drew hugged her with his free arm. "I know it seems overwhelming, but I'll help you get things back together. Contractors, plumbers…. whoever else you need. You do have insurance, right?"

"Yes, thank God. And I think it's pretty good. But I've never had to use it."

"C'mon," he said. "It's almost dark. We have to string up the tarps while we can still see."

They carried her things out to the truck and put them in the jump seat. Jed had already untangled ropes and unfolded three enormous sheets of heavy plastic. Beth leaned against the hood and watched as her Good Samaritans struggled and cursed and finally managed to get the first tarp in place. Gradually they encased the broken portion of the house in a shroud of overlapping layers.

It wasn't airtight. And it wouldn't keep out varmints, animal or otherwise. But hopefully it would protect her personal belongings from the weather. If she had to, she would rent a storage unit and move her things out of the house until the repairs were done. Since most of her furniture was thrift shop in origin, she wasn't too worried.

Darkness closed in on them. As Drew and his brother tied off the last corners and used duct tape to secure vulnerable spots, Beth wandered over to the storm cellar. Squatting, she opened one side of the double doors. Without wind to contend with, it was as easy as raising a window. Nothing was visible down below. But she remembered. She would always remember.

Drew lowered the ladder and shoved it into the bed of the truck. His eyes were on Beth. She seemed so alone, it made his chest hurt.

Jed tossed a canvas bag of supplies on top of the ladder. "So what's the deal with you and Beth Andrews?"

Still watching Beth, Drew shrugged. "We're neighbors. That's all."

"C'mon, Bro. I wasn't born yesterday. This *thing* you two have between you is more than surviving a tornado."

Drew shot his brother a disgusted look. "Have I butted in about you and Kimberly? Drop it, Jed."

"Fair enough. But be careful. Sometimes women mistake kindness for something else. It wouldn't be fair to lead her on."

"One budding relationship in your pocket and suddenly you're an expert. Get over yourself. I can handle my love life without your help."

Jed grinned smugly. "Who said anything about love?"

Muttering under his breath, Drew strode over to where Beth stood looking at the mass of metal and tires that had once been her car. "I've got an old rattletrap of a pickup out at the house," he said. "We use it sometimes to run errands on the ranch. But you're welcome to it for as long as necessary."

Finally, she faced him. "I hate taking charity," she said, her gaze stormy. "I'm already staying in your house. This is too much."

"What does it matter, Beth? It's not your fault the tornado struck here. It's a whim of fate or whatever you want to call it." He felt guilty that his place had been mostly spared. He would do whatever he could to help rebuild Royal. And he would start with Beth's little bungalow.

It was so dark now he could barely see her face. "Let's go." She allowed him to take her arm and steer her toward the truck, but he knew she was struggling to deal with the blow to her life, her livelihood, her dreams.

As they pulled up in front of Willowbrook, Jed excused himself and walked away. Drew helped Beth down from the truck, his hands lingering a second longer than was necessary at her narrow waist. "I think I'm ready for that pie now. You want to join me? We can take it in the den and watch some TV."

Beth nodded. "Sure."

The kitchen was dark, the housekeeper gone for the night. But she had left the pie front and center on the table. Drew grabbed a couple of plates and cut two big slices. Beth looked askance at hers. "Seriously?"

He grinned at her, feeling the stress of the day melt away. "You're still catching up on calories. It won't hurt you. Besides, you know you're a knockout."

She blinked twice as if his words had shocked her.

Taking the can of topping, he spritzed both desserts with a fancy swirl. Since Beth was still mute, he dared to tease her. "Maybe when we know each other a little better, I'll let *you* use the whipped cream."

"In your dreams," she shot back.

But he had made her smile.

They carried their plates to the comfy den. Drew lowered the lights to a gentle glow and sat down on the sofa with a sigh of contentment. Beth took a seat beside him, but at the other end. They both kicked off their shoes and propped their feet on the coffee table.

Someone had already built a fire in the fireplace. Everyone on Drew's staff knew that as soon as the thermometer dropped below fifty for the first time in the fall, he wanted firewood and matches ASAP. It was a comfort thing to him, not so much for warmth as for the sound and smell. The pop and crackle—and the scent of burning wood. Fires reminded him of happy times with his dad…the many occasions the older Farrell had taken Jed and Drew camping in the Texas hill country.

The silence in the room was comfortable. He and Beth ate pie in harmony. It was, perhaps, a temporary détente, but he was content to enjoy the moment. Now that he was seated, the full weight of exhaustion rolled over him. Between the sleepless night and the hard, emotionally draining work in Royal today, his body felt battered.

He finished his dessert and set the plate aside. Closing his eyes, he let his head drop back against the sofa.

Beth's voice caught him just as he hovered on the edge of sleep. "How bad was it in town?"

Not bothering to move his body, he turned his head to look at her. "Bad. As bad as I've ever seen in person."

Beth was pale, her teeth worrying her bottom lip. "What did you and Jed do today?"

"Helped with the search and rescue teams. The houses we went to were all empty, but I heard that one of the crews this afternoon found a mom and two kids trapped in a bathtub with a mattress over them. They'd been yelling for help off and on for hours. But with their house crumpled on top of them, it took the dogs to sniff them out."

"But they're going to be okay?"

"Yes, thank God."

"I want to go with you tomorrow," she said.

"I understand. And there will be plenty of stuff to help with. But I'll come back for you after lunch. Jed and I have a meeting at the Cattleman's Club in the morning. Did you call the building inspector I told you about?"

Beth didn't seem entirely pleased. "I did, but I feel bad about it. Jumping to the head of the line seems rude."

"It's not rude at all. That's what friends do."

"But he's not *my* friend."

Drew sat up, rested his elbows on his knees and rubbed his eyes with his fingertips. Was he doomed to surround himself with stubborn women? He counted to ten. When he thought he had his temper under control, he glared at her. "I *know* you're an independent woman. I know you can take care of yourself. But why not let me smooth the path when I can? I guarantee that if you try to find an inspector on your own, your house will sit there for a long time. Half of Royal is going to be in the same boat."

Beth felt the pinch of shame. Drew was only trying to help. And she was being less than gracious. "I'm sorry," she said stiffly. Her mother had raised two kids on government assistance, leaving Beth with an aversion to asking for or taking help. "You're right. I'll be happy to meet with him. Thank you."

The sharp planes of Drew's masculine face softened. He reached across the cushioned no-man's-land between them and twined his fingers with hers, playing with the silver ring on her right hand. "Now, was that so hard?"

She managed a smile though she was distracted by the curve of his mouth and the way his sexy, humorous grin left her breathless. She tugged her hand away. "It must be gratifying to be able to hand out help without thinking of the consequences."

Now he frowned. "Why does that sound like an insult?"

"I wasn't being sarcastic. I'm serious. You have the means to help people without worrying about the bottom line. I imagine you find that rewarding."

He released her and returned to his earlier position. Perhaps her impulsive statement had offended him.

Shaking his head in what appeared to be disgust, he frowned. "I won't apologize for having money." The words were flat. "If you weren't so stubborn, and if you would let yourself think outside the box, you might realize that our dispute over the road could be handled in a way that would help your bottom line immensely."

This time the silence that descended was awkward. He had shut her out deliberately. Maybe she had not been entirely truthful about her lack of sarcasm. It was possible she had some passive-aggressive issues to work through when it came to the inequity between their lifestyles. But if he thought he could *buy* her automatic compliance, he was mistaken.

Drew was champagne and Rolex and jetting to Paris. Beth drank tap water, used the clock on her cheap flip phone and had never been outside of Texas. Was it any wonder that she felt at a disadvantage when it came to dealing with a macho, Texas-born-and-bred billionaire?

"May I ask you something?" she said, wanting to get inside his head and understand what made him tick.

His gaze was wary. "I suppose."

"When we were in the storm cellar, you started to tell me something about your engagement, but I cut you off. I'd really like to hear what you were going to say."

He shrugged. "It's not anything noteworthy."

"Then tell me."

He linked his hands behind his neck, staring into the fire. "Her name was Margie. We met at an equine convention in Dallas. Shared a few laughs. Tumbled into bed. We had a lot in common."

Beth pondered his response for several long seconds. "And that was enough for an engagement?"

"We went back and forth seeing each other for six months. Her condo in Houston. My place here in Royal. By the end of the seventh month, it seemed like the right time to settle down. Start a family. So I proposed. She was pleased that I asked."

"No grand passion?"

"I wouldn't call it that. No."

"Ah."

"We made it a couple of months with a ring on her finger before the problems began to crop up. She was stubborn. Extremely bull-headed."

"And so are you."

"Exactly. We locked horns about everything. If I said the sky was blue, she said it was green. Soon, every time we ended up in bed turned out to be for make-up sex."

"Some couples thrive on that."

"Not me. I started to realize that I had made a huge mistake."

"So what happened?" Beth was curious, more than she cared to admit.

Drew inhaled sharply, letting the breath out slowly. "I introduced her to a buddy of mine. Deliberately. He was from Houston. A handsome, charming veterinarian. They hit it off. Six weeks later she gave me back my ring."

"Ouch."

"But don't you see? That was what I was after. People showered me with sympathy over my "broken" engagement. I felt like a complete and utter fraud."

He turned away, perhaps already regretting his honesty. "So now you know my dirty little secret."

Several minutes passed in silence as Beth tried to analyze her confusing response to his tale. Jealousy? Relief? Sympathy? Eventually, a slight noise alerted her to a change in the status quo. Drew had fallen asleep. Poor guy.

In slumber he seemed slightly less intimidating. She studied him intently, trying to see through the handsome package to the man beneath. For months he had harassed her about selling her property to him. Even yesterday, he had approached her with fire in his eyes. But in the midst of incredible danger, he had taken control in the best possible way and made the experience of surviving a killer tornado bearable.

His dark lashes fanned out against his tanned cheeks. The broad chest that rose and fell with his regular breathing was hard and muscular. Below his belt, a taut, flat abdomen led to long legs and sock-clad feet.

Part of her was disappointed that the evening had so obviously ended. Her attraction to Drew made her want to spend time with him. But the snarky, inner Beth said *danger, danger, danger*. A girl could get her heart broken by a man like Drew Farrell.

She wondered what had happened to Jed. Drew told her he was visiting from Dallas. But the man was like a phantom. If he was in the house tonight, he was keeping to himself. Too bad. It would certainly help to have a third party around. Someone who might be able to keep Beth and Drew from either strangling each other or tumbling into bed without weighing the consequences.

A gentle snore from the man on the couch made her smile in spite of her unsettled emotions. Drew was out for the count. He would probably sleep better in his own bed, but Beth definitely didn't feel comfortable poking his leg and suggesting that he move. In lieu of that, she stood quietly, removed the fire screen, and added a couple more logs to the blaze.

Warming her hands, she studied the dancing flames. Already, she felt the pull of Willowbrook Farms. It was a warm, welcoming place, something she had never experienced growing up. She'd never slept on the street, but a home was more than brick and mortar. A home meant security and comfort. Beth and her brother had battled uncertainty and fear more times than not.

Shaking off the bad memories, she turned for one last wistful look at her would-be benefactor. She couldn't afford to depend on Drew. She'd already had one man give her a helping hand. But at least back then, she'd been a broke college student, so there was some basis for taking what had been a huge gift.

Now, she was an adult woman who paid her bills on time and took care of herself. If she weakened and let Drew do too much, her self-respect would become an issue. Not only that, but there was a good chance he was trying to soften her up. Maybe he thought if she were beholden to him it would be easier to sway her to his way of thinking. Because she was attracted to him, the situation was even more fraught with pitfalls. If and when the two of them ever pursued what she now knew was a definite spark, she wanted a level playing field. A relationship of equals.

Unfortunately, that was never going to happen. No matter how you spun the fantasy, she didn't belong in Drew's world. She was the girl from the wrong side of the tracks.

Six

Drew struggled to stay focused on the conversation ping-ponging around the large conference table. Every man and woman in the room was a friend of his. And they were all well-respected members of the Texas Cattleman's Club. At Sheriff Nathan Battle's request, the informal group had convened to discuss the coordination of cleanup efforts and the utilization of volunteers now that the county had been designated a disaster area.

Nathan looked as if he hadn't slept at all. Drew himself had awakened at 3:00 a.m. to a cold, empty living room. The fire had long since burned out, and Beth was nowhere to be found. He'd dragged himself to his bed and managed a few more hours, but he'd been up at first light, eager to get into town and assess the situation.

The trouble was, though he was here, all he could think about was Beth. He'd left the keys to the truck he had promised her with the housekeeper. And Allan was supposed to be at Beth's place at 10:00. But even so, Drew felt a churning in his gut that told him he was more invested in Beth's situation than was wise.

Forcing himself to concentrate, he was startled when his buddy Whit Daltry whispered in his right ear.

"I helped rescue Megan's daughter, Evie, from the day-care center yesterday. It was chaos. All those terrified parents and kids. I can't imagine what Megan was going through."

Drew muttered softly in return. "I thought you and Megan were mortal enemies."

"Very funny." Whit rubbed two fingers in the center of the forehead as if he had a headache. And he probably did. "Things change, Drew. Especially now."

The talk at the table had moved to an even more sober topic. Funerals. There would be a number of them over the next week. Fortunately, the mortuary and Royal's three main churches had sustained only minimal damage.

Drew spoke up at one point. "Jed and I would like to donate $100,000 to start a fund for families with no insurance." One by one, people jumped in, offering similar amounts as they were able. A representative from social services suggested designating a point person to triage which needs were most urgent.

Shelter would be the first priority. And then cleanup.

The enormity of the task was mind-boggling. Drew looked around the table at Royal residents he had known since childhood, people who pulled together in times of trouble. The town had never faced a catastrophe of this magnitude. But together they would rebuild and help the helpless.

The building in which they sat, the Texas Cattleman's Club, was an icon in Royal. Built in the early 1900s, it had served as a gathering place for movers and shakers, primarily ranchers whose families had owned their property for decades. Though once upon a time a bastion for the *good ole boys,* the club in recent years had moved into the twenty-first century.

Despite opposition from the old guard, the club had begun admitting female members. Not only that, the TCC had opened an onsite day care center. Times were changing. The old ways were beginning to coexist with the new. Both had something to offer.

As a historical and social landmark, the TCC was an integral part of the town's identity. Fortunately, the main building had survived the tornado, but downed trees had damaged many of the outbuildings. Broken glass and water damage seemed to be the worst of the problems.

Gil Addison was on his feet now. "I think I speak for everyone in this room, Nathan, when I say that we'll do whatever it takes, for however long it takes. As each of you leaves in a few moments, my assistant will be at a table outside taking volunteer sign-ups for shifts on various work details. I know most of us will have some personal issues to deal with, but I appreciate whatever you can do for the town. Because we *are* the town."

Applause broke out as the meeting ended.

Jed ran a hand through his hair and turned to Drew. "I brought work clothes with me. What if you and I grab a bite of lunch and then I'll stay here while you go get Beth?"

"Sounds like a plan. Do you think Kimberly will want to help, too?"

A funny look crossed Jed's face. "I don't think she's free this afternoon."

Drew felt as if there was something going on there, but he had too much to juggle on his own without sticking his nose into Jed's life. He was just glad his brother had been in Royal and not Dallas when the tornado hit. It felt good to have Jed's support at a time like this.

On the way out, Drew paused to speak to friends: Stella Daniels from the mayor's office, who was playing a key role dealing with the media, and Keaton Holt, who co-owned and ran the Holt Cattle Ranch. Everyone's demeanor was the same. Grief, determination, and beneath it all, a pervasive sense of loss. The tragedy had stripped away a semblance of security and left them all floundering.

Drew signed up for a shift later in the day and spoke briefly with Nathan, reporting the damage to Beth's home. When he finally made it to his truck, he waited for Jed to grab his things. "I think I'll take a pass on lunch," he said. "I want to catch Allen, the inspector, if he's still around and hear the report on Beth's house."

Jed nodded. "I'll give you a rain check. Say hi to Beth for me…and don't do anything I wouldn't do."

Beth felt a trickle of sweat roll down her back. There wasn't a cloud in the sky, with temperatures reaching the lower eighties. That was Texas for you. A veritable smorgasbord of weather. For the first hour, she had been banned from the house while the inspector, hardhat in place, went over the structure with a fine-tooth comb.

At last, he permitted her to enter. He took her around, pointing out spots that would require repair. Fortunately, the foundation was intact. That was a huge relief.

Beth put her hands on her hips and frowned. "So if I had to sleep here, I could?"

Drew's buddy frowned. "Well, in theory, yes. But it should be a last resort. You'd be breathing in bits of insulation and maybe mold in the short term. I wouldn't recommend it." He clicked a few more times on his hand-held tablet and pursed his lips. "I should be able to get you this report by tomorrow morning. If you call your insurance immediately and give them my contact info, we can get the ball rolling. Hopefully, you'll be near the front of the line."

"Thank you for coming."

He climbed in his car and lowered the window to say goodbye. "It won't be so bad. To a layperson, this might look daunting, but a professional carpenter will have you back to rights in no time. I'll be in touch."

As the inspector drove back down the driveway toward the shared road that had been a bone of contention between Beth and Drew, she wondered for a bleak half second if she should simply sell her land to Drew and relocate. She'd poured what little capital she had into making a go of Green Acres. It would take months to recover from this setback. Maybe it would be smarter to look for a small house in town.

She had worked at the bank before. It wasn't her passion, but it paid the bills.

As she stood there pondering her options, a second vehicle arrived, this one an ancient green Pinto with a muffler that was shot. The car shuddered and snorted to a stop. Beth's stomach clenched. The last thing she needed today was a run-in with her deadbeat brother.

The car door opened and Audie stepped out. He weighed barely a hundred pounds sopping wet. Numerous jail sentences over the last ten years had hardened him. Mostly B&E, with a few disorderly conducts and a handful of public drunkenness thrown in. Audie had his mother's alcoholic tendencies. Unfortunately, she'd let him drink his first beer at age twelve. It was a wonder he wasn't already dead from liver failure.

Audie had been in and out of rehab repeatedly. But apparently this last time had produced some success. Though Beth found it difficult to trust anything he said, Audie had supposedly been clean for six months now.

Beth had done her best to rise above the stigma of her upbringing. Hanging out with her brother didn't help matters. But as much as she hated his behavior and his lack of backbone, she couldn't ignore the fact that he had a wife and child.

Angie, Audie's bride of four years, was a cheerful woman-child with less street smarts than most kindergarteners. What she saw in Audie was anyone's guess. The baby was small and sad-eyed, but as far as Beth could tell, little Anton was healthy. Angie had picked out the decidedly non-Texan name. She liked having three *A*s in the family.

Angie and Anton remained in the car, so that meant this visit was business and not pleasure. Beth's stomach knotted. She had called her brother to check on him only this morning and gotten his answering machine.

When she made no effort to approach the parked car, Audie ambled in her direction. "Hey, sis." When he smiled, the usual sly calculation in his gaze was missing. He appeared clear-eyed and sober. "Looks like the house is okay."

She raised her eyebrows, incredulous. "An entire section is gone."

He shrugged. "Still standing. Our apartment is toast. Thought we might stay with you for a while."

"Audie…." She struggled for words. Bringing in a homeless stranger would be an easier task than dealing with her sibling's personality.

"C'mon," he said, slinging an arm around her shoulder. "We're family. You wouldn't let a baby sleep on the streets, would you?"

Feeling boxed in and frustrated, Beth evaded his grasp. "There are shelters set up in town."

"Those are for people who don't have relatives to help out. I got you, babe." His snickered reference to an old song didn't amuse Beth in the least.

"I'll have to get repairs done. Construction debris is no place for a child."

"We can stay out in the shed. It has electricity and a sink. And a utility shower."

It was clear that Audie had made up his mind. Beth knew from experience he would continue to harangue her until she gave in. Perhaps she shouldn't stay in Royal at all. Sometimes the temptation to move far away and make a new start was compelling. This setback in her fledgling farm endeavor might be a sign.

But in the same instant, she thought of Drew. And of her friends and neighbors in Royal who faced a long road ahead. This corner of Texas was all Beth had ever known. Though her memories of growing up weren't entirely positive, Royal was home. Audie would always be her brother, no matter how hard she tried to tell herself they were nothing alike. They shared DNA and a difficult past.

Audie had made different choices in life than Beth had. Poor choices in many instances. She felt no real compunction about letting him bear the consequences of his actions. But she couldn't turn her back on an innocent child and a waiflike woman with no common sense at all.

"Fine," she said. "Have it your way. You can stay. But you'll have to bring in some kind of camp stove and a mini fridge."

"Why didn't you take care of that?" he asked.

"I'm not staying here," she said evenly. "Drew Farrell has invited me to Willowbrook Farms for as long as it takes me to get the repairs done."

Audie frowned. Apparently he had assumed Beth would be responsible for everything. "Well, that's convenient. Seems like you always have men hanging around to look after you."

The implication in his voice and in his words made her furious, but she wouldn't let him see that he could get to her. Keeping her expression bland, she lifted an eyebrow. "Audie…"

"Yeah?"

"For once in your life, try to think of someone other than yourself. If this turns out to be too uncomfortable for Angie and Anton, please be a man and find a solution."

"Easy for you to say."

She refused to let him make her feel guilty. "I'm leaving now." She headed toward the green Pinto to greet her nephew and sister-in-law. But before she got there, a familiar dark truck turned off the highway and approached the house. *Well, this day just keeps getting better and better.* Grim-faced, she watched Drew Farrell park and get out of his vehicle.

He lifted a hand as he approached. "Has Allen already come and gone?"

She nodded. "I'm surprised you didn't pass him. It hasn't been that long."

Drew stopped short, seeing Audie and the car. He held out a hand. "I'm Drew Farrell. Don't believe I know you."

Audie wiped his palm on his jeans before returning the gesture and shaking Drew's hand. "I'm Audie Andrews, Beth's brother."

Beth knew Drew well enough by now to see that he was surprised. But he hid it well. "I suppose you're checking up on your sister."

Audie seemed nonplussed, possibly because the notion of worrying about anyone other than himself was foreign to him. "Um…yeah."

"Did she tell you what happened?"

"You mean the tornado?"

Drew smothered a smile, exchanging a quick look with Beth. "Not just that. Obviously the farm took a direct hit. But we were trapped in the storm cellar overnight. The car pinned us inside." The vehicle in question still sat in a forlorn heap. Beth wondered if it was worth anything as scrap metal.

Audie's eyes shifted from Drew to Beth. "You two must be kinda close."

"We're neighbors." Drew's wry smile dared Beth to disagree. "I had come over to discuss a few things with Beth when the sirens went off."

"And now she's staying at your house."

It was hard to miss the insinuation. Beth's cheeks burned with humiliation. There were about a thousand places she would rather be right now than in the midst of this awkward confrontation.

Drew ignored the provocative statement and returned his attention to Beth. "What did Allen have to say?"

"He hopes to have his report to me by tomorrow morning. The foundation is sound. He says the other stuff won't be as bad as it looks to repair."

"That's great."

"It is."

Surely Drew was confused about her lack of enthusiasm, but she was barely holding it together. Her nerves were shot. Dealing with Audie always had that effect on her. She grimaced as she faced her brother. "I have to go now. Make yourself at home."

Drew gaped. "They're staying here?"

Audie cocked his head toward the car. "I'm between jobs at the moment. Our place in town was trashed by the storm. But we were only rentin' anyway, and it's the end of the month. Beth is going to let us bunk down out in the shed. It's in pretty good shape. We'll be fine."

Beth noticed he didn't bother to mention that he'd been fired from his last two places of employment for showing up drunk.

Drew seemed baffled. This unfortunate intersection of the haves and the have-nots illustrated more than anything else the gulf between Beth's world and the Farrell empire.

She interceded, hoping to end the regrettable interlude. "I have to go, Audie. Drew and I are volunteering in town this afternoon."

Excusing herself, she went to say hello to Angie and Anton and then returned quickly to Drew's side. "Shall I follow you?" she asked.

Drew's gaze went from Beth to Audie and back again. "We can change our plan," he said, his expression troubled.

"It's not necessary. I want to go into town and do something useful."

A long silence stretched to thirty seconds. Maybe more. For once, Audie kept his mouth shut. Finally, Drew's shoulders lifted and fell. "Okay, then. We'll stop by the ranch to grab a bite to eat and drop off the clunker. Then we'll go."

Perhaps it escaped Drew's notice that his version of a *clunker* was several notches above Audie's car.

Beth wiped sweat from her forehead with the back of her hand, wishing she had thought to bring water. "Goodbye, Audie."

He nodded. "Thanks for letting us stay."

Beth took Drew's arm. "Let's go."

When they were out of earshot, he opened her door and muttered beneath his breath. "Are you sure we don't need to do something for them? They're your family."

She closed her eyes briefly and took a deep breath, settling her hands on the steering wheel. "Audie always lands on his feet. He's the perfect example of *give him an inch and he'll take a mile*. Don't worry about them. They'll be fine. I swear."

Turning the key in the ignition, she made her wishes clear. "It's getting late."

To her dismay, Drew stood at her window for several long seconds. He must think she was a heartless bitch. But for the life of her, she didn't have the energy to explain why Audie was a barnacle on the ship that was her life.

The truth was, he was *worse* than a barnacle. Barnacles didn't actually do any damage. But Audie wreaked havoc in his wake. Even sober, he was an opportunist and a liar.

Without another word, she raised her window, turned on the air conditioning and spun gravel as she shot down the drive and onto the road. Her eyes burned with tears. She swallowed hard, blinking them away. She refused to let Drew see how much her brother upset her.

Drew couldn't possibly understand what it was like to crawl out of a dismal past and reach for something cleaner, something better. Was that a crime?

The thought of Audie staying at Green Acres outraged her, despite the fact that the house was ripped apart and vulnerable. She knew there was a good chance that before she managed to eventually evict him, he would steal anything worth pawning. It had happened before...far too often.

Angie would never know. She was so clueless, it never occurred to her to ask where Audie got the money he spent so recklessly. And Beth wouldn't say a word. Because she had *been* Anton once upon a time. A helpless child at the mercy of a parent too selfish and irresponsible to make sure she was safe.

The only way to cope at the moment was to compartmentalize. This afternoon, she and Drew were going to offer assistance where they could. In the midst of tragedy they would extend a helping hand. If Drew wanted to talk about Audie, Beth would deflect the conversation.

Seven

Drew followed Beth back to Willowbrook, wondering what in the hell was going on. Beth had never mentioned Audie, but now that Drew thought about it, she *had* alluded to her family not being close. Maybe her brother was the only family she had. Clearly, the two of them didn't get along.

Was she embarrassed for Drew to meet Audie? Maybe she thought Drew was the kind of man to pass judgment on others. He knew full well that he was a very fortunate guy. He'd been born into a loving family, one with considerable financial assets. Though his parents had retired early and moved to Padre Island, all of the Farrells were a close-knit group, even the cousins and aunts and uncles.

As he parked and got out of his truck, Beth was already hurrying up the front steps. By the time he reached the kitchen, he found her talking to the housekeeper, who was quickly setting out lunch.

Suddenly starved, Drew sat down and dug into a thick corned beef sandwich. The afternoon would be more about physical labor than the morning had been. Breakfast was a long time ago. Beth seemed equally hungry, but she barely glanced at him as she ate.

She finished before he did and gave him a smile that didn't reach her eyes. Blotting her mouth with a napkin, she stood. "If you'll excuse me, I want to freshen up for a moment before I leave. I'll see you back here tonight."

He caught her wrist. "It doesn't make sense for both of us to drive. I'll take you anywhere you want to go."

Not a muscle in her body moved. She stared away from him. Beneath his thumb, her pulse was rapid. "Fine. If you're sure."

Releasing her reluctantly, he nodded. "I'll be ready in fifteen minutes."

She disappeared, leaving him to ponder the odds that she would actually wait for him. Maybe she was upset about dealing with her brother. Families could be complicated. Most likely, Audie's unemployment made things worse.

When Drew stepped out onto the front porch two minutes ahead of his deadline, Beth was perched on the top step. Despite the heat, she was wearing faded jeans that would protect her legs. A yellow cotton sunhat perched on top of her head. Her long, blond curls were tucked up in a jaunty ponytail. She smelled of sunscreen.

He touched her shoulder briefly. "Let's go. Where would you like me to drop you?"

Beth shot him a sideways glance as they climbed into the overly-warm cab of the truck. "I'd like to check on Megan at the animal shelter."

Drew cranked up the A/C, wondering if Mother Nature realized that it was October. The temperature was supposed to be winding down. "Are the two of you friends?"

"Recent friends." Beth's gaze was pensive as she stared through the windshield. "When I first moved to the farm, it felt lonely at night. Megan helped me adopt a sweet puppy. His name was Gus. Half cocker spaniel, the other half pure mischief. I built a fenced-in enclosure, but he got out one day. One of my customers ran over him."

Without thinking about it, Drew reached across the small space that separated them and touched her hand. "That sucks. I'm really sorry."

She didn't look at him, and she moved her hand. "I felt so guilty."

"You shouldn't. That's what puppies do. They get loose. And run out into the road. Sometimes it doesn't end well. Did you ever think about getting a second dog?"

"For about two seconds. Love can't be transferred automatically, you know. I loved Gus. But maybe I don't need a pet. I'm having a hard enough time taking care of myself."

She said it matter-of-factly, and now Drew was the one who felt guilty. Here was a woman who had battled long odds to pursue a dream. But he'd overlooked her hard work and dismissed her modest success in his single-minded determination to safeguard his horses and his business.

From Beth's perspective, he must have seemed like an arrogant jerk. He chewed on that unpalatable bone until they pulled up in front of Royal Safe Haven. The animal shelter was located near the hospital in an industrial area of town.

Beth scanned the premises. "It looks like they've been spared."

"It's hard to believe, because the hospital lost an entire wing. But it was the oldest section, so maybe it wasn't up to modern codes."

The grounds of the shelter were covered in tree limbs and foliage and debris carried in from parts unknown. But the single story brick structure appeared solid.

Megan McGuiness, the owner, greeted them with a harried expression. "Thank God. I hope at least one of you is here to lend a hand. People have been dropping off strays all morning." The green-eyed, curvy woman was pale beneath her sprinkling of freckles. Her straight, bright red hair framed her face in tangles.

Beth hugged her, despite the assortment of stains on the other woman's clothing. "Drew is committed to a work detail in town. But I can stay for a while."

"Bless you." Megan arched her back and winced. "The animals went nuts. Clearly there was no way to get them all in a storm shelter. I'm grateful we escaped the worst of it."

Beth turned to Drew. "I still want to see the damage in the rest of Royal. And help if I can. But I'd like to stay here with Megan for a couple of hours. Would you mind coming back to get me?"

"Of course not." He focused his attention on Megan. "Is there anything you need in terms of supplies? Anything I could round up in town?"

"Some tarps would be great, but I have a feeling those are going to be scarce as hen's teeth. Still, I'll take what you can get. And a roll of twine."

He grinned. "Beth can text me if you think of anything else."

Megan's smile turned sly. "What I really need is adoptive homes. How would you feel about taking a couple of cats, Drew?"

He grimaced. "I'm allergic to cats."

"They're barn cats. You have a barn. It's a match made in heaven."

Beth held up her hands when Drew blanched. "Don't look at me," she said. "My house is barely standing. It's no place for an animal right now."

Drew gave in with good grace. He and Megan had gone out once about a hundred years ago, so he cared about her…though more as a sister. "Fine. Two cats. No more. I'll send one of my guys to pick them up this afternoon if I can find anyone who's not working cleanup."

Megan went up on tiptoe to kiss his cheek. "I knew there was a reason I liked you."

He rolled his eyes. "Flattery doesn't work on me. I've already agreed to the deal. You don't have to oversell it."

Beth chuckled. "You'd better run, Drew. The last time I was here she had two iguanas and a python. I think you're getting off easy."

Beth smiled at her friend as Drew drove away. "I should have already asked. How is Evie?" Beth had met the four-year-old when Beth had adopted the puppy. Evie's precocious charm had won her over immediately.

Some emotion flickered in Megan's eyes. "She's good. She's fine."

Since the other woman's tone of voice indicated she didn't want to talk further about her child, Beth backed off. "Tell me what to do. I know you're overwhelmed."

For the first time, Megan took a deep breath, her gaze sober. "Is it true that your house is badly damaged?"

Beth nodded. "My place took a direct hit. The fields are ruined. One corner of the house is a shambles. Drew and I were trapped in the storm cellar overnight when my car decided to land on top of us."

"Dear Lord."

"Yes. We were lucky. I still get shaky thinking about it."

"Well, I can take your mind off your troubles, I guarantee. Come on inside and you can help me decide how to rig up some extra cages. I won't be able to use the outdoor dog runs until I get help clearing everything the storm dropped on top of us."

Within the walls of the building, chaos reigned. Dogs howled. Cats screeched. It was as if the animals realized that a disaster of epic proportions had swept the county. And perhaps they did.

When Beth voiced the thought, Megan nodded. "They understand, they really do. Dogs and cats are remarkably intuitive. Of course, right now most of them are cranky because their routines have been altered. But they'll settle down soon. I hope."

For the next couple of hours, Beth worked until her back was sore and her legs ached. Feeding and watering the clientele took a long time, not to mention finding places for the new residents displaced by the storm.

At one point, pausing to catch her breath, she leaned down and picked up a tiny puppy with matted golden-brown hair. He reminded her a lot of Gus. The little dog curled into her arms with what she could swear was a sigh of relief. Murmuring to her newfound friend, she stroked his ears. "If you don't have a name, I'll call you Stormy. I know…it's cliché. But all the little girl dogs will think you're cute."

Megan returned from outside where she had been hosing out buckets. "Looks like somebody loves you."

Beth's heart turned over in a wistful flip of longing. "Do me a favor, Megan."

"Of course."

"If no one comes to claim this sweet fella, will you keep him for me? Until I'm back in my house?"

"I doubt Drew would care if you brought a dog home. He's not allergic to those. The man has a Golden Retriever and a couple of Bluetick hounds."

"All the more reason to leave Stormy here. Drew is already feeding and housing me. I can't trespass on his good nature any further than that."

Megan lifted an eyebrow. "You're *staying* with Drew? I thought he was the big bad wolf trying to gobble up your farm."

Beth held Stormy more tightly. "It's not like that. When

he saw that my house was going to need major repairs, he offered me a room. That's all."

Megan grinned. "And how many other homeless females has he taken in?"

"None."

"I rest my case."

At that exact moment, a horn honked outside, signaling Drew's return. He carried in the supplies Megan had requested and glanced at Beth with amusement. "You both look like you've been dragged through a bush backward."

"Some of us have been working hard," she said.

He didn't rise to the bait. "You ready to go?" He scratched Stormy's tummy gently. The puppy practically rolled his eyes in ecstasy. Beth understood entirely. Drew's big hands gave a woman naughty ideas.

Beth looked at Megan and handed over the small dog. "I'll come back again, I promise."

Megan tucked the pup under her arm and glanced at her utilitarian watch. "No worries. We've had lots of volunteers. Thanks for all you've done."

Drew pointed the truck toward downtown. "You sure you want to do this?" The farther they drove, the more damage they witnessed. Beth stared in silence. At one point he saw a single tear slide down her cheek. But she didn't wipe it away.

"How can it happen so fast?" she asked, the words heartbroken.

He understood that it was a rhetorical question. Though he had already seen the devastation yesterday and twice today, the senseless destruction still took his breath away. The random patterns of the storm's fury played out much like what they had seen at Beth's farm. Some streets were still impassable, cordoned off by orange and white barricades. Power poles had been tumbled like matchsticks.

But in the midst of chaos, here and there, a potted plant survived…a child's bicycle, a glass shop front. Signs of hope in the midst of incredible sorrow. Drew pointed to a family of four sifting through what was left of their modest two-story home. "Everywhere I've gone so far, people have been amazing. They're putting it in perspective. Grateful to have each other." Left unspoken was the thought that not everyone had survived.

"Where are we going?" Beth asked, her voice subdued.

"The high school. They've set up a large shelter area in the gym. How do you feel about reading books to kids?"

"I have no idea. I'm never really around little ones very much."

"I'm in the same boat, but this came as a direct request from the shelter coordinator. They've provided phone service and internet connections so parents can deal with insurance details and anything else. But it's hard for the children to be cooped up. Schools are going to be closed for at least a week, probably longer. The principal is lining up volunteers to plan activities and give some structure to the days."

"I'll do whatever I can."

When they entered the gym, normally open to the community for basketball games and carnival nights, the scene was a cacophony of loud voices and crying children. Cots lined the floor in neat rows. It struck Drew that if he hadn't asked Beth to stay with him, she might have been a resident here as well. He couldn't imagine trying to keep a family together and entertained in the midst of such chaos.

Thankfully, it appeared that social services and law enforcement were handling this very personal disaster efficiently and compassionately. Emergency preparedness training had kicked in, and relief efforts were functioning like a well-oiled machine.

Drew steered Beth toward a far corner that served as command central. The site coordinator's face lit up when she saw them. "You're a gift from heaven," she said. "The TCC members have been amazing. We've already started three age groups with other volunteers. I'd like the two of you to take the eight, nine and ten-year-olds to classroom 107. There are fifteen of them in all. You'll find signs in the hallway directing you. Someone will deliver afternoon snacks." She handed Beth a copy of *Charlotte's Web* and two other books. "Thank you."

That was the extent of their training. Drew smiled at Beth ruefully. "Ready for this?"

She was rumpled and hot and her ponytail was awry. But her beautiful eyes sparked with mischief. "I can handle anything you dish out. Bring it on."

In moments, they were surrounded by a gaggle of youngsters chattering excitedly—except for the few whose sober faces reflected a very adult understanding of all they had lost. One little boy with a crooked haircut and pants that were too short held Drew's hand as they walked down the hall.

Beth took the lead, playing the role of Pied Piper as they led their charges to the assigned spot. It didn't take long to get the kids settled into their desks. The furniture was designed for adolescents, which was a novelty in itself. When a momentary quiet reigned, Beth lifted an eyebrow, holding up one of the books.

Drew shook his head. "I'll be bad cop, if necessary. You take the wheel."

Shaking her head with a wry smile, she took the teacher's chair, pulled it from behind the large oak desk and sat down facing her audience. If she was nervous, she didn't show it. After reading quietly through the first few paragraphs, she found her rhythm and injected a note of drama into Fern's character, particularly the girl's outrage when she found out the small pig was going to be killed.

At that moment, Drew realized his role as disciplinarian was going to be unnecessary. The children hung on Beth's every word. She read nonstop for forty-five minutes, creating voices for each new actor in the beloved story. Even Drew found himself caught up in the classic tale.

But after a while he went from listening to watching. The curve of Beth's lips as she smiled. The nuances of expression on her face. The way she made eye contact with each child, as if assuring every boy and girl that she was reading just to him or her.

It struck him that Beth Andrews would make an amazing mother. Drew hadn't spent much time thinking about marriage and babies and home and hearth. After all, he was only thirty-two. He had plenty of time.

But the storm's havoc made him reassess a lot of things. Watching families pull together in the last forty-eight hours had shown him the importance of being grounded. Jed lived in Dallas, their parents in south Texas. Drew travelled often. Though his work was satisfying and he had a wide circle of friends and extended relatives, for the first time he wondered if he was missing something very important. Maybe he needed to think about the bigger picture.

Beth ended a chapter as the promised refreshments arrived. Supervising snack time was a sticky, rowdy mess, but it reminded him of what it was like to be a kid. When the apples and peanut butter disappeared faster than a snowflake in the hot sun, he helped clean up the debris. Another volunteer arrived to shepherd the group of children back to their parents.

Drew straightened one last row of seats and grinned at

Beth. "Your talents are lost on farming. You should have been either a librarian or an actress."

Tucking wayward strands of hair behind her ears, she perched on the teacher's desk, her legs swinging. "To be honest, kids give me the heebie-jeebies. They scare me to death. One wrong word or move, and you've scarred them for life. It's too much responsibility. And as for being an actress, well…let's just say I prefer digging in the dirt."

He yawned and stretched, feeling tired but content. "It's hard to believe that forty-eight hours ago we were running for our lives."

"I know. It seems like a dream until you look outside. Then it smacks you in the face. I feel so sorry for all the people taking shelter here. Especially the ones with children. My house is damaged, but at least I have only myself to worry about."

"And your brother."

Beth's face closed up. "I don't want to talk about Audie."

"We're one man short at the stables. I could offer him a job. It's grunt work…doesn't pay much. But it would be better than nothing."

Despite the stuffy air in the classroom, Beth's pink cheeks paled. "That would be a very bad idea. Trust me." Her soft lips firmed in a grim line.

"It's not that big a deal. I really am looking for somebody."

"Then look somewhere else."

He stood, nonplussed, and wondered with a sick feeling in the pit of his stomach if Beth was as stubborn and intractable as his ex-fiancée. Whatever happened to sweet, amenable women?

Beth jumped down from the desk and walked toward the door. "We should see if they need us anywhere else."

"Wait." The command came out more urgently than he had intended.

Beth stopped and turned. Her posture was wary. "What's wrong?"

He went to her and rubbed a thumb over her cheek. "I've been wondering if those first two kisses were a fluke."

When her gaze went to his mouth, a tingle of something hot and heady settled in his gut.

She bit her lip. "Perhaps not flukes, but probably mistakes. Adrenaline…the will to live. That's all."

"Don't kid yourself, Beth. I haven't been able to stop thinking about them." He slid one hand beneath her hair, prepared to draw back if she made a protest. Instead, she looked up at him with curiosity and something more. It was that second emotion that stole his breath and made his hands shake.

Lowering his head, he found her lips with his. She tasted like peanut butter and cherry Kool-Aid. At first, her arms hung at her sides. He explored her mouth gently, his tongue brushing hers. The only other place their bodies connected was where his left hand cupped her chin.

In the storm cellar, emotions had run high. Now, in the broad light of day, he felt the same jolt of arousal. "Touch me," he said.

Slowly, her arms came up and twined around his neck. She stretched on her tiptoes, straining to get closer.

Lifting her off her feet, he strode to the teacher's desk and sat her there, moving into the V of her thighs. Now they were perfectly matched. He cupped her breast through her shirt. The door was unlocked. They were in a public building. Though he rubbed his thumb over her nipple, he knew he dared not go any further.

"I don't know what to do with you," he muttered.

She rested her forehead on his collarbone. "I have a few ideas."

Her droll humor startled a laugh from him. "I hope we're on the same page."

Her answer was to kiss him so sweetly that an entirely inopportune erection was the result. Breathing heavily, he stepped away, trying to elude temptation. "I think one of us is supposed to say this is going too fast."

She shrugged, leaning back on her hands. "I've had a terrible crush on you for over a year, even when you *were* being an obnoxious, overbearing plutocrat."

"Ouch." His wince was not feigned. Hearing her description of his less-than-stellar qualities made him squirm. "I thought we called a truce."

"Under duress and the threat of apocalypse."

"Then I'll say it again," he muttered quietly. "For the moment, I'm not going to fight with you or try to make you see reason."

She crooked a finger. He went to her like a kite on a string, hoping she didn't recognize the hold she had on him.

Beth kissed him again, but in a naughtier fashion this time. She pulled back and smiled, her lips swollen. "We're consenting adults. I'm staying at your house temporarily. Seems like the universe is giving us a sign."

He curled a hand behind her neck and pulled her mouth to his, no longer as in control as he would have liked. "If you believe in that kind of stuff."

"Are you turning me down?"

He jerked. "Hell, no. Besides, this was *my* idea."

"To-*may*-to, to-*mah*-to. But if we're going to share the credit, then we'll both share the blame when we crash and burn."

"Why would you say a thing like that?" He stole half

a second to nip her earlobe with sharp teeth. Her groaned sigh was his reward.

"You're you, and I'm me," she whispered with inescapable logic.

"So?"

"Don't ruin the moment, Farrell. We're the definition of short-term."

He sighed. "I don't want to argue about what ifs. Surely the tornado taught us that. Live in the moment. Carpe diem. Any cliché you want to choose. I've never come that close to disaster. I feel foolish saying it, but it changed me."

Beth stared at him, her green eyes bright. He wondered what she was thinking.

Finally she responded. "I think it's too soon to make a statement like that. Give it a week. A month. You'll be your old self."

"That's pretty cynical."

"People don't change, Drew."

"Are we talking about your brother again?"

"Let me get one thing straight. If you and I are contemplating a hook-up, there have to be ground rules. Number one is *forget about my brother.*"

"That's pretty cold."

"Take it or leave it. I don't tell you how to run your ranch. Please respect my wishes."

"And if it turns out to be more than a hook-up?"

"It won't. I won't let it. I like you, Drew. A lot. When you're not trying to push me around, you're funny and sexy and way too handsome for your own good. But long-term relationships are built on shared backgrounds and values."

"You think we don't have the same values?"

She stood up and straightened her clothing. "I think we're done here." She walked past him to the door and turned. "Are you coming with me?"

He grimaced. "I'll be a few minutes behind you."

She looked confused until she noticed the front of his pants. Her face flushed. "Ah. Well then. Okay."

Despite his physical discomfort, he had to chuckle when she left the room. Beth Andrews tried so hard to pretend she was a badass, but he knew the truth now. Her tough exterior concealed a woman who had perhaps been hurt one too many times. What she didn't know, however, was that Drew Farrell was a patient man. Sooner or later he would prove to her that the two of them were much more alike than she thought.

And when they ended up in bed during the process, he was pretty sure there were going to be fireworks and bells and enough heat to rival the Texas sun.

Eight

Beth navigated the gym, stopping to talk to a few people she recognized. Despite the circumstances, the large room felt comfortable and safe. Because so many families were in the same boat, a sense of camaraderie permeated the air.

Nobody was perfect. Tempers flared occasionally, and children fussed when they were tired and hungry. Without asking, Beth joined the line of volunteers helping serve a simple spaghetti dinner. Folding tables—hastily set up— accommodated the large crowd in shifts. She watched the hallway that led to the school proper and knew the moment Drew reappeared.

His eyes scanned the room. She couldn't tell if he saw her or not. Instead of crossing the gym in her direction, he spoke with the site coordinator and was soon climbing a very tall ladder to replace lightbulbs on the ceiling.

Beth loved the way he walked and moved. He was confident, masculine and strong. Drew was the kind of man who should have at least a couple of kids, maybe more. He would be an incredible father. Beth had no memory of her father, so she didn't have much personal basis for comparison. But she knew that things like compassion and generosity and gentleness were important.

While she had read *Charlotte's Web* to the group of children, one small boy had climbed without fanfare into

Drew's lap. Far from seeming uncomfortable, Drew had murmured something to the kid and curled an arm around his waist.

Witnessing that moment had twisted something in Beth's heart. But she ignored the wistful stab of longing. Perhaps because she was unable to decide if the pang was because of all *she* had missed as a child or because she was pretty sure she didn't have what it took to be a parent.

A request for a refill pulled her back to the present. It was clear that people in this room were dealing with a host of emotions. Obviously, they were grateful for the meal and the shelter. But many of the men and women gathered under this one big roof were unaccustomed to accepting handouts. They seemed shell-shocked, as if still not quite believing they had lost their homes and most of their possessions.

Beth had an advantage there. She had learned at an early age that *things* could be taken away. One dismal January when the rent was due and money was nonexistent, Beth's mother had done the unthinkable: she pawned the two shiny new bicycles a charity group had provided for Beth and Audie at Christmas. Audie wailed, but Beth never shed a tear, her grief and anger too deep to articulate. From then on, she understood that happiness was not to be trusted if it depended on accumulating material belongings.

She liked nice things. But she wasn't driven to purchase them for herself. It was far more satisfying to put time and effort into her fields and to watch new life grow. Her house had been ripped apart, and there was a good chance that her brother would rob her blind. But she had to let it go. Those realities were out of her control.

In the end, Audie could only hurt her if she valued what he took. She had no childhood mementos. No much-loved antiques that had been her grandmother's. No school trophies. No heirloom jewelry.

All she had was herself and her determination to make a good life. A clean life. A life worth living. It was a truth she shared with many in this room.

When the last of the refugees had been served, Beth and her co-workers sat down to eat. Drew snagged the seat beside her at the last minute. They ate quickly. It had been a long time since lunch.

Beneath the table, his thigh pressed against hers. The chairs were crunched closely together because of the confined space. It was impossible to ignore him even if she had wanted to.

He reached over and used his napkin to wipe a dab of sauce from her chin. "You about ready to go home?"

She nodded, feeling breathless suddenly. Drew's gaze was warm and intimate. Did he mean for the evening to conclude in a very special way? They were both dirty and sweaty. Nothing in their current situation could be construed as romantic by any stretch of the imagination. But when his hand brushed hers, her throat constricted and her body felt hot and achy.

For months she had seen him as an adversary. A very sexy, gorgeous man, but someone to keep at bay, nevertheless. Now, the lines were blurred. They had shared a terrifying experience. Not only that, but they were working side by side in the town they both loved.

Comrades in arms often developed deep friendships during time spent in battle. Beth and Drew found themselves serving in the trenches, as it were. Their physical closeness had accelerated the formation of a definite bond. But as much as she liked and respected Drew, she definitely wanted more than friendship.

Wanting was okay. Crossing a physical line was okay. As long as she understood he wasn't hers to keep.

Drew was bone tired and yet still aroused. He admired Beth so much. Despite personal losses, she had plunged headfirst into helping her neighbors. Instead of fretting about her own disaster, she acted as if nothing were wrong.

On the way back to the ranch, he glanced at his silent partner. "Do you want to stop by your house and check on things?"

"No." She didn't dress up her refusal.

"Are you sure? It won't take but a minute."

"I said no."

The snap in her voice pissed him off. He could have found any one of a number of topics to chat about, but her stubbornness shut him up. Surely her brother's situation weighed on her. It was easily within Drew's power to erase all that stress. He had a legitimate job available for Audie. If Beth had asked, Drew would even move Audie and his family to Willowbrook temporarily.

So either Beth didn't *want* to help her brother, or Beth didn't want to accept Drew's help. Come to think about it, she hadn't exactly been enthused about staying at Willowbrook Farms herself.

Pulling up in front of the home where he had lived since birth, Drew shoved the gearshift into park, got out, and slammed the door. Hard. If Beth didn't want his assistance, he wouldn't force it on her. He had better things to do than wrangle with a hardheaded woman.

He unlocked the front door, not waiting to see if she had followed him. The house echoed with emptiness. The housekeeper had gone home, as had all of Drew's staff except for the handful of guys who kept watch over the animals at night. Now he and Beth were alone. The thought tormented him.

He went straight to his bedroom, stripped off his filthy clothes and stalked toward the shower. The erection rearing thick and hungry against his belly made him grit his teeth. How in the hell could he want a woman so badly and at the same time feel the urge to shake her until her teeth rattled?

Usually he appreciated the luxury of triple showerheads. Tonight, the marble enclosure made him feel isolated and alone. That simple realization shook him. Since when did he *need* a woman? For sex, sure. He understood that drive. But the burning in his gut was about more than getting laid. He thought he and Beth had made progress toward becoming friends. Apparently, he was wrong.

He was so wound up in his righteous indignation that he didn't notice at first when the glass door opened.

"Need some company?"

He whirled around so fast his feet nearly slid out from under him. That would have topped it all. Ending up ass-first, naked and wet at her feet.

"Beth…." He eased off on the hot water. Steam made it difficult for him to see, and he definitely didn't want to miss a moment. "What are you doing here?"

It was a stupid question. Even he admitted that. She was wearing her shirt from today. And nothing else. The hem of the rumpled garment ended at the top of long, shapely legs. She had taken her hair down. Her toes curled against the stone floor, so maybe she wasn't quite as blasé as she wanted to appear.

"We started something earlier," she said. "At the school. I'm sorry I ruined the mood by arguing with you."

Some mysterious constriction in his chest eased. He

picked up a curl that lay on her shoulder. "So soft," he muttered.

"Do you still want me?"

"Oh, yes." Slowly, he unbuttoned her top. She'd had the foresight to remove her bra already. Soon nothing stood between him and the lush female flesh waiting to be touched, stroked, mapped with every hill and valley noted.

Beth seemed frozen, barely breathing. She watched him, eyes downcast, as he traced her collarbone, played lightly with her tight nipples, lifted and plumped her soft breasts. He was trying his damnedest to go slow. But when she closed her eyes and shuddered, he almost lost it.

Gently, he tugged at the cotton shirt until it slid down her arms. He pulled it free and tossed it out of the shower. "Come inside," he said hoarsely. "We're getting the bathroom floor wet."

His prosaic request sounded awkward to his ears. But coherent speech was difficult if not impossible. All the blood in his body had run south, leaving him lightheaded and perilously lost to reason.

Beth looked up at him. She laid a hand, palm flat, against his stubbly cheek. "Will you wash my hair?" she asked. Her big shadowy eyes held secrets…feminine wiles. She was so close to him their thighs brushed. His sex throbbed against her belly, eager to see action.

"Of course," he said gruffly. "Turn around."

Her creamy skin was flawless. Until now, he had never realized that shoulder blades could be sexy. But when they pointed the way to a nipped-in waist and a butt shaped to fit a man's hands, the view was mouthwatering. He kissed the nape of her neck before reaching for a plastic bottle. His shampoo was scented with pine. He had a feeling that from tonight forward, this particular smell was going to provoke a Pavlovian response.

Easing her backward a step, he covered her eyes with his hand and directed the stream of water until it darkened and straightened her thick, vibrant hair. When every strand was soaked, he adjusted the spray in the opposite direction and pulled her flush against him until her bottom nestled in the cradle of his thighs.

It was a very perverse form of self-torture, but things got worse when he began rubbing soapy liquid into her hair. His fingers caressed her scalp. Beth groaned—a sexy, visceral sound that tightened every muscle in his body despite the warm shower. It was the most effective form of foreplay he had ever tried.

Beth seemed to be enjoying it, but more to the point, the gentle massage actually sent *his* libido into a state of high alert. He reached around her with both arms and slid his hands across slick breasts. Was *she* panting, or was it he?

It occurred to him—despite his mental faculties being sluggish—that the sooner he finished this project, the sooner he'd have Beth in his bed where he wanted her. Exercising admirable control, he returned to the task at hand and began rinsing her hair. Tiny soap bubbles clung to his fingers, even as strands of dark gold wound themselves around his wrists.

Beth remained silent. Since he was behind her, he couldn't see her expression. Finally, after interminable minutes, he decided his job was complete. He had to clear his throat to speak. "All done," he said.

She turned slowly, her lips curved in a smile of feminine amusement. "You have hidden talents, Mr. Farrell."

"I'm only getting started."

"That's nice to know." The air that surrounded them was thick with moisture and charged with anticipation.

Without asking for permission, she reached for the soap and a washcloth. Something about the lazy movements of her hands as she rubbed the plain white bar against the navy cotton square mesmerized him. "I think I was already clean before you joined me," he pointed out, eager to move things along.

Beth reached up to kiss him, her lips clinging just long enough to drive him insane.

"I should make sure you didn't miss any spots," she whispered. "Put your hands behind your neck and spread your legs."

He obeyed instinctively. Compliance was a foregone conclusion.

Without realizing it, he closed his eyes. When Beth touched him on the upper thigh, he flinched…hard. Her husky laugh sent desire raging through his veins. "Hell, Beth. Warn a guy, why don't you?"

Warm, rough strokes were her answer. Somehow she managed to avoid his erection. She dragged the wet, soapy cloth over and around his thighs and between his legs. His teeth dug so hard into his lower lip he tasted the tang of blood.

"Enough," he groaned.

"If you say so." She aimed the water at his abdomen, creating a waterfall that cascaded down his groin. In some dim, barely reasoning corner of his brain, he registered the fact that his next water bill was going to be outrageous.

Without warning, slender fingers closed around his shaft. *Holy hell.* He was so close to coming that his vision blurred.

With her free hand, she stroked his chest. "Don't fight it, Drew," she whispered. "Let go. Enjoy."

He grabbed her close, clutching her against him as he came with an audible groan that encompassed shock, amazement and physical nirvana.

* * *

Beth scarcely knew herself. It had taken great courage to invade Drew's privacy impetuously. But earlier today, they had turned up the heat. The wanting and needing had remained on a slow boil all afternoon and evening. It was only her stubbornness that had caused the rift.

Drew wanted to do everything he could for her. He was generous to a fault. And even Beth acknowledged that providing assistance to those in need should not always be predicated on whether or not the recipient *deserved* the help.

But Audie was a different story. Beth had been burned too many times in the past to believe that her brother had really changed. She loathed the idea of Drew taking a peek into her life, her gene pool. How could he look at Audie and *not* make some judgments about Beth, even if they were unconscious?

Since she didn't want to get into complicated explanations of why she wanted to keep Drew far away from her brother, she did the next best thing. She let Drew see how much she wanted him, and how far she was willing to go.

Even in the aftermath of an impressive orgasm, he was quick on the uptake. He hustled them both out of the shower and made her stand still while he dried her from head to toe with a thick towel. Remaining passive beneath his touch was no hardship. His gentle care was at once soothing and arousing.

"Open your eyes, Beth."

She obeyed reluctantly, fearing what she might see on his face. Taking the lead in sex the way she had in the shower was not her M.O. Some men would not like the tables being turned. It was programmed into male DNA to be the pursuer.

Drew stared at her, his eyes glittering with unveiled

hunger. "I applaud your inventive enthusiasm, but this next time I'm not leaving you behind."

"I can live with that."

He scooped her into his arms and carried her into his bedroom. She had been so nervous going into this that his masculine domain had barely registered. Now, particularly after he turned on a small lamp on the chest, she saw a room that was both elegant and comfortable.

The navy carpet alone was hedonistic. Thick and soft, it invited toes to flex in its luxury. The bed was massive, a dark mahogany four-poster king covered in ivory damask. There was nothing remotely feminine about the decorating scheme, but Beth fell in love with the ambiance.

Drew appeared to hesitate for a moment. She looked up at him. "Is there a problem?"

His lips curled in a smile that sent shivers down her spine. "Not at all. I was merely counting up how many times and ways I want to take you and where to start."

Her mouth dried. Feverish and needy, she raked her fingernails across his shoulder. "Swear you mean that."

"Every word."

Dumping her on her feet without ceremony, he threw back the covers and ripped open a drawer in the bedside table to find protection. The handful of packets he dropped on the tabletop was impressive.

He crooked a finger, his flash of white teeth wicked. "It's your turn now, little tease. Prepare to be ravished."

Without protest, she allowed him to draw her toward a mattress that seemed a mile wide. She shrieked when he lifted her without warning and tossed her onto soft sheets. Scrambling to appear worldly rather than awkward and ungainly, she curled on her side and pulled a corner of the sheet over her.

With one quick jerk of his hand, her modesty was history. "Don't hide from me, Beth."

"I wasn't."

His knowing smile acknowledged her lie. "Put your hands behind your neck and spread your legs."

Somehow, when Drew repeated the command she had spoken to him in the shower, the words took on a whole new meaning. She melted from the inside out, every muscle in her body turning to heat and energy.

He watched with hooded eyes as she forced herself to comply. Deliberately exposing her sex to his hungry gaze took more courage than it had to invade his shower. "Be gentle with me," she joked, jittery with nervous anticipation.

"The first time."

Wow. How could a man infuse three syllables with such delicious intent and promise? She sucked in a deep breath and exhaled as he lowered himself next to her, his body radiating heat. "Why have we waited so long to do this?" he asked, teasing her navel with a fingertip.

She writhed and panted. "Because I'm a thorn in your side."

"I can't remember why." He bent his head and kissed her flat tummy.

"That's because you're not thinking with the correct portion of your anatomy."

"Damned straight. We're in the midst of a truce. So I propose that you stay in my bed for as many hours as it takes for us both to get tired of each other."

"How long will that be?"

He parted the folds of her sex with his thumbs. Her back arched instinctively.

"I'll let you know," he muttered.

After that, conversation halted in favor of sheer, carnal

pleasure. Drew's expertise was unmistakable. He touched her reverently, like a man examining a newfound treasure.

When she wanted him to go fast, he slowed down. When she craved more pressure, he gave her butterfly caresses. Pleasure built. Wanting multiplied. Her climax hit with the force of a thunderstorm, drenching her with delirium.

She reached for him. "Drew. Drew...."

He did what had to be done and moved between her legs, sliding his hands beneath her thighs and opening her even further to his possession. Feeling the blunt head of his sex as he pushed into her was in some ways more frightening than the tornado. How could she survive this? She had been halfway in love with him for months, disguising her silly unrequited crush as indifference.

Apparently, one of the reasons she had argued with him about her produce stand and her customers was to keep him coming back again and again. How pathetic was that? She'd lied to herself and not even seen the truth. If it had not already been far too late for second thoughts, she might have run from the room. With every stroke of his body inside hers, he left his imprint. She would never be the same.

But as he loved her slowly and tenderly, fear gave way to wonder and hesitation became assurance. Nothing so wonderful could be a mistake. She gave herself up to the deep, drugged pleasure of his lovemaking.

Muscles bunched in his arms as he struggled to keep his weight off her. "Tell me you won't regret this," he demanded.

"I came to you, remember?"

"Doesn't matter. I see your eyes. You're already running scared."

His perspicacity embarrassed her. She couldn't deny the truth.

So she arched her back, driving him a fraction deeper,

clenching his hard length with inner muscles. "I'm here now. Don't stop, Drew. Please." She teetered on the brink of a spectacular finish.

His answer was to give her everything she wanted. No more nuances. No more time for talk. He was big and hard and determined to push her off the ledge. "Come for me, darlin'," he muttered.

She did as he asked, but only because she had no choice. If she had ever experienced such pure, crystalline pleasure, she couldn't remember it. The ripples went on and on, leaving her breathless and lost.

Drew was seconds behind her, his climax signaled by a harsh shout and thrusting hips. With her legs wrapped around his waist, Beth clung to his wide shoulders and held on as her universe tumbled out of control.

Nine

Drew lay perfectly still, waiting for his thundering heartbeat to return to a normal cadence. Beth had fallen asleep immediately, worn out by their long day and his crazed lovemaking. As promised, he had taken her more than once—the second time sitting in an armchair with Beth straddling his lap, and finally, bending her over the foot of the bed and making the last coupling slow and sweet.

By all rights, he should be exhausted as well. But adrenaline pumped through his veins. Being with Beth tonight had been far more than physically gratifying. The connection they forged had opened his eyes to what was missing in his life. Falling in love with a woman had been something for the future…the kind of thing a man did when he was ready to settle down.

Apparently, unbeknownst to him, love had grown in spite of his self-deception. As incredible as it seemed, his frequent trips to Beth's place of business had been about far more than her patrons spooking his horses.

He had been irresistibly drawn to her spirit and her beauty. The storm's wrath had ripped away wood and metal and shingles, but it had also laid bare an astonishing truth. Drew Farrell had feelings for Beth Andrews. Deep, messy emotions.

Her head lay pillowed on his shoulder. He combed her

curls with one hand as contentment slid through his veins like honey. Tomorrow she would probably fuss about how her hair looked because she had not dried it. But Drew liked the wild tangle. It was a reflection of the intimacy they had shared.

She had let down her guard with him tonight. For a woman so fiercely independent, he understood very well what a gift she offered. They had met as equals and by her choice. What he didn't know was the outcome of tonight's excess.

Tomorrow would be the test. Would he see the real Beth, or would the walls be up once again?

Beth awoke at first light, disoriented, but very relaxed. It took a handful of seconds for reality to come crashing in. Drew's room. Drew's bed. Drew's big, muscular body wrapped around hers.

What have I done?

The wanting had been building for over a year. No surprises there. But why had she acted on it? Why now?

She could tell herself it was because of the storm or because she was staying in Drew's house or even because she was lonely and displaced. But the truth was far simpler. Yesterday, she had felt the relentless pull of sexual need, and she had given in. Not only that, she had wallowed in it without shame or regret.

The truth was shocking but impossible to ignore.

Gingerly, she lifted his heavy arm and scooted away from him. He stirred, grumbling, but buried his face in his pillow and continued to sleep.

Fortunately, gathering her things was not an issue. One shirt. That was it. One shirt to protect her modesty as she scuttled back to her room. She had no idea how early the household staff arrived, but surely not at this hour.

When she made it without incident to the relative safety of her own suite, she debated what to do. It would probably be a good idea to wet her hair and dry it again before getting dressed. But a yawn caught her by surprise. It had been a harrowing three days. Removing her one item of clothing, she tossed back the covers on the decadently luxurious bed and climbed naked beneath the sheets.

It was a warm autumn in Texas, but the crisp cotton felt chilled after snuggling with Drew all night. Her body was pleasurably sore as she settled into a comfy spot. Remembering Drew's attentions was not a good idea. After a long hiatus, her libido was alive and well.

Closing her eyes, she gave herself over to the numbing drug of sleep. She had acted rashly, impulsively, totally without forethought. The results had been amazing, but it was time to retreat and regroup.

She knew now what it was like to be with Drew. It was good. Really good. Before she got in too deeply, she had to set some ground rules for herself. Drew's amicability was only temporary. When she was living in her house again, they would revert to the same impasse. Drew had the time and the money and the determination to badger her until she gave in to his wishes. Plus, the storm had weakened her resolve and her certainty about the farm as her life's work.

Equally depressing was the fact that Audie would always be a millstone around her neck. She came from questionable roots. Everyone in the horse business knew that breeding was everything.

Even if a tornado had thrown Beth and Drew together—literally—they had nothing in common but sharing a frightening ordeal. That wasn't enough on which to build a relationship.

After an hour of tossing and turning, she gave up and

got out of bed. Perhaps a hot shower would settle her jangled emotions. The prospect of coming face to face with Drew made her ridiculously nervous. What would she say to him?

She dressed in a pair of faded jeans and a comfortable sky blue polo shirt. No need to make a good impression. There was work to be done.

After a quick call to her insurance agent to follow up on Allen's report, she went in search of breakfast. If she were lucky, Drew would be somewhere out on the ranch tending to business. The thought of a hot cup of coffee with a side of morning solitude was irresistible.

Unfortunately, only half of her order was on the menu. When she entered the kitchen, she pulled up short, dismayed to find it full of people, or so it seemed. Though the housekeeper excused herself to go tend to the laundry, the kitchen table was occupied. Drew and Jed and a woman who looked strangely familiar were helping themselves to bacon and sausage and eggs as well as pancakes and grapefruit.

"Sorry to intrude," she said quietly. "I'll just grab a cup of coffee."

Drew stood up and pulled out a chair. "Don't be silly. Join us." The look in his eyes dared her to disagree.

With her cheeks warm and her legs quivering, she sank into the chair and tried not to flinch when Drew's hand brushed her shoulder. Had the motion been deliberate? The last thing in the world she had expected or wanted was an audience for their inescapable morning after.

Jed touched the woman's arm. "Kimberly, this is Beth Andrews. Her house was damaged by the tornado, so she's staying here at Willowbrook for a bit."

The brunette smiled. "I know who you are, but you probably don't remember me. I came to Green Acres several times last summer to buy vegetables. Your heirloom tomatoes were so good."

"Thank you," Beth said. "And yes, I do remember you now. You used to come into the bank when I was working there…you made deposits for the dress shop."

"Yes, I did."

"So," Drew said, changing the subject and lifting an eyebrow as he stared at his brother. "I'm always glad to have guests for breakfast, but I'm sensing your visit has a particular agenda."

Jed looked at Kimberly. She motioned for him to do the honors. Jed took her hand and faced his brother. "Kimberly and I are going to get married." After noting the shocked silence from Drew and Beth, he continued. "We had planned to do something quick and easy at the courthouse, but obviously that's out of the question. And we're not sure it's appropriate to have a marriage ceremony at all with so many people suffering."

Jed and Kimberly sat shoulder to shoulder, their fingers entwined. Between them shimmered an almost palpable tenderness. Beth couldn't help but feel a twinge of envy. Jed looked at Kimberly as if she were the answer to all his prayers wrapped up in one lovely package.

Drew cleared his throat, obviously emotional about his younger brother getting hitched. "Congratulations, you two."

Beth nodded and smiled. "And from me as well. But I have to say, I think a wedding might be the perfect occasion to bring some joy and cheer to what have been pretty bleak days in Royal."

"You could have the ceremony here," Drew said. "We'll invite all our friends."

"I'd be honored to help any way I can," Beth said. "Though to be honest, I don't know much about planning an event like that. But I am pretty organized if that counts for anything."

Kimberly's smile held gratitude. "You're both being very sweet about this, but the thing is…" She trailed off, biting her lip.

Jed picked up where she left off. "The thing is…an affair like that takes time to put together."

Drew frowned. "What's the rush, Jed? Can't Dallas do without you for another six or eight weeks? You could fly back and forth if you needed to."

Jed's cheekbones flushed with color. The look he gave Kimberly was so fiercely and intimately personal, Beth felt as if she were witnessing something very private.

"Go on," Kimberly whispered, her cheeks rosy as well. She gazed at Jed with starry-eyed adoration.

Jed kissed her gently on the cheek before turning back to his brother. "Kimberly and I are going to have a baby. In about six months."

Beth had seldom seen Drew speechless, but he couldn't have looked any more surprised if someone had whacked him over the head with a two by four. "A baby? Why didn't you tell me before now?"

Jed and Kimberly exchanged wry glances. "I only found out myself right before the storm hit. I had just asked her to marry me when all hell broke loose."

Beth laughed softly. "That must have been some proposal."

Drew stood up and tugged his brother and Kimberly to their feet, hugging them fiercely. "I'm damned happy and excited for the both of you." He kissed Kimberly's cheek gently. "Welcome to the family. Jed's a lucky man."

After that, the conversation escalated, everyone talking at once and making plans. Beth glanced at her watch.

"Oh, shoot. I've got to run. I promised Megan that I'd help her again today."

Drew's brows drew together as he frowned. "I'll take you."

Beth stood her ground. She needed a little personal space. It was hard to be rational with Drew in touching distance. "It will be better for me to drive myself," she said. "I don't know how long I'll be there. And besides, the three of you have lots to talk about. I'll be back by suppertime."

She cut and ran before he could argue. With his brother and soon to be sister-in-law in his kitchen, he couldn't very well chase after her.

By the time she reached the shelter, she had made a firm decision not to think about Drew for the rest of the day. It was a good goal if she could stick to it.

Megan was delighted to see her. "Beth, you're wonderful to come help when you have your own problems. How are things going with your house?"

"Believe it or not, and thanks to Drew who got me in with a building inspector, it looks like I may have a check in hand by the middle of next week. Now all I have to do is line up a contractor."

"You two are being awfully chummy considering your history. Couldn't you ask Drew to help with that, too?"

Beth shook her head. "I'm sure he *could,* but I'm not going to let him. I'm a grown woman. My house is my responsibility. Besides, he—" She stopped short, realizing that Jed and Kimberly might not want their business blabbed all over the county.

Megan cocked her head, her arms full of wriggling kittens. "He what?"

"You have to promise me you won't say anything. I don't know if this news is ready to go public yet."

The other woman mimed locking her lips. "I'll take it to my grave."

"Drew's brother Jed is getting married. To Kimberly Fanning. And the wedding will be at Willowbrook, I think. Drew is going to be plenty busy without me playing the helpless female."

"That's exciting. But I'm sure no one looks at you as a helpless *anything,* Beth. Look at how you started your farm from scratch."

"Well, the tornado took care of that. I'll bet my pumpkins ended up smashed to bits all over the county."

"At least you can joke about it."

Beth shrugged. "I'm one of the lucky ones. I wasn't injured, and my house is not a total loss. I can't complain."

"You certainly have a great attitude about all of this. I suppose it helps to have a handsome rancher in your back pocket."

"I told you before. Drew is only being kind." The excuse was not quite as easy to stand behind today. Not with everything that had happened in Drew's bed last night. She felt her cheeks heat. Her vow not to think about the sexy billionaire was shot already, which didn't say much about her willpower.

Megan deposited the kittens in front of a large bowl of milk and touched Beth's arm. "Your new friend has been waiting for you." She pointed to a cage nearby.

"Oh, Stormy." Beth's heart melted. The little dog looked healthy, but his mournful eyes seemed to say he had hoped Beth would come back. She unlocked the mesh door and scooped him up for a hug. "I didn't forget about you, I swear. You are the sweetest thing."

Stormy burrowed closer with a bark of happiness.

Megan grinned. "He knows a soft touch when he sees one."

"Has anyone asked about him?"

"No. I traced the number on his collar and spoke with his owner. Turns out they dumped him on my doorstep because they couldn't afford dog food anymore. Stormy is an orphan."

"What is his real name?"

"Do you honestly want to know? Or would you rather think of him as Stormy?"

"Good point. Will it confuse him if I call him that?"

Megan laughed. "As long as you agree to be his mama, I think he'll let you do anything you want."

Drew was happy for his brother and Kimberly. He really was. But a man had a finite amount of patience for wedding details—unless of course, it was his own woman bubbling over with joy. With one ear he listened to Jed make suggestions to his newly-minted fiancée about ways to use the elegance of Willowbrook Farms for a romantic occasion. Even keeping things simple, the timetable would be a challenge.

Drew chimed in when appropriate, but in truth, all he could think about was Beth. Wet and willing in his shower. Naked and naughty in his bed. Limber and luscious in any number of heart-pounding scenarios. The previous night was etched in his memory. Probably forever. He knew they were attracted to each other. What he hadn't expected was the feelings that went beyond the physical.

The raw need and urgent passion Beth stirred in his gut alarmed him. It had been a long time since a sexual encounter turned him inside out. He'd felt invincible.

But when he woke up this morning, Beth was gone. He told himself there was no need to jump to conclusions. Maybe she was bashful about rehashing their experience in the cold light of day…or perhaps embarrassed that someone might see her come out of his room.

Or maybe it hadn't been good for her.

He refused to believe that. Beth had been like sunshine in his arms…passionate, teasing, warming him in every way possible. When he showered this morning, his body had reminded him painfully of last night's excess. His sex hardened as he remembered the feel of her hands on his body.

Instead of hunting her down in her room, he'd done the gentlemanly thing and waited for her in the kitchen. Then all his plans had gone awry when Jed and Kimberly showed up. Drew had not had a single opportunity to talk privately with Beth. In fact, she'd barely made eye contact with him.

And now she was gone for the day. He could drop by the shelter again, but he had no real excuse for doing so. He'd never lacked confidence when it came to women. But he'd rather not have witnesses to a post-coital confrontation that might not turn out the way he hoped.

He glanced at his watch and stood up. "You two lovebirds stay as long as you want. But I promised to help at the courthouse today. They're trying to recover as many documents as possible before it rains again. I may try to speak to Colby Richardson, too. Offer my sympathies. He's come back to town to bury his brother, Craig, and to be supportive of Craig's widow, Paige. That and dealing with the ranch will be a lot for one man to handle."

Jed nodded. "Yeah, it will. I'm supposed to work a shift later. I'll see you down there."

Drew hugged Kimberly, stunned to realize that the thought of being an uncle was pretty damned exciting. "Welcome to the family."

* * *

As Drew neared the turn to Green Acres, he pondered Beth's attitude toward Audie. *Forget about my brother.* Surely she didn't really mean that. He turned his truck onto Beth's road, calling himself all kinds of a fool. But try as he might, he couldn't ignore the fact that Audie needed a job and Drew could help. Surely that would ease some of Beth's emotional burden. She didn't need to be worrying about her brother in addition to everything else she was juggling.

The house looked much the same. Fortunately, the moderate temperatures had continued, so no one was in any danger of freezing to death, even if the shed wasn't heated. Audie sat on a tree stump smoking. He didn't move when Drew put the vehicle in park and got out.

Drew lifted a hand. "Thought I'd stop by and check on you."

Audie's nodded. "Where's sis?"

"Helping out at the animal shelter. I'm sure she'll see you later."

"Wouldn't count on it." Audie paused to flick a mosquito off his knee. "Can I help you with something?"

"Actually, I might be able to help you. One of my stable hands quit last week, so I have a job available. It's not glamorous work. The pay is decent but not great. But since you're staying here, you could save up a deposit for another place in town."

"Does Beth know you're here?"

A warning flag went up. "No. This is between us."

"She won't like it. She doesn't believe I've really changed."

"Changed how?"

"I've been a drunk most of my life. But I finally started

going to AA, and now I've been sober for six months. My history is why I've had trouble getting a job."

"How bad is it?"

Audie shrugged. "I've had a few run-ins with the law. Nothing major. I had to clean up my act when the baby came along."

"We run a tight ship at Willowbrook. You would be answering to my manager. I'm doing this for your sister, but I expect a lot from my men."

"I hear what you're saying."

"In that case, do you want the job?"

Audie took off a stained baseball cap and scratched his head. "I don't much like gettin' up early."

Drew winced inwardly. He was beginning to see why Beth had issues with Audie. "The job is 7:30 to 4:00 with half an hour for lunch and two fifteen minute breaks. No smoking anywhere on the property."

"Okay. I guess I can live with that. I appreciate you taking a chance on me."

"Let me be straight with you, Audie. I could have a dozen guys lining up for the chance to work at Willowbrook. My stable hands are the best in the business. You'll learn a lot from them. The only reason I'm offering you this job is because I care about your sister."

Audie nodded. "I bet you do."

Drew inhaled sharply. With two hands, he took Audie by the collar and lifted him to his toes— wishing he could put his hands around his neck.

Audie went the color of skim milk when Drew got in his face and snarled, "You will *not* disrespect your sister. Are we clear?" When the man nodded, Drew released him, chest heaving.

Beth's skinny sibling got to his feet, grabbed up his dust-covered ball cap, and had the audacity to ask for more.

"I'll need a way to get to work. Can't leave the wife and kid without a car."

This time Drew had to count to ten. "One of my guys passes here every morning. I'll see if he's willing to pick you up. Now do you want the job or not?"

"Yeah. I appreciate it. I really do. But Beth may get her feathers ruffled. She's not big on taking help."

"Are you the only family she has? I know your parents are gone. But no aunts and uncles? Cousins?"

"Wouldn't know on my dad's side. Mama was an only child. Me and Beth aren't bosom buddies. She's a little uppity. Thinks she's better than me."

"I warned you."

Audie took two steps backward. "I gotta check on things."

"You'll be ready in the morning?"

"Yup."

"Don't waste this opportunity."

"I won't, Mr. Farrell. You won't be sorry."

Ten

Drew brooded about the unsettling encounter with Beth's brother all the way into town. No wonder Beth had warned him off. Audie's reinvention of himself might or might not be the real deal. Only time would tell. But Drew was determined to insert himself between Beth and the stress of looking after her brother. She didn't need to worry about Audie and his family if Drew was around to help. It was the least Drew could do.

In Royal, reality hit once again. Sifting through the wreckage of Town Hall was a distraction, but not a welcome one. Knowing people had lost their lives on this very spot was sobering. A pall of tragedy lay over the site. Though at least two dozen volunteers worked side by side in an attempt to recover valuable records, there was no joking, no camaraderie. Faces were grim. Eyes were shadowed with grief.

Lord knew how anything would ever get back to normal.

In the midst of the backbreaking work, once again Drew realized how lucky he and Beth had been. Imagining her snatched from his side by a killer tornado made him queasy. And it could have happened. So easily....

Today, the skies above were innocent and blue, nothing at all like what he remembered from the day of the storm. He had a feeling that many in Royal would experience post-traumatic stress in the weeks and months to come. Thankfully, the calendar said they were on the tail end of tornado season, but next spring would be another story. Every thunderstorm promised to be nerve-wracking, especially for the children who didn't really understand these things.

Pausing to take a swig of water, he noticed a piece of paper flapping in the breeze, anchored by a chunk of concrete block. He squatted to pick it up and saw that it was a fragment of a marriage license. Neither of the names was familiar to him. But for a moment, he was struck by how many people would be affected by this mess at Town Hall. Were any of the computer records recoverable?

After his long, difficult shift wrapped up, he acknowledged he wasn't going to have any peace of mind until he had it out with Beth. He was hot and tired and second-guessing himself about getting involved with Audie. Sooner or later he would have to confess to Beth what he had done. His job offer had been motivated by a desire to help Beth, perhaps even to earn her gratitude. But he was coming to realize that she didn't always see things the way Drew did. He would postpone that hurdle for as long as possible.

Cell service was pretty good now. He thought about calling or texting, but instead, he drove over to the shelter, arriving just as Beth walked out the front door. She didn't notice him at first. Her head was bent as she talked softly to a little bundle of caramel-colored fur.

Drew closed the distance between them. "I remember that little fellow. What's his name?"

Beth halted abruptly, seeming startled but pleased to see him. "I call him Stormy. It turns out his owners abandoned him the other day. I may adopt him as soon as my house is finished."

"Lucky dog." He toyed with the puppy's ear. "We need to talk about last night."

Beth's cheeks turned pink. "Lower your voice, for Pete's sake. And if you mean the sex—" She stopped abruptly.

He smoothed her hair behind her ear. She hadn't worn it up this time. The long gold waves danced in the breeze. "What *about* the sex?"

Her head ducked as she focused all her interest on the dog. "It was good."

"Good? That's it? Not much of an affirmation."

"What do you want from me, Drew?" She shot him a sideways glance that told him she wasn't accustomed to discussing her sex life so matter-of-factly.

Come to think of it, neither was he. But he wanted to be sure that last night was not a one-time thing. "I've thought about you all day," he murmured, thankful that Megan was not in earshot. "I was disappointed to wake up and find you gone."

"I wasn't thinking very clearly. I didn't want to make a mistake."

"And did you?"

At last she raised her chin. Squaring her shoulders, she met his gaze full on, her smile small but genuine. "I'll let you know."

He shook his head with a rueful grin, glancing at his watch. "You're a hard woman, Beth Andrews." Her stubbornness worried him on another count. Drew planned to tell her he had hired Audie. And to explain that his intention in doing so was to make life easier for Beth…because he cared about her.

But her pride and her aversion to taking help might be Drew's downfall. This *thing* between the two of them was fragile. Before confessing, he had to be sure she wanted him enough to overlook the fact that he had gone behind her back.

"I came by with a proposition," he said. "How would you feel about a quick trip to Dallas?"

"Don't we have plenty to do here?"

"Of course we do. But Jed is supposed to be present at a meeting tomorrow morning at his headquarters. He doesn't want to leave Kimberly right now, so I said I would take his place since I sit on his board. If you come along, we can spend the night, have a nice dinner, take a break from all of this."

"I don't have anything to wear."

"I thought you might say that. Kimberly works at a clothing store in town."

"A very high-end establishment," Beth said wryly. "Not my price range at all."

"She's already picked out several outfits with her discount. You can return any you don't like."

"Has anyone ever told you how bossy you are?"

"It might have come up." He kissed her cheek. "C'mon, Beth. Say yes."

"Isn't it a little late to be booking a flight?"

"I have a helicopter."

Well, of course you do. Beth gaped, although why she was surprised, she didn't know. Drew was an incredibly wealthy man. "I see." She wrinkled her nose, deciding how honest she was willing to be. "After the tornado, I'm not sure I'm up for riding in anything that whirls in the sky."

Drew chuckled. "My pilot is one of the best. You have nothing to worry about."

Except being wined and dined and treated like a queen and falling in love with the king. That kind of stuff could go to a girl's head. "Okay. But I've never flown before, so if I freak out, it's all your fault."

He wrapped his arms around her from behind and nuzzled her ear. "I'll take care of you, Beth. I swear."

He was warm and tall, and his hard, muscled arms folded her close. Instinctively, she leaned into him, her back against his chest. Her heart began to jump and race. Stormy wriggled in her arms, ready to get down and play. Beth swallowed hard. "I should see if Megan needs anything else."

Drew nipped her earlobe. "Come home with me, now. Kimberly promised to have the dresses at the ranch by dinnertime. She and Jed are going to eat with us. After that, I'm planning on an early night."

Beth peeked over her shoulder, their lips almost touching. "Because you're exhausted from working all day?"

Drew's eyes flashed with barely concealed hunger. His jaw, covered in dark stubble, was carved in granite. Clearly, he hadn't shaved that morning. "I could be comatose," he said gruffly, "and I would still want you in my bed. But don't count on getting much sleep. You can nap at the hotel tomorrow while I go to the meeting."

An odd lethargy stole through Beth's muscles, making her limbs weak. He smelled of sweat and warm male. Not a combination she'd ever found erotic before now. But then again, Drew Farrell was one of a kind.

"Let me tell Megan I'm leaving," she whispered, ruefully aware that his sexuality drew her despite her determination to establish boundaries. She didn't even *want* to resist. Not anymore.

Drew waited in his truck with the engine running while she said her goodbyes and tucked Stormy back into his cage. The puppy settled onto his soft, warm blanket and rested his chin on his paws, regarding her with mournful eyes.

"Don't give me that look," she said, laughing at the small animal's innate ability to make her feel guilty. "You're going to live with me. But not yet."

With one quick word to Megan, who was struggling to coax a large Labrador into eating unfamiliar food, Beth grabbed her purse and her water bottle and ran outside. Drew's impatience was palpable.

Grinning to herself—equally eager for the night ahead—she pulled in behind him and followed him back to the ranch.

An hour later, standing in the beautiful bedroom Drew had given her, Beth stared at herself in the mirror and bit her lip. "I don't know, Kimberly. Isn't it a little…um… skimpy?"

Kimberly laughed, handing her a mist-gray shawl that was soft as a butterfly wing. "The dress is perfect. It showcases your assets."

If by assets the other woman meant breasts, then yes. No question there. The black cocktail dress dipped low in the front and even lower in the back. The silk and jersey blend clung to every curve of Beth's body as if it had been sewn onto her. Narrow rhinestone straps were its only embellishment.

"This must be horribly expensive," she said. How could she justify purchasing anything so frivolous and impractical when her house was partially demolished? She was playing dress-up with a man who was way out of her league.

"I'm giving you my discount. You can afford all of this stuff and not break the bank." Kimberly obviously picked up on Beth's ambivalence. She shook her head and folded her arms across her chest. "I think I know what's going on. You have a thing for Drew, but you don't want to get hurt."

"You have to admit that we're an unlikely couple. His prize thoroughbreds have a better lineage than I do."

Kimberly took her arm and steered her toward a chair, forcing her to sit. The other woman stretched out on the bed on her side, propping up on one elbow. "Let me tell you a story, Beth. It might help."

"I'm not sure I understand."

"Jed and I were high school sweethearts."

"I had no idea."

"Well, it was a long time ago. Up until this summer when he came home for our reunion, I hadn't seen him in a decade."

"That must have been odd."

"Odd and awkward. Because I was the one who broke up with him."

"Ouch."

"Yeah. We were madly in love. He was headed off to college, but he wanted to give me a ring before he left."

"And what about you?"

"I didn't have the money to go to college. My parents and younger brother were killed in a car accident when I was fifteen. There was only a tiny life insurance policy. My grandmother lived with us and was in poor health. So, all during high school I was her caretaker. It was everything I could do to keep my grades up, go out with Jed occasionally and make sure Grammy was looked after."

"That must have been terrible."

"Not terrible, exactly. Just a lot of hard work. But by the time graduation rolled around, I realized that Grammy was sliding into dementia. Jed was brilliant. He had multiple acceptance letters from colleges and universities all over the country. But he chose to go to Austin so he would be able to come home and see me regularly."

"So why did you break it off?"

"I knew it was an impossible situation. He deserved to do all the things young men are supposed to do when they get out on their own. I couldn't bear the thought of dragging him down."

"I see."

"I don't think you do. I made assumptions about his feelings for me. I told myself it was puppy love. That he would meet lots of girls in college—suitable females with family backgrounds similar to his. I did the noble thing and let him go."

"And?"

"I broke his heart," Kimberly said flatly, her eyes shadowed with remembered grief. "And I broke my own. All because I had issues with self-esteem and a chip on my shoulder about my circumstances."

"Why are you telling me all this?"

Kimberly's smile was gentle. "Royal is a small town when all is said and done. I know there have been unkind people over the years who have slandered your reputation. And I remember your mother. She wasn't much of a parent."

"Don't forget my wonderful brother," Beth quipped. Hearing Kimberly voice the truth hurt. A lot.

Kimberly shook her head. "No one who takes the time to know you will ever believe that you are anything but a strong, talented, amazing woman."

Beth refused to cry, though her eyes burned. "Thanks for the pep talk."

"I'm serious, Beth. If there's something between you and Drew…something real, don't be as stupid as I was. Don't throw away love."

"Who said anything about love?"

"I saw the way he looked at you this morning."

"That was lust. There's a difference."

"And which is it for you?"

The pointed question put a lump in Beth's throat and made her stomach hurt. "The man is a billionaire."

"The man is a *man*. We all need someone to love. I've been lucky enough to get a second chance. I don't care how much money Jed has. He loves me, and I love him, and we're having a baby. That's something money can't buy."

Beth jumped to her feet, stripping off the dress and putting on a clean pair of jeans and a long-sleeved lavender top. "Thank you for bringing the clothes. If you'll give me the receipt, I'll write you a check."

Kimberly nodded. "I'll get it to you tomorrow. And listen, Beth, take things slow if you're scared, but don't run away. You and Drew could easily have been killed, but you weren't. Haven't you wondered why?"

"Mother Nature is random in her violence."

"True. But those of us who survived owe a debt to the ones the storm took. We have to live. And be happy. Don't you see?"

Beth understood what Kimberly was saying. And she agreed with it up to a point. Life was precious. To have survived a killer storm was no small thing. But she wasn't sure she trusted her feelings. Or Drew's. Not yet.

Sexual attraction was fickle. It could burn out rapidly.

She glanced at the small pile of clothes on the bed. Kimberly had included everything Beth would need for a quick trip to Dallas and a romantic evening. Jed's fiancée had exquisite taste. Beth would not feel out of place appearing in public with Drew Farrell, the polished and sophisticated businessman.

But donning a costume of sorts only transformed the

outside. Did Drew want to know the real Beth? Or maybe the bigger question was—was Beth willing to trust Drew with her heart and her emotional baggage?

"Thank you, Kimberly," she said. "I don't know how you did it, but everything you brought is perfect."

"I've had a lot of experience." Kimberly smiled. "But that doesn't include maternity clothes. I'm getting close to needing them. My pants are already tight."

"I'm sure your hunky groom-to-be would help you shop."

"I know he would. But there's so much to do after the storm. And we want to get married as soon as possible. I have my eye on a wedding dress downtown with a high waist. Hopefully, the style will disguise the fact that I'm *increasing,* as the old women used to say."

"Drew and I will only be in Dallas overnight. As soon as I get back, I'll pitch in and help you any way I can."

Kimberly hugged her. "I wonder if we'll end up being sisters-in-law?" she said archly.

For a moment, Beth allowed herself to dream. Kimberly was a sweetheart, and Beth had never had a sister. "Let's take care of one romance at a time. You and Jed deserve your special day. Don't worry about Drew and me."

Drew fidgeted in his chair wondering how one simple dinner could last for ten hours. That's how long it seemed. Everyone at the table was in a jolly mood, everyone except him. Jed beamed, happier than Drew had ever seen him. Kimberly glowed visibly, wrapped in the love of her fiancé and the knowledge that a baby was on the way. Even Beth, who often guarded her feelings, laughed and joked and enjoyed the impromptu dinner party.

All Drew cared about was getting Beth naked. The sooner, the better.

The housekeeper had made a pumpkin spice cake for dessert before she went home for the day. The women dished it up, added ice cream, and made coffee while the brothers conferred over what Drew would say in Jed's place tomorrow. When that was nailed down, they stood to help carry bowls and cups to the table.

Drew sat down beside Beth and frowned. "Not to dampen the mood, but I heard some news today about the mystery woman who came to Beth's stand right before the storm."

"Don't keep us in suspense," Jed said.

Beth jumped in. "What about her? Is she worse?"

"No, but they've identified her as Skye Taylor. Her parents still live in Royal and were shocked when the authorities contacted them. She left town four years ago—ran away with Jacob Holt. It was a big scandal. The two families have been feuding for decades. But no one knew Skye was back, and no one has a clue why Jacob isn't with her. Everybody's assuming the baby is Jacob's but no one knows for sure."

"How sad," Kimberly said. "To miss the birth and the bonding time."

For a moment they were all silent. Skye had missed those moments as well, since she'd been in a coma.

Drew grimaced. "Sorry. I shouldn't have brought it up. We're celebrating."

Kimberly patted his hand. "We can't avoid sobering news these days. But life goes on." She gazed askance at the large scoop of vanilla bean in front of her, clearly trying to change the subject. "Is it bad that I'm already having cravings? I could eat this whole bowl and then some."

Jed grinned. "More of you to love."

Drew rolled his eyes. "Does that line really work with women?"

"If it's sincere." Kimberly shook her spoon at him and took another bite. "Am I right, Beth?"

Beth swallowed, dabbed her mouth with a napkin, and frowned slightly. "Yes. I suppose. But I'm more interested in finding a guy who waits on me hand and foot and cooks all my meals and cleans the house."

Laughter greeted her comeback. Drew paused to think about what she had said. The Farrells employed almost a hundred workers at Willowbrook—counting the stable staff, financial managers and the housekeeping crew. In his entire life, Drew had never cooked anything more complicated than a scrambled egg on a propane stove.

His dad had made sure the two Farrell boys could take care of themselves in the wilderness. But on a daily basis, Drew had the luxury of concentrating on business, free from worry about meals or dust bunnies or muddy footprints on the hardwood floors. His life had been, and still was, so very different from Beth's. What she had accomplished all on her own was little short of a miracle.

She would make some man a very good wife.

He sat back in his chair, dessert uneaten, and tried not to let on that he'd just had an epiphany of gigantic proportions. Maybe it was seeing Jed in love. Or perhaps it was the literal earth-moving force of the tornado that had knocked some sense into him. But whatever the impetus, suddenly, he saw his life more clearly.

Willowbrook was a family enterprise. The ranch was far more than a business, it was his heritage, a place made for children. He wasn't getting any younger. He'd spent the last year and a half squabbling with Beth, but maybe underneath it all, he'd been falling for her.

He watched her interact with Kimberly and Jed. She was funny and witty and smart. Jed already treated her like a sister. Drew had acknowledged long ago the physical pull between Beth and him. But now he paused to consider everything he liked about her. Love? Yes. It was possible. All he needed was time to think it over.

Jed insisted on clearing the table. Drew jumped up to help. The women immediately began poring over the notebook and magazines Kimberly pulled from a large tote bag.

Kimberly shook her head when Beth pointed to a picture. "We want to keep this very simple."

The men rejoined them. Jed took Kimberly's hand and squeezed it. "I've done some thinking, sweetheart. If we try to invite a handful of close friends, we're going to end up leaving out people who would love to be here. I grew up in Royal. Drew has lived here all his life. You have, too. I say we call it an informal ceremony and reception and open it up to anyone who wants to come. People could use a breather from the work and the sadness and the stress. It doesn't have to be complicated."

Kimberly paled. "But the businesses in town were hit hard. I don't know that we could find a caterer."

Drew spoke up. "Jed and I have a buddy in Austin who does this kind of thing all the time. He has the chairs and the tents and the food ideas. If you'll trust him, he'll handle it all. You won't need to do a thing except show up."

Kimberly turned to Beth. "What do *you* think?"

Beth nibbled her bottom lip. "Well…."

"Tell me the truth," Kimberly insisted.

"You want to get married right away because of the baby, correct?"

"Yes."

"And we all agree that Royal could use an excuse to concentrate on something other than relief work and insurance claims."

"True."

"Then I say if your future husband and brother-in-law are willing to feed the entire town, let them do it."

Kimberly shook her head, her expression dazed. "I'm not sure I'm ready to be a Farrell."

Jed kissed her cheek. "No choice now. You're mine, honey. I sure as hell am not going to lose you again."

Eleven

Drew closed the front door behind his brother with an inner sigh of relief. Jed was staying at Kimberly's again tonight. Which left Drew alone with Beth, just the way he liked it. He found her in the kitchen tidying up. "Leave that," he said.

"It won't take a minute." She continued putting things away.

Leaning in the doorway, Drew watched her. Tall and leggy, she was beautiful enough to be a model. But there was something so real about her. She was a poster child for the girl next door. Which in Drew's case was literally true.

He moved behind her, slipping his arms around her waist and linking his hands over her belly. "I want to make love to you tonight."

Beth turned suddenly, startling him. Wary eyes looked into his. She scanned his face as though looking for some kind of answer to a question he didn't understand. "I want that, too. But I haven't been entirely honest with you. I'd like to clear the air before we go any further."

His arousal plummeted. Releasing her, he grabbed a kitchen chair, turned it backward and straddled the seat, resting his arms on the back. "I'm listening." He couldn't imagine what she was going to say, and it rattled him.

She remained by the sink, arms wrapped around her

waist, her body language defensive. "It's no secret that I came from the wrong side of the tracks. My dad left when I was three. My mom was an alcoholic who made it from day to day with odd jobs and public assistance. People around Royal knew her, because she wasn't above begging on street corners. She wasn't intentionally abusive to my brother and me, but let's just say that by the time I was a teenager, I knew I wanted more for my life."

"Where is she now?"

"She died of pneumonia when I was a senior in high school. Her health was in such bad shape that she couldn't fight it off."

"I'm sorry, Beth."

"It's a scary world when the only parent you've ever known, even a bad one, leaves you. But I was lucky to have good teachers who helped me get a scholarship to the University of Texas at Austin."

He kept his expression impassive, though his response was gut deep. "So far this doesn't sound like a tale of defeat."

"Be patient. I'm getting there. While I was in school, I did work-study and also two other part-time gigs, one waitressing and the other tutoring kids in math."

"Math?"

"Don't sound so surprised. That was my major. I minored in marketing."

"I'm impressed. No wonder everyone knows about your produce stand."

"Well, anyway," she said, "by the time I graduated, I was missing Royal. Not my family in particular. As I told you before, we're not close. But I grew up in Royal, all eighteen years before I went off to school. As wonderful as Austin was, it wasn't home. I guess I had deeper roots here than I realized."

"So you came home."

"Not yet. You're getting ahead of me." She continued her story, her quiet voice drawing him in. "I met a man."

Drew stiffened, hoping she didn't notice. For some inexplicable reason, he wasn't sure he wanted to hear this part. He liked the notion of Beth Andrews as sweet and untouched. What did that say about him? She was twenty-eight years old. A truly extraordinary woman in every way, particularly when it came to her stunning looks. It didn't make sense to think that no man had ever staked a claim.

He prompted her. "Tell me about him."

The long silence grew heavy. "He was older."

"How much older?"

"Eighteen years. We patronized the same video store, back when there were such things. One day he chatted me up and invited me out for coffee."

"So he was forty?"

"Almost. But his wife had died of leukemia when they were both little more than newlyweds. He never remarried."

"And then you entered the picture." He was really trying not to be critical, but this unknown bum sounded like a guy hitting on a college girl while in the midst of a midlife crisis. It made no difference that Beth had been of legal age.

She picked up on his ambivalence. "It's not what you think. We genuinely cared about each other. I've always been mature for my age, and he was lonely."

"I'll bet."

The sarcastic retort silenced her.

Drew grimaced. "I'm sorry. I was being a jerk. Tell me the rest. What was his name?"

"Richard," she said. "His name was Richard."

"Finish your story, please."

"Are you sure you want to hear it?"

"I really do."

She wished the recounting put her in a better light. At the time it hadn't seemed so bad. But in retrospect, the decisions she had made were ones she mostly regretted.

"We became close," she said.

"Physically intimate?"

"Yes."

"Was he your first lover?"

"No. I'd had one boyfriend in college. Nothing too serious. My lack of experience was really ironic, because somehow in high school I gained a reputation for being easy."

"I don't understand."

"Guys wanted to go out with me because I had nice breasts and blond hair. I also came from a part of town and from a family that gave people certain impressions of me. When boys realized that I didn't put out on a date, they were embarrassed, because they thought I had been fooling around with their buddies. So to save face, they made up stories. Denying them only drew attention to me, so I kept my mouth shut."

She had no clue what Drew was thinking. Some people assumed that all scandalous gossip had basis in fact.

His gaze was steady. "I'm sorry, Beth. That must have been excruciating."

The sincere caring in his voice brought tears to her eyes, but she blinked them away rapidly. She had long since come to terms with her past. That was one reason her little house and farm were so special. There, she was her own person.

"Well, anyway…back to Richard. He was a lovely man, decent and kind. Though he definitely wasn't a father figure, he was a mentor, I suppose. While I was with him, he taught me about life in many ways. Simple things such as how to choose a wine, but deeper stuff, too, like not settling for a man who treated me poorly."

"Where is he now? Why did you break up?"

"We didn't break up. He knew I wanted to come home to Royal. But I still had a few student loans. Without a car and cash to make the move, I was stuck."

"Did he ask you to stay with him?"

"He wanted to, I think. But he was the sort of man who put others' needs ahead of his own. He told me that the road was wide open in front of me…that I would have experiences and opportunities to find my passion in life. He knew before I did that I *loved* him, but I wasn't *in love* with him. And I respected him too much to pretend."

"So what happened?"

Here was the part she wanted to skip. But Drew had heard everything else. "He opened a checking account for me and deposited twenty-five thousand dollars. Then he bought me a car, gave me his blessing and sent me on my way."

She saw and heard Drew inhale sharply. What was he thinking? She wanted badly to know. In all fairness, what she had done *could be* construed as sex for money. It wasn't. Not at all. She knew that. But the facts were open to interpretation.

"What did you do with the cash?"

Though she listened carefully, she was unable to detect any note of judgment in his question. "I used the least amount possible to make it back here to Royal. Took only what was necessary to put down a deposit on an apartment. I'd been home five days when I landed a job working at one of the banks downtown as a teller. It wasn't what I wanted, but it paid the bills."

"And the rest of Richard's gift?"

"It stayed in my account for several years until I used it as a down payment to buy the farm."

Drew sat in silence absorbing the details of Beth's remarkable story. Though he still wasn't happy with the unknown Richard, the man deserved kudos for doing what was best for Beth.

The one thing Drew hadn't questioned was the status of the relationship today. Were Beth and Richard still friends? Did they call and text and visit occasionally? Beth was twenty-eight, which meant that the mysterious Richard had to be about forty-six. Still plenty young enough to remarry and start a family, especially with a younger wife.

It was entirely possible that in the intervening years Beth's feelings toward her benefactor might have changed…deepened. On the other hand, the way she kissed Drew didn't suggest an attachment to another man.

He stood up. What she shared with him suggested a level of trust. He was humbled by her openness, especially since his treatment of her in the past had been questionable at best.

Beth watched him walk toward her. "So, do you still want me…knowing the truth? I might be a gold-digger luring you into my bed so I can get my hands on your money."

"For the record, that has never crossed my mind." He grinned. "And to be perfectly clear, you can put your hands on anything I've got." He tilted her mouth to meet his. Her lips were soft and eager, her body pliant in his embrace. The scent of cinnamon and spices lingered in the air. Drew's arousal built from gentle enjoyment to flat-out desperation at warp speed.

He scooped her into his arms and strode down the corridor toward his bedroom. "As for whether I still want you? I think you know the answer to that."

Beth laughed softly. With one hand she traced the shell of his ear. The fact that an innocent touch could inflict so much damage to his self-control told him things were different. *Beth* was different. The ball was in his court, though. He was determined to show her how much they had to give each other.

He kicked open the bedroom door so hard it bounced off the wall. Never pausing, he strode to the bed and went down with her, tumbling in a melee of arms and legs.

"We have our shoes on," Beth protested. "You'll ruin the spread."

"Screw the spread," he groaned. But to pacify her, he toed off his cowboy boots and waited impatiently until she managed to get rid of her ballet flats.

She sat cross-legged and stared at him. "Don't move. I want to unbutton your shirt."

Breathing harshly, he leaned back on his elbows and waited. She knelt beside him with an endearingly serious look on her face. Slender fingers worked the buttons free of their buttonholes. Everywhere her fingers brushed his skin, he burned.

When she was done, she sat back on her heels. "You are a very handsome man," she said quietly.

Her solemn praise made him uncomfortable. He worked outside much of his life, sometimes shirtless, and never thought twice about it. His naturally golden skin was permanently tanned. But having the woman he wanted study him so closely threatened his equilibrium.

He scooted back against the pillows and feigned relaxation with his hands tucked behind his head. "Your turn. Take off your shirt. And go slowly. I plan to enjoy this."

Though she didn't respond verbally, Beth met his challenge with an innocent strip tease that dried his mouth. When she slid her arms out of the top and tossed it aside, all that was left was a sheer bra whose delicate fabric did nothing to conceal her rose-colored nipples.

"Come here," he groaned, extending his arms. "I can't wait anymore."

She went to him willingly, settling half across his chest, kissing him teasingly. "I think we're overdressed," she muttered, her hips pressed to his.

He was hard and ready. His chest heaved with harsh pants. "We have a fifteen minute pants-on rule in this bed. Otherwise, I'll embarrass myself."

They kissed for hours it seemed. Exploratory. Urgent. Passionate. Tender. Every flavor and permutation of lip-to-lip known to man. Like teenagers necking in the back-seat of a car.

Beth must have lost some weight in the aftermath of the tragedy. He was able to slide his palm down inside her jeans and underwear, finding the firm swells of her butt and caressing them. She buried her face against his neck, biting his collarbone.

He flinched. Desire roared in his head, blinding him to everything but the need to possess her. "I want you naked," he muttered.

"I thought you'd never ask." She scooted away from him and removed the rest of her clothes.

He raced her instinctively. When they were both bare as the day they were born, they met in the center of the bed—kneeling—breathless....

"I can't believe it's taken me this long to realize what I was missing." He rubbed a thumb across her flushed cheek. "I want you so much it's insane."

"Insane bad? Or insane good?" The sparkle in her eyes made him uncomfortable. Beth Andrews knew exactly what she did to him. Of course, in this particular scenario, it was difficult to hide.

He cupped her neck with two hands. "You're important to me, Beth. This isn't casual sex."

He said it to reassure her. Instead, she bit her lip, a sure sign of her agitation. "Don't say things you'll regret later, Drew. Our whole world is topsy-turvy right now. But that's no reason to make a grand gesture. I'm here because I want to be. For now. Let's leave it at that."

Several arguments sprang to mind, but when both her hands closed around his erection, he found it was impossible to string words together. His body tightened in helpless pleasure. When she flinched, he realized he had gripped her shoulders too tightly. "Sorry."

"I like it," she said, grinning. "I like knowing I drive you crazy."

If the situation hadn't been so loaded with physical and emotional baggage, Beth might have laughed out loud. Apparently she had shocked him.

She wanted to say, *I like knowing you're mine.* But that might have been over the line.

Even so, she let the concept roll around in her head while they eased by unspoken consent down onto the mattress. Drew paused only long enough to take care of protection. When she was flat on her back with him looming over her on one elbow, she took a deep breath and exhaled slowly, trying to steady her nerves. No one had ever made her feel this way. No one.

She wanted to crawl inside his skin until there was no more him and her, but only them. After a lifetime of guarding her emotions and holding back in every relationship, sexual or otherwise, she wanted to open herself to Drew. "I don't want to scare you," she said softly, "but I think you're pretty wonderful."

His grin, a flash of white teeth and cocky confidence,

revealed his playful side. "A compliment from my arch rival?" He kissed her nose. "I thought we survived the tornado, but maybe the world is coming to an end."

"Smart ass." She lifted her hips, hoping he would get the idea. "I argued with you on numerous occasions, but that didn't stop me from ogling your butt and wondering what you would be like in bed."

He shifted, rubbing his sex in the notch of her thighs. "Why, Ms. Andrews. How naughty of you."

Dizziness, the wonderful kind, made her eyes close for a moment. Her senses intensified. Inhaling the spicy aroma of his aftershave…feeling the warmth of his breath on her skin. Every second took on new meaning. The hoarseness in his voice told her that he felt the same alluring possibilities.

"Go slow," she pleaded. "I don't want it to end."

A low, raw curse underscored his ferocity as he entered her in one forceful thrust that shook the bed.

She was so primed she nearly came. Her breathing shallow, she managed a weak question. "You call that slow?"

He rested his forehead on hers. "Sorry. I'll do better."

"Any better, and you'll kill us both."

A laugh rumbled through his chest. "Is it really possible to die from too much pleasure? My life insurance is up to date, but I'm sure Jed's expecting us to be at the wedding."

The wedding. For one weak, poignant second, Beth allowed herself to imagine a *double* wedding. What would it be like to know that a man like Drew loved her unconditionally? Enough to put a ring on her finger.…

Pushing away the inopportune fantasy, she concentrated on the delicious present. "I know CPR," she whispered, nipping his bottom lip with her teeth. "If we climb too high, I'll take care of you."

The notion that Drew needed *anyone's* care, much less

hers, was almost comical. He had everything as far as she could tell. Maybe not a wife with a baby on the way. But home and hearth weren't a lure for every bachelor. Drew jetted all over the world. He probably had women available on every continent. She believed he cared about her. She really did. If nothing else, the tornado had proved what kind of man he was. He had literally saved her life.

"You *do* make me crazy," he muttered.

It didn't sound like a compliment. She squeezed him intimately where her body clasped his. How long could he hold out? She had asked for slow, but already she regretted that request. Inside her he was thick and ready, pulsing with an energy that promised to consume her. "I changed my mind," she panted. "I don't want to wait."

"Patience is a virtue."

Since he said it through clenched teeth, she didn't put too much stock in the platitude. "Virtue is overrated. Take me, Drew. Hard. Please."

Her about-face snapped whatever chains held him in place. "Whatever the lady wants." Withdrawing slowly, he thrust again, setting up a rhythm designed to drive them both mad. She clung to his shoulders, her legs wrapped around his waist. Reveling in his wildness, she took everything he had to give and responded in kind.

She grabbed his hair and pulled. "More," she cried. "More."

He hit a pleasure point one last time and she came apart, flying into the dark without a net. Dimly, she heard him shout his own release.

It was too much and not enough. But in the end, all she could do was cling to him and live in the moment.

Drew slept, but he kept a tight hold on Beth. Even his subconscious knew that she was a flight risk. She felt right in his bed. As though they had been together forever. He needed time to think, to plan.

Toward morning he made love to her one last time. Slow and sweet, their coupling built on soft touches, quiet gasps, shuddered completion. It was all he could do to force himself to let her go.

"I never want to leave this bed," he said, smoothing a hand down her back. "But the chopper is going to be here in an hour." He kissed her shoulder. "I'll have one of the staff put a suitcase outside your door in the next half hour. Can you get ready that quickly? Throw your things in the bag. We'll have someone at the hotel press whatever you need." The fact that she grumbled and lingered despite the timetable was gratifying.

"Lucky for you I'm low maintenance," she said. She nuzzled her face in the side of his neck, her breasts pressed against his chest. "I'm going, I'm going."

He was treated to a brief but memorable naked tableau as Beth grabbed up her things and dressed rapidly. She shot him a glance over her shoulder as she dashed for the door. "Shouldn't you be moving?"

"Didn't want to miss the floor show." He was still laughing when she disappeared.

Drew shouldn't have been surprised when his houseguest was true to her word. Beth met him in the foyer at five minutes before her allotted deadline. He almost did a double take. He was so accustomed to seeing her in casual clothes that he was stunned to see an entirely different woman.

Her long hair was twisted up in one of those fancy styles on the back of her head. Kimberly's fashion choices had been spot on. The pencil skirt and short jacket in navy pinstripe showcased Beth's narrow waist and curvy bosom.

And her legs. Wow. Pin-up girls would kill to have those gams. Taupe pumps with four-inch heels drew attention to shapely calves and trim ankles.

He whistled long and low, eyeing her from head to toe. "For a farmer, you clean up real nice."

Beth turned in a slow circle, smiling. "We have Kimberly to thank for that. She turned a pumpkin into a fancy pie."

"You're too modest. And if that was a Cinderella reference, I'll have to buy you a book of fairytales when we get to Dallas. Anyone who botches a classic that badly needs a refresher course."

Her smile faded. "I know the story, Drew. Every little girl does. But we aren't exactly going to a ball, now are we?"

The front door swung open without warning, and two of the ranch hands came in to collect the bags. "Your ride is here, Mr. Farrell. Whenever you're ready," said one of the men respectfully.

Drew took Beth's arm as they made their way to the concrete pad. The grassy expanse between the house and their destination was uneven and not easily traversed in couture footwear.

The pilot had shut off the rotors, so there was no wind to contend with. But the high step presented some problems for Beth. Drew didn't wait for the inevitable argument. He lifted her by the waist and set her inside the doorway of the chopper.

She looked down at him and shook her head. "I'm not a package. You could have asked first."

"I know you. We'd have spent fifteen minutes dithering while you tried to figure out how to climb aboard in that skirt. I merely speeded up the process." He climbed in as well, greeted the pilot, and handed Beth a set of headphones. "Fasten your seat belt, honey. And hang on."

Beth left her stomach somewhere down at the ranch along with her determination to appear poised and confident. She felt like a kid on a ride at the amusement part, half thrilled, half scared spitless. The ground fell away so fast her knuckles turned white as she held on to the edge of her seat.

Drew leaned into her and shouted. "What do you think?"

Gazing at the vista below, she shook her head in amazement. "I love it."

She wasn't sure if he heard her or not, but they exchanged a smile that made her stomach flip. It would have been nice to blame the woozy feeling on the combination of speed and altitude. But in truth, when Drew took her hand in his and gripped it tightly, she experienced a flash of perfect joy...one of those brief moments that linger in the heart always.

For a girl from the wrong side of the tracks who had never been more than ten feet off the ground, it was heady stuff.

The trip was over far too quickly. They landed atop one of Dallas's tallest buildings on a helipad marked with red and black paint. The pilot set them perfectly within the lines. When the rotors stilled at last, the lack of noise was jarring.

Drew tapped her chin. "Close your mouth, country mouse. You'll catch flies."

His gentle teasing made her blush. "I can't believe this is commonplace to you. I feel like a movie star."

He jumped down onto the pad and reached up to help her out. "You look like one, too. C'mon. I've got twenty minutes to spare. I'll get someone to call a cab and take you on to the hotel with our luggage."

"Can't I stay with you during the meeting? Or would that be a faux pas?"

"But wouldn't you rather relax?"

"I want to see you in action," she said. "Especially if you're stepping in for Jed. I've been on the receiving end of your Big-Bad-Wolf routine, remember?"

Drew scowled. "Jed is no pussycat, despite his present lovesick condition. I'm more or less a silent partner. He's the shrewd businessman."

She patted his arm as they stepped into the building via an industrial gray metal door. After the bright sunshine, she was momentarily blinded. "Does that mean you see love as a weakness?"

He paused in the shadows to kiss her quickly. "Don't put words in my mouth."

His lips were firm and warm. She inhaled the scent of starched cotton and expensive cologne. Seeing him in a suit and tie this morning had weakened her resolve not to weave daydreams. The cowboy businessman managed to look both professional and sexy at the same time. His arm was hard against her back, dragging her so close they touched in all sorts of interesting places.

"I stand corrected," she said, when he allowed her to breathe.

Now that her eyes had adjusted to the dim lighting at the top of the staircase, she could see that his gaze was unusually dark and fathomless.

"I admire my younger brother more than any other man I know. And I am happy for him, honest to God happy for him. You and I should be so lucky."

All the breath left her lungs. Though it took courage, she felt recklessly brave. "What does that mean?"

He kissed her again, before glancing at his watch with an imprecation. "I think you can figure it out, Beth. But it will have to keep."

Life had taught Beth some tough lessons about expectations and their demise. But hearing Drew's cryptic answer filled her with a quiet, warm jubilance. She felt no need to press. It was enough to hoard the amazing surprise and wait for things to develop. Drew was not the kind of man to make promises he didn't intend to keep.

Besides, the next few days were all about Jed and Kimberly. No one should steal their thunder, least of all Beth and Drew. If there were things to be said, Drew was right. It could keep. After all, anticipation was the best part of the journey.

It was eye-opening to watch him in action. The sleek boardroom in the sophisticated high rise where Jed had his offices was a pleasing blend of modern with old Texas. The enormous windows offered breathtaking views of the Dallas skyline. Though the furniture was unmistakably twenty-first century, the dark wood and a definite streak of tradition still made a statement.

Drew settled into the chair at the head of the table. Beth quietly took a seat along the wall with a dozen young men and women who were apparently staffers or interns. Jed, a financial genius according to Drew, managed funds for a large consortium of Texas ranchers. This quarterly meeting was routine but important.

After a brief apology for Jed's unavoidable absence— without going into inappropriate personal detail—Drew launched into the agenda. Beth watched him carefully, seeing him as others did. He wielded an air of command and confidence that was not only a product of his privileged upbringing but integral to who he was as a man.

The wealthy and influential ranchers seated around the

table, Jed's board of directors, afforded Drew respect and careful attention. What she hadn't expected was the wit and humor Drew infused into dry numbers and projections. His relaxed style produced laughter, camaraderie and a speedy conclusion to what could have been an endless discussion.

He didn't draw any kind of attention to Beth, and she was glad. Being a fly on the wall was all she wanted. By the time Drew adjourned the meeting and spoke to numerous individuals afterward, her stomach was growling. They had been up early, and it was almost one o'clock.

At last, as the room emptied, he joined her. "Well, how did I do?"

She linked her arm through his. "You were a lot nicer to this group than you ever were to me. But maybe that's because none of them own land you want to steal."

Pressing his hand over her mouth, he shook his head in mock disgust. "Why are you the only person who thinks of me as a villain?"

She twisted free, gazing at him almost eye-to-eye thanks to her borrowed footwear. "If the twirly mustache fits...."

With a chuckle, he ushered her in front of him. "Let's get out of here. I'm off the clock, and I promised you some fun."

Drew wanted to skip lunch and anything else in his way and take her straight to the hotel. Beth deserved more than that, though. She'd shown him bits and pieces of her difficult childhood, but the parts she left out were pretty clear when he read between the lines. Except for college—where she had lived on a shoestring budget—Beth had led a narrowly confined life. No travel. No cultural opportunities.

He felt a moment of shame for taking so much of his

life for granted. Despite his physical hunger, he wanted to please Beth…to make her happy. And that's what he set out to do.

After an intimate lunch, they started with one of the art museums. Two hours later when Beth expressed an interest in Dallas's sobering Kennedy history, they headed for Dealey Plaza.

Drew couldn't remember the last time he had played tourist. He'd forgotten how much fun it could be. As the day progressed, the truth cemented itself firmly in his gut. He no longer wanted to fight with his neighbor. He wanted to make peace, even at the expense of his own endeavors.

They went back to the hotel only long enough to shower and change for dinner. Beth refused to give him a peek at her dress. As he waited impatiently in the suite's opulent sitting room, she finally came through the door.

"Wow." It was the only word he could muster. The black dress she wore revealed lots of skin. Beautiful, creamy skin.…

The quiet pleasure in her eyes warmed him. He kissed her cheek, unwilling to do more for fear they wouldn't make it out the door. "I've never enjoyed a business trip as much as I did today," he said, trying to make light of the emotions bombarding him. His heart pounded.

Beth smoothed her skirt with both hands and wrinkled her nose, betraying a hint of nerves. "I've had fun, too."

"C'mon," he said gruffly. "I promised you dinner and dancing. Your chariot awaits."

Twelve

Beth was living a fairytale. She knew it. And acknowledged it wouldn't last. But she decided to enjoy herself and appreciate the moment.

When Drew helped her step into the sleek black limo parked at the curb of their upscale hotel, she felt like a princess. As they glided through the heavy Dallas traffic, he served her a glass of champagne. "To the future," he said, clinking his glass gently against hers.

She took a sip of the sparkling liquid, relishing the crisp bite and feeling the bubbles tickle her nose. "To the future."

Their toast covered a host of possibilities. Though the storm had decimated much of Royal, the town would rebuild and emerge stronger than before. Jed and Kimberly were getting married. Soon, Drew would have a niece or nephew. But did his quiet words hold a deeper meaning?

They sat on opposite ends of the wide seat. Drew seemed distracted, his attention focused now on the passing view.

She finished her drink and twirled the stem of the glass in her fingers, wishing she had the guts to slide across the space separating her from Drew and put a hand on his thigh. The open window behind the driver stifled the impulse. Not only that, but Drew's dark suit made him seem less approachable than the man she knew as a down-to-earth cowboy. A very wealthy cowboy, but a man of the land, nevertheless.

This Drew she had met in Dallas was more sophisticated, perhaps even a bit more dangerous. She would give a lot to know what he was thinking.

Their destination was a private club. Inside, the lighting was romantic and the décor stunning. A supercilious maître d' led them to a table for two tucked away in an intimate corner.

Beth barely tasted her fork-tender beef, though it was some of Texas's finest. Drew talked. And she talked. They flirted. They laughed. Books. Movies. Politics. Nothing about her family or his. Nothing about the storm.

When the last bites of cherry tart were nothing but crumbs, Drew held out his hand. "I've been waiting all night for this."

The polished hardwood dance floor in the center of the room was covered in shards of light from the priceless chandelier overhead. Couples of all ages moved in time to the vintage band that played classic romantic tunes. The common denominator in the room was wealth and tradition.

When Drew took her in his arms, he settled one big, warm palm on her back. She leaned into him, resting her cheek on his broad shoulder. She'd never had much occasion to dance formally, but his confidence steered them smoothly.

Letting the music wash over her, she floated—mentally and physically—her thoughts flitting as comfortably as her feet followed his. Publicly acceptable foreplay. That's what it was. He held her so close she felt the heat of his body. Their heartbeats seemed in sync.

It was impossible to miss his arousal. Hers was easier to

hide but no less urgent. Her muscles were lax with sensory overload. Every cell in her body trembled with anticipation.

When he spoke, his warm breath teased her ear. "I could hold you like this all night. But whenever you want to leave, say the word."

"One more song," she pleaded. "One more dance...."

It must have been late. She had lost all track of time. If it weren't for the promise of what lay ahead, she might have chosen to dance until the club closed down. Drew's fingers stroked her bare back above the edge of her dress. The gentle caress was at once soothing and sensual.

The band took a break, waving at the crowd and exiting the stage. Beth pulled away and smiled. "I think that's our cue."

On the ride back to the hotel, she and Drew did not sit apart. He tucked his arm around her and pulled her close.

"More champagne?" he asked.

"No, thank you." She wanted to remember every second of the night ahead. Alcohol would only make her sleepy.

Somehow they made it from the limo to the elevator to their suite. But the details were fuzzy. In the sitting room, Drew ripped off his tie and discarded his jacket, tossing both on a chair. Beth stepped out of her shoes and wiggled her toes in relief. The plush carpet felt wonderful. For a woman used to tromping around farm fields, an entire evening in high heels was torture.

She and Drew stood half a room apart. When he crooked his finger with a wicked smile, her stomach did a free-fall. Fingering one of the rhinestone straps of her dress, she lifted her chin, determined to be his match, at least in the bedroom. "You seem to think I'll coming running whenever you ask."

Two masculine eyebrows went up. "I'm perfectly willing to reverse the roles if the lady wishes."

Damn him. She smothered a grin. It was impossible to win a battle of wits with Drew. At least when it came to sex. She decided to call his bluff. Slowly, watching his eyes darken and glaze with hunger, she slipped the narrow jeweled straps off her shoulders. The dress didn't fall. It fit snugly around her breasts.

With one hand she lifted her skirt and carefully peeled off a pair of naughty undies, stepping out of them with flair.

Drew's Adam's apple bobbed conspicuously. She was pretty sure she saw a sheen of sweat on his forehead.

Tossing the scrap of black silk in his direction, she sauntered into the bedroom.

Drew shuddered, blinking his eyes to clear his vision. He forced himself to count to ten…and then to fifty. His blood pressure went up, not down. Unbuttoning his cuffs as he walked, he made his way slowly to the room where Beth waited for him. The lack of speed was intentional. He had to gather himself, needed to clear his head.

When he paused in the open doorway, all his plans were for naught. Beth stood naked beside the bed with her back to him. She whirled around, the dress clutched to her chest. "Hello."

Perfect white teeth dug a furrow in her bottom lip. Her slender body, what he could see of it, was healthy and shapely. For one long moment, he literally couldn't speak. She dazzled him. Finally, he cleared his throat. "Hello."

Their stilted conversation might have been humorous if the mood in the room hadn't been heavy with sexual tension.

She sat on the edge of the bed, still covering her interesting bits with the dress. "Is there something you wanted to say to me?"

The overhead light was off, but the bedside lamp glowed. He shrugged. "It occurred to me you might think I invited you along on this trip so I could have wild, crazy sex with you."

"Well, didn't you?"

"Yes. I mean no. Oh hell, Beth. It's way more than that and you know it." He was frustrated…and as awkward as a teenage boy courting his first girl. "You know the saying, 'actions speak louder than words'?"

"Of course."

"That's what I'm going with." The time for talking was over.

While she sat and watched, he undressed…completely. He saw Beth assess his condition. Color flooded her cheeks. He was fully erect. In fact, he'd been hard to one degree or another most of the day. Right now, he felt like a man who hadn't had a woman in years.

He sat down beside her, their hips touching…sans clothing. Beth didn't protest when he tugged the dress out of her grasp and flung it aside. But she had trouble meeting his eyes.

Rubbing her bare knee, he spoke to her softly. "I don't think you can come close to imagining how much I want you at this very moment."

Her quick sideways glance held a hint of hesitation. "You've been with a lot of women."

It could have been an accusation, but it sounded more like a statement of fact. "I'm thirty-two years old," he said quietly. "I've had a number of relationships. But none in the last year."

"Why not?"

"It's been a busy time. We've expanded the ranch operations. I've courted new clients around the world. I suppose

I've become more selective when it comes to sex. Casual hook-ups don't do it for me anymore."

"I still think we're not a good match."

He debated what to say…how to get around the walls she was erecting. "I respect your opinion, Beth, but I reserve the right to prove you wrong."

His gentle teasing finally coaxed a smile from her. "Fair enough."

Without moving away from him, she reached up and began removing the pins from her hair. Thick strands tumbled onto her shoulders. He wrapped one silky blond curl around his fist, waiting until she was finished to pull her close for a kiss. "Come here, Beth."

She slid her arms around his neck, clinging tightly. "Is this where you try to change my mind?"

He laughed roughly. "I'll do my best."

His tongue dueled with hers. Despite her air of toughness, Beth had an innocence about her that made him want to set the moon at her feet, to wrap up the world as a gift and place it in her keeping. She deserved everything he could offer.

Scooping her into his lap, he chuckled when she tried to keep his hands from roaming.

"That tickles," she complained.

He played with one raspberry nipple until it puckered enticingly. "You have the most amazing body." When he switched to the other breast, Beth caught her breath and moaned in a low, throaty gasp that made his skin tighten.

Reading her verbal clues, he eased her down onto the bed and splayed her legs. Her eyes were closed. He was able to take her by surprise. Pinning her thighs with his hands, he bent and tasted her center.

Beth cried out, struggling instinctively.

"Easy, darlin'." He rested his head on her belly and

reached down to stroke her with his fingertips, sliding them back and forth on either side of her most sensitive spot.

Her fingernails scored his forearm. *"Drew!"*

He paused instantly, alarm skittering down his spine. "What's wrong?"

She reared up on her elbows, hair tousled, eyelids at half-mast, lips swollen from his kisses. "How do you know I like that?"

"Was I supposed to ask permission?"

Her expression was one part petulance and two parts reluctant excitement. "I don't think it's a good thing for a man to know so much about women. It gives you an unfair advantage."

"How so?" he asked, genuinely curious.

"What if we have incredible, earth-moving sex, you ruin me for other men, and then we break up?"

He pushed her back onto the bed, chuckling at her imaginary scenario. "I guess that's a risk we'll have to take."

The risk is all mine. She knew it, and she didn't care. Not when Drew made love to her so very well. She closed her eyes a second time and let sensation wash over her. His fingers were both delicate and precise. One moment she hovered on the edge and the next he drew her back, playing with her masterfully.

Hot need coalesced deep in her abdomen. Her body wept for him, moist and ready. As she hovered on the verge of violent release, he thrust two fingers inside her passage and found the spot that triggered her climax.

"Drew. Drew...."

She lost her voice in the middle of the storm. Wrenched with physical pleasure that was incredibly intense, she had no recourse but to let him hold her tightly until everything was calm.

Shaken and bemused, she felt something inside her shift and settle. Drew. It was always going to be Drew for her. That was a damned scary future to contemplate. She felt as fluttery and faint as a Victorian maiden. Of course, most women would be a little woozy after an orgasm like that.

So maybe if he was really serious…maybe she could learn how to be married to a wealthy Texas rancher. Things like entertaining and hobnobbing with the rich and famous. Still, one part of her held back…the little piece of her heart that had survived disappointment after disappointment while she was growing up. Trust was hard. For two years Drew had tried to force her to submit to his wishes concerning their disputes.

Though it was difficult to admit, a tiny suspicion remained. What if he was softening her up so he could persuade her to leave the farm? Even the thought of it made her ill. She had worked hard to make something of her life, despite her upbringing. Surely Drew wouldn't be so cavalier. Surely he respected her feelings.

He scooted her up in the bed. "Your skin is freezing, woman. Let's get under the covers."

She followed his lead, settling into his arms with a sigh of contentment, pushing her doubts aside. The elegant duvet was thick and fluffy. It felt wonderful to cuddle with her sexy, um…*lover? Neighbor? Friend?* What should she call him? Or did it really matter?

Smiling to herself, she roved beneath the covers until her hand encountered hard male flesh. Drew's only reaction was a hissed intake of breath. Lazily, she circled the head of his shaft, feeling the drops of fluid that signaled his excitement. Even without that evidence, his rigid muscles and harsh breathing told her everything.

She stroked him gently, feeling his erection flex and thicken even more. Despite her recent carnal excess, Drew's arousal rekindled a buzz in places she had been sure were sated. Nipping the side of his neck, she moved her hand lower, cupping him intimately. "How do you want me?" she whispered.

He let out a broken laugh. "Six ways to Sunday," he said, humor in his voice despite the tension gripping him. "But I'll settle for good ol' missionary right now. You make me a little nuts, so I'd like to play to my strengths this first time."

Pleased by his wry admission, she shifted onto her back and lifted her arms toward the ceiling. "Take me, I'm yours," she said in her best dramatic voice.

He rolled on a condom and moved on top of her in a nanosecond. "Has anyone ever told you you're a brat?"

"Not recently."

He settled between her thighs, his weight mostly supported on his elbows. "You make me happy, Beth."

She hadn't expected that. Tears sprang to her eyes. His gaze was unguarded, intimate.

"You're not so bad yourself," she said. The flip answer embarrassed her. "Sorry. You took me off guard." Pausing, she searched for the right words. "I admire you, Drew. But more than that, I *like* you. And it doesn't hurt that you're sexy and smart."

"Who knew?" he said with a wry grin.

"Who knew what?"

"That dueling neighbors could end up like this."

She put her hands on his buttocks, feeling his muscular flanks. "But remember, it took a tornado to get us together."

"I suppose that means we're both pretty stubborn."

"True."

"You do something to me I can't explain."

Her heart stopped. She wasn't sure she could respond in kind. Not because it wasn't true, but because the words made her so very vulnerable. Finally, when the silence became too painful, she whispered, "I care about you, too."

He entered her slowly, giving her tenderness and understanding despite her reservations. He was big and dominant and determined.

There was no talking after that. Drew moved in her with barely restrained ferocity. He rolled suddenly, settling her on top of him. "Come with me," he demanded. "Both of us…together." He used his thumb to tease the little bundle of nerves, making her squirm. "I can wait."

"It's too soon."

"Think positive."

Ripples of sensation rolled through her lower abdomen. "Drew…." She swallowed hard.

"Yes, darlin'?"

"You get started. I'll catch up."

He took her at her word. Hard masculine fingers gripped her butt as he urged her up and down. Every stroke took her temperature higher. Drew groaned and shook, nearing the finish.

"Now, baby," he muttered. "Let it go."

The moment took her by surprise, jerking her over the top without warning. Sending her into the abyss. But as she tumbled, she clung to Drew. Sated at the end, they rolled into each other's arms and slept.

Drew frowned in his sleep. Some noise, a damned annoying ping, had dragged him from a deep, wonderful slumber. He opened his eyes, marginally aware that faint light shone in through a crack in the draperies. Beth lay on her side facing away, but curled against him, her bottom bumping his hip.

He touched her hair lightly. Glancing at the digital clock on the bedside table blearily, he managed to make out the numbers. *7:15?* Who in the hell was texting him at this hour of the morning? Yawning, he reached for his phone. Jed's cell number appeared with a message:

Come home as soon as you can. Wedding day after tomorrow. Caterer's only open date. God help us. J J

Jed really must be in love. Drew couldn't remember a single other instance where his brother had used a smiley face, much less two.

Beth sat up, the sheet clutched to her breasts. "Is something wrong?" With her hair tumbled around her face, she looked sexy and adorable.

He handed her his cell phone. Her eyes widened as she read the words. "Day after tomorrow? Seriously? Kimberly must be frantic."

"I knew we had to go home today, but I didn't expect it to be quite so abrupt. Especially since checkout is not until eleven."

"And how did you plan to spend those last three hours?"

He took the phone and dropped it on the carpet. "The same way I'm going to spend the next thirty minutes."

Beth dressed more casually for the return trip. But the navy slacks and pale gold silk blouse were still a far cry from her usual wardrobe. Because Drew had been so inventive in delaying their departure, they barely had a chance to shower and pack their bags. By the time they checked out, grabbed a cab and returned to the office building where the helipad was located, they were several minutes past their agreed upon rendezvous.

The pilot was unfazed, choosing to lean against the building and have a smoke while he waited.

Beth felt as if the morning's sexual antics were emblazoned across her crimson cheeks. Drew merely laughed at her and slid an arm around her shoulders as they lifted into the sky. The sudden whoosh stole her breath and make her insides quiver, not unlike the experience of Drew's lovemaking, now that she thought about it.

She studied his profile as he gazed out the large, curved window. Everything about him was exceptional. He was wildly successful in business, widely liked and respected in Royal. There was even talk that he might be the next president of the Texas Cattleman's Club when Gil Addison's term ended.

The man wasn't perfect. Thank God. Who wanted to live with that? But he was pretty darn close. And he wanted Beth.

Even as she told herself she could adapt to his world, doubt crept in. Audie would never leave her alone if she were married to Drew. He would want money and favors and anything else he thought he could get from his sister married to the big shot. She knew how his brain worked.

Thankfully, the noise of the helicopter meant she didn't have to talk to Drew. After yesterday, last night and this morning, she didn't know what she would say. Maybe she spent too much time worrying, too many minutes trying to predict the future. In the greater scheme of life, there were few things she could control. Not her own destiny, and certainly not the man who was in so many ways her opposite.

He reached for her hand, turning her heart to mush. She had never been much of a girlie girl. No time for hearts and flowers and doodling a guy's name on notebook paper.

But with Drew, she found herself softening, enjoying the many ways he showed her he cared.

He was a man. Arrogant. Always sure he was right. But he gave her something she had never found with anyone else. Not even Richard. Drew gave her the unshakable conviction that she had found the person who was her other half.

It might not be the same for him. It might not be forever. But it was the most exhilarating feeling she had ever experienced.

Leaning into his shoulder, she closed her eyes and dreamed. The helicopter closed the remaining distance to Royal rapidly. Soon they'd be back to life at Willowbrook. And Audie living on her farm. And all the heartaches from the storm. But with Drew at her side, she knew she had the support to deal with whatever came her way.

At last, the pilot set them gently on Drew's home turf. Drew jumped out and reached up to lift her down, his hands lingering a bit longer than necessary at her waist. He kissed her cheek. "You ready to enter the house of crazy?" he asked.

She chuckled. "From everything I've heard, weddings are always a little bit out of control."

"True. But since Jed and Kimberly have invited the entire town of Royal, *crazy* may be only the beginning."

Thirteen

Drew was chagrined to find that his joking description was painfully accurate. The serenity of Willowbrook farm had morphed into a state of total chaos. In addition to Drew's own fairly large staff, several dozen outsiders had converged on the ranch. There were tents to be erected, chairs to be lined up, barbeque grills to be stationed.

And that was only the beginning.

Since Jed seemed to have things under control, Drew spent his time in the stables. Recently, he'd had offers for two of his stallions. The money would help finance the next big expansion. A month ago, that expansion had been all he thought about. After the storm, things looked very different.

To his frustration, Drew barely saw Beth after their return from Dallas. She was swallowed up in the responsibility of being Kimberly's de facto wedding planner, coordinating everything from menu items to the bride's clothing. Kimberly walked around with a beaming smile on her face, nothing at all like the bridezillas Drew had heard about. Jed, on the other hand, was snappy.

Drew caught him by the arm as he passed in the hall. "What in the hell is wrong with you, man? You're acting like a horse with a burr under his saddle."

Jed leaned against the wall, rotating his head and rubbing the back of his neck. "I know this was partly my idea, but God in heaven, I never expected it to snowball like this. I should have kidnapped Kimberly."

"Oh?" Drew tried to remain neutral, even though he was in his brother's court.

"I want Kimberly. That's all."

Suddenly, Drew understood. "You mean you *want* Kimberly."

"Isn't that what I said?" Jed snarled.

Drew managed not to laugh, but it was tough. His brother was suffering from sexual frustration. Kimberly had kicked him out of her apartment in town. Beth was her new roommate as the women took care of final wedding details.

By the same token, Drew had been deprived of Beth's company. As much as he missed her presence in his bed, however, for him it was a temporary relief. With Beth spending the bulk of her hours in Royal, Drew didn't have to worry every minute about her learning the truth about Audie.

Drew was going to confess. Hopefully, she would be grateful that he was helping get Audie back on his feet. He wanted to ease Beth's troubles. That had been his intent all along. He wasn't a liar by nature, and even though he knew Beth was going to be pissed, he had to tell her.

But when the wedding was over....

The day after the Dallas trip was a blur. Everyone had a question for Drew. *What about this? Can we do that? Where will we find those?*

While he was happy to help, no one seemed to acknowledge or care that he had a ranch to run. The pandemonium only increased. Thankfully, by sundown on the eve of the wedding, a brief lull fell over Willowbrook.

At long last, he and Jed kicked back in the den to drink beer and eat steak and baked potatoes. With no womenfolk in the house, they decided to have their own impromptu version of a bachelor party. The meal began in silence as they watched a play-off game on the big screen TV.

Sometime later, Jed set his empty plate on the coffee table. "Thanks, Drew."

"For what?"

"Keeping me sane."

Drew grinned. "I like having you here. You know that. It seems like old times. What does Kimberly think about the move to Dallas?"

"She's excited, I think. The Cattleman's Club there is going to have a reception for us pretty soon after we get back."

"So things at the club are going well?"

"They are. It's not as big as the one here, of course, but we're getting new members all the time."

"Good." Drew put his dishes aside as well. "You want another beer?"

"Sure."

When Drew returned from the kitchen, Jed sat with his elbows on his knees, his head in his hands. Drew put the open beer beside him and resumed his seat. "You okay, baby brother?"

Jed looked up at him, his eyes glazed. "I don't know the first damn thing about being a father. I've tried not to let Kimberly see, but I'm scared, Drew. What if I mess things up? I'm not worried about Kimberly and me. We're solid now. But I'm going to be responsible for a human life."

Drew nodded. "I could tell you it will all be fine, but what do I know? I guess most of it comes instinctively. Like in the animal kingdom."

"True, but that's usually the female of the species.

Human dads in the twenty-first century are supposed to be hands-on."

"I've known you your whole life. You never walk away from a challenge. You've got this, Jed. You and Kimberly. You'll be fine."

The tension in Jed's shoulders visibly relaxed. "You're right. As long as I have her, I've got everything I need."

Beth was exhausted but exhilarated. The morning of Kimberly and Jed's wedding day dawned perfectly. The weather forecast promised blue skies, a light breeze and temperatures in the upper seventies.

Kimberly was sleeping in, so Beth tiptoed around the apartment as she fixed a cup of coffee. She had been taken aback when it became clear that Kimberly wanted to include her not only in the preparations, but also in the small wedding party. Kimberly's lack of family plus the fact that her two best friends from childhood had married and moved far away in the last two years meant that this extremely quick wedding left her with few options for female support.

In a normal situation, with months to plan, her friends would have flown back to Royal, of course. But despite how much they loved Kimberly, it just wasn't possible on such short notice.

So Beth set out to do everything in her power to make this day wonderful for the bride.

As much as Beth was embroiled in last minute details, she couldn't stop thinking about Drew. They had barely seen each other since the helicopter brought them back from Dallas. She knew she had to make some decisions soon. She believed Drew had strong feelings for her. So why did she still have doubts?

All this wedding fever put ideas in her head. She

couldn't deny it. But it was never good to make important life decisions in the heat of the moment. First the storm, and now Kimberly and Jed's baby news. A quickie marriage ceremony. Would life ever get back to normal? Until it did, Beth wasn't sure she could make any kind of commitment to Drew even if he asked.

Two hours later, she and Kimberly loaded Beth's loaner truck with everything they would need for the day. The two of them had put together a detailed list so nothing would be overlooked. Kimberly was pale but calm. Drew had orders to keep Jed occupied while Beth smuggled Kimberly into Beth's suite of rooms at Willowbrook.

On the drive to the ranch, Kimberly stared out the window, her hands resting protectively over her almost nonexistent baby bump.

Beth envied her in many ways. Having a baby was an incredible blessing. Kimberly's sweet spirit would translate well to maternal devotion. Then there was Jed, who so very clearly adored his high school girlfriend. The two of them seemed meant for each other. Which was a statement Beth couldn't make about herself and Drew.

Doggedly, she put her own agenda out of her mind for the moment. This was Kimberly's day. Beth was honored to be a part of it.

Fortunately, they made it inside the house without detection. No bad luck to endure because the groom saw the bride before the ceremony. While Kimberly showered, Beth read through texts and emails on her phone.

One from Drew made her heart race, though it had nothing to do with romance.

Kimberly came walking out of the bathroom wearing a thin robe, a towel in her hand as she dried her hair. "What's wrong?"

Beth realized that her face must have revealed more than she intended. "Um, nothing."

Kimberly sat on the edge of the bed. "I'm not a fragile flower. Tell me what you just read."

Beth bit her lip and gave her the bottom line without dressing it up. "According to Drew, over four hundred people have RSVP'd by phone, text or email that they're coming to the wedding. And that's not counting the ones who will show up without letting us know."

Kimberly's eyes widened. "Oh. My. God. What happened?"

"Apparently your idea worked. People are so overwhelmed and sad and tired from the cleanup, they jumped at the chance to have some fun."

"Is there enough food?"

"Drew says he and Jed have it under control. The caterer is catatonic, but I heard two helicopters land while you were in the shower. Drew and Jed are reveling in the moment, I think. You know. Macho men handling impossible logistics."

"Better them than me."

Beth laughed. "I think you and I have the easy part. All we have to do is get you dressed and walk down the aisle."

The ceremony was scheduled for four o'clock. At twenty till, the housekeeper came to say that all the guests were in place. Many of them, apparently, were perched on hay bales hastily pressed into service for additional seating.

Beth touched Kimberly's shoulder. "You look beautiful. Are you ready?"

Kimberly's lip wobbled. "It was supposed to be casual and fun."

"And it still is," Beth said firmly. In light of the town's tragedy and given the impromptu nature of the nuptials,

Jed and Kimberly had opted for nontraditional clothing. The men were wearing pressed dress jeans with crisp white shirts and bolo ties made from polished petrified wood that had been found on Willowbrook land back in the early 1900s. Hand-tooled boots, of course, completed their rig.

Kimberly had chosen as her bridal gown a simple, strapless, knee-length dress in cream silk and lace. Her only adornment was a stunning strand of pearls Jed had given her as a wedding gift. The elegant jewelry once belonged to his grandmother. Because of the tornado, Kimberly didn't even have an engagement ring, but Jed swore to remedy that as soon as they got to Dallas.

Beth's maid-of-honor dress was Kimberly's choice as well. It echoed the bride's in style, but was a shade of pale green, to complement Beth's eyes.

The two women stared at each other. "We'd better go," Beth said. "Don't want to give the groom a heart attack."

Drew stood beside his brother in front of the minister beneath a trellised arch woven with blush pink roses and gazed out over the guests. In addition to the extended Farrell family, half the town had showed up, it seemed. So many familiar faces dotted the crowd. Nate Battle, the sheriff and his wife, Amanda, who ran the diner; Sam and Lila Gordon, whose courtship had gotten off to a rocky start but who now had a set of twins; Ryan Grant, the rodeo star, and his better half Piper, who worked out of the hospital as a paramedic. The list went on and on. Families Drew and Jed had known since childhood, along with newer friends.

A string quartet had played for a long time as the guests were seated, but now the music changed. The crowd rose to its feet with a murmur of approval. As the notes of Pachelbel's Canon lifted on the autumn breeze, Drew's eyes strained until he saw a familiar figure appear and begin to walk down the endless satin runner.

His heart stumbled to a halt. Beth. She walked toward him with a small smile on her face. Their eyes locked. Something sweet and deep passed between them. The bride followed only a few steps behind, but Drew never saw her. His whole focus was on the woman who had become as necessary to him as oxygen and food.

The dress she wore made her look like a gift of spring, even though the calendar said otherwise. Her hair, shiny and glowing in the sun, floated around her shoulders. The small posy of rosebuds she carried was held at exactly the correct angle.

Everything about her was perfect. At last, she reached the front and took her place opposite Drew.

Vaguely, he was aware that Jed stepped forward and took Kimberly's hand. But Drew continued to stare at Beth, even as the small wedding party turned as one to face the minister.

Later, he couldn't remember a single thing that was said. Vows were exchanged, rings blessed and finally the pronouncement. With the citizens of Royal clapping and cheering, the newlyweds made their way back down the aisle.

At the appropriate moment, Drew took Beth's arm in his. His chest bursting with love and pride, he walked her toward the house, smiling broadly.

Jed and Kimberly stepped inside the ranch house for a moment of privacy. Drew dragged Beth to a sheltered corner of the porch out of sight. "God, I've missed you," he muttered. He wrapped her in his arms and kissed her roughly, rejoicing when she gave him eager passion in return.

"Enough," she said finally, breathing heavily. "We have to go back for pictures."

"Pictures?" He parroted the word, unable to think about anything but getting her naked and under him ASAP.

"C'mon, Drew. It's their day. We can't ruin it."

He understood Beth's point and applauded the sentiment. But a beast raged inside him. Beth was his. He wanted to tell the whole world. And he never wanted to spend a night apart from her again.

Today, however, social convention demanded he live up to his role as host.

What followed was a combination of high spirits, ample food and drink and a celebration of life in the wake of what could have been death for those in the crowd. The tornado had marked everyone in attendance in one fashion or another. There was still much to do. Sorrow had visited households that would need time to recover. But today was about joy.

Hours later, Drew waved as Jed and Kimberly departed via helicopter for their honeymoon. At the same moment, the last of the guests and caterers rolled away in a string of vehicles down the road to Royal. Soon, he and Beth were alone, standing near the front of the house.

The tents and chairs were still up…and the grills. But cleanup would finish tomorrow. Dark closed in.

He reached for Beth's hand, feeling a heady mix of contentment and anticipation. "Alone at last."

The words had barely left his mouth when one of his two top guys approached, his mouth grim. "I hate to bother you, boss. But we've had an incident. Someone left a gate open. Inkblot got out and injured his leg."

Inkblot was one of Willowbrook's prized stallions— worth a couple million dollars, not to mention the stud fees.

"No one on my staff is stupid enough to let that happen."

"It was the new guy."

Beth cocked her head and stared at Drew. "The new guy?"

The foreman responded. "Audie Andrews. He's your brother, right? No offense, ma'am, but I didn't expect him to screw up this fast."

Beth clapped a hand over her mouth, but she was unable to muffle a sound of distress. Drew reached for her. She backed away, her face white. The foreman stood watching them both, a look of confusion in his gaze.

Drew clenched his teeth, damning the timing. "Go get Andrews. I want him in my office immediately."

The foreman strode away at a rapid clip, clearly aware that something more was going on. Drew turned to Beth. "I can explain."

Dull acceptance replaced her look of disbelief. "I told you," she said. "I warned you. Did you not believe me?"

"You weren't specific. He told me about his alcoholism and his six months sober. I assumed you had trouble believing he had changed. I thought if I gave him a job he could prove himself and get his own place sooner. I was trying to *help* you," he said through clenched teeth. "Is it really such a hell of a big deal?"

Beth's eyes flashed. "You tell me. You're the one with a damaged horse. You're so arrogant and bossy you can't bear to stay out of my business. After the storm, I decided maybe I had misjudged you, but apparently not." She whirled and ran for the steps to the house.

"Where are you going?" he shouted, desperation and anger dueling in his chest.

"To pack."

He stalked after her. "And go where?"

Facing him from the porch, she wrapped her arms around her waist. Her eyes glittered with pain. "I have a key to Kimberly's apartment. I'll stay there. I never should have come to Willowbrook at all."

She disappeared into the house. Drew let her go. Once she had a chance to calm down, he could make her see reason.

Beth slung clothes into the bag she had taken to Dallas. It wouldn't hold everything she had brought from her house after the tornado, but she could ask the housekeeper to box up the rest later and send it to Kimberly's address.

She didn't have a plan after that. Embarrassment and anger sent tears rolling down her cheeks as she gathered up her toiletries in the beautiful bathroom. Today had been perfect. Until Audie ruined things. Like he did every other time.

But the weird thing was, Audie wasn't the focus of her fury and disappointment. Audie was simply being Audie. She had learned to expect nothing more from him.

Drew was another story. He had given her a roof over her head so she wouldn't have to live in a half-demolished house. He had made love to her as if she was the only woman on the planet....

But the one thing she asked him to do—stay away from her brother—had apparently been too much. He'd deliberately ignored her wishes. Audie would never have had the initiative to go to Drew about a job. Clearly, Drew had sought out Audie. But why, when he knew what Beth had said about her brother? Because the mighty Drew Farrell always knew best. And he didn't give a damn if anyone else thought differently.

Well, it didn't matter now. This debacle was exactly the reason she didn't belong in Drew's rarefied world. Audie was her brother, and as such, he would always be a millstone around her neck. Even in the short time Beth had stayed at Willowbrook, she had come to understand the value of Drew's horses. The one injured today, Inkblot, was a wildly expensive cornerstone of Willowbrook's breeding program.

Thanks to Audie, the valuable animal had been hurt.

Wiping her face with the back of her hand, she finished packing and debated whether or not she would bother saying goodbye to Drew. Part of her wanted to show him that she was poised and coldly angry. The better decision, though, seemed to be a quick escape.

But she couldn't resist one last chance to see him before she left. Tiptoeing down the hall, she approached Drew's office. If he was finished reprimanding and probably firing Audie, perhaps she would say something. But as she drew closer, she realized that her brother was still with his boss.

She eavesdropped unashamedly.

Drew spoke sternly. "I gave you a chance, Andrews. And you blew it."

"Somebody's trying to pin this on me, Mr. Farrell, I swear. I never left that gate unlocked. You gotta believe me."

"One of the men saw you leaving the stall area just before the wedding."

"Yeah, that's true. One of my buddies from town wanted to see your horses. I guess I'd been braggin' a little about workin' here. So I took him back for a look. But that's all we did, I swear. I know it was a dumb thing to do."

Silence reigned for a few seconds. Then Drew spoke again. "Beth tried to warn me about you, but I thought she was overreacting."

Audie's angry voice ricocheted off the walls. "She never

gives me a chance. Nobody does. And for a rich guy, you aren't too smart."

Beth leaned against the wall just outside the door and put a hand over her eyes. Audie was an idiot with a bad temper.

Drew's voice could have frozen lava. "Not that I really care, but would you like to elaborate on that remark?"

"My sister," Audie yelled. "She's playing you for a fool. And it isn't the first time. She's already had one sugar daddy bail her out. Now, after the tornado, all she had to do was bat those long eyelashes at you and suddenly, she's tucked up in your little palace here being treated like a queen. I know she's sleeping with you."

Moments later Audie wailed.

Beth couldn't help herself. She peeked into the room and saw Drew nursing his fist. His chest heaved, and his face was flushed with anger. Audie lay flat out on the floor with a giant purplish red spot on his cheekbone.

Drew looked up and saw her standing there. Everything inside Beth melted in despair. She'd been the one to tell Drew about Richard. Now, Audie's vindictive accusation painted her in the worst possible light.

She ran.

Out of the house. To the battered pickup truck. Down the road to town.

As she drove, hands shaking on the steering wheel, humiliation choked her. Her budding relationship with Drew was too new to withstand this wretchedly embarrassing incident with her brother.

Even worse, maybe Drew thought she had lied about her relationship with Richard. Maybe in light of Audie's words, Drew thought Beth had *used* Richard. And now was using him.

Glancing in the rearview mirror, she stepped on the gas

a bit harder, half expecting at any moment to see Drew's vehicle hot on her heels. But the road was empty.

In Royal, she headed for the only place guaranteed to provide refuge. She holed up in Kimberly's apartment and cried. By nightfall, she accepted the truth.

Drew was done with her. How did she know? He didn't try to follow her. He had let her go without protest.

And that was the cruelest blow of all.

Three days later, she finally attained a fragile state of calm acceptance. It helped that the insurance money had come through. She'd hired a contractor, and with a professional's help, began making the string of decisions that governed the remodeling of her home.

But she conducted all meetings in town. Until Audie was off her property, she was not going back there. And she surely wasn't going to risk a run-in with Drew. Not under any circumstances.

Deep in one little hopeful corner of her heart, she believed he would come for her. That tiny bit of positive energy told her he would eventually understand that she had given him her heart...that she didn't sleep with every man with money who came along.

But the hours passed, and Drew didn't come.

At the seven-day mark, she regretted looking in the mirror. She hated being a pitiful, grieving mess. Each morning she forced herself to dress and put on lip gloss and mascara so she could pretend to the world that she was normal. But it was only an act. She ate barely enough to keep from starving. Her stomach hurt from bouts of sobbing. The tears came at night when there was no one else to see. Desperation lurked with each new sunrise.

Kimberly and Jed were returning to Royal tomorrow afternoon. Though they would soon be moving to Dallas, they planned to stay at Kimberly's place in the meantime. Neither of them knew Beth had moved out of her room at Willowbrook.

Beth couldn't be in residence when the newlyweds came home.

But where was she to go?

Every motel and hotel and B&B in town was full of refugees from the storm. She knew. She had checked.

That night she packed her things. The weather was still pleasant. If she drove out toward the interstate, she could park at the rest area and sleep in the truck. It was a plan, but not much of one.

It took her two trips to load her stuff into the cab. She had accumulated a small stash of food. The cooler she purchased yesterday would keep it edible. She shivered when she realized that her preparations exhibited a sad familiarity. Once more she had been reduced to living as a nomad.

With one last look around to make sure everything was spic and span, she took a deep breath and told herself she could exist without Drew.

She had lived self-sufficiently and by her wits for a long time, remarkably so after her troubled upbringing. No need to suffer a broken heart simply because one man didn't want her like she wanted him. Another day, a fresh start. First on the list was a trip to the local furniture store to buy a new kitchen table and chairs. The manager promised to hold it for delivery until the contractor had finished the repairs.

Picking up her keys and her cell phone, she opened the door.

Drew stood on the sidewalk.

He watched the color drain from her face. It was some small comfort to see that she had suffered as much as he had. His stupid mistake had started the whole mess, but Beth had been the one to cut and run without fighting for what they had.

"Hello, Beth," he said quietly.

Her expression was hunted. "I have an appointment," she said, the terse words just short of outright rudeness.

"Let's get something straight. I knew you were here the whole time. But I thought we both needed some time to think."

"There you go again. Assuming you know what's best."

The comeback lacked her usual heat.

"Jed and Kimberly are coming home tomorrow."

"I know. That's why I've moved out."

"Moved out to where?"

"None of your business."

He studied her intently, noting the changes. Though she had lost weight after the storm, now her cheekbones were even more sharply defined. She wore jeans and a casual shirt, looking much like the woman who had battled a tornado with him.

She scrunched her eyes against the sun and pulled out a pair of sunglasses. "I really have to go," she said.

Now he couldn't read her gaze at all. He took one of her hands, disturbed to find it ice cold. Did she despise him? Had his careless actions, his lack of respect for her feelings cost him everything?

"Please," he said urgently. "Give me one hour. Then if you still want to go, I won't stop you. In fact, I'll never speak to you again if that's what you want."

He saw the way her throat worked. Recognized her agitation in white knuckles and beautiful lips pressed in a firm line.

"Why?" she asked, her voice sounding dull.

"Because I need to apologize."

"So do it."

He held on to his patience. "I'm sorry for not listening to you about Audie. But I can't believe you thought I would let his nasty allegations sway me."

She took off the sunglasses, her eyes stony and blank. "They were true. Every word."

"So you don't love me?"

Her jaw dropped and her eyes widened. "That's ridiculous."

"Am I supposed to believe that the only reason you had sex with me was so I would give you room and board? That's absurd. I *know* you, Beth. And I choose to believe that you feel something for me. Don't you? Just like I feel something for you. Something I'm pretty sure is love."

He cupped her cheek, ignoring her move to evade him. "I'm sorry, Beth. Sorry for everything. Sorry I didn't have the courtesy to listen to your opinions and preferences. Sorry that I gave you so little confidence in our relationship that you had to run."

Finally, she spoke. "Why did you wait so long to come find me?"

He tugged on her hand. "One hour. Please. I want to show you something."

That she accompanied him was a miracle. But maybe she thought it was the only way to be rid of him. He had brought a car, not his truck this time. In the trunk he had a few necessities in case things went his way, but mostly he wanted her to be comfortable.

He opened the passenger door, helped her in, then ran around to his side, not entirely sure she wouldn't bolt.

Unwilling for her to guess his intentions, he drove around several blocks in town before heading out toward Willowbrook. When it was time, he turned onto Beth's road.

When he reached the edge of Beth's fields, in sight of her house and the storm cellar, he stopped the car and helped her out.

He led her toward what used to be her produce stand and positioned her with gentle hands. "Take a look."

Beth blinked in astonishment. Her flattened produce stand had been rebuilt. The structure still smelled of new wood. A jaunty, brightly colored sign announced "Green Acres—Good Food at Good Prices." Even more astonishing were the piles of pumpkins artfully arranged. Dozens of pumpkins, maybe hundreds.

Artificial fall leaves and real corn shocks decorated every available space.

"I don't understand," she said, thinking the whole thing must be a mirage.

Drew stood shoulder to shoulder with her, his hands shoved in his pockets. "I want you to be happy, Beth. Even if it's not with me. I've tried to reset the clock to the day before the storm hit. I wasn't able to put the pumpkins back in the field for photo ops, but you're all ready to reopen whenever you want to."

She bent down and picked up a mini pumpkin, its color the perfect orange. "I don't know what to say." When she stood again, she stared at him face-to-face for the first time. He looked worse than the day they had both survived a killer tornado. Shadowed eyes, grim lines around his mouth.

He took her hands in his, forcing her to meet his eyes. "Audie is not staying here anymore. I made him help me with all this, and then I booted him out of your shed. He says he wants to apologize to you for all the things he said that day in my office. But I told him it might be best to wait a little bit. I wasn't sure you could handle seeing him yet."

"Angie and Anton?"

"I found them an apartment. They moved this morning."

"He won't appreciate your kindness the way he should."

"I did it for you."

When her bottom lip trembled, she bit down on it. Hard. "How is your horse?" She had worried about Inkblot every day.

"He's doing well. And I think you should know, Audie is still working for me. It turns out he was telling the truth."

"Then who left the gate open?"

"One of the wedding guests. A horse-crazy thirteen-year-old girl. When the family got home that night, the daughter confessed she had been sneaking around my stables. She went into Inkblot's stall to pet him, but the stallion scared her and she ran. She knew she had left the gate open. The father called me and apologized."

"Did you tell him the horse was injured?"

"No. I didn't want to make him feel worse."

"Well, I'm glad it wasn't Audie."

"Tell me what you're thinking," Drew said, gently brushing a strand of hair from her cheek.

She flinched. And saw him suffer.

He backed away. "God, Beth. I'm sorry. I know you don't want to hear it, but I love you. I'm sorry I went behind your back."

She lifted her shoulders and let them fall. "I don't care about that anymore. But don't you see…?" She paused, her throat thick with tears. "Audie will never go away. If I agree to a relationship with you, he'll be an embarrassment to your business and to your family. I can't be responsible for that."

"Because why?"

"Because I love you, too. And you deserve a wife with some family credentials. Someone who knows how to plan a dinner party for three dozen people or at least a woman who can tell one end of a thoroughbred from another."

He grinned. "You are such a snob."

She frowned. "I certainly am not."

He pulled her close and kissed her soundly, ignoring her halfhearted attempts to escape. Finally, he held her at arms' length. "The only wife I want is you," he said, breathing heavily, his gaze intent. "If you turn me down, I'll be a pitiful, aging bachelor with no one to love me."

She brushed her fingers over his lips, wondering if happiness really was in reach. "You are such a scoundrel." Closing her eyes, she nestled against him with a smile, resting her head on his chest and feeling his heart beating beneath her cheek. "But what about Audie?"

"I can handle your brother, Beth." Drew's big hand was warm on her back. She soaked in the moment, unwilling to rush ahead when anticipation was so very sweet. Arousal and exhilaration danced in her blood.

Apparently, her patience was greater than his. "Now what do you say to my proposition?" he asked.

"Have you actually posed a question yet?" She could feel his impatience in the way his body shuddered against hers.

Without warning, he went down on one knee, looking up at her with such naked love it made her chest ache. "Beth Andrews, will you marry me?"

The sky was bluer, the breeze sweeter, the sun as warm and perfect as the love in her heart. She feathered her fingers through his hair. "Yes, I will. Under one condition." She pulled him to his feet. "I want to offer you a wedding gift."

"Okay." He appeared mystified.

"A man like you has everything. So I'm giving you Green Acres."

He shook his head instantly. "No, Beth. I can't take your farm. I can't bulldoze the roots you've worked so hard to put down. This is important to you."

She went up on tiptoe and kissed him, lingering long enough to feel her pulse race as his arms tightened around her. "*You're* important to me, Drew. I want to make babies with you and learn the horse business and be a part of Willowbrook. Those are my conditions."

The stunned shock in his blue eyes gave way to mischief. "How soon can we start on the making babies part?"

"I'd like a ring on my finger, first. You Farrell men are so darned impulsive."

He picked her up in his arms and carried her back to the car. "Did I mention I have a blanket in the trunk? And a picnic?"

"I love you, Drew." She kissed his chin.

"And I love you, my stubborn, beautiful Beth. It may have taken a killer storm to bring us together, but I'm never letting you go."

"I can live with that."

And so she did…

* * * * *

SHELTERED BY
THE MILLIONAIRE

BY
CATHERINE MANN

USA TODAY bestselling author **Catherine Mann** lives on a sunny Florida beach with her flyboy husband and their four children. With more than forty books in print in over twenty countries, she has also celebrated wins for both a RITA® Award and a Booksellers' Best Award. Catherine enjoys chatting with readers online—thanks to the wonders of the internet, which allows her to network with her laptop by the water! Contact Catherine through her website, www.catherinemann.com, find her on Facebook and Twitter (@CatherineMann1), or reach her by snail mail at PO Box 6065, Navarre, FL 32566, USA.

To my parents, Brice and Sandra Woods.
Thank you for the joyous gift of always
having pets in my life as a child.

One

The airbag inflated. Hard. Fast.

Pain exploded through Megan Maguire. From the bag hitting her in the face. From her body slamming against the seat. But it wasn't nearly as excruciating as the panic pumping through her as she faced the latest obstacle in reaching her daughter after a tornado.

A *tornado* for God's sake.

Her insides quivered with fear and her body ached from the impact. The wind howled outside her small compact car on the lonely street, eerily abandoned for 4:30 on a weekday afternoon. Apparently she was the only one stupid enough to keep driving in spite of the weather warnings of a tornado nearby. In fact, reports of the twister only made her more determined. She had to get to her daughter.

Megan punched her way clear of the deflating airbag to find a shattered windshield. The paw-shaped air freshener still swayed, dangling from her rearview mirror and releasing a hint of lavender. Files from work were scattered all over the floor from sliding off the seat along with the bag containing her daughter's Halloween costume. Then Megan looked outside and she damn near hyperventilated.

The hood of her sedan was covered by a downed tree. Steam puffed from the engine.

If the thick oak had fallen two seconds later, it would have landed on the roof of her car. She could have been crushed. She could have died.

Worst of all, her daughter would have become an orphan for all intents and purposes since Evie's father had never wanted anything to do with her. Panic pushed harder on Megan's chest like a cement slab.

Forcing oxygen back into her lungs one burning gasp at a time, she willed her racing heart to slow. Nothing would stop her from getting to her daughter. Not a totaled car. Not a downed tree. And definitely not…a…panic…attack.

Gasping for air, she flung open the door and stepped into the aftermath of the storm. Sheeting rain and storm winds battered her. Thank heaven she'd already left work to pick up her daughter for a special outing before they announced the tornado warning on her radio. If she'd been at the shelter when the warning sirens went off she wouldn't have been able to leave until given the okay.

But if she'd left at 1:00 to go to the movie as they'd originally planned, Evie would have been with her, safe and sound.

As a single mom, Megan needed her job as an animal shelter director. Evie's father had hit the road the minute Megan had told him about the unexpected pregnancy.

Any attempts at child support had been ignored until he faded from sight somewhere in the Florida Keys. She'd finally accepted he was gone from her life and Evie's. She could only count on herself.

Determination fueled her aching body. She was less than a mile from her daughter's Little Tots Daycare. She would walk every step of the way if she had to. Rain plastered her khakis and work shirt to her body. Thank goodness her job called for casual wear. She would have been hard pressed to climb over the downed tree in heels.

At least the tornado had passed, but others could finger down from the gathering clouds at any minute. With every fiber of her being she prayed the worst was over. She had to get to her daughter, to be sure she was safe.

The small cottage that housed Little Tots Daycare had appeared so cute and appealing when she'd chosen it for Evie. Now, she could only think how insubstantial the structure would be against the force of such a strong storm. What if Evie was trapped inside?

Sweeping back a clump of soggy red hair, Megan clambered over the tree trunk and back onto the road strewn with debris. She took in the devastation ahead, collapsed buildings and overturned cars. The town had been spun and churned, pieces of everyday life left lining the street. Glass from blown-out windows. Papers and furniture from businesses. Pictures and books. The tornado's path was clear, like a massive mower had cut through the land. Uprooting trees, slicing through lives, spewing a roof or a computer like it was nothing more than a blade of grass sliced and swept away.

She picked her way past half of a splintered door. Wind whistled through the trees, bending and creaking the towering oaks. But she didn't hear the telltale train sound that preceded a tornado.

Thoughts of Evie scared and waiting dumped acid on Megan's gut. Even knowing the Little Tots Daycare workers were equipped to handle the crisis didn't quell her fears. Evie was her daughter.

Her world.

She would trudge through this storm, tear her way through the wreckage, do anything to reach her four-year-old child. The roar of the wind was calling to her, urging her forward until she could have sworn she actually heard someone speaking to her. *Megan. Megan. Megan.* Had she sustained a concussion from the wreck?

She searched around her, pushing her shoulder-length hair from her face, and spotted a handful of people every bit as reckless as her venturing outside for one reason or another. None of them looked her way…except for a looming man, a familiar man, charging down the steps of one of the many buildings owned by Daltry Property Management. For three and a half years, Whit Daltry had been a major pain in the neck whenever they'd crossed paths, which she tried to make as infrequently as possible.

The fates were really ganging up on her today.

Whit shouted, "Megan? Megan! Come inside before you get hurt."

"No," she shouted. "I can't."

His curse rode the wind as he jogged toward her. Tall and muscular, a force to be reckoned with, he plowed ahead, his Stetson impervious to the wind. Raindrops sheeted off the brim of his hat, as his suit coat and tie whipped to and fro.

He stopped alongside her, his brown eyes snapping with anger, warm hand clasping her arm. "I couldn't believe it when I saw you through the window. What are you doing out in this weather?"

"Dancing in the rain," she snapped back, hysteria threatening to overwhelm her. "What do you think I'm doing? I'm trying to get to Evie. I had already left the shelter when the tornado hit. A tree fell on my car so I had to walk."

His jaw flexed, his eyes narrowing. "Where is your daughter?"

She tugged her arm free. "She's at Little Tots Day-care. I have to go to her."

And what a time to remember this man was the very reason she didn't work closer to her daughter's pre-school. When the shelter had decided to build a new facility shortly after she'd signed on as director three and a half years ago, Whit had started off their acquaintance by blocking the purchase of land near his offices— which also happened to be near the day care. The Safe Haven's board of directors had been forced to choose an alternate location. Now the shelter was located in a more industrial area farther from her daughter. Every single work day, Megan lost time with Evie because of an arbitrary decision by this man.

And now, he could have cost her so much more if something had happened to Evie.

Whit grasped her arms again, more firmly this time, peering at her from under the brim of his hat. "I'll get your daughter. You need to take shelter until the weather clears. There could be more tornadoes."

"You don't know me very well if you think I'll even entertain that idea." She grabbed his suit coat lapels. "There's no way I'm sitting in a gas station bathroom hugging my knees and covering my head while my Evie is out there scared. She's probably crying for me."

"Look at the roads—" He waved to the street full of branches and overturned vehicles. "They're blocked here too. Only a truck or heavy-duty SUV would stand a chance of getting through."

"I'll run, walk or crawl my way there. It's not that much farther."

He bit off another curse and scrubbed his strong jaw with one hand. "Fine. If I can't convince you, then we might as well get moving. Hopefully, my truck can four-wheel it over the debris and drive that last two blocks a lot faster than you can walk. Are you okay with that?"

"Seriously? Yes. Let's go." Relief soaked into her, nearly buckling her knees.

Whit led her back to the redbrick building and into the parking garage, his muscular arm along her back helping her forge ahead. Time passed in a fugue as she focused on one thing. Seeing her daughter.

Thumbing the key remote, Whit unlocked the large blue truck just ahead of them and started the engine from outside the truck. She ran the last few steps, yanked open the passenger door and crawled inside the top-of-the-line vehicle, surprisingly clean for a guy, with no wrenches or files or gym bag on the floor. No child's Halloween costume or box of recycling like what she had in her destroyed car, and— Oh, God, her mind was on overdrive from adrenaline. The warmth of the heater blasted over her wet body. Her teeth chattered. From the cold or shock? She wasn't sure and didn't care.

She could only think of her child. "Thank you for doing this, Whit."

"We may have had our differences, but these are ex-traordinary circumstances." He looked at her intensely for an instant as he set his hat on the seat between them. "Your daughter will be fine. That day care building may look small but it's rock solid, completely up to code. And that's me speaking as a professional in property management."

"I understand that in my mind." Megan tapped her temple. "But in my heart?" Her hand trembled as it fluttered to her chest. "The fears and what-ifs can't be quieted."

"You're a mother. That's understandable." He shifted the truck into four-wheel drive and accelerated out of the parking lot, crunching over debris, cracked concrete and churned earth. "How did the shelter fare in the storm?"

Her gut clenched all over again as she thought of all the precious charges in her care. "I wasn't there. I'd already left to pick up Evie when the warning siren went off. The kennel supervisor is in charge and I trust him, completely, but telephone service is out."

She felt torn in two. But she had a stellar staff in place at the shelter. They were trained to respond and rescue in disaster scenarios. She'd just never expected to use that training to find her child.

Already the rain was easing, the storm passing as quickly as it had hit. Such a brief time for so much change to happen. And there could be worse waiting for her—

The worst.

Her chin trembled, tears of panic nearly choking her. "I was supposed to take the whole afternoon off to go to a movie with Evie, but we had a sick employee leave early and a mother dog in labor dumped off with us… If I had kept my promise I would have been at the afternoon matinee with Evie rather than copping out for a later show. God, she must be so terrified—" She pressed her wrist to her mouth to hold back a sob.

"You can't torture yourself with what-ifs," he said matter-of-factly. "There was no way to see this coming and no way to know where it would be safe. You were doing your job, supporting your child. Deep breaths. Be calm for your kid."

She scrubbed her wrist under her eyes. "You're right. She'll be more frightened if she sees me freaking out."

Whit turned the corner onto the street for the Little Tots Daycare. The one-story wooden cottage was still standing but had sustained significant damage.

The aluminum roof was crunched like an accordion, folded in on the wooden porch. Already other parents and a couple of volunteer emergency responders were picking through the rubble. The porch supports had fallen like broken matches, the thick wooden beams cracked and splintered so that the main entrance was completely blocked.

Megan's heart hit her shoes.

Before she could find her breath, Whit had already jogged to her side of the truck and opened the door.

"No," she choked out a whisper. She fell into his arms, her legs weak with fear, her whole body stiff from the accident. Pain shot up her wrists where, she realized, she had burns from the airbag deployment.

None of it mattered. Her eyes focused on that fallen roof. The blocked door. More acid churned in her stomach as she thought of her little girl stuck inside.

"I've got you," Whit reassured her, rain dripping from the brim of his Stetson.

"I'm okay. You can let go. I have to find my daughter."

"And I'm going to help you do that. I have construction experience and we need to be careful our help doesn't cause more damage."

No wonder the other parents weren't tearing apart the fallen debris to get inside.

"Of course, you're right." Hands quaking, she pressed a palm to her forehead. "I'm sorry. I'm not thinking clearly."

"That's understandable. We'll get to your daughter soon. You have my word."

Whit led her past the debris of the front porch, then around to the side, where the swing sets were uprooted, the jungle gym twisted into a macabre new shape. Painted Halloween pumpkins had scattered and burst. He called out to the handful of people picking at the lumber on the porch, offering advice as he continued to lead Megan around to the back of the building. The gaggle of frantic parents listened without argument, desperate.

She couldn't imagine a world without her daughter.

In her first trimester, she'd planned to give her baby up for adoption. She'd gotten the paperwork from a local adoption agency. Then she'd felt the flutter of life inside her and she'd torn up the paperwork. From that point on, she'd opted for taking life one day at a time. The moment when she'd seen her daughter's newborn face with bright eyes staring trustingly up at her, she'd lost her heart totally.

Evie was four years old now, those first sprigs of red hair having grown into precious corkscrew curls. And Megan had a rewarding job that also paid the bills and supported her daughter. It hadn't been easy by any stretch, but she'd managed. Until today.

Whit guided her to the back of the building, which was blessedly undamaged. The back door was intact. Secure. Safe. She'd been right to come with him. She would have dived straight into the porch rubble rather than thinking to check....

Megan yanked out of Whit's grip and pounded on the door. Through the pane she could see the kids lined up on the floor with their teachers. No one seemed in a panic.

The day care supervisor pulled the door open.

"Sue Ellen," Megan clasped her hand, looking around her to catch sight of her daughter. "Where's Evie?"

"She's okay." The silver-haired supervisor wearing a smock covered in finger paints and dust patted Megan's hand. The older woman seemed calm, in control, when she must be shaking in her sensible white sneakers. "She's with a teacher's assistant and three other students. They were on their way to the kitchen when the tornado sirens went off. So she's at the other end of the building."

Sue Ellen paused and Megan's heart tripped over itself. "What are you not telling me?"

"There's a beam from the roof blocking her from coming out. But she's fine. The assistant is keeping the kids talking and calm."

Megan pressed a hand to her chest. "Near the porch? The collapsed roof?"

Whit gripped her shoulder. "I've got it."

Without another word, he raced down the corridor. Megan followed, dimly registering that he'd clasped her hand. And she didn't pull away from the comfort. They finally stopped short at a blocked hall, the emergency lighting illuminating the passageway beyond the crisscross of broken beams and cracked plaster. Dust made the image hazy, almost surreal. The teacher's assistant sat beside the row of students, Evie on the end, her bright red curls as unmistakable as the mismatched orange and purple outfit she'd insisted on wearing this morning because the colors reminded her Halloween was coming.

"Evie?" Megan shouted. "Evie, honey, it's Mommy."

"Mommy?" her daughter answered faintly, a warble in her voice. "I wanna go home."

Whit angled past Megan and crouched down to assess the crisscross of boards, cracked drywall and ceiling tiles. 'Stand back, kids, while I clear a path through."

The teacher's assistant guided them all a few feet away and wrapped her arms around them protectively as fresh dust showered down. With measured precision, Whit moved boards aside, his muscles bulging as he hefted aside plank after plank with an ease Megan envied until finally he'd cleared a pathway big enough for people to crawl through. Evie's freckled face peeked from the cluster of kids, her nose scrunched and sweet cherub smile beaming. She appeared unharmed.

Relief made Megan's legs weak. Whit's palm slid along her waist for a steadying second before he reached into the two-foot opening, arms outstretched. "Evie, I'm a friend of your mommy's here to help you. Can I lift you through here?"

Megan nodded, holding back the tears that were welling up fast. "Go to Mr. Whit, honey."

Evie raised her arms and Whit hauled her up and free, cradling her to his chest in broad, gentle hands. Megan took in every inch of her daughter, seeing plenty of dirt but nothing more than a little tear of one sleeve of her Disney princess shirt, revealing a tiny scrape. Somehow she'd come through the whole ordeal safely.

Once they reached the bottom of the rubble, Whit passed Evie to her mother. "Here ya go, kiddo."

Evie melted against Megan with one of those shuddering sighs of relief that relayed more than tears how frightened she had been. Evie wrapped her tiny arms around Megan's neck and held on tightly like a spider monkey, and it was Megan's turn to feel the shudder of relief so strong she nearly fell to her knees.

Thank you, thank you, thank you, God. Her baby was safe.

"You're okay, sweetie?"

"I'm fine, Mommy. The t'naydo came and I was a very brave girl. I did just what Miss Vicky told me to do. I sat under the stairs and hugged my knees tight with one arm and I held my friend Caitlyn's hand 'cause she was scared."

"You did well, Evie, I'm so proud of you." She kissed her daughter's forehead, taking in the hint of her daughter's favorite raspberry shampoo. "I love you so much."

"Love you, too, Mommy." She squeezed hard, holding on tightly as Whit helped the other students through.

Once the last child stepped free, Whit urged everyone to file away from the damaged part of the building. He led them down the hall to where Sue Ellen had gathered the children in the auditorium, playing music and passing out cookies and books to the students whose parents hadn't arrived to pick them up. The school nurse made the rounds checking each child, dispensing Band-Aids when needed.

Whit's hand went to the small of Megan's back again with an ease she didn't have the energy to wonder about right now.

"Megan, you should see the nurse about your scratches from the accident. The air bag has left some burns that could use antiseptic too—"

She shook her head. "I will later. For now she's got

her hands full with the children and they need her more."

Evie squirmed in her arms. "Can I get a cookie? I'm reallllly hungry."

"Of course, sweetie." She gave her daughter another hug, not sure when she would ever be okay with letting her out of her sight.

Evie raced across the gym floor as if the whole world hadn't just been blown upside down. Literally.

Whit laughed softly. "Resilient little scrap."

"More so than her mom, I'm afraid." Megan sagged and sat down on the metal riser.

"All Evie knows is that everyone is okay and you're here." Whit sat beside her, his leg pressing a warm re-assurance against hers. "Maybe we should get you one of those cookies and a cup of that juice."

"I'm okay. Really. We should go back to clearing the debris outside." She braced her shoulders. "I'm being selfish in keeping you all to myself."

"All the children are accounted for and the teachers have them well in hand. It's getting dark. I think cleanup will be on hold until the morning."

What kind of carnage would the morning reveal? Outside, sirens had wailed for the last twenty minutes. "I should take Evie and check back in at the shelter. Local animal control will need our help with housing displaced pets."

"Civilians aren't allowed on the road just yet and you don't have a car." He nudged her with his shoulder. "Face it, Megan. You can actually afford to take a few minutes to catch your breath."

The concern in his brown eyes was genuine. The warmth she saw there washed over her like a jolt of pure java, stimulating her senses. Why hadn't she ever noticed before what incredibly intense and expressive eyes he had? Sure, she'd noticed he was sexy, but then any woman who crossed his path would appreciate Whit Daltry's charismatic good looks. And in fact, that had been a part of what turned her off for the past three years—how easily women fell into his arms. She'd let herself be conned by a man like that and it had turned her life upside down.

But the warmth in his eyes now, the caring he'd shown in helping her get to Evie today presented a new side to Whit she'd never seen before. He might not be romance material for her, but he'd been a good guy just now and that meant a lot to a woman who didn't accept help easily.

She slumped back against the riser behind her. "Thank you for what you did for me today—for me and for Evie. I know you would have done the same for anyone stranded on the road." As she said the words she realized they were true. Whit wasn't the one-dimensional bad guy she'd painted him to be the past few years. There were layers to the man. "Still, the fact is, you were there for my child and I'll never forget that."

He smiled, his brown eyes twinkling with a hint of his devilish charm. "Does that mean I'm forgiven for refusing to let the shelter build on that tract of land you wanted so much?"

Layers. Definitely. Good—and bad. "I may be grateful, but I didn't develop amnesia."

He chuckled, a low rumble that drew a laugh from her, and before she knew what she was doing, she dropped her hand to his shoulder and squeezed.

"Thank you." She leaned to kiss his cheek in a heartfelt thank-you just as he turned to answer.

Their lips brushed. Just barely skimmed, but a crackle shot through her so tangibly she could have sworn the storm had returned with a bolt of lightning.

Gasping, she angled back, her eyes wide, his inscrutable.

She inched along the riser. "I need to get Evie…and um, thank you."

She shot to her feet, racing toward her daughter, away from the temptation to test the feeling and kiss him again.

That wasn't what she'd expected. At all. But then nothing about Whit had ever been predictable, damn his sexy body, hot kiss and hero's rescue. She'd been every bit as gullible as her mother once. And while she could never regret having Evie in her life, she damn well wouldn't fall victim to trusting an unworthy man again. She owed it to Evie to set a better example, to break the cycle the women in her family seemed destined to repeat.

And if that meant giving up any chance for another toe-searing kiss from Whit Daltry, then so be it.

Two

Six Weeks Later

The wild she-cat in his arms left scratches on his shoulders.

Whit Daltry adjusted his hold on the long-haired calico, an older female kitten that had wandered—scraggly and with no collar—onto the doorstep of his Pine Valley home. Luckily, he happened to know the very attractive director of Royal's Safe Haven Animal Shelter.

He stepped out of his truck and kicked the door closed, early morning sunshine reflecting off his windshield. Not a cloud in the sky, unlike that fateful day the F4 tornado had ripped through Royal, Texas. The shelter had survived unscathed, but the leaves had been stripped from the trees, leaving branches unnaturally bare for this region of Texas, even in November. The town bore lasting scars from that day that would take a lot longer to heal than the scratches from the frantic calico.

He should have gotten one of those pet carriers or a box to transport the cat. If the beast clawed its way out of his arms, chances were the scared feline would bolt away and be tough as hell to catch again. Apparently he wasn't adept at animal rescue.

That was Megan's expertise.

The thought of seeing her again sent anticipation coursing through him as each step brought him closer to the single-story brick structure. Heaven knew he could use a distraction from life right now. For six weeks, ever since they'd shared that kiss after the tornado, he'd been looking for an excuse to see her, but the town had been in chaos clearing the debris. Some of his properties had been damaged as well. He owned multiple apartment buildings and rental homes all over town. And while he might have a lighthearted approach to his social life, he was serious when it came to business and was always damn sure going to be there for his tenants when they needed him.

He'd thrown himself into the work to distract himself from the biggest loss of all—the death of his good friend Craig Richardson in the storm. It had sent him into shock for the first couple of weeks, as he grieved for Craig and tried to find ways to help his pal's widow. God, they were all still in a tailspin and he didn't know if he would be in any better shape by the memorial service that was scheduled for after Thanksgiving.

So he focused on restoring order to the town, the only place he'd ever called home after a rootless childhood being evicted from place after place. And with each clean-up operation, he thought back to the day of the storm, to clearing aside the rubble in the day care.

To Megan's kiss afterward.

Sure the kiss had been impulsive and motivated by gratitude, and she'd meant to land it on his cheek. But he would bet good money that she'd been every bit as affected by the spontaneous kiss as he was.

Granted, he'd always been attracted to her in spite of their sparring. But he'd managed to keep a tight rein on those feelings for the three and a half years he'd known her because she'd made it clear she found him barely one step above pond scum. Now, he couldn't ignore the possibility that the chemistry was mutual. So finally, here he was. He had the perfect excuse, even if it wasn't the perfect time.

And Megan wouldn't be able to avoid him as she'd been doing since their clash over the site where she'd wanted the new shelter built. A battle he'd won. Although from the sleek look of the Safe Haven facility, she'd landed on her feet and done well for the homeless four-legged residents of Royal, Texas.

Tucking the cat into his suit coat and securing her with a firm grip, he stepped into the welcoming reception area, its tiled surfaces giving off a freshly washed bleach smell. The waiting area was spacious, but today, there were wire crates lining two walls, one with cats, the other with small dogs. They were clean and neat, but the shelter was packed to capacity. He'd heard the shelter had taken in a large number of strays displaced during the storm, but he hadn't fully grasped the implications until now.

The shelter had a reputation for its innovative billboards, slogans and holiday-themed decor, but right now, every ounce of energy here seemed to be focused on keeping the animals fed and the place sparkling clean.

He closed the door, sealing himself inside.

The cat sunk her claws in deeper. Whit hissed almost as loudly as the feline and searched the space for help. Framed posters featured everything from collages of adopters to advice on flea prevention. Painted red-and-black paw prints marked the walls with directions he already knew in theory since he'd reviewed the plans during his land dispute with Megan.

A grandmotherly woman sat behind the counter labeled "volunteer receptionist." He recognized the retired legal secretary from past business ventures. She was texting on her phone, and waved for him to wait an instant before she glanced up.

He swept his hat off and set it on the counter. "Morning, Miss Abigail—"

"Good mornin', Whit," the lady interrupted with a particularly thick Southern accent, her eyes widening with surprise. The whole town knew he and Megan avoided each other like the plague. "What a pleasant surprise you've decided to adopt from us. Our doggies are housed to your right in kennel runs. But be sure to peek at the large fenced-in area outside. Volunteers take them there to exercise in the grassy area."

She paused for air, but not long enough for him to get in a word. "Although now I see you're a cat person. Never would have guessed that." She grinned as the calico peeked out of his suit jacket, purring as if the ferocious feline hadn't drawn blood seconds earlier. "Kitties are kept in our free roam area. If you find one you would like to adopt, we have meet-and-greet rooms for your sweetheart there to meet with your new feline friend—"

"I'm actually here to make a donation." He hadn't planned on that, but given all the extra crates, he could see the shelter needed help. So much of the post-tornado assistance had been focused on helping people and cleaning up the damaged buildings. But he should have realized the repercussions of the storm would have a wider ripple effect.

"A donation?" Miss Abigail set aside her phone. "Let me call our director right away—oh, here she is now."

He pivoted to find Megan walking down the dog corridor, toward the lobby, a beagle on a loose leash at her side. He could see the instant she registered his presence. She blinked fast, nibbling her lip as she paused midstep for an instant before forging ahead, the sweet curves of her hips sending a rush of want through him.

Her bright red hair was pulled back in a low ponytail. He ached to sweep away that gold clasp and thread his fingers through the fiery strands, to find out if her hair was as silky as it looked. He wanted her, had since the first time he'd seen her when they crossed paths in the lawyer's office during the dispute over a patch of property. He'd expected to smooth things over regarding finding an alternate location for the new shelter. He usually had no trouble charming people, but she'd taken to disliking him right away. Apparently her negative impression had only increased every time she perceived one of his projects as "damaging" to nature when he purchased a piece of wetlands.

He'd given up trying to figure out why she couldn't see her way clear to making nice. Because she had a reputation for being everyone's pal, a caring and kind-hearted woman who took in strays of all kinds, ready to pitch in to help anyone. Except for him.

"Megan," the receptionist cleared her throat, "Mr. Daltry here has brought us a donation."

"Another cat. Just what we were lacking." Megan's smile went tight.

He juggled his hold on the fractious fur ball. "I do plan to write a check to cover the expense of taking in another animal, but yes, I need to drop off the stray. She's been wandering around in the woods near my house. She doesn't have a collar and clearly hasn't been eating well."

"Could have been displaced because of the storm and has been surviving on her own in the wild ever since, poor girl. Animals have a knack for ditching their collars. Did you take her to a vet to check for a microchip?"

"I figured you could help me with that. Or maybe someone has come by here looking for her."

"So you're sure it's a girl?"

"I think so."

"Let's just pray she's not in heat or about to have kittens."

Oh, crap. He hadn't thought about that.

Megan passed him the dog leash and took the squirming cat from his arms. Their wrists brushed in the smooth exchange. A hint of her cinnamon scent drifted by, teasing him with memories of that too-brief kiss a month ago.

She swallowed hard once; it was the only sign she'd registered the brief contact, aside from the fact that she kept her eyes firmly averted from his. What would he see in those emerald-green eyes? A month ago, after her impulsive kiss, he'd seen surprise—and desire.

He watched her every move, trying to get a read on her.

"Hey, beautiful," she crooned to the kitty, handling the feline with obvious skill and something more…an unmistakable gift. "Let's get a scanner and check to see if you have a chip. If we're lucky, you'll have your people back very soon."

Kneeling, she pulled a brown, boxy device from under the counter and waved the sensor along the back of the cat's neck. She frowned and swept it over the same place again. Then she broadened the search along the cat's shoulders and legs, casting a quick glance at Whit. "Sometimes the chip migrates on the body."

But after sweeping along the cat's entire back, Megan shook her head and sighed. "No luck."

"She was pretty matted when I found her yesterday." He patted the beagle's head awkwardly. He didn't have much experience with pets, his only exposure to animals coming with horseback riding. The cat and dog were a helluva lot smaller than a Palomino. "I combed her out last night and she's been pissed at me ever since."

She glanced up quickly, her eyes going wide with surprise. "You brushed the cat?"

"Yeah, so?" He shrugged. "She needed it."

Her forehead furrowed. "That was kind of you."

"Last time I checked, I'm not a monster."

She smiled with a tinge of irony. "Just a mogul land baron and destroyer of wetlands."

He raised a hand. "Guilty as charged. And I hear you have need of some of my dirty, land-baron dollars?"

He looked around, taking in a couple of harried volunteers rushing in with fresh litter boxes stacked in their arms. The dog sniffed his shoes as if checking out the quality of his next chew toy.

The stuffing went out of her fight and she sagged back against the wall. "Animal control across town is full, and we're the only other option around here. People are living in emergency housing shelters that don't allow pets. Other folks have left town altogether, just giving up on finding their animals." He could hear the tension in her voice.

"That's a damn shame, Megan. I've heard the call-outs for pet food, but I hadn't realized how heavy the extra burden is for you and the rest of your staff."

"Let's step into my office before your kitty girl makes a break for the door. Evie's in there now, but it'll only take a second to settle her elsewhere so we can talk." She rested a hand on the front desk. "Miss Abigail, do you mind if Evie sits with you for a few minutes?"

"Of course not. I love spending time with the little darlin'. You don't let me babysit near enough. Send her my way."

Megan looked at Whit, something sad flickering in her eyes. "Evie's taking the day off from school. Come this way."

He followed her, his eyes drawn to the gentle sway of her hips. Khaki had never looked so hot. "I'm sorry to add to your load here, but I meant it when I said I want to make a donation to help."

She opened a metal baby gate and ushered the beagle into the room. It was a small room with a neat bookshelf and three recycling bins stacked in a corner. Two large framed watercolors dominated the walls—one of an orange cat and the other of a spotted dog, both clearly painted by a child. The bottom corner of each was signed in crayon. *Evie*.

The little minx peeked from under the desk, a miniature version of her mom right down to the freckles on her nose. "Hello, Mr. Whit."

She crawled out with an iPad tucked under her arm, then stood, her red pigtails lopsided. Evie's face was one hundred percent Megan, but the little girl had a quirky spirit all her own. Evie wore a knight's costume with a princess tiara even though Halloween had already passed and Thanksgiving was rapidly approaching. Her mother smoothed a hand over her head affectionately, gently tightening the left pigtail to match the one on the right. "Miss Abigail wants you to sit with her for a few minutes, okay? I'll be through soon."

Evie waved shyly, green eyes sparkling, then sprinted out to the front desk, carrying her iPad and a foam sword.

Megan gestured for him to step inside the small office, then closed the gate again. "You mentioned writing a check, and I'm not bashful about accepting on behalf of the animals. I'll get you a receipt so you can write it off on your taxes."

"Where will you put this cat if you're already full?" he asked as the beagle sniffed his shoes.

"I guess we'll learn if she gets along with dogs since she'll have to stay in my office for now." She crouched down with the cat in her arms. The pup tipped his head to the side and the cat curled closer to Megan but kept her claws sheathed. Nodding, Megan stood and settled the cat onto her office chair.

"She likes dogs better than she likes me, that's for sure." He shook his head, laughing softly.

"I guess not every female in this town likes crawling into your arms." She crinkled her freckled nose.

He would have thought she was jealous. She *had* been avoiding him since the tornado. He would have attributed it to her being busy with cleanup, but his instincts shouted it had something to do with that impulsive kiss. "I feel bad for adding to your load here. Could you use more volunteers to help with the extra load here? I'm sure some of my buddies at the Texas Cattleman's Club would be glad to step up."

"We can always use extra hands."

"I'll contact Gil Addison—the club president—and get the ball rolling. Maybe they'll adopt when they're here."

"We can only hope." Her hand fell to the cat's head and she stroked lightly. The cat arched up into the stroke, purring loudly. "I'm working on arranging a transport for some of the unclaimed pets to a rescue in Oklahoma. A group in Colorado has reached out to help as well, but we're still trying to find a way to get the animals there. And since the Colorado group is a new rescue, I need to look over their operation before entrusting our animals to their care. Except I don't know how I'll be able to take off that much time from work for the road trip, much less be away from Evie for that long. She's still unsettled from the trauma of last month's storm. But, well, you don't need to hear all about my troubles."

"My personal plane is at your disposal," he said without hesitation.

"What? I didn't realize you have a plane. I mean I know you're well off, but...."

Her shoulders braced and he could almost see another wall appearing between them. He appreciated that she wasn't impressed by his money, but also hated to see another barrier in place.

Still, the more he thought about flying the animals for her, the more the idea appealed to him. "Make the arrangements with the rescue and whatever else needs to be done as far as crating the animals. I assume you have procedures for that."

"Yes, but...." Confusion creased her forehead. "I

don't know how to say thank-you. That's going above and beyond."

"There's nothing to thank me for. This is a win-win." He got to help the animals, score points with Megan and spend more time with her to boot.

"But the cost—"

"A tax write-off, remember? Fly animals as far as you need them to go and your time away will be reduced considerably." This idea just got better and better, not only for the animals, but also by giving him an "in" to see Megan, to figure out where to take this attraction. "This isn't a one-time offer either. You're packed with critters here. If there's help out there, take it and my jet will fly them there."

"I can't turn you down. The animals need this kind of miracle if we're going to find homes for them by the holidays." She exhaled hard. "I need to get to work placing calls. There are rescues I hadn't considered before because of the distance and our limited resources. Rescue work happens fast, slots fill up at a moment's notice."

"And this little gal?" He stroked the cat's head and for once the calico didn't dig her claws in. Perched on the back of the chair, she arched up into his hand and purred like a race car.

"Are you sure you don't want to keep her?"

He pulled his hand away. "I can't. I'm at work all the time, which wouldn't be fair to her."

"Of course." Megan looked disappointed in him, even though he'd just offered her thousands of dollars' worth of flight hours.

But then, hadn't he said it? Offering his plane was easy. Taking care of another living being? Not so easy.

"I should let you get to work on lining up those rescues." He pulled a business card from his wallet and plucked a pen from the cup on the edge of her desk. He jotted a number on the back of the card. "This is my private cell number and my secretary's number. Don't hesitate to call."

When he passed her the card, their fingers brushed. He saw the flecks of awareness sparkle in her eyes again. He wasn't mistaken. The mutual draw was real, but now wasn't the time to press ahead for more.

"Thank you again." She flipped the card between her fingers, still watching him with suspicion, their old conflicts clearly making her wary. "Would you like to name your kitty cat?"

"That's not my kitten."

"Right," she answered, a smile playing with her plump lips that didn't need makeup to entice, "and she still needs a name. We've had to name so many this past month, we're out of ideas."

He thought for a second then found himself saying, "Tallulah."

"Tallulah?" Her surprise was a reward. He liked unsettling her. "Really, Whit? I didn't expect such a… girly name choice."

"That was the name of my mom's cat." She was briefly theirs, but when they'd moved, the cat ran away. Then his father had said no more pets. Period.

"It's a lovely name."

He nodded quickly then turned to leave.

"Whit," she called, stopping him short, "about what happened after you helped me get to Evie that day…."

Was she finally acknowledging the impulsive, explosive kiss? The thought of having her sooner rather than later… "Yes?"

"Thank you for helping me reach my daughter." She

looked down at her shoes for an awkward moment before meeting his eyes again. "I can never repay you for that...and now this."

"I don't expect repayment." The last thing he wanted was to have her kiss him again out of gratitude.

The next time they kissed—and there would be a next time—it would be purely based on mutual attraction.

The stroke of Whit Daltry's eyes left her skin tingling.

Standing at the shelter's glass door, Megan rubbed her arms as she watched Whit stride across the parking lot back to his truck. His long legs ate up the space one powerful step at a time. His suit coat flapped in the late afternoon breeze revealing a too-perfect, taut butt. Her head was still reeling from his surprise appearance, followed by the generous offer she couldn't turn down.

After six weeks of reliving that brief but mind-blowing kiss, she'd seen him again and would be spending an entire day with him. Somehow, because of that day they'd gone from avoiding each other to.... What? She wasn't sure exactly.

Maybe he'd gotten the wrong idea from that kiss and thought she was looking for something more. But she didn't have time in her life for more. She had a demanding job and a daughter, and both had taken a hard hit from last month's tornado.

And speaking of her child, she'd left Evie long enough. Thank goodness Miss Abigail had been so accommodating about helping with Evie. The retired legal secretary had even babysat a couple of evenings when Megan got called out to assist with an emergency rescue. Evie had been particularly clingy this past month.

And she couldn't blame her. That nightmarish day still haunted Megan as well; she often woke up from dreams of not reaching her daughter in time, of the whole roof of the preschool collapsing.

Dreams that sometimes took a different turn with Whit arriving, of the kiss going further....

Megan watched his truck drive away, a knot in her stomach.

It would be too damn easy to lean on those broad shoulders, to get used to the help, which would only make things more difficult when she was on her own again. Megan turned away from the door and temptation, returning to reality in the form of her precious daughter sitting on Abigail's lap as they played on the iPad together. Evie's knight's armor was slipping off one shoulder, her toy sword on the ground beside her tiara.

Megan held out her arms. "Come here, sweetie."

She gathered Evie into her arms and held her on her hip. Not much longer and her baby girl would be too big to carry around. This precious child, who wanted to be a "princess knight" for Halloween and cut through tornadoes with a foam sword. Megan had hoped her daughter would relax and heal as they put the storm behind them, but now Thanksgiving was approaching and Evie was still showing signs of trauma.

The holidays were tough anyway, reminding her that she was the sole relative in Evie's life. She was a thirty-year-old single mom.

And damn lucky to have landed in this small town full of warmhearted friends.

"Thank you, Abigail, for helping out even after the school finished repairs. You've been a lifesaver."

The roof of Little Tots Daycare had been reconstructed quickly, but the dust and stress had taken its toll on the kids and the workers. Some had gotten the flu.

Others, like Evie, had nightmares and begged to stay home. Her daughter conquered pretend monsters in iPad games and dress-up play.

Abigail rocked back in her chair. "My pleasure. She's a doll." She pinched Evie's cheek lightly. "We have fun readin' books on the iPad. Don't we, Evie?"

Bringing her daughter to work wasn't optimal, but Megan didn't have any choices for now. "Thanks again."

"I'm always a call away. The benefit of being retired. Maybe we'll see Mr. Daltry again tomorrow. Now wouldn't that be nice if he became a regular volunteer?"

As much as Megan wanted to keep her distance, she couldn't ignore all the amazing things Whit had done for her.

Evie patted her mother's cheek with a tiny palm. "Where did the nice man go?"

"He brought a kitty to stay with us here."

She stuck out her bottom lip. "We don't like people who dump their pets. Does this mean I can't like him anymore?"

"He didn't dump the kitty, sweetie. He saved her from being cold and hungry in the woods." Although she had to admit she was disappointed he hadn't offered to keep the cat. She struggled not to resent his wealthy lifestyle. Everyone knew he was a self-made man who'd worked hard to build a fortune before his thirty-fifth birthday. "Tallulah lost her family and had nowhere else to go. We're going to help her find them again."

"'Lulah?"

"Right. That's her name."

"She can come home wif us and live in our house. I'll get her a costume too."

They already had three cats and two dogs, all of which Evie had been dressing up as part of her medieval warrior team. The costumes transformed them into horses, elves, queens and even a unicorn.

Their house was full.

And Megan was at her limit with work and her daughter. "You can visit Tallulah here while she waits to find her family. We have our kitties and doggies at home to take care of and love."

Evie patted Megan's face again. "Don't worry, Mommy. I'll tell Mr. Whit to keep 'Lulah."

If only it worked that easily. "I need to work a little longer, just a few phone calls and then we can go home for supper. We'll make a pizza."

"Can Mr. Whit share our pizza?"

Abigail laughed softly from her perch behind the counter. "I think Mr. Whit wants to share a lot more than pizza."

Evie looked up, frowning. "Like what?"

Megan shot Abigail an exasperated look before kneeling to tell Evie, "Mr. Whit is sharing his airplane to help send some of the puppies and kitties to forever homes before Thanksgiving."

"He shares his plane? See. He is very nice. Can I play my games, please?" Evie squirmed down with her iPad, her foam sword tumbling from her hand. "I'm gonna play a plane game this time." Her daughter put on her tiara and fired up a game for touring the states in a puffy airplane.

Megan glanced at the receptionist. "I don't want to hear a word about Whit's visit today, Abigail. And no gossiping."

She glanced over her shoulder to see if other volunteers were listening in. Luckily, most of them were occupied with exercising animals, folding laundry and washing bowls. The only person even remotely close enough to hear was Beth Andrews, Megan's favorite volunteer.

"Gossip?" Beth chimed in. "Did I hear the word gossip? That would surely never happen in the town of Royal where everyone stays out of each other's business. Not."

Beth wasn't a known gossip, but was definitely known for helping out everywhere; she was very involved in the community. The leggy blonde owned Green Acres, a local organic farm and produce stand. Beth's business had taken a big hit from the tornado. That made her generosity and caring now all the more special, given how rough life had been for her lately. The homemade goodies she brought to the animals were always a treat. Beth had that willowy thin, effortless beauty that would have had women resenting her if it weren't for the fact she was so darn nice.

Abigail stroked her phone as if already planning a text. "It's a gift having a community that cares so much. Like how Whit Daltry just showed up to make a big donation."

Beth arched a blond eyebrow. "You two are speaking to each other?"

Megan shrugged her shoulders and examined her fingernails. "He's helping with the overflow of animals. I can work with anyone for the good of the animals."

"Everyone's had their lives turned upside down since the twister. To lose over a dozen lives in a blink…to have our friend Craig gone so young…." She paused with a heavy sigh. "No one has been exempt from the fallout of this damn storm. Even our mayor was critically injured. And that poor Skye Taylor…"

"What tragic bad luck that she came back to town after four years on such a terrible day. How is she doing?" Megan rubbed her arms again, feeling petty for stressing over her life, thinking of Skye Taylor, found seriously injured and unconscious after the storm, her baby delivered prematurely. And since Skye was still in a coma, she hadn't even met her child. Megan shivered again, even though she didn't know the woman personally. As a mother, she felt a bond. Thank God Evie was safe. That's what mattered most. She would figure out how to heal her daughter's fears.

Clearly agitated, Beth thumbed a stack of shelter flyers. "Drew checked in with the family and Skye is still in a medically induced coma and the baby girl— Grace—is in the neonatal intensive care unit."

Abigail sighed. "And the doctors still don't know who the father is?"

Did this qualify as gossip? Megan wasn't sure, but if the talk could help find the father, that would be a good thing. "I've never met her, but I heard a rumor Skye ran off with the younger Holt brother despite their parents' protests. So I assumed he was the dad."

Beth tucked a stray curl back into her loose topknot, scrunching her nose. "I recall hearing mentions of an age-old feud between the Holts and Taylors. Abigail, do you have any idea who started it?"

"I haven't a clue. Quite frankly, I'm not sure they do either, anymore."

Beth shook her head slowly. "How sad when feuds are carried on for so long." She stared pointedly at Megan. "So what's this with Whit Daltry coming to the shelter to see you? And you actually spoke to him rather than running out the back exit?"

"Running out the back? I wouldn't do that." Okay,

so maybe she had avoided him a time or two but hearing it put that way made her sound so…wimpy. And she didn't like that one damn bit. "I think we've all done some reevaluating this past month. If he wants to offer his private plane to transport homeless animals to new homes, who am I to argue?"

Beth laughed softly. "About that flight… Look how neatly he tied in a way to see you again. Coincidence? I don't think so."

Not even having a clue how to respond to that notion, Megan clasped her daughter's hand and retreated to her office. The second she closed the door, she realized she'd done it again. Run away like the coward she'd denied being.

But when it came to Whit Daltry and the way he flipped her world with one sizzling look, keeping her cool just wasn't an option.

Three

Whit parked his truck in the four-car garage of his large, custom-built home in Pine Valley. With a hard exhale, he slumped back in the seat. He'd spent the whole day at work thinking about seeing Megan at the shelter when he'd brought in the cat. Knowing he'd locked in a reason to see her again pumped him full of excitement. Life had sucked so badly the past month. Feeling alive again was good. Damn good.

He reached for the door and stepped out into the massive garage, all his.

Growing up, he'd lived in apartments half the size of this space, which also held a sports car, a speed boat and a motorcycle. He liked his toys and the security of knowing they were paid for. Since the day he'd left home, he'd never bought anything on credit. His college degree had been financed with a combination of scholarships and two jobs. Debt was a four-letter word to him.

His father had showered his family with gifts, but too often those presents were repossessed or abandoned as the Daltry family fled creditors yet again. His parents had passed away years ago, his dad of a stroke, his mom of a broken heart weakened from too many years of disappointment after disappointment.

Every time they'd moved to a new place, his mother wore that hopeful expression that this time would be different, that his father wouldn't gamble away the earnings from his new job, that they could stay and build a life. And every time she was wrong. Most times that hope would fade to resignation about a week before his dad announced the latest cut-and-run exit for the Daltry family. Whit came to appreciate the advance warning since it gave him the opportunity to tuck away some things before the inevitable pack-and-dash.

He'd built this house for himself as a tribute to leaving that life behind. But he'd waited to start construction. He'd refused to break ground until he had the money to pay for every square foot of it. People viewed him as lighthearted and easygoing—true enough, up to a point. No way in hell was he sinking himself into debt just to make a show of thumbing his nose at the past. He knew the pain of losing everything as a kid and he refused to go through that again. He'd been damned lucky his home in Pine Valley hadn't sustained any damage from the storm.

As he stepped from the garage into the wide passageway, he thought of all this empty space. He made a point of donating to charities, even throwing in elbow grease as well when called for, like pitching in with the never-ending cleanup after the tornado.

And now working with the animals? Except he

wasn't. He'd left that cat at the shelter. He'd meant everything he said about not having time for a pet, but Megan had asked about temporary fostering and he'd rejected that out of hand. He knew he'd disappointed her with his answer. Or rather confirmed her preconceived negative notions about him.

Maybe if he got a couple of cats to keep each other company. Cats were more independent, right?

As he opened the door to the kitchen, his cell phone rang. He fished it out of his pocket and the caller ID showed…Megan Maguire?

His pulse kicked up a notch at just the sight of her name. Damn, he needed to get a grip. Pursuing her was one thing. Giving her this much control over how he felt? Not okay. He needed to keep things light, flirtatious.

He answered the phone. "Hello, pretty lady. What can I do for you?"

"Seriously?" she asked dryly. "Do you always answer the phone that way?"

"Megan?" he answered with overplayed surprise. "Well, damn, I thought it was my granny calling."

She laughed, her voice relaxing into a husky, sexy melody. "You have a granny?"

"I didn't crawl out from under a rock. I have relatives." Just really distant ones who had cut ties with his branch of the family tree long ago because of his father. "Actually, my grandmother passed away ten years ago. My cheesy line was totally for your benefit, I just didn't expect it to fall so flat. So let's start over."

That might not be a bad idea: to call for a do-over in a larger way, erase the past three and a half years.

"Sure," she said. "Hello, Whit, this is Megan Maguire. I hope I didn't disturb your supper."

"Well, hey there, Megan." He opened the stainless-steel, oversized refrigerator and pulled out an imported beer. "What a surprise to hear from you. What do you need?"

He sat in a chair at the island where the cooking service he'd hired left a dinner in a warmer each night. He couldn't cook. Tried, but just didn't have the knack for more than grilling and he worked too late to grill. He twisted open the beer and waited for her to answer.

"I was just loading my dishwasher, and this weird panic set in that maybe you weren't serious earlier."

"About what?" He tipped back a swig of the imported brew.

"Did you really offer your plane to transport animals?"

"Absolutely. I don't make promises I can't keep." His father was the king of broken promises, all smiles and dreams with no substance.

"Whew," she exhaled. "Thank goodness. Because I asked a contact in Colorado to check out the rescue. I also spoke with the veterinarian the rescue uses and everything appears perfect. So I called them and they can still take a dozen of our cats, a huge help to us and to local animal control. Am I being pushy in asking how soon we can transport them because I would really like to see them settled before Thanksgiving?"

"Not pushy at all." This was Thursday, with turkey day only a week away. He had a meeting he couldn't miss on Friday, but the notion of spending the weekend with her was enticing as hell. He'd hoped this would work out. He just hadn't realized how quickly the plan would come together. "Glad they have space to accommodate. I could see you're stuffed to the gills."

"Feeding and caring for so many animals is depleting our budget in a hurry." Her voice was weary, tempting him to race over to her house with his pre-cooked dinner. "We try our best to plan for disasters, but having just built the new shelter, we're stretched to the max."

He couldn't feed her tonight, but he could lighten some of her load. "I also meant it when I said I'll talk to the Cattleman's Club about rolling up their sleeves and opening their wallets. We can help. We're about more than the Stetson hats and partying."

"I honestly don't know what to say to all of this generosity. You've really come through for us with so much, especially offering your plane. Thank you."

"Glad to help. Can you have the animals ready to fly day after tomorrow? I'm free to fly them to Colorado on Saturday."

She gasped. "*You* are flying the plane? I thought you would have a pilot...."

Had he failed to mention that part of his offer? Would she go running in the opposite direction? Not with the cats' well-being at stake. But might she try to send someone else from the shelter in her place? Had he just roped himself into a weekend with her kennel supervisor?

That didn't change his promise. He didn't break his word.

But he would definitely be disappointed to miss out on the chance to get closer to Megan.

He clicked speakerphone and placed his cell phone on the slate island. "I do have a pilot who flies me around if I need to have a meeting or entertain enroute. But I'm a licensed pilot too, quite proficient, if I do say so myself. What do you say? Let's make a week-end out of it."

"A weekend away together in Colorado?" The shock in her voice vibrated through the phone line. "Are you trying to buy your way into my life?"

"Now that stings." And oddly enough, it really did. He wanted her to think well of him. "I will concede that I'm trying to get your attention, and bringing the cat today offered an excuse to see you again, but it's not like I concocted a fake stray to meet you. Flying the other cats to Colorado is the right thing to do for the shelter and for our community. Even a hard-ass like me can see that. If you doubt my motives, bring your daughter along. She's a great kid."

The silence stretched and he checked the menu card with his meal—balsamic skirt steak with corn polenta—while he waited. Her answer was suddenly a lot more important than it should have been. But he wanted more time with her. Hell, he flat-out wanted her. He had since the first time he'd seen her. The tornado had just made him reevaluate. Life was too short and too easily lost to put off pursuing goals.

And right now, his goal was to discover if the chemistry between him and Megan was as explosive as that one kiss led him to believe.

"So, Megan? About Saturday?" He rolled the beer bottle between both palms, anticipation firing in his gut.

"Without question, Evie would love the adventure. I'm not able to offer her much in the way of vacation or special trips. She's also been hesitant to stay at the sitter's...." Megan drew in a shaky breath. "Saturday it is then."

A thrill of victory surged through him, stronger than any he'd experienced in a damn long time.

"Excellent. And hey, feel free to make more calls and line up a place for the extra dogs and we can make it a weekly outing. Wait—before you accuse me of using the animals to get to you, the offer still stands if you want to send one of your staff in your place."

She laughed dryly. "Let's take it one week at a time."

But he knew she wouldn't be able to turn down the offer. He'd found the perfect in with her. "And by the way, a trip that long won't all fit into one day. Be sure to pack an overnight bag."

Megan held a clipboard and cross-referenced the information on the printout with the card attached to each cat carrier lined up inside Whit's aircraft. The plane could easily hold a dozen or more people, but those sofas and lounge chairs were empty. The kitty cargo had been creatively stashed beneath seats and strapped under the food station bar.

Most of the felines were already curled up and snoozing from the sedative she'd administered prior to crating them. Three of the cats, though, were staring back at her with wide, drugged eyes and the occasional hiss, hanging on to consciousness and looking at her suspiciously. Sheba, an all-black fluff ball, had come from a home where she was an only pet and queen of her domain, but after her owner passed away, the extended family had dumped their mother's beloved pet at the shelter. Sheba had been freaked out and terrified ever since. She needed a home environment, even a foster setting, until an adopter could be found. Skittles, an orange tabby stray, had been found at the shopping mall with no name tag, no microchip and no one to claim her. If she went much longer without a home setting, Megan feared Skittles would turn feral. And the third of the cranky passengers, Sebastian, was a gorgeous, very huge Maine Coon cat that desperately needed more space to move around than the shelter could offer.

Provided the Colorado group was as wonderful in person as her contact and the vet indicated, by evening the twelve cats would be with a rescue that only operated with foster homes until adoptive homes were found. No more shelter life for them.

She rested a hand on top of a crate, exhaustion from the past month seeping through her. Maybe now that she had some help in sight, her body was finally relaxing enough to let all those extra hours catch up with her. She still could hardly believe this was happening—and thanks to Whit Daltry, of all people. The last man she would have expected to go the extra mile for her.

But the very man who'd done more than that for her when he'd helped her reach Evie after the tornado.

Megan stole a quick glance to check on her daughter, currently sprawled out asleep on one of the leather sofas. They'd had to get up early to ready the cats at the shelter. Evie had insisted on wearing a cowgirl outfit today—with the ever present tiara, of course.

Footsteps sounded outside on the metal stairs, and a second later Whit filled the hatch. He looked Texas-awesome, with broad shoulders—as if Texas ever did anything half way. He wore a chambray button-down with the sleeves rolled up. And his jeans—Lord help her. The well-washed denim fit him just right. Her mouth watered. He ducked and pulled off his hat to clear the hatch on his way inside.

"Everything's a go outside whenever you and Evie are ready to buckle in." His boots thudded against the carpeted floor as he walked to Megan and rested a hand on her shoulder.

Static sparked through her so tangibly she could almost believe crackles filled and lit the air. Whit's clean soap scent brought to mind the image of a shared morning shower, a notion far too intimate to entertain, especially when they had to spend the next two days in close confines. She eased away from him under the guise of flipping the page on her clipboard. Except it was already the last page so she looked too obvious.

Quickly, she flipped all the papers back into place.

Whit stuffed his hands in his jean pockets. "We might as well talk about it."

"Talk about what?" How she couldn't peel her eyes off his strong jaw? Could barely suppress the urge to step closer and brush her cheek along the fresh-shaven texture of his face? She was having a hard time remembering why she had to stay away from this man.

"When you kissed me."

"Shhhh!" she whispered urgently. "Do you want someone—Evie—to hear?" Her daughter was a great big reason she needed to tread warily with any man she let into their lives.

He stepped closer. "Okay, how's this?"

His voice rumbled over her like the vibration of quiet thunder in a summer rain. Desire pooled low in her belly, her breasts tingling and tightening as if the first drops of that summer storm were caressing her bare skin.

Damn. She was in deep trouble here.

She clutched the clipboard to her chest. "I didn't kiss you that day. Not exactly."

"I remember the day well. Your lips on mine. That's a kiss," he bantered with a devilish glint in his eyes.

"But just so that we're clear, none of this trip today is contingent on there being another kiss."

"I meant to kiss your cheek as…a thanks." A mind-melting, toe-curling thanks. "You're the one who turned your face and made it into something more."

He dipped his head and spoke softly, his breath warm against her ear. "And you're the one who smells like cinnamon and has this sexy kitten moan. I dream of hearing it again."

She fought back the urge to moan at just the sound of his voice and the memories his words evoked. "I thought you were taking the animals on this flight as a totally philanthropic act."

"I am."

She tipped her chin and stood her ground. "Then what's this flirting about?"

"I'm a multitasker." He knocked on the clipboard still clasped against her breasts. "Let's get strapped in and ready to roll."

An hour later, Megan rested her arm along the sofa back and watched the puffy white clouds filling the sky. The plane cruised as smoothly as if they were cushioned by those pillowy clouds, not a bump yet to disconcert her.

Shortly after takeoff, Evie had asked to join Whit. Megan had started to say no, but apparently he'd heard and waved her daughter up front to the empty co-pilot's seat. As a single parent, Megan was so used to being the sole caregiver and primary form of entertainment for her daughter—especially since the tornado. This moment to relax with her thoughts was a welcome reprieve.

Hell, to relax at all seemed like a gift.

The cats were all happily snoozing now in their tranquilized haze. No more evil eye from the three stubborn ones that had stayed awake the longest.

Her gaze shifted back to her daughter up front. Evie, rejuvenated from her nap, was now chattering to Whit. He sat at the helm, piloting them through the skies with obvious ease and skill. His hands and feet moved in perfect synch, his eyes scanning the control as he seamlessly carried on a convoluted conversation with her four-year-old daughter.

"Mr. Whit, I'm a cowgirl," Evie declared proudly.

"I see that," he answered patiently as if she hadn't already been peppering his ear with accounts of every detail of her life from her best friends at school—Caitlyn and Bobby—to what she ate for breakfast this morning—a granola bar and chocolate milk in the car on the way to the shelter. "Last week, you were a knight with a sword."

"A princess knight," she said as if he was too slow to have noticed the difference.

Megan suppressed a smile.

"Right," Whit answered. "You always wear that pretty tiara."

"This week, I'm keeping the monsters away with my rope." She patted her hip where the miniature lasso was hooked to her belt loop. "It's a lassie."

"Lassie? Oh, lasso. I see," he said solemnly. "You're going to rope the monsters?"

Megan swallowed down a lump of emotion at how easily he saw through to her daughter's fears.

"Yep, sir, that's right," Evie answered with a nod that threatened to dislodge her tiara. "Rope 'em up and throw 'em in the trash."

He stayed silent for a heart-stopping second before he

answered with a measured calm, "You're a very brave little girl."

Evie shrugged. "Somebody's gotta do it."

Megan choked back a bittersweet laugh as her daughter parroted one of her mommy's favorite phrases.

Whit glanced at Evie. "Your mommy takes very good care of you. You're safe now, kiddo."

"But nobody takes care of Mommy. That's not fair."

Megan blinked back tears at the weight her little girl was carrying around inside. He didn't seem to have a ready answer to that one. Neither did Megan.

Evie hitched up her feet to sit cross-legged, picking at the Velcro of her new tennis shoes. They hadn't been able to afford cowgirl boots, not with new shoes to buy. "I'm not sure what I'll be next. Gotta look through my costume box and see what'll scare the monsters."

"Where are these monsters?"

"They come out of the sky with the wind." Evie pointed ahead at the windscreen and made swirly gestures with her spindly, little-girl arms. "So I'm riding wif you in the plane. I'll get 'em before they scare other kids."

Megan tipped her head back to hold in the tears. She had seen this flight as a welcome distraction for her child. She hadn't considered Evie might be afraid, and certainly not for this particular reason. But it made perfect sense, and somehow Whit had gotten more information on the fears in one simple conversation than Megan had been able to pry out of her strong-willed child in the past month.

Evie wiggled her feet. "I got new shoes. They light up when I walk."

"Very nice."

"My princess sneakers got messed up in the tora-na-do." She pronounced the word much better these days than a month ago.

They'd all had lots of practice with the word.

Whit glanced at Evie for an instant, his brown eyes serious and compassionate. "I'm so sorry to hear that."

"They were my favorites. But we couldn't find ones just like 'em. I think these lights are a good idea. I coulda used the lights the day the tora-na-do made the school all dark."

Megan's stomach plummeted as surely as if the plane had lost serious altitude. Was every choice her child made tied into that day now? Megan had thought the shoe-shopping trip had been a fun day for Evie, and yet the whole time her daughter had assessed every choice using survivalist criteria. Megan blinked back tears and focused on listening to Evie.

"Mommy says lots of little girls lost their shoes too and we need to be glad we gots shoes."

"Your mother is a smart lady."

Was it her imagination or had he just glanced back at her out of the corner of his eye? A shiver of awareness tingled up her spine.

"I know, and I wanna be good like Mommy so Santa will come visit my house."

His head tipped to the side inquisitively. "Santa will see what a very good girl you've been today. I suspect you're always a good girl."

"Not as good as Mommy."

Megan frowned in surprise, her heart aching all over again for what her daughter had been through and how little Evie had shared about that. Until now. Somehow Whit had a way of reaching her that no one else had. Megan was grateful, and nervous to think of him gaining more importance in her life.

Whit waited a moment before answering, "Why do you think that about yourself, kiddo?"

Evie just shook her head, pigtails swishing and tiara landing in her lap. "Let's talk about something else. Caitlyn and Bobby are my bestest friends. Are you Mommy's new bestest friend?"

Four

As the sun set at the end of a chilly day, Whit cranked the heat inside the rental car, an SUV that had been perfect for transporting the twelve cats to their new foster families with the Colorado rescue group. They'd just finished their last drop-off. Mission complete.

Megan had insisted on inspecting every home in spite of the long day and the Colorado cold. But in the end, she was satisfied she'd found a great new rescue to network with in the future.

Glancing at the rearview mirror, Whit watched Megan strapped her daughter into the car seat, a task he'd learned she never allowed anyone else to take over no matter how many stops they made. Evie had been patient, excited even, over seeing her mom in action. And the couple of times the kid had gotten bored, she'd been easily distracted by the snow flurries—which had necessitated a side trip to pick up a warmer snow suit and snow boots.

Evie had been hesitant about covering her costume and her trepidation stabbed Whit clean through with sympathy for the little tyke. Finally, he'd been able to persuade her even cowgirls needed cold weather gear more appropriate for Colorado—which was a helluva lot colder than Texas.

Megan tucked into the passenger side as they idled outside a two-story farmhouse belonging to an older widower inside who'd made a fuss over his feline visitor. She rubbed her gloved hands together in front of the heat vent and then swiped the snowflakes off her head.

"I miss Texas," she said between her chattering teeth. "If you ever hear me complain during the winter, just remind me of this day."

That implied they would keep in contact after this weekend. He was making progress in comparison to their previous standoff. Did this mean she'd forgiven him for claiming the land she'd wanted for the shelter? He wasn't going to push his luck by asking. He intended to ride the wave of her good mood today and build some more positive memories.

Megan deserved to have some fun and recreation.

He'd seen firsthand how she carried a ton of worries around for one person, between taking care of her daughter alone and spreading her generous heart even thinner for these homeless animals. Who looked after Megan? Who gave her a break from life's burdens?

He turned his heater vents in her direction as well. "You accomplished a lot in one day."

"It's a relief to have them settled, and so quickly." She reached back to Evie and squeezed her daughter's hand. "Did you have fun?"

"I like the plane and the snow." She kicked her feet. "And my new boots that Mr. Whit bought me."

"Good, I'm glad, sweetie. We'll get a Happy Meal before going back to the…hotel." She swallowed, her eyes darting nervously to Whit. "Thank you again for arranging everything."

He put the SUV into drive and pulled out onto the tree-lined suburban road, leaving the last foster home behind. "What about other rescues? Did you find more places that can help out with some of the animals back home?"

Her green eyes lit with excitement. "I have a line on a couple of breed-specific rescues that might be able to take a few of our beagles and our German Shepherd." She touched his arm lightly; it was the first physical contact she'd initiated since that kiss. "But I can't keep asking you to take off work to fly around the country."

"I have a private pilot and I'm guessing if you already know the reputation of the rescue, then the animals can fly alone with him." While the obvious answer would be to lock in their weekends with more of these flights together, he also knew a more subtle approach would win Megan over. Just as he'd told Evie, her mama was smart and Whit was drawn to that part of Megan as well. So he opted for a smoother approach. "This doesn't always have to be about us spending time together. Not that I'm complaining. What? You look surprised."

He bit back a self-satisfied smile and steered out onto the rural mountain road into a smattering of five o'clock traffic.

She tipped her head to the side, the setting sun casting a warm glow over her face. "You would pay your pilot to fly just one or two dogs at a time?"

"Sure, although I've also got an idea for recruiting some of my friends to help out." He accelerated past a slow-moving vehicle backing up traffic. "A number of them own planes, short range, long range, and we all like to pitch in and help. Sometimes we just need pointing in the right direction."

"Even if you don't get to see me and make moves to follow up on…." She glanced up at the rearview mirror and watched Evie playing with her iPad. "Even if you know there won't be a replay of what happened a month ago."

"I can separate work and personal, just as I can separate personal and philanthropic. And," he ducked his head closer to hers, "I can also blend them when the situation presents itself. Like today."

Evie kicked the back of her mother's seat. "Can I have my Happy Meal, please? 'Cause if I have to wait much longer, I'm gonna starve and then it would be a Sad Meal."

Whit choked on a laugh. God, this kid was a cute little imp. "Absolutely, kiddo, we can get supper for you. And then after supper, I have plans."

Megan sat up straighter. "Plans?"

Damn straight. He had an agenda full of fun for a woman who didn't get much in the way of recreation. "Unless you have an objection, we'll have dinner and ice skating before we turn in for the night."

Ice skating.

Megan never would have guessed the mega-wealthy, smooth operator Whit Daltry would plan a night of ice skating and burgers. Granted, they were the best burgers she'd ever eaten. But still, the laid-back quality of fun appealed to her.

He'd also taken Evie into account, something else that set him apart from other men who'd asked her out for a date—except wait, this wasn't a date. She didn't have time for dating.

Right?

She sat on a bench by the outdoor skating rink, eating the last of her sweet potato fries and watching Whit lead her daughter carefully as she found her balance on the children's skates. Moonbeams and halogen lights created the effect of a hazy dome over the crowded ice, which was full of people getting into the Christmas spirit early. His patience was commendable. A person couldn't fake that. He genuinely had a knack with kids.

Megan could see her daughter's mouth moving non-stop as she chattered away, her breath puffing clouds in tiny bursts. Whit nodded periodically. Other skaters whipped past, but he kept up the slow, steady pace with Evie, making sure to keep her safe.

She stopped and tugged his hand, so cute in her puffy pink snowsuit next to Whit, who towered over her in his blue parka. He knelt, listening intently. Then he stood, scooping her up and skating faster, faster, faster still. Evie's squeals of delight carried on the wind, mixing with music piping through the outdoor sound system. Megan's heart softened, a dangerous emotion because this could be so easy to get used to, to depend on. To crave.

Him.

She exhaled a very long stream of white vapor. She needed to steel herself and tread warily. She ate three sweet potato fries. Fast. Feeding her stomach because she couldn't address the deeper hunger.

Whit and her daughter circled the rink twice before he skidded to a stop in front of Megan's bench. He held Evie confidently. Her cheeks were pink from the cold, her little girl's smile wide and genuine for the first time since the twister tore apart their lives.

Megan scooted over on the bench to make room for them to join her. She patted the chilly metal with her gloved hand. "You're very good at ice skating for a Texan."

Whit lowered Evie to sit between them. "My parents moved around a lot when I was growing up, all over the U.S., actually. I spent some time ice skating on ponds because we couldn't afford the admission to a rink."

That explained why his accent wasn't as strong as others who lived in Royal. But she'd assumed he still came from a privileged background because he fit so seamlessly into the elite Texas world typified by the TCC members. She tried to picture him as a kid fitting in at all those new places. He'd earned all that confidence the hard way. She understood that road well.

"What other skills did you pick up over the years?" Megan passed her daughter the box of fries.

"You'll have to wait to find out." He stretched his arm along the back of the bench and tugged a curly lock of her hair.

"A man of mystery." Had she actually leaned into his touch? The warmth of his arm seared her through her coat and sweater and the temptation to stay right here burned strong.

"Just trying to keep you around."

Evie dropped her fry and looked up with worried green eyes. "Where's Mommy going?"

"Nowhere, sweetie." She gathered her child close to her side, love and the deep importance of her role as Evie's mom twining inside her. "I'm staying with you."

Her daughter continued to stare up at her. "Are you sure?"

"Absolutely."

Evie looked down at her ice skates, chewing her lip before turning to Whit. "You said I could pick somethin' from the gift shop."

Megan gasped, ducking her head to meet her daughter's eyes. "Evie! You shouldn't ask Mr. Daltry to buy you things. He's already been very generous with this trip for the kitties and then entertaining us with ice skating."

He squeezed Megan's shoulder. "It's okay. Evie's right. I offered, downright promised. And a person should always do their best to keep their promises."

Megan raised her gloved hands in surrender. "Sounds like I'm outvoted."

"Yay!" Evie giggled.

Whit hefted her up, keeping his balance on the ice skates. "Did you have something already picked out, kiddo?"

She bobbed her head, pigtails swinging around her earmuffs—which she had instead of a hat so she could still wear her tiara. "I wanna get the snow princess costume so I can freeze the monsters."

Megan's stomach plummeted. This night may have felt like a magical escape from real life. But she couldn't afford to forget for a second that her everyday reality and responsibilities were still waiting for her once this fantasy weekend was over.

This night was all she could have with Whit.

The more time he spent with Megan on this trip, the more Whit was certain he should take his time with her, get to know her. Win her over gradually once they got home.

For now, here in their cozy ski chalet, he needed to

keep his distance. He needed to bide his time. Rushing her tonight could well cost him all the progress he'd made. Megan wasn't the type to be interested in a one-night stand, and quite frankly, he couldn't imagine that once with her would be enough.

The chalet was a three-bedroom in Vail, with a full sitting room and kitchen that overlooked a lake. He'd originally gotten three bedrooms to assure Megan that he respected her privacy, while still leaving their options open. But that timetable had changed.

He'd just finished building a fire in the old-fashioned fireplace when Evie's bedroom door opened and Megan stepped out. Her hair was loose and curlier than normal around her face after their evening at the windy ice rink. She still wore her jeans and green fuzzy sweater, no shoes though, just thick socks. Her toes wiggled into the carpet as if she was anchoring herself in the room. Finally, he had her alone and today of all days he'd resolved to bide his time.

It would take all his restraint to keep himself in check.

Tucking aside some extra logs to keep the fire burning for a few more hours, he stepped behind the wet bar and pulled out a bottle of sparkling water. "Would you like something to drink? The bar is stocked. There's juice and some herbal tea…"

"Any wine? Preferably red." She slid a band off her wrist and tugged her hair back to gather it into a low ponytail. "One glass won't incapacitate me."

"Oh, sure," he said, surprised. He scanned the selection and found a good bottle from a reputable California vineyard. He poured a glass for her, water for himself. He passed her the crystal glass.

She savored a sip and smiled, sinking down in the

middle of a pile of throw pillows on the sofa. She could have chosen the chair, but she'd left room for him to sit, even sweeping aside one of the pillows to clear a space. Intentional or not? He kept his silence and waited while she gazed into the fire for a long moment.

"Thank you for everything, Whit. For bringing us here, for going to so much trouble to arrange such a special evening for Evie too." Megan tucked her legs to the side, the flames from the fire casting a warm glow on her skin. "It was an incredible way to end an already wonderful day."

As she shifted, her socks scrunched down to her ankles, revealing a tiny paw print tattoo. How had he never noticed that before? Did she have others hidden elsewhere on her body? His gaze fixed on that mark for an instant before he took his tumbler and sat in the leather chair beside her.

Was that a flicker of disappointment in her eyes?

"No trouble at all," he said. "This has been a nice change of pace from eating alone or playing darts at the club."

"You aren't fooling me for a second." Her green eyes twinkled with mischief. "Your life is much more fast-paced than that."

"If you're asking if I'm seeing anyone, the answer is no." Although the fact that she would ask gave him hope he was on the right track playing this cool, taking his time. "You have my complete and undivided attention."

Her eyes went wide and she chewed her bottom lip. "Really?"

He angled back, hitching a booted foot on his knee. "That was impressive seeing you in action today. You were amazing interviewing the foster families and sifting through all that paperwork. I had no idea how much detail went into ensuring the animals are safe and well cared for."

"I'm just doing my job, a job I'm very happy to have. I get to do the work I love in an environment that is flexible about letting my daughter join me. It's the best of both worlds and I intend to be worthy of keeping the position."

"Well, I don't know a lot about the animal rescue world, but from what I can tell, whatever they're paying you can't be nearly enough for how much heart you pour into saving each one of those cats and dogs."

"We're all called to make a difference in the world. This is my way," she said simply and sipped her wine, her eyes tracking him with a hint of confusion.

Keep on course.

And he found himself actually wanting to get to know her better. Staying in the chair and finding out more about Megan wasn't such a hardship. "What made you choose this line of work?"

"I've always loved animals."

"But it must be more than that."

She eyed him over the rim of her glass. "Most people accept the simple answer."

"I'm not most people."

He stared back, waiting even though he wanted to close the space between them and lay her down along that sofa. He burned to cover her, kiss her. Take her.

"Well, while other girls were reading *Little House on the Prairie* or Nancy Drew novels, I devoured everything I could find on animals, their history, how to care for them, how to train them." The more she spoke, the more she relaxed on the throw pillows piled on the corner of the sofa. "I had these dreams of going to the big dog shows with my pup Snickers. I watched the shows over and over again so I could train him to do all the moves."

She was so buttoned up and proper, all about the rules, he hadn't expected such a quirky story from her. He wanted to know more. "What happened?"

Megan rolled her eyes and lifted her glass in toast. "Somehow I missed the memo that the dog show was just for purebreds."

"What kind of dog did you have?"

"A Jack Russell-Shih Tzu mix. Absolutely adorable and somehow unacceptable." She shook her head. "Wrong."

"I'm sorry you didn't get to have your big show with that pup."

Her gaze narrowed to a steely determination he'd seen before, except he'd been the cause of her ire then.

"Oh, I made sure Snickers still had his moment in the sun. I trained him to ride a skateboard, made a video and sent it into the *Late Night* show. Imagine my mom's surprise when they contacted us. I went on the show. And my dog was famous for a week."

He leaned back with a chuckle of admiration. "If you did that today, you'd get a reality show."

"You could be right."

"You were famous for more than a week. I remember that story now...."

"I ran the talk show circuit until my fifteen minutes of fame was up."

He blinked in surprise. "Somehow I didn't guess you were a limelight seeker. I envisioned you more as the studious type, the crusader in a more conventional way. Now I see where Evie gets her showmanship."

She laughed. "We've never really spent enough time with each other to form opinions."

"You must have been fearless." His mind filled with images of her as a child, as quirky and incredible as little Evie. "Most kids would be scared to put themselves in front of the camera that would broadcast them to the whole world."

"I was hoping my father would see me." She sipped her wine and stared into the flames crackling in the fireplace.

"Your dad?" he prompted.

"My biological father wasn't in my life. He made child support payments and sent a birthday card with a check each year, which puts him one step ahead of Evie's dad, who hasn't so much as bought her a pair of shoes." She cleared her throat. "But back to my father. I know he saw the show because he mentioned it in my next birthday card. He'd noticed, but it didn't change a thing." She shrugged. "I found out later he was married. I worry about Evie, since her father's chosen not to be a part of her life."

"I imagine it doesn't help to hear that missing even a minute with Evie is his loss."

She held up a hand. "Stop, I don't want sympathy. I love my daughter and I've worked hard to build this life. I just want her to have an easier path, to find a man who will value what a gift she is."

"That makes sense."

She leaned forward, elbows on the arm rest. "I'm not sure you're hearing me though. I can't afford to make another mistake in a relationship. I have to be a good example as her mother, as a woman."

Was she tossing him on his ass before they even got started? He angled forward, and suddenly the space between them wasn't so great after all. "That doesn't mean you can't have a social life."

"I need to be careful for my daughter." She nibbled on her bottom lip. "So things like dating, especially now, need to be on hold."

She half rose from the sofa and her mouth was a mere inch away from his as he sat in the leather chair beside her. Her pupils widened with unmistakable arousal. But she'd just said she wasn't interested in dating. He had to be misreading her…unless…she wanted a one-night stand, which was ironic as hell since she was the first woman he'd had serious thoughts about dating in a very long time. Before he could wrap his brain around that thought—

She kissed him.

Five

Shimmers of desire tingled through her.

Megan settled her mouth against his. It was no impulsive "thank you" this time. She'd thought it out, planning to make the most of this evening with Whit. She could indulge in this much before returning to everyday life and responsibilities.

She'd spent so much of the past three and a half years annoyed at Whit, resisting the attraction. Until now. She'd been tempted, seeing the altruistic side of him that she'd heard about but he'd done his best to keep hidden from her. Then watching him with her daughter totally slayed her.

Just one night. That's all she could have. And she intended to make the most of it.

Her lips parted against his, encouraging... *Yes.* His tongue traced along her mouth, sweeping inside to meet hers. Kissing. She'd longed for a man's kiss, the bold give and take, the hard planes of a masculine body.

Of his body.

Whit.

She'd been attracted to him from the start, and resented those feelings since they'd been at odds over the property dispute. Not to mention he wasn't particularly known for being environmental friendly. She'd given him an earful once over his purchase of a piece of wetlands.

However, even if they hadn't been adversaries, she'd been wary of dating because of her little girl, who was less than a year old then. The memory of Evie's father's betrayal had still been so fresh. She'd been struggling to put her life together and Whit had threatened to rock that. She'd been tempted though, then deeply disappointed when he quickly squelched those fantasies by being a ruthless land baron, causing her constant headaches.

The ache was lower now, pooling between her legs.

She thrust her fingers into his hair, and something seemed to snap inside of him. His muscular arms wrapped around her, hauling her closer until her chest pressed to his and she sat on his lap. She wriggled against him and straddled his legs, kneeling on the leather chair. His low growl of approval rumbled against her, flaming the heat inside her higher, hotter.

His hands slid down her back in a steady caress to cup her hips. The steady press of his fingers carefully sinking into her flesh had her writhing closer. It had been so long since she'd languished in these sensations of total, lush arousal. Maybe she was feeling emotional in the wake of the storm's destruction, leading her to want something more.

And judging from his response, he felt the same. She'd known he was attracted to her too. She couldn't miss that in his eyes. But feeling the thick length of his arousal against her stomach sent her senses reeling.

His mouth moved along her jaw, then down her neck, his breath caressing along her overheated skin. Her head fell back to give him better access and with each breath she drew in the scent of his aftershave mixed with the sweet smell of fragrant smoke wafting up from the fireplace.

He stroked her arms, then ran his hands up over her shoulders to cup her face. The snag of his callused fingertips sent a thrill through her. He was a man of infinite finesse and raspy masculinity all at once. Would they go to her bedroom or his? She had condoms in her purse. Always. She loved her daughter but she wouldn't risk an unplanned pregnancy.

The thought threatened to chill her and she sealed her mouth to Whit's again, her fingers crawling under his sweater to explore the solid wall of his chest. His touch trailed back down her arms in a delicious sweep until he clasped her wrists.

And pulled her hands away from him.

She blinked in confusion. "Whit?"

He angled back, his brown eyes almost black with emotion. "You're beautiful. I've fantasized about what your hair feels like so many times."

Then he cradled her hips in his palms again and shifted her off his lap and onto the sofa. Were they going to take things further out here? She opened her mouth to suggest they go to her room when she realized he wasn't sitting down again.

She reached up for him, ready to follow him wherever. He took her hand and pressed a kiss to her palm.

His eyes held hers. "Thanks for an amazing day. I look forward to tomorrow." He squeezed her hand once before letting go. "Goodnight, Megan. See you in the morning."

Cool air chilled over her flaming face. The first time she'd kissed him she could write off as an accident and save her pride. But not now. And he'd clearly been turned on and into the moment. So why the rejection?

Damn it all, she didn't have time in her life for games. Anger took root inside her, fueled by frustrated desire. As far as she was concerned, he could take his mixed signals and stuff them.

She would communicate with him on a professional level for the animals. But beyond that, she was done throwing herself at Whit Daltry.

As Whit landed his plane on the runway back in Royal, he couldn't help but compare this journey home to their flight out to Colorado. Yesterday's trip had been full of chatter and fun. The whole day had been one of the best he could remember. And he wanted more of them—with Megan and with Evie. Which meant he had to stay the course. As much as he'd wanted to follow through on Megan's invitation last night, he sensed she wasn't as ready as her kiss indicated.

So today, he sat up front alone at the plane's helm, while Evie stayed in the back napping beside her mom. The craft glided along the runway, slowing, slowing, slowing. He taxied up to the small airport that serviced their little town, the only place that had ever felt like home.

Megan had stayed quiet all day for the most part, giving only one or two answers to his questions about her work. Had he offended her last night? He'd only intended to ramp her interest, to take his time rather than rush her and risk her bolting. And now she'd bolted anyway after one of the most explosive kisses of his life. Only a kiss, damn it.

A cinnamon-scented moment.

The memory of that instant with her had him hard and wanting her now. But from the steely set of her jaw and straight spine, another kiss wasn't welcome. He had some serious backpedaling to do.

He steered the plane into the appointed parking spot. His employees converged outside to service the plane, unload the luggage and all the empty animal crates. He opened the hatch and lowered the steps while Megan unbuckled her napping daughter. Megan hefted Evie up into her arms and paused by Whit, her eyes scrubbed free of any emotion.

"Thank you for everything," she said with a careful smile.

He touched her elbow. "It was a good weekend."

"I should get home to relieve the pet sitter. Evie and I need to tackle washing before Monday hits." She nibbled her bottom lip, anger flickering in her eyes.

Well, hell. That cleared up any questions. He didn't have to wonder if he'd upset her by giving her time and space. And in the process, he'd denied them both an incredible night together for no reason at all. He needed to let her know he wasn't rejecting her, just…giving her time to adjust to the change in their relationship. "Do you need help with anything? I'll have the crates delivered back to the shelter."

"Thank you," she said tightly, then looked away for a second, adjusting her hold on her daughter before meeting his gaze head-on again. "Listen, about last night when I kissed you—"

He tapped her lips. "Would you like to spend Thanksgiving together?"

Her eyes went wide with shock. "What?"

"Let's spend Thanksgiving together." He hadn't planned on that particular offer, per se, but it made perfect sense now as a way to show her he was serious. "Last night wasn't a game to me. Your place or mine, whichever you want. I don't expect you to cook for me."

"What is going on with you? You're giving me whiplash." She cupped Evie's head. "You plan to make the meal?" She laughed skeptically.

"If you don't mind ptomaine poisoning." He scratched the back of his neck. "Actually, I have a cooking service and they'll cater Thanksgiving. Unless I got a better offer from you and Evie."

"No." She shook her head without hesitation. "I'm sorry. But no. Spending the holiday together would give Evie the false expectations about the two of us."

She was turning him down?

Okay, now he was truly confused. "We just spent the weekend together. How is an afternoon of turkey a problem?"

"You didn't hear me. It's Thanksgiving. A holiday. That's for families." Her throat bobbed with a quick swallow. "Last night, I, uh, I didn't mean to give you the wrong impression with that kiss."

"What impression was I supposed to get?" He braced a hand on the open doorway, trying to get a read on her. She'd kissed him, made it clear she was ready for sex but didn't want anything—close. Damn. She'd wanted a quickie with him and nothing more.

Now he was mad.

"Whit, you don't have to worry about me throwing myself at you anymore."

"Seriously?" he said, unable to believe he'd so misread this woman. "You expect us to go back to avoiding each other after the weekend we just spent together?"

"Not at all. I can behave maturely as I trust you can too. We both have to live in this town." Without another word, she descended the stairs and stepped out into the sunshine. The rays streamed over her hair, turning it into a beacon, and he couldn't peel his eyes away.

Damn, she was hot when she was all fired up. Of course she was hot any time. And while he'd misjudged her intent with the kiss Saturday, he hadn't misread her interest. For some reason she thought a one-night stand would suffice, but she was wrong.

He would give her some space for now. Holidays were tough. He got that. But after Thanksgiving?

They would not be ignoring each other.

Monday morning, Megan carried her sleepy daughter with her into work. The familiar chorus of barking dogs greeted her, reminding her of her responsibilities here, to all of the animals still in need of homes. Saturday's placement of twelve cats had been an amazing coup for such a small shelter. She couldn't afford to turn down Whit's generous offer of his plane, but she also couldn't put her heart at risk again.

The weekend with Whit had been better than she could have dreamed. He'd been charming, helpful, generous. He'd been amazing with her daughter.

And he'd been a perfect gentleman.

She was the one who'd gone off the rails and kissed him. She'd literally thrown herself at him. Again. Sure, he'd responded, but then he'd pulled away. She was starting to feel silly.

Except she knew she hadn't misread the signs. He wanted her too. So why did he keep pulling away? She'd all but promised him a night of no-strings sex and he'd still walked.

Usually guys bailed out because she had a kid. Those guys were easy to spot. They were awkward with Evie. But Whit wasn't that way.

Had he freaked out that there was a child in the picture at the last minute anyway? She didn't think so. His eyes had still smoked over her at every turn Sunday. But she hadn't felt up to the embarrassment of doing a postmortem on how he'd walked away from taking that kiss to its natural conclusion.

Damn it, she didn't have time for these kinds of games in her life. Which was the very reason she'd wanted one night, just one night with him.

She nodded to Beth at the front desk and walked past to settle Evie in her office on the small sofa. Evie had chosen a doctor's costume today, to cure all the people and animals hurt in the tornado. The post-Halloween sales had filled Evie's costume box to overflowing. Every time Megan or one of her friends offered to buy her a toy, Evie shook her head and picked another outfit. Megan had thought about counseling, even discussed it with the preschool director. Sue Ellen had pointed her in the direction of some videos the other children in the preschool had watched together, but so far those hadn't effected any changes in Evie.

Megan sagged against the open door frame.t

Beth waved from the desk. "Good morning. How was your weekend?"

She dodged the question that she didn't even really know how to answer. "You're here early."

Beth cradled a mug of herbal tea, the scent of oranges and spices drifting across the room. "The kennel supervisor let me in. I wanted to see your face when you came to the shelter today."

Alarms sounded in Megan's mind. "Is something wrong?"

"Things are very right." Beth set aside her mug. "A dozen guys—and women—from the Cattleman's Club spent the weekend volunteering."

Another reason to be grateful to a man she'd spent the past three and half years resenting. "Whit said he intended to ask them to help out...."

And she was grateful. She'd assumed a couple of them would come by to play with the dogs.

"Well, they did more than help out. In addition to doing the regular cleaning and exercising the dogs, they fixed the broken kennel run and cleared an area behind the play yard that's been full of debris. They said they'll be back after Thanksgiving weekend to build an agility course for the dogs and add a climbing tree for the cat house." Beth winked, her eyes twinkling with mischief. "You must have really impressed him."

Megan's knees felt wobbly. He'd coordinated all that effort this weekend while she'd been thinking about a quick fling? She'd had Whit Daltry all wrong. All. Wrong.

"Whit mentioned putting in a call, but I had no idea how much they would do. Especially when everyone is still dealing with the upheaval in their own lives."

"They care about each other and our community. They just needed pointing in this direction to help. It's okay to ask for help every now and again, Megan. You don't have to be a superwoman."

She nodded tightly. "For the animals, absolutely."

"For yourself."

Megan stayed silent, uncomfortable with the direction of the conversation. She was happy with her life, damn it. She was looking forward to spending Thanksgiving with her daughter, eating turkey nuggets and sweet potato fries.

Memories of Evie's laughter at the ice skating rink taunted her with all she might be missing.

"So?" Beth tipped back the office chair and sipped her tea. "How did things go with you and Whit on the great kitty transport?"

"Fantastic. The rescue is all foster-home-based, so every cat is now placed with a family until an adopter is found." Megan opted for impersonal facts. She walked to the shelves by a small table and straightened adoption applications and promotional flyers. After Thanksgiving, she would need to put up a small Santa Paws tree for donations. So much to do. She didn't have time for anything else. "I even made some notes for our shelter on how they handle their foster system."

"Sounds like Whit is really bending over backwards to mend fences with you."

Megan crossed her arms over her chest that still yearned for the press of Whit's body against hers. "As you said, we all need to do what's best for the community right now."

"Sure, and sometimes it's personal." Standing, Beth said, gently, "Like now."

"I never even implied—"

"You don't have to. You're blushing!" Beth pointed, her nails short and neat. She stepped closer and whispered, "What happened while you were in Colorado? Come on. I tell you everything. Spill!"

"There's nothing to tell." Sadly. Megan had wanted more and still didn't know why he'd pulled away. "My daughter was with me. How about we discuss your love life? Yours definitely has more traction than mine. How are things with you and Drew Farrell? Have you set a date?"

"Weeellll, a Valentine's wedding would be nice, but we'll see." She set aside her mug with a contented sigh. "For now, we're enjoying being together and in love. Repairs are still going on at my house. Once they're done, we'll decide if I'm going to sell or stay at Drew's."

"How's Stormy?"

Beth had adopted a cocker spaniel mix from the shelter, similar to her dog Gus that had died. Stormy had stolen Beth's heart when she'd volunteered after the tornado. "Full of mischief and a total delight."

"And the cats?" She stalled for time.

When Drew first dropped Beth off at the shelter after the storm to help Megan with cleanup, Megan encouraged Drew to take a couple of cats home with him. He'd insisted he was allergic to cats, but Megan could tell he and Beth were both enchanted. Since the kittens had come from a feral litter, placing them would have proved difficult at a time when they were already packed. Megan had mentioned the possibility of him needing barn cats—and it was a match made in heaven.

"They spend more time indoors than in the barn. Drew pops a couple of antihistamines and watches ball games with them in his lap." Home-and-hearth bliss radiated from her smile. "It's adorable."

Megan didn't begrudge Beth that joy, but God, it stung today of all days. "I'm happy for you both. For Stormy and the cats too. Thank you for taking them."

"Our pleasure."

Hearing how easily Beth said "our," Megan couldn't help but ask, "You and Drew were enemies for so long. How did you overcome that negative history so easily?"

"Who said it was easy?"

"Oh, but—"

Beth rested a hand on hers. "It's worth the effort." She sat back with a sigh. "I'm still in the 'pinch me' stage with this relationship. It's everything I didn't dare to dream of growing up."

Beth was a jeans-and-cotton-shirts kind of girl, with a causal elegance she didn't seem to realize she had. If anything, she was a little insecure in spite of all her success, sensitive about her past and the whole notion of having grown up on the wrong side of the tracks.

Megan gave Beth an impulsive hug. "It's real." She leaned back with a smile. "I've seen the way he looks at you and I'm so happy for you, my friend."

"Thank you." Beth hugged Megan back. "By the way, I noticed you dodged answering my question about Whit. I only ask because I care. I want you to be happy. You deserve to have more in your life than work."

"I have my daughter." Megan sat at the table set up for people to fill out adoption applications, the Thanksgiving holiday suddenly looming large and lonely ahead of her.

Beth walked to the table and sat in the chair across from her. "And when Evie grows up?"

"Then you and I can have this talk again." She fidgeted with a pen, spinning it in a pinwheel on the table.

Beth's eyes turned sad. "I'll respect your need for privacy." Standing again, she started to return to the front desk, then looked back over her shoulder. "Oh, in case you wanted to tell the Cattleman's Club thank-you in person, this weekend they're having a big cleanup in preparation for Christmas decorating."

Whit couldn't remember having a crummier Thanksgiving. Thank God it was finally over and he could spend the weekend helping out at the club with cleanup and decorating.

His invitation to spend Thanksgiving with Megan and her daughter had been impulsive—he'd originally just planned to send some flowers as part of his gradual pursuit. So he'd been surprised at the level of disappointment when she'd turned him down for dinner. That frustration had gathered steam with each day he waited and she didn't return his calls.

His catered turkey meal had tasted like cardboard. He'd ended up donating the lot to a homeless shelter. There had been invitations from his buddies in the Cattleman's Club to join them and their families for the holiday, but he hadn't felt up to pretending. No doubt part of his bad mood could be chalked up to the memorial service planned for Craig next week.

He just wasn't up to being everyone's pal today, either, but he'd promised to help and so many of them had chipped in to volunteer at the shelter. This club was the closest thing to family he had.

Launched by some of the most powerful men in town, the Texas Cattleman's Club had stood proud in Royal, Texas for more than a century. The TCC worked hard to help out in the community while also being a great place for members to get away from it all and to make contacts.

To be invited into the TCC was a privilege and a life-long commitment. And for a man who'd grown up as rootless as he had, that word—commitment—was something he didn't take lightly.

He climbed a ladder to hook lights along a towering tree outside the main building, an old-world men's club built around 1910. The tree was taller than the rambling single-story building constructed of dark stone and wood with a tall slate roof. Part of that roof had been damaged by the tornado, as were some of the out-buildings.

Looking in through the wide windows, he could see other club members and their families decorating the main area, which had dark wood floors, big, leather-up-holstered furniture and super-high ceilings. TCC president Gil Addison was leading a contingent carrying in the massive live tree to be used inside.

What would Megan think of all the hunting trophies on the wall? He'd never thought to consider her feeling on that subject given her work in animal rescue. But he sure as hell hoped it wasn't a deal breaker.

He hooked his elbow on the top of the ladder, look-ing out over the stable, pool, tennis courts and a re-cently added playground. Evie would love this place. He could almost envision her in her tiara, fitting right in with the rest of the kids. Except a person had to be a member to have full use of the facilities.

How had he gotten to the point in his mind where he was envisioning Evie and Megan here?

"Whit?"

A voice from below tugged his attention back to the present.

He looked down to find one of his pals from the Dal-las branch of the TCC, Aaron Nichols, partner in R&N Builders. Aaron had been overseeing the repairs to the club, but didn't appear to be in any more of a merry-making mood than Whit was. But then given the fact Aaron had lost both his wife and his kid in a car ac-cident several years ago, Whit could see how holidays must be particularly tough.

Which made him a first-class ass for feeling sorry for himself over being alone for Thanksgiving.

Whit hooked the lights along the top of the tree, wrapping and draping. "Hey, buddy, what can I do for you?"

Aaron handed up more lights, controlling the strand as it unrolled. "Just here to help. Shoot the breeze. Everyone's asking about you inside."

"Yeah, well, somebody's gotta take care of the tree out here." That had always been Craig Richardson's job.

Aaron nodded with an understanding that didn't have to be voiced. "Have fun on your big rescue mission?"

As if Whit hadn't been asked that question a million times already. Folks had expected him to bring Megan today. He'd entertained that notion himself while in Colorado, but she'd shut him down.

"We helped place a lot of cats, eased the burden on the shelter. It was a good day." He kept the answer brief and changed the subject. "Thanks for the cleanup at the shelter last weekend." Whit hooked the light over a branch. "I appreciate so many of you pitching in."

"We help our own," Aaron said with a military crispness he hadn't lost in spite of getting out of the service. "We would have gone sooner if we'd realized how tough things were at the shelter."

And Megan wasn't one to ask for help easily. He admired her independent spirit, her grit, the way she fought for her daughter and the animals. He just hadn't realized how much he would flat-out enjoy being with her too.

He hauled his attention back to the present rather than daydreaming like a lovesick teenager. "Everyone's been up to their necks in repairs. Sometimes it's difficult to tell where to start."

As he reached for Aaron to feed him more lights,

Whit caught a glimpse of a car approaching with a woman at the wheel.

There was a time when women weren't allowed at the club unless they were accompanied by a male member. But a few years ago the TCC had started allowing women to join, a huge bone of contention that caused great friction in the organization.

Now, however, almost ten percent of its members were females. Two years ago they'd added an on-site day-care center, which had created even greater discord. But this year, things had finally begun to settle down and feel normal for the TCC members. Watching everyone pull together today, Whit could see there was a real sense of camaraderie the club hadn't experienced in a long time.

So a woman coming to the club on her own wasn't a surprise or big deal. Except this woman had unmistakably red hair. Whit knew her from gut instinct alone, if not sight. His pulse sped up and he decided that this time, he wouldn't just bide his time. He'd known and wanted her for years. Aaron Nichols's presence had served to remind him how fast second chances could be taken away.

Whit tossed aside the strand of lights, leaving them tangled in the tree branches for now, and climbed down the ladder. Because he'd found the perfect distraction to lift his holiday mood and make him feel less like Scrooge.

Megan Maguire had come to the Texas Cattleman's Club.

Six

Megan told herself she was not coming to the Cattle-man's Club to see Whit. Absolutely *not*.

Holding a Tupperware container full of homemade brownies, she exited her new-used compact purchased after the tornado took out her other car and hip-bumped the door closed.

Evie had wanted to bake on Thanksgiving so they would be like a real family. Real? The comment had sent Megan into a frenetic Betty Crocker tailspin that produced dozens of brownies.

She was proud of the life she'd built, damn it. She was an independent woman with a satisfying career and a great kid.

This morning hadn't been very easy though. Evie had thrown a screaming fit over the thought of wearing regular clothes to a playdate with Miss Abigail's great nieces. The counseling videos and books recommended by the preschool director just weren't working with

Evie. Finally, Megan had surrendered to the request for a homemade costume made out of cut up sheets. In the big-picture view of things, it was most important that Evie wanted to play with other kids again without her mom present. But Megan had had to draw the line somewhere. When Evie had wanted to be a zombie, Megan suggested she be a mummy instead. Somehow a mummy princess seemed more benign than a zombie princess. What four-year-old knew about zombies?

Megan adjusted her hold on the container of brownies and picked her way around the big trucks and SUVs in the parking lot. Halfway to the looming lodge, as she was passing a golf cart loaded down with fresh evergreen boughs and spools of red ribbon, she felt as if she was being watched. She tracked the sensation to a towering pine tree with a ladder beside it. Whit stood at the base, his boot on the bottom rung, Stetson tipped back on his head.

Of course she'd known he would be here today.

But she didn't know what she would say to him. At all. She'd been off-kilter this week, questioning herself. She'd spent all of Thanksgiving imagining what it would have been like to share the day with him. Had he been alone on the holiday because of her decision?

His offer to spend the day together had intrigued her the more she thought about it. But it also had her reliving their kiss in Colorado. Had she really thought she could just sleep with him for one night and then walk away? This was a small town. They would run into each other.

Often.

That was good motivation to tread warily, because if things exploded between them, there could be lasting fallout. Not just the upheaval it would cause for

Evie to lose a male figure in her life, but Megan also had to think of her job and how a big blow-up between her and Whit could make living in this town together awkward. She had to put Evie first and her daughter was happy here.

"Hey, hello, Megan," a female voice called out from a row of cars over.

Megan turned to see Stella Daniels waving as she got in her sedan to leave. The administrative assistant from the mayor's office had become an unexpected hero after town hall had taken a direct hit in the tornado. With Mayor Richard Vance still in the hospital, Stella was serving as the unofficial leader of Royal, giving interviews to the major networks and making heartfelt pleas for federal aid. Her quiet calm was just what the town needed in a crisis.

Megan could use some of that calm for herself.

Waving back, she smiled, then grappled to keep the plastic container from tumbling out of her arms. Stella ducked into her car; the organized woman was likely headed back to the office or off to inspect more cleanup efforts, even on the weekend.

Megan balanced the brownies again, turning back to the ladder only to find Whit gone. But it wasn't more than a second before Whit's broad hands came into view, sliding underneath the container.

"Can I help you with that?" he asked, his broad flannel-clad shoulders angling beside hers, their elbows bumping lightly as he shifted to help.

"Thank you. I brought these to thank the club for all their hard work at the shelter." She handed the three dozen turtle brownies to Whit.

"That's what we do." He glanced back over his shoulder. "Right, Aaron?"

Startled, she looked past Whit, surprised she hadn't even noticed Aaron Nichols was there as well. Just as she hadn't noticed Stella until the woman had called out. Megan had been one hundred percent focused on speaking to Whit. She'd seen that easy smile too many times in her dreams. Remembered the feel of his touch on her waist. Her hips…

Aaron clapped a hand on Whit's shoulder. "We can finish up later." He tipped his head to Megan. "Good to see you, Megan. Be sure this bozo doesn't keep all the brownies for himself. See you inside." He pivoted away and went into the lodge.

And then Megan was alone with Whit for the first time since before Thanksgiving. She searched for something to say to fill the awkward silence, finally asking, "What was Stella Daniels doing here?"

She tried not to let her gaze roam all over Whit. No easy task, that.

"She came to ask for help out at town hall. They're still plowing through debris and there's concern about lost files."

"If anyone can restore order in the chaos, Stella can." The town was lucky to have someone so competent leading recovery efforts during such a tumultuous time. "She's done some great work in organizing reconstruction during the mayor's recovery."

Mayor Vance had suffered massive injuries while working out of the town hall when the tornado hit. Stella seemed unsure of herself at times, but she was proactive in rounding up help where it was needed. And the Cattleman's Club was definitely the place to check, full of powerful movers and shakers in the community.

"The club is all in to do what we can." Whit's molten brown eyes held her for another long instant, making her skin tingle. "How was your Thanksgiving?"

She swallowed hard, thinking about how she'd been too much of a coward to return his calls. "Evie and I had a feast of chicken nuggets and sweet potato fries, then made turkey paintings using our handprints. The front of my refrigerator is full of artwork." She paused for an instant before asking, "How was your Thanksgiving?"

"Lonely," he said simply, without even a hint of self-pity, more like a statement of fact.

Surprise kicked through her, quickly followed by guilt that he'd spent the day alone after reaching out to her. "You didn't spend the day with friends?"

"They have families, like you do." He shrugged his broad shoulders. "But hey, it wasn't a total wash. I watched ball games and ate a catered meal."

The Whit she'd spent time with recently, the Whit who was standing here with her now, didn't fit the image of the man she'd known for over three years. She wasn't sure what to make of him now. She'd been so sure he was a wealthy, ruthless charmer.

Maybe he really was just a nice guy who wanted to be with her. What the hell was wrong with her that she'd been upset because the man had acted like a gentleman and didn't jump all over her during their trip? "I'm sorry you spent the day alone. After all you did for the shelter it was small of me not to include you in my Thanksgiving."

"I didn't want you to include me in your holiday out of gratitude." He looked past her, trees rustling overhead. "Where's Evie today?"

"Playing with Miss Abigail's great nieces." She took the brownies back from him under the guise of securing the lid but really to occupy her jittery hands. It had been Evie's idea to give the extra brownies to Whit, but Megan had been wary of showing up on his doorstep. Bringing baked goods to the whole Club offered her a face-saving option.

A smile played with his mouth, a sexy mouth that kissed like sin. "What's our princess dressed as today?"

Our? Had he noticed the slip of the tongue?

"She wanted to be a zombie, but I thought that was a little dark for a kid that young. We opted for a mummy, like 'Monster Mash.'"

"Good call." He frowned, his hand tucking under the brim of his Stetson to scratch his head before he settled the hat back into place. "She's still having a tough time?"

"I've talked to the day-care director about it. Sue Ellen suggested some videos and books with tips on how to promote discussion with a child after a traumatic experience. I have the name of a counselor too." She swallowed hard. "I hope we won't need to use it. I figured I would give her another week to ease back into a routine. Hopefully she'll get excited about Christmas celebrations at school."

"Hopefully," he echoed.

She should go. She reached and opened the container, releasing the intoxicating scent of chocolate. "Would you like an advance sampling of the brownies as an olive branch? Well, a chocolate kind of olive branch?"

She took one out to offer it.

He leaned in to bite off a corner of the brownie while she still held it. "Hmmm…" He hummed his appreciation as he chewed. "Damn, these are good."

His praise warmed her on a chilly day. "I'll take that as a compliment, coming from a man who can afford to eat at the best of the best restaurants."

"The cooking service I use has never brought anything as good as this." He popped the rest of the brownie in his mouth and reached for another.

"Over-the-top flattery." She scrunched her nose and set the container aside on the golf cart. "That can't be true."

"Sure it is." His smile was as bright as the dappled sunlight in the tree branches. "A cooking service is a luxury, but it's a necessity for me unless I want to eat at a restaurant every night, which I do not. I get to kick back in front of my television at night like a normal guy."

"A normal guy with a cooking service." She toyed with a strand of lights dangling off the cart.

"A cooking service I may have to fire since apparently they have been feeding me substandard brownies."

Damn it. How could she not like a guy who said things like that? She couldn't hide a smile.

"Evie and I will make some more just for you to thank you for the flight." The offer fell from her mouth before she could overthink it.

"I should say no, given how busy you are. But I'm going to be utterly selfish and accept." He finished off the second brownie.

"It's the least I can do after all your help. And you were so patient with Evie last weekend."

"That's a good thing. So why are you frowning?"

And there was the crux of things, her real reason for coming here with the brownies when she knew she would run into Whit. "My daughter is hungry for a father figure in her life. I just don't want her to build false hopes based on some nice gestures from you."

"Is that why you turned down my request to spend Thanksgiving together?" He raised an eyebrow.

"Yes, in part," she said carefully.

"You gotta know I think she's a great kid and I enjoy her company as well."

Yet another reason to like Whit. His affection for Evie was genuine.

Megan sagged back against a fat oak tree, bark rough even through her thick sweater and jeans. "She's a kid in a fragile state of mind. I'm not…comfortable risking anything upsetting her."

"Okay, okay…." Exhaling hard, he pressed a hand to the tree trunk, just above her head. "I can see where you're coming from on that, given the tiara and tornado-butt-kicking costumes."

"I'm glad you understand my predicament. I'm her mother. I have to put her needs first."

"You're a great mom too, from everything I've seen." His head angled closer. "I have to wonder though. Why did you kiss me in the hotel? Call me arrogant, but I wasn't mistaken in thinking you're interested…." He stroked her loose hair back over her shoulder. "Unless you were using me as a one-night stand. In which case you should be upfront about that. I'm not passing judgment. Just asking for honesty."

His touch sent a shiver down her spine. "Point taken."

"Exactly." His hand glided down to her shoulder blade, his fingers tangled in her hair.

Thank heaven everyone was inside, though the possibility that someone could catch sight of them through a window helped keep her in check. And heaven knew she needed all the help she could get to restrain her from throwing herself at him again. Her daughter's well-being had to be first and foremost in her mind.

"Whit, I'm just asking you not to use her to get to me.

She's a little kid who still believes in fairy tales where princesses can always win in the end."

"What about her mom?" He cupped the back of her neck, massaging lightly. "What does *she* believe in?"

His question stunned her silent for three heartbeats. "What does that matter?"

"Because, honest to God, I want to get to know you better."

His words filled the space between them with so much hope and possibility, she was scared as hell to step out on that ledge and risk a big fall.

So she settled for sarcasm. "You want to sleep with me."

"True enough." He eased his hand around to palm her cheek, caressing with his thumb. "Can you deny you're attracted to me?"

"Your ego is not your most attractive quality."

He chuckled softly. "What is, then?"

"Searching for compliments?" She tipped her chin. "I wouldn't have expected that from you."

He ducked his head. "Megan, I'm searching for a way to get through to you, because make no mistake, I want to spend more time with you. A lot more. I always have." His words and eyes were filled with sincerity. "I was able to keep my distance when I thought the feeling wasn't mutual. But now that I know you're attracted to me too? I'm all in."

Her breath hitched in her chest. "What does that mean?" Nerves made her edgy.

"A regular date, dinner with me."

Dinner scared her a lot more than the notion of no-strings sex. "I can't leave Evie alone and she can't stay out that late."

"What time does she go to sleep?"

She chewed her bottom lip, already seeing where he was going with this. "At eight."

"Then how about getting a sitter and we go out after she falls asleep."

"And this gossipy small town we live in?"

"There are plenty of places other than Royal to find dinner. We can get to know each other better talking during the drive."

She hesitated, wanting to agree but unable to push the words past her lips.

A smile stretched across his handsome face, giving him a movie-poster twinkle in his eyes. "I'll take that as a yes. See you tomorrow at eight-fifteen." Stepping back, he picked up the brownies again. "Let's take these inside so we can get started making plans for the evening."

The next day, after finishing up at the Cattleman's Club, Whit rushed home to shower and make plans for his evening with Megan. God, he needed her and not just for the distraction of forgetting about Craig's upcoming memorial service. But for the chance to be with her, talk to her, find out why she had this tenacious hold over his thoughts.

She'd clearly had reservations, but she'd still agreed. She'd been emphatic though that he couldn't arrive until after eight once she had Evie in bed.

As if he didn't understand how important it was to be careful of the little girl's feelings.

But one victory at a time.

He finished his shower and pulled out a suit, more ramped for this date than he could remember being... ever.

An hour later, he shifted his sports car into park

outside Megan's cute three-bedroom bungalow south of downtown. He'd left the truck at home tonight and opted for his silver Porsche. He wanted to make the evening special for her. He had things back on track to win Megan over. Tonight was a big step in the right direction.

He'd considered bringing her flowers, but didn't want to be obvious. So he'd opted to buy her a catnip plant. He'd actually bought two, one for her and one for his greenhouse even though he didn't have a cat. He'd also picked up a citronella plant that repelled mosquitoes to give him an excuse to stop by the shelter.

Walking up the flagstone path, he took in the multi-colored lights on the bushes and a little wooden sign that read *Santa, please stop here.* He climbed the steps and knocked twice just under the holly wreath on the door.

Dogs barked inside and he could hear Megan shushing them just before she opened the door. The sight of her damn near took his breath away. She wore a Christmas-red dress, the wraparound kind with a tie resting on her hip. Those strings made his fingers itch to untie the bow, to sweep aside the silky fabric and reveal the hot curves underneath. His gaze raked down her body, all the way to her bare feet, that tiny paw tattoo on her ankle tempting him all the more.

And he would have told her just how incredible she looked with her hair flowing loose to her shoulders except two dogs ran circles around his legs. He planted one hand on the door frame and gripped the terra-cotta pot with the catnip plant in the other. Some kind of Scottie mix in an elf sweater yapped at him while a border collie bolted out around the porch, then back inside.

"Sorry for the mayhem." Megan rolled her eyes.

"Piper and Cosmo just need a good run in the back yard before I go."

"No problem." He passed her the plant. "Catnip."

"Thank you, how thoughtful. Truffles, Pixie and Scooter will have a blast with it." Her smile was wide and genuine, her lips slicked with gloss. "Come on inside. Evie is asleep and Abigail should be here soon to watch her. Beth helps out, but since she's with your friend Drew...I just want to keep any talk to a minimum."

He swept off his Stetson as she stepped aside to let him in. He focused on learning more about her from her house to distract himself from the obvious urge to keep staring at her.

Her home was exactly how he would have imagined: warm and full of colors. A bright red sectional sofa held scattered throw pillows and three cats. Her end tables were actually wood-encased dog crates. A toy box overflowed in a corner.

And there were photos everywhere. Of her with Evie. Of them with the dogs. The cats too. Years of her life not just on the mantel but also in collages on the walls.

She held up the sprig of catnip. "I'm just going to water this."

He followed her into the kitchen and sure enough, the refrigerator front was decorated in finger-painted turkeys and a cotton ball snowman. He noticed her recycling station tucked just inside the laundry room, with its neat stacks of bundled newspapers and rinsed milk jugs in labeled bins. "I should take lessons from you on recycling."

"You should," she said pertly.

Chuckling softly, he looked past all those precise

labels, and saw a large crate with a familiar calico cat inside.

"Is that the same cat I brought to the shelter?" He pointed. "Tallulah? I thought she was staying in your office."

"Tallulah came down with an upper respiratory infection, so I brought her home to keep a closer watch over her." She turned off the water and set the plant on the counter. "I've been crating her to keep her separate from the other animals."

He knelt beside the extra-large enclosure, wriggling his fingers through the wire. The kitty woke, arching her back into a long stretch. She was a damn cute little scrap. "Is she going to make it?"

"She's doing much better now." Megan leaned a hip against the doorframe, crossing her arms over her chest as she watched him with curious eyes. "She's on medication. I've been keeping her at home with me at night to make sure she's eating and hydrated."

As if on cue, Tallulah went to the double bowl and lapped up water.

Whit stood again, inhaling Megan's cinnamon scent. "Do you often take animals home from work?"

"We all do. There are never enough foster homes, especially right now."

"And I added to that burden by bringing in Tallulah. I'm sorry about that."

"You're a confusing man, Whit Daltry." She studied him intently.

"If it makes you feel better, I'm not even close to understanding you yet either. But everything I've seen so far, I like." Unable to resist for another second, he tipped his head and brushed his mouth against hers.

The soft give of her lips and that sweet moan of hers

had him reaching for her. She didn't lean in, but she wasn't pulling away either. So he moved slowly, carefully. And savored the feel of her.

He slid his hands behind her, along her waist, the silkiness of her dress teasing his hand with thoughts of how silky her bare skin felt. He tasted her, drawing her closer and just enjoying the moment. Things couldn't go any further, not with the babysitter due to knock on the door at any second.

So he enjoyed just kissing Megan, learning more about the way the two of them fit together. Her arms slid around his neck and she pressed those sweet curves against him as her fingers toyed with his hairline. Such a small gesture, but each brush of her fingertips sent his pulse throbbing harder through his veins.

He backed her against the door and she stroked her foot up the back of his calf. A growl rumbled in the back of his throat, echoing the roar in his body to have this woman, to take her even though his every instinct shouted he would lose her if he moved too fast.

The doorbell rang, jarring him back to his senses.

For now.

A date.

She was on a no-kidding, grown-up date.

Megan couldn't even bring herself to feel guilty. Her child was asleep and well cared for and she was enjoying an adult evening out with a sexy, fascinating man.

The valet drove away to park the Porsche as she and Whit climbed the steps of the restored mansion-turned-restaurant. She had heard about the French cuisine at Pierre's, but never had the spare cash or free time to try it for herself. Her heels clicked on her way up the stairs and she couldn't miss the way Whit's eyes lingered on her legs.

A rush of pleasure tingled through her.

Sure, she loved being a mom and enjoyed her job, but it was nice to slip into a dress that wasn't covered with ketchup or cat hair. She tucked her hand into the crook of Whit's arm as they stepped over the threshold into the warm, candlelit restaurant. Her fingers moved against the fine weave of his suit jacket.

A string quartet played classical carols in the foyer, elegant strains swelling up into the cathedral ceiling. She was so preoccupied with taking it all in she almost ran smack dab into an older couple. She started to apologize, then realized—damn it—they weren't the only Royal residents who'd ventured outside the city limits.

She forced herself to relax and smile at Tyrone and Vera Taylor. "Good evening. Imagine running into you two here."

She'd hoped to keep her relationship with Whit out of the public eye a while longer, but she should have known that would be next to impossible, in most any local restaurant given their wide circle of friends.

"Whit?" Tyrone said. "What are you—? Oh, well, hello, Ms. Maguire."

"Good evening, sir," Whit answered the silver-haired man. Tyrone had a reputation for riding roughshod over people, but Whit met him face on without a wince.

Megan considered asking them about their newborn grandbaby in the NICU, about their daughter Skye still in a coma, but rumor had it Vera wasn't enthused about being a grandmother. The possibility of that poor little baby being unwanted hurt Megan's already vulnerable heart. So she simply said, "You and your family are in my thoughts."

"Thank you," Vera answered tightly before turning to her husband. "Tyrone?"

The blustery man clapped Whit on the shoulder. "We'll let you get to your meal. I'll see you at the town hall cleanup…and of course at Craig Richardson's memorial service."

"Yes, sir." Whit nodded curtly.

Megan wondered if the others noticed the tension in Whit's shoulders at the mention of his dead friend. She tucked her hand into the crook of his arm again and squeezed a light reassurance.

The maître d' arrived and saved them from further awkward conversation by leading the Taylors to their table while the hostess guided Whit and Megan to theirs—thankfully on the other side of the room.

Megan settled into her seat, the silver, crystal and candlelight a long way from chicken nuggets and fast food on the run. Music from the quartet filled the silence between them until their waiter took their order. They both settled on the special: rack of lamb, white grits and Texas kale.

As she stabbed at her salad, she realized just how quiet Whit had gone and knew with certainty that the mention of his friend Craig had hit him hard.

"Are you okay?" She rested a hand over Whit's. "We don't have to do this tonight."

"I want to be here with you." He flipped his hand over to squeeze hers. "I'm good."

"You don't have to be Mr. Charming all the time." In fact, she sometimes wanted a sign to know what was real about him, what she could trust, because lately he seemed too good to be true. "We can call it a night and reschedule."

His thumb caressed along the sensitive inside of her

wrist. "No. I need a distraction and you're a damn fine one."

"Thank you, I think." She tipped her head to the side. "I'm just so sorry for your loss."

"Me too. It was just so...." The tendons in his neck stood out, and even in the dim candlelight, she could see his pulse throbbing along his temple. "Losing him in that tornado was just so unexpected."

She agreed on many levels. The whole town of Royal, Texas, had been tipped upside down by that storm. "Do you think we're both just reacting to all that life-and-death adrenaline?"

His gaze snapped up to meet hers. "What I feel for you has nothing to do with a natural disaster."

"But I kissed you that day and that changed things between us."

"Lady," a smile finally tugged at his handsome face, "I was attracted to you long before that kiss."

She'd suspected, but hearing that gave her a rush far headier than it should have. "I thought I was just a great big pain in the butt since I moved to town."

He glanced down again. "Craig used to tell me I should just sweep you off your feet."

"You told him how you felt?"

Whit shook his head. "I didn't have to. Craig guessed. He said it was obvious every time I looked at you." And his eyes held hers again now, full of heat and intensity. "But you shut me down cold right from the start. And I can't blame you. We had our disagreements. I thwarted your business plans. And you were quite vocal in your disapproval of my company buying wetlands. I thought I was saving us both a lot of grief by steering clear. Then you kissed me, and all bets were off. I would have acted sooner but when we got the news about Craig...."

The confirmation that he'd been wanting a relationship with her for so long rattled her more than a little. "You've been grieving."

"I have...still am." He glanced down for a couple of heartbeats before swallowing hard and looking back up at her. "But that doesn't stop life from happening. And it doesn't stop me from thinking about what happened between us that day. We can't ignore it."

Her face flamed. "I'm embarrassed that I kissed you."

"But you liked it." He leaned back in his chair, watching her over the candlelight. "So did I."

She couldn't deny it to him or to herself any longer. She wanted Whit, and she wanted him for more than just one night. "Obviously I liked it."

He leaned closer, took her hand across the table, the heat in his eyes smokier than the candle between them. "Then let's do it again."

Seven

After Whit's suggestive comment, dinner had passed in a blur of anticipation as she waited for this moment. To be in Whit's sports car heading to his house. To be alone. Together.

A part of her knew she'd done a grave disservice to the fine cuisine, but she could only think of the promise in Whit's eyes. Now they were finally at his house for after-dinner drinks and whatever else came next.

The garage door slid closed behind them, sealing them inside one of the four bays, where they were surrounded by other signs of his luxurious lifestyle. She'd seen the truck, but there was also a boat. A motorcycle. She gulped back a nervous shiver and concentrated on the man in the seat next to her instead. He was about more than expensive toys and an extravagant lifestyle. Whit was real. This was real. She was going to act on her feelings for this man. The attraction that had been simmering between them for days—weeks, years—would finally be fulfilled. She'd ached for him, dreamed of him.

Shifting in her seat, she smoothed her fingers over the red silk hem where it had ridden up one knee just a little. She'd dressed with care, wanting to be noticed. Yet the silk fabric had teased her too, clinging and skimming along her skin every time she moved.

Whit turned to her, the leather seat creaking. Her temperature spiked and heart pounded. She met his gaze and knew what was coming. She'd been waiting all evening....

He sketched his mouth over hers lightly. Once. Twice. Nipping her bottom lip and launching a fresh shower of sparks through her veins.

Then he eased back and looked into her eyes. "Going inside doesn't commit to anything more than you want."

She angled her head to the side and lifted an eyebrow. "Really? Are you going to kiss and bolt again?"

"Not a chance." He tucked his hand behind her head, his fingers massaging a sensual promise into her scalp. "I just want you to know I care about you."

The simple words were filled with layers of meaning she wasn't ready to delve into just now. Still, she held them close, savoring the heady warmth of being cared about by this handsome, magnetic man.

"I want to see the inside of your house." She stroked his face with one hand and reached for her door handle with the other. "So let's go."

"Yes, ma'am." He scooped up his Stetson. "I'm happy to oblige."

As she stepped out of the low-slung sports car, Whit was already holding the door open for her like the perfect gentleman he'd been all evening. His palm low on her back, he guided her past his Porsche and truck toward the door. The warmth of his hand seared through her silky dress. The silence wrapped around her as they climbed the three stairs into his house.

And holy cow, what a house.

Mansion would be a more appropriate word. She slipped off her heels and padded barefoot down the corridor leading to the main foyer. She wriggled her toes against cool marble, then into the plush give of a Persian rug. She tipped her head back to stare up the length of the stairway, up to the cathedral ceiling with a crystal chandelier. The scent of lemony furniture polish and fine leather teased her nose. Whit stood silently at her side.

God, the place was quiet compared to the constant mayhem of her home, with Evie's laughter, dogs barking, and kids' television shows playing. Curious to learn more about this man full of contradictions, Megan glanced at the dining room to her left, with its heavy mahogany table set, then turned to the living room on her right. She stepped through the archway, taking in the tan leather sofas and wingbacks, tasteful while still being oversized for a man. She trailed her fingers along the carved mantel above the fireplace.

"What do you think?" he asked from behind her, his footsteps thudding on the hardwood floor.

"It's…" She searched for a word to describe the surroundings that had clearly been professionally decorated, just as his meals were professionally prepared. The place was pristine. High-end gorgeous. Yet missing all the touches that made a place a home. There was no clutter, no scars on the furniture from the wear and tear of making memories.

And there were no pictures, just knickknacks on

the shelves and gallery artwork on the walls. But no photos. That tugged at her heart as sad, so very sad. "You have a lovely home."

His hands fell to rest on her shoulders, his chin against her hair. "It's a damn study in beige and I never realized that until I compared it to your place tonight. Kinda like how your brownies taste better than anything the best catering service could offer."

With every word, he made her heart ache more for him. She turned in his embrace and slid her arms around his neck. She saw so much in his eyes. So much caring and even a hope for things she wasn't sure she could give him.

But she couldn't think about that now. She refused to ruin this night by borrowing trouble from what might come. For now, she just wanted to enjoy this new connection and all the heady promise of his touch.

She stroked the back of his neck along his close-cropped hairline. "Do you really want to talk about paint swatches and recipes? Because I have something a lot more interesting in mind." She gripped his shoulders, her fingers flexing against hard male muscle. "The only question in my mind is, do you prefer the leather sofa or your bedroom?"

Megan's proposition fueled Whit's already smoldering need for her. Dinner had been a delicious torture as he waited to get her in his home, in his bed.

Although right now, the sofa sounded fine to him.

He skimmed the back of his fingers along her face. "You're sure this is what you want?"

"Are you kidding?" She tugged his hair lightly. "I thought I'd made my wishes abundantly obvious."

"I just want you to be clear." He cupped her face,

resting his forehead on hers. "This won't be a one-night thing."

She hesitated, but only for an instant before whispering, "I hear you."

"And you agree." He needed to hear her say it. He'd waited too long to have this woman in his arms to wreck it all now.

"How about this." She angled closer into his embrace, her cinnamon scent filling his every breath. "It isn't a one-night stand, but we're still going to take it one night at a time."

He'd wanted more, but she hadn't said no outright. He was a smart man. He'd made progress, and he wasn't going to wreck his chance with this amazing woman.

He wrapped his arms around her and pressed her soft body to his. "I can live with that for now."

"Good, very good." She swept her hands into his suit coat and shrugged his shoulders until the jacket fell to the floor. "Because you've been filling my dreams for a very long time."

"I would bet not as long as you've been in mine."

"Really?" Her green eyes went wide, her voice breathy. "Tell me more."

"Yes, ma'am. I'd heard about the hot new director at the shelter, then I saw you and you were—are—so much more than hot." He took a step toward the wide leather sofa, then another step. "But you shut me down cold because of the property dispute."

"I noticed you all right." She tugged at his tie, loosening it and pulling it free from his collar. "But yes, you made my life more than a little difficult by putting up roadblocks for the original shelter plans. And you're right that I don't approve of your company's history of buying up wetlands. But, to be honest, there's more. I was still wrapped up in getting my feet on the ground with Evie and being a mom."

"It didn't have to do with trusting men because of Evie's father?" he couldn't resist asking.

"This conversation is getting too serious." She backed toward the sofa, their feet synching up with each step. "Can we return to the part where you tell me I'm beautiful and I tell you I admire your abs?"

"You like my abs, do you?"

Her fingers stroked down again until she cupped his butt. "I like a lot about you, Whit Daltry."

"Nice to know." He leaned down to kiss her just as she arched up to meet him.

The taste of their after-dinner coffee mingled with the flavor of pure Megan. A taste he was coming to know well and crave more with each sampling.

Every time he held her, it was only more intense. He leaned forward at the same time she fell back. They landed on the leather sofa in a tangle of arms and legs and need. The sweet give of her curves under him sent desire throbbing through him, making him ache to be inside her. The silk of her dress as she writhed against him only tormented him with the notion of how much better her skin would feel. He wanted her now on the sofa and again upstairs. But he also wanted to make this moment perfect for her. No rushing.

Although that was getting tougher to manage with her tugging his shirt from his pants and working his belt buckle open. He toyed with the hem of her dress, his knuckles brushing the inside of her knee and drawing a husky moan from her lips.

He'd been fantasizing all evening long about untying her wraparound dress, and he intended to fulfill that fantasy. Soon. For now, he lost himself in the pleasure of kissing her, stroking along her creamy thigh. Taking his time. Taking them both higher and higher still until the need was a painful razor's edge.

Drawing in a ragged breath to bolster himself, he lifted off her. The image of her kissed plump lips, her flame-red hair splayed across the buff-colored sofa, was pinup magnificence.

She looked up at him with a question in her sparkling green eyes. She extended a hand. "Whit? Where are you going?"

"To carry you to my bedroom." He scooped her into his arms and against his chest.

Her gasp of surprise made him smile.

She got past her surprise quickly, though, and toyed with the top button of his shirt. "Luckily for both of us, that's exactly where I want to be."

He headed back into the foyer and past the stairs with long-legged strides that couldn't eat up the distance to the master suite fast enough.

Finally, finally, he crossed the threshold into his room. He'd never thought of it as more than a place to sleep. Houses—homes—weren't things to get attached to.

Just short of the four-poster bed, he set her on her feet. As she slid down his body, she thumbed free two more buttons on his starched cotton shirt.

She angled back as if to sit on the edge of the bed and he stopped her with a hand to the waist.

"Wait," he said, "we'll get there soon enough."

He dropped to his knees, his hands grazing over her breasts on his way to hug her hips. Her husky sigh urged him on as he eyed the tie of her dress, the loops right there for the taking, releasing. He took one end of the sash between his teeth. He looked up at her, holding her gaze with his. Her hands fell to his shoulders, but not to push him away. In fact, she swayed a bit, her fingers digging into his back, as if she was bracing herself to keep her balance. She dampened her lips with her tongue.

He tugged, slowly, imprinting the moment on his mind. Her dress parted and with a shrug of her shoulders she sent it slithering off into a pool at her feet. His breath lodged in his chest, then he exhaled in a long, slow sigh of appreciation.

The sweet swell of her breasts in red lace, the curve of her hips in crimson satin panties had him throbbing harder with the urge to be inside her. Now. And thanks to her bikini undies, he found the answer to his question about whether she was hiding more tattooed paw prints. She had a tiny trail along her hip bone. He took the edge of her panties in his teeth and let it lightly snap back into place.

"Megan, you are…beautiful beyond words. More than I even imagined, and what I imagined was already mighty damn awesome." His hands trembled as he reached to stroke her arms. Sure, he'd touched before but the feel of naked flesh was so much more intimate now that her curves were bared.

A flush swept over her lightly freckled skin. "And you, Whit, are seriously overdressed for the occasion."

She tugged him back up to stand again and unbuttoned his shirt the rest of the way, one deliberate move at a time, kissing each inch of exposed skin. Her licks and nibbles had him bracing a hand against one of the bed posts to keep from stumbling to his knees again. He kicked off his shoes while she made fast work of unzipping his pants and shoving them down and off. Her eyes widened with appreciation and she stroked the length of him. He gave up and let gravity take them both onto the mattress.

Whit laid her back on the bed, his bed. In his room. His house. Finally, he had her here after three and a half long years.

He stretched out on top her, hot flesh meeting flesh. Her curves melded to him, enticed him, made him ache all the more to be inside her.

The thick comforter gave underneath them. He stroked up the creamy satin of her skin, cupping her lace-clad breasts. Her nipples tightened against his palms. A low growl rumbled in his chest and he took one of those hard pebbles in his mouth, teasing and circling with his tongue through the fabric.

He reached a hand behind her and unhooked her bra. Then, yes, he took her in his mouth again, bare flesh this time, and she tightened with pleasure at the stroke of his tongue. Her fingers dug deeper into his shoulders, cutting tiny half moons in his skin.

The moment was so damn surreal. He'd been hoping for this chance to be with Megan since the day he'd met her. He'd held himself in check because she'd shut him down cold for so long.

She wasn't cold now. Not even close.

Megan matched him stroke for stroke, taste for taste, exploring him as he learned the landscape of her naked body. Each panting breath came faster and faster, hers and his, and he knew restraint was slipping away. He angled off her to reach into the bedside drawer and pull out a condom.

She smiled a thanks before plucking the packet from him. She tore the wrapper open, her eyes intent but her hands trembling. He understood the feeling well. She pressed a hand to his shoulder and nudged him onto his back.

With a smooth sweep of her leg, she straddled his legs. Her fiery red hair tumbled over her shoulder in a gorgeous tangled mess of curls. He reached to cradle her breasts in his palms, his thumbs circling. Her eyes fluttered closed for a second before she looked at him again and rolled the condom over him, one deliberate inch at a time, never taking her eyes off him.

He cupped her hips and drew her closer until his erection pressed against her damp cleft. She rocked against him and his fingers dug deeper into her flesh. Much more and this would be finishing too soon.

He lifted her from him and lowered her back to the bed, sliding on top of her again. She hitched a leg around his, gliding her foot along his calf and opening for him. He nudged against the warm, moist core of her, pressing and easing inside with a growl echoed by her sigh. He thrust deeper as she arched up with a with gasping "yesss."

Her hips writhed against his, her arms looped around his shoulders and holding him close. She gasped and whispered in his ear, nonsensical words that somehow he understood. He moved inside her, the velvety clamp of her body around him so damn perfect. Like her.

The need to pleasure her, to keep her, pulsed through him along with each ragged breath. He linked fingers with her, their clasped hands pressing into the comforter as they worked together for release. Damn straight he'd been right to wait for her, because being with Megan was more than special. This woman had him tied in knots from wanting her.

And even as he chased the completion they both craved, he was already planning the next time with her, and the next. But first, he had to be sure she felt every bit as rocked by the moment as he did. Whatever it took. He pulled a hand free and hitched her leg higher around him, kissing and stroking as he filled her.

Her head dug back into the pillow, thrashing, her gasps coming faster and faster, the flush on her chest broadcasting how close she was to…flying apart in his arms.

She arched against him, her arms flinging up to lock tighter, draw him closer and deeper as she dug her heels in and rode through each shivering echo of her orgasm.

The bliss on her face sent him over the edge with her.

He growled as his release shuddered through him again and again, each ripple of pleasure reminding him how much and how long he'd wanted this woman.

And how damn important it was to keep her.

Good sex mellowed a person.

But great, incredible, unsurpassable sex?

That made Megan nervous. She'd been looking for a brief, no-strings affair. What she and Whit had just shared made an already complicated relationship even more tangled.

Megan sat on a barstool at Whit's kitchen island, wearing his white linen shirt, while the man himself foraged in the refrigerator. He'd tugged on a pair of jeans and nothing more and heaven help her, he offered up an enticing view. His perfect butt in denim…his broad, bare shoulders… She swallowed hard and looked away.

She'd just had the best sex of her life. She should be rejoicing. Instead, she kept thinking about all the ways this could go so horribly wrong. And if it did, that failure would be in her face every single day because living in such a small town made it all but impossible to ignore each other.

Regardless of her intention to keep things light, tonight was a game changer. She knew that. To protect herself and her daughter, Megan would have to tread warily. Easy enough to do since her feelings for him made her jittery.

For now? Her best move would be to get to know as much about him as possible and figure out quickly whether or not to run.

Whit grabbed two bottled waters and closed the refrigerator. He opened a cabinet and pulled out two cut crystal goblets. He poured them each a glass and set them on the island just as the microwave dinged. He'd warmed their crème brulee dessert they'd brought home rather than waiting any longer at the restaurant.

He snatched up a potholder, pulled out the warm pudding and placed it on the island. The image of him all domestic and sexy had her mouth watering.

She eyed the empty bottles and walked to the counter, letting her hip graze his as she passed. "I'll just toss these for you. Where's the recycling?"

"Thanks. Check the door beside the pantry."

She tugged open the door to reveal a line of high-end built-ins, labeled with brass plates. "Be still my heart. This is amazing."

She smiled over her shoulder at him, then opened the bin marked *glass*. She found it empty and pristine, clearly never used. She tamped down disappointment and tossed the two bottles inside. She turned back to find him standing right behind her with a sheepish grin on his face.

Whit slanted his mouth over hers. "Forgive me?" He kissed her again, then teased her bottom lip lightly between his teeth. "I promise to try to be more earth-friendly in the future. Scout's honor."

"I wish you would do it because it's a good thing to do and not just to impress me." She enjoyed the bristle of his five o'clock shadow, savoring the masculine feel of him. "But I'll take the win for our planet however I can get it."

He chuckled softly against her mouth. "I appreciate your willingness to overlook my shortcomings."

His hands tucked under the hem of the shirt, cupping her hips in warm, callused hands. Goosebumps of awareness rose on her skin and she stepped closer, her feet between his as she flattened her palms to his bare chest. His heartbeat thudded beneath her touch, getting faster the longer the kiss drew out.

In a smooth move, he lifted her and set her on the island, his fingers stroking along her legs as he stepped back. "Food first. Then maybe we could share a shower—in the interest of conserving water, of course."

His promise of more hung in the air between them. He opened the silverware drawer and passed her a spoon.

Megan tapped the caramel crackle on top of the crème brulee, Whit's shirt cuffs flopping loosely around her wrists. "So I told you why I went into animal rescue. What made you decide to go into property development?"

He raised an eyebrow, his spoon pausing halfway to his mouth. "You say that like it's a something awful."

"I'm sorry. I didn't mean to sound…judgmental." She winced as she set her spoon down and folded back the shirt cuffs. "But I guess I wasn't successful in holding back."

"Well, I do have three and half years' worth of cold shoulders from you to go on."

"Help me to understand your side." She spooned up a bite and her taste buds sang at the creamy flavor. Of course, her senses were already alive and hyper-aware after both of the spine-tingling orgasms Whit had given her.

"I like building things. I like helping businesses and people put down roots." He stood at the bar beside her, so close he pressed against her thigh.

"You can build things anywhere. Why destroy wet-lands with high-rise office buildings?" Damn it. There came her judgmental tone again. But she had values. She couldn't hide what she believed in just because it might stir old controversies.

"I'm not destroying the wetlands around here." He said with an over-careful patience. "I'm relocating them, responsibly and legally. Tell me how that's a problem."

At least he was asking. He'd never opened the door to discussion before, just shut her down.

But then hadn't she done the same?

Now was her chance. "By relocating you're creating a manmade, imitation version of something that already exists in nature. Why not leave nature alone?"

He scooped up a spoonful of the crème brulee. "I guess we'll have to agree to disagree on the word imi-tation."

"You say you care about the animals and environ-ment by relocating the wetlands." Frustration elbowed its way into her good mood. She set her spoon down and tried another approach to help him see her side of things. "In order to save animals, I needed the best fa-cility and location possible, which you blocked. Legal and ethical aren't always the same."

He quirked an eyebrow. "You landed on your feet. The animals are cared for. I made sure of that."

"What?"

"I made sure the piece of land you ultimately built on was affordable."

She wasn't quite sure what to do with that piece of information. She rubbed a finger along the rim of her crystal goblet. "Are you saying you offered up a diversion so I would back away from the property you wanted?"

"Do we have to rehash this now?" He tempted her with another spoonful of his caramel custard dessert.

"I think we do." She took the spoon from him, licked it clean and set it down. "I would have been closer to Evie the day of the tornado if the shelter had been built where the original plan called for."

"Fine." He leaned back and crossed his arms over his chest. "I can't make business decisions based on personal convenience and be successful."

"I understand that. Obviously." She searched his eyes for a sign of easing, but his expression was inscrutable. "But you also shouldn't pull your heart and humanity out of your job."

His eyes narrowed and chin tipped up as he reached to skim her hair over her shoulder, his hand lingering to stroke the sensitive spot behind her ear. "How can I make you get over that grudge?"

"I'm not sure. Show me you've changed…." She struggled to think, tough as hell to do with his touch enticing her to just sink into his arms again. "Or convince me you didn't do anything wrong."

"Megan," he said, exasperation dripping from that one word. Then he kissed her in an obvious attempt to distract her. "You're trying to pick a fight with me so I won't get closer. Am I wrong?"

His breath was warm along her face.

She whispered, "You're not wrong."

He nodded, then pulled back, his hand trailing along her arm. "Tell me how teaching your dog to ride a skateboard led you to become a shelter director rather than, say, a lion tamer?"

She grasped the safe topic with both hands, grateful for the reprieve. "I was always the little girl bringing home stray kittens and lost dogs. My mother was terrified I would get bitten or scratched, and looking back I can totally see her point." She shrugged. "But nothing she said stopped me—you may have noticed, but I'm very stubborn. So my mom signed me up for this thing called 'Critter Camp' at our local Humane Society. It was a summer camp for kids. We learned about animal care, animal rights, responsible ownership and yes, animal rescue."

"Sounds like a great program."

"My mom had to work overtime to pay for it." The memory pulled her under, back to those days of her mother scrimping to support her child. Megan understood the fear and weight of that responsibility well. "I didn't realize that until I was older, begging to go to the camp for the fifth year in a row. But I was hooked. I looked into the animals' eyes and they needed me. But they also saw how much I needed them. People don't always realize that they save us just as much as we save them."

"Why haven't you started a critter camp here? I'm certain it would be a huge success."

A dark smile tugged at her mouth and she dropped

a hand to his knee, squeezing. "Are you sure you want the answer to that?"

"I wouldn't have asked unless I wanted to know." His hand fell to her leg, his calluses rasping along her sensitive inner thigh.

She swallowed hard and tried to think past the delicious sensation. "Lack of space because of the plot of land we had to take as the consolation prize when you blocked the purchase of our original choice."

"You said you were content with the second location." Concern creased his forehead, but his hand inched higher.

She clamped his wrist. "It's farther from the schools, which makes logistics tougher for after-school programs. There are a host of other reasons—"

"Such as?"

"We need space to enlarge the dog park, and then there's the budget." She moved his hand back to the counter. "But if you start writing checks to the shelter and offering flights for animals, while generous, that does not buy you time with me. If you want to make a donation, I'll gratefully accept as the director. But we have to keep that separate from me—Megan, the woman."

He clasped her hand and brought it to his mouth, kissing her knuckles. "That said, will Megan, the *sexy* woman, have dinner with me again?"

Another brush of his mouth along the inside of her palm made it tough for her to think, but then that was a problem even when they weren't touching. She needed time to get her head together. She needed to figure out if it was even possible to let this play out regardless of the consequences.

That wasn't something she could figure out now.

"I'm helping with the town hall cleanup tomorrow afternoon while Evie naps. We can talk about it then." She slid off the barstool. "I should get dressed and go home. I have to think about all that's happened between us."

He held on to her hand. "Remember what I said about one-night stands. I don't do them."

Could she trust in those words when neither of them knew what the future held? She searched his eyes and saw he believed what he said. For now.

Somehow that only made matters more complicated. "I remember." She let go. "I'll see you tomorrow—at town hall."

Eight

The next day, Whit spent hours sifting through the rubble inside a town hall office, his buddy Aaron helping, but there was still no sign of Megan. This whole place was a lot like the mess of his life. His evening with Megan had been right on track. He'd been so certain they were making progress.

Then somehow things had derailed near the end for reasons that went a helluva lot deeper than his unused recycling bins. He still wasn't sure how they'd steered off course. It was as if they'd both self-destructed by discussing things guaranteed to drive a wedge between them.

And she still hadn't shown up for the town hall cleanup effort as they'd planned.

After their argument last night, they'd both thrown on their clothes and he'd driven her home, silence weighing between them in the dark evening streets. It was around one o'clock when they arrived, and he'd insisted on walking her to her door, where he gave her one more searing kiss. But she'd drawn the line there. She didn't want him to come inside where Abigail waited, babysitting Evie.

Work boots scuffling through dusty and crumbled brick, he took another garbage bag from Aaron. The job was too mindless to take his thoughts off Megan and what had happened last night. He trusted Abigail to keep her word to stay silent about their date until they— until Megan—was comfortable revealing the news to the town. But this had gone beyond Abigail. Given that they'd run into the Taylors at the restaurant last night, the whole town would know soon enough anyway.

As if there wasn't enough to keep everyone occupied. Like rebuilding the town.

The perimeter of town hall had been secured but there was no quick fix to all the destruction, especially inside in the few areas of the building still standing. Town hall had been almost totally destroyed. Only the clock tower had survived unscathed, but since the tornado, the time had been perpetually stopped at 4:14. The planning committee had decided to rebuild on the same location, but the cleanup effort would take time. They had to be careful sorting through the mess. Even in the digital age, there was so much damn paperwork.

Outside, Tyrone Taylor was barking orders to people as if it was his place to take charge. The guy seemed to think he ran the town. Luckily for them, Stella Daniels was there, and she had a quieter approach. A far more effective one at that. She let Tyrone bluster away and quietly followed up behind him giving direction and thanks.

Whit scanned the crowd outside the cracked window, over the parking lot, looking for Megan but she still hadn't shown. He hadn't heard from her since he'd driven her home. He'd called in the morning to offer her a ride over, but she hadn't answered. Was this a replay of the day the tornado hit when she'd shut him out after the kiss?

Being with Megan had been even more incredible than he'd expected. And his expectations had been mighty damn high.

He ground his teeth and focused on what he could fix. "Hey, Aaron, wanna help me lift this bookshelf and put it back against the wall?"

"Sure thing." Aaron squatted and braced both hands under one side of the walnut shelf. "Okay, Whit, on three, we lift. One. Two. Three."

Whit braced his feet, hefting and pushing alongside his friend until the bookcase was standing upright again. Files and thick hardbacks littered the floor where it had fallen. They were dry, but some had been soaked in the past, their pages curled and dirty brown. "We can put the undamaged items on the shelf again and stack the ruined stuff on the desk. The staff can decide what's crucial to keep."

"Sounds like a plan to me." Aaron scooped up two large volumes and paused, half standing, then pointed to the window. "Check out who just arrived—your shelter director lady friend."

Whit pivoted fast, then realized he'd given himself away with how damn eager he was just to see her. But he kept looking as she picked her way around a trash dumpster and a pile of broken boards. The sun streamed down on her fiery red hair, which was held back in a loose ponytail. Her jeans and shelter sweatshirt might as well have been lingerie now that he knew what was underneath. She could have been wearing a burlap sack and he would still want her.

Aaron stepped up beside him at the window. "So you and Megan Maguire have made peace with each other."

"We weren't at war." His denial came more out of habit than anything else; he was still focused on Megan, who was now talking to Lark Taylor, a local nurse passing out surgical masks for people to wear in the dusty cleanup.

"Like hell you two weren't constantly at odds," Aaron said. "You can't rewrite history, my friend. We all know how contentious things got over that land dispute when she wanted that site for the shelter. What I can't understand is how you got her to overlook how you buy up wetlands to build. She went ballistic last time it was mentioned."

As if Megan could hear their conversation—or feel the weight of Whit's stare—she turned, her eyes meeting his through the window with a snap of awareness as tangible as a crackle of static. He waved in acknowledgment, then turned back to cleanup detail. "We stay away from controversial topics these days."

Aaron didn't let him off the hook so easily. "Ah, you are seeing her. I always thought you had a thing for her under all that bickering."

Whit didn't like being transparent but he couldn't outright deny the obvious. "Why are you so all fired up to know about my personal life?"

"Oh, I get it. Who's trying to keep it quiet?" His friend elbowed his ribs like they were in freakin' high school. "You or her?"

Whit leveled a stare at his pal, who was grinning unrepentantly. "Do you want my help with this mess or not?"

"Somebody's touchy."

Touchy? That was one way to put it.

He was frustrated as hell that Megan appeared to have returned to their old ways of avoiding each other. Damn it, last night had been a game changer.

Ignoring each other simply was *not* an option anymore.

Megan said bye to Lark and went in search of Beth. She wasn't sure if she wanted advice or a buffer, but she just wasn't ready to face Whit yet, and she couldn't stand out here shuffling her feet indefinitely.

A voice whispered in the back of her mind, asking her why she'd bothered to come here if she really wanted to avoid him.

Truth be told, Megan wanted to rush into town hall and find Whit, to touch him or even just look at him. And the strength of that desire was the very reason she had to stay away until she found her footing again. No man should have the power to rock her with just a simple glance through a window.

She needed to get her head on straight fast because given the way people kept looking at her and whispering to each other, she suspected that Vera Taylor hadn't wasted any time in spreading the word about seeing her with Whit at the restaurant last night. Vera liked to pretend she was the expert on couples and marriage and everything else, but the senior Taylors were poster children for all the reasons marriage made people miserable.

But then on counterpoint, she saw the Holt family patriarch and matriarch bringing refreshments to the volunteers. Watching David and Gloria Holt lodged an ache in Megan's chest. Seeing them resurrected dreams she'd buried five years ago when Evie's father had walked out, leaving Megan pregnant and alone. The Holts were such a team, married for decades and still so deeply in love. Word around town was that David still brought his wife flowers every week. And Megan was glad Gloria had delivered her baked goods to boost the TCC's spirits after Megan's brownies. It was no contest: Gloria was renowned for her blue ribbon fruit pies.

Finally, she spotted Beth's blond head. Just last week, she and her friend had decided to create compost heaps for rubbish wherever possible. It wouldn't take care of all the recyclable debris, but it would help.

"Sorry I'm late," Megan said, kneeling beside a box of moldy computer paper that had been soaked by rain.

Beth swiped a wrist over her forehead, brushing back her hair. "The Holts are adorable, aren't they? Real soul mates."

"If you believe in that kind of thing, I guess." She tugged on the facemask Lark had given her and passed another to Beth.

Her friend pulled the elastic bands around her ears. "You don't believe in soul mates?"

"Years ago I did. I imagined finding him, getting married and starting a family." She looked up and shrugged, tossing a moldy ream of paper into the pile. "It's obvious things didn't work out that way. But I have my daughter. I love her and I don't regret having her for even a second."

But she couldn't deny life was tougher. Choices were more difficult.

"You don't mention Evie's father often. I've never wanted to pry, but it's tough not to feel judgmental of the guy when you're working so hard to do everything on your own."

"Thank God I found out what a selfish jackass he is before I married him." Still, the fallout for her daughter wasn't so clear-cut. "My only regret is the pain Evie will feel when she realizes he abandoned her. She doesn't ask about him now, but someday, she's going to want answers. Telling her he lives very far away won't be enough."

"There must have been some positives that drew you to him in the first place."

The oak tree branches rustled in the afternoon breeze as Megan tugged on work gloves. "I was blinded by his charm." She dug deeper into the rubble to move past bad thoughts. "He went out of his way to romance me with dinners and trips, gifts that seemed thoughtful as well as extravagant. It was like a Cinderella fantasy after the way I grew up."

"You're a big-hearted person who sees the best in people." Beth reached to give her arm a quick squeeze. "The only person I've ever heard you criticize is Whit."

"And people who abandon their animals." She scrunched her nose under the mask.

"Surely he ranks a level above them."

"Of course he does." Megan kicked through layers of dirt until she found more paper goods for the compost heap and some limp file folders that could go to the recycling pile. "I just don't want to repeat the past. I let myself believe in love at first sight. I was wrong. It takes time to get to know a person, to trust them."

"You've known Whit a long time." Beth loaded branches into a wheelbarrow for a bonfire later. "There's no issue with love at first sight here."

"I didn't say I love Whit Daltry." The L word. Her chest went tight. She tore off the mask to breathe deeper.

"I never said you did. You're the one who got defensive." Beth pulled off her surgical mask and guided Megan toward a park bench. "Where there's smoke, there's fire. And I'm seeing lots of smoke steaming off the two of you."

Megan sat down beside her friend, toying with the mask and snapping the elastic ear bands. "I've learned the hard way that attraction isn't enough. And I have Evie to consider now."

"You're not the only single mom to have been in this situation before, you know." Beth squeezed Megan's wrist. "There's happiness out there for you."

She looked out over the volunteers who'd turned up in droves, a town full of people who'd welcomed her into their fold. "I am happy with the life I've built."

"Fair enough. Still, there can be love and a partner for you. There can be a man who wants to be a father to that amazing daughter of yours. But you'll never know if you don't try."

Megan heard the logic in Beth's words, but accepting what she was saying was easier said than done. "I think we're all just feeling our mortality because of Craig and the others who died. We're all reacting out of grief and adrenaline, a need to affirm life."

"Or the tornado could have torn away your defenses and is making you face what you've been feeling all along."

"Okay, Dr. Freud." Megan bumped shoulders with her friend. "Do you think we can back off analyzing for a while?"

The crunch of footsteps on downed branches gave her only a second's warning. She looked over her shoulder and found Whit approaching. Denim and flannel never looked so good. She smoothed back the wisps of loose hair into her ponytail before she could stop herself.

Beth stood abruptly as Whit leaned against the bench. "I think I'm going to head inside and see if Drew needs help. Good to see you, Whit." She scooped up her mask and jogged toward the clock tower.

The sounds of traffic being routed around town hall mixed with birds chirping. The world was almost normal again.

Almost.

Whit gestured to the scarred bench. "Mind if I sit?"

"Of course I don't mind." That would be silly, and she didn't even one hundred percent understand the turmoil inside her.

"I noticed that your car's blocked in so I'm offering you a ride if it's not clear when you're ready to leave." His hard thigh pressed against hers. He pointed to where utility vehicles had recently arrived and boxed in her compact.

She eyed him suspiciously. "Did you have something to do with my car getting blocked in?"

"Why would I do that?" He palmed his chest in overplayed innocence.

"You're funny." And she was being prickly for no reason. She rested her hand on his knee.

He covered her gloved hand with his. "Just trying to keep you happy. When are we going to make it official and tell folks we're seeing each other? They all know anyway."

Panic made it tough to breathe even without the surgical mask. "I need time to figure out what to tell Evie."

"Well, people are already talking so you should figure that out soon before someone says something in front of her."

"I know, I know." She sagged back on the bench, accepting she'd reached a crossroad with Whit. Beth's words knocked around in her mind. Had Megan just been hiding from her feelings for Whit all along? She tugged off her work gloves. "We just need to be careful with Evie. She's fragile right now."

His thumb stroked the inside of her wrist. "Do you think she's going to be jealous of the time we spend together?"

"Just the opposite. She likes you." And that had a whole different set of potential landmines. "You're really good with her and that's scary too. Her heart's going to be broken when we—"

Irritation flickered through his dark brown eyes. "You're dooming this before we're even off the ground yet."

Was she? She reminded herself of the conversation with Beth. "I want to try. I just need time. Okay? Let's finish helping out and then you can drive me home if I'm still blocked in."

"Evie will be there. What will you tell her?"

She chose her words carefully. This was such a damn big step for her. She hoped he understood just how much. "That you're Mommy's very good friend." She tugged another surgical mask from her pocket and passed it to him. "Let's get back to work."

Whit hadn't had a role in blocking Megan's car but he was more than happy to ride the good luck that fate had dealt him. Now he had time alone with her to figure out why she was so spooked.

Not spooked enough to avoid him altogether though, because she could have asked Beth to bring her home. But she hadn't. Instead, Megan had worked beside him tirelessly at town hall, as if she didn't already carry a full load at the shelter, and agreed to a lift in his truck when they were done.

Sun dipping into the horizon, he pulled up and parked outside her cottage. "You fit right in here. You'd think you've lived here all your life."

"It's a welcoming town." She dusted off the knees of her jeans. She'd really dug in to help at town hall today.

She worked hard all the time and he couldn't help but want to make things easier for her.

Whit angled toward her, enjoying the way the setting sun brought out highlights in her hair. "Are you planning to stay in Royal?"

She blinked in surprise. "I don't have any plans to leave."

"That's not the same as planning to stay." He stroked a loose strand behind her ear.

"What about you?" she countered. "What if your business expands and there's a great opportunity to take things global or something?"

"No matter how large my company grows, Royal will always be where I've planted my roots," he said without hesitation. "This is the only place I've ever been able to call home. That's not something I'm willing to throw away."

She shook her head slowly. "Home is family, not a place. If I got an offer from another shelter for a significant pay raise, I would have to consider it, for Evie's future." She cupped his face. "Why are we discussing this now? It's a what-if that may not ever happen. Let's focus on this moment."

"Right, of course." His hand slid behind her head and he guided her to him and kissed her. It was just one of those simple kinds of kisses. But he was finding there were so many ways to savor this woman and they'd barely even begun.

She eased back and smiled. "I need to let Miss Abigail go. Do you want to come inside and have supper with Evie and me? It's nothing fancy. Just hot dogs, macaroni and cheese, maybe apple slices with peanut butter."

"Peanut butter?" He kissed her nose. "Now that's an offer I can't turn down." He stepped out of the truck.

She was trying, and that was more important than he wanted to admit to himself right now. He needed to keep his focus on the moment.

He followed Megan into her house, the warm space full of color and clutter reminding him again how his place didn't come close to feeling like a home. Tails wagging, Piper the Scottie and Cosmo the Border Collie raced across the room to sniff his shoes. The cats Truffles, Pixie and Scooter lounged on the back of the red sectional sofa in the same spots he'd seen them last time, as if they hadn't moved.

Evie jumped up from her Barbie house, wearing an angel costume with a halo and tiara, the two headpieces jumbled on top of each other. She ran to her mother and flung her spindly arms around Megan's waist. "Mommy, I missed you." She peeked up, a little bit of gold garland from the halo dropping over one eye. "Hello, Mr. Whit."

Miss Abigail scooped up her purse and sweater from the sofa beside one of the snoozing cats. "Well, hello, Whit. This is a surprise."

Megan kept her arms around her daughter. "My car was blocked in. Whit offered to bring me home."

"Right." Abigail winked. "Have fun, sweetie, and

call if you need me to babysit. Anytime." She patted Whit on the cheek. "Treat her well."

The door closed behind the retired legal secretary. He took heart in the fact that Megan hadn't even bothered denying Abigail's assumptions.

Megan eyed him nervously, then blurted, "Would you mind keeping an eye on Evie while I change and cook supper?"

He could tell what that cost her. "Thanks, of course I can." He looked over at Evie's toys. "We'll play—"

"Tea party," the little girl squealed, and ran to the coffee table.

Megan's laugh tickled his ears as she left the room.

Whit sat on the sofa. "How's Tallulah?"

Evie arranged a tiny pink plate in front of him and one on her side, then placed two more on the table and whistled for Piper and Cosmo, both of whom were apparently familiar with the game and sat beside her. "My mommy's taking very good care of your kitty cat."

He didn't bother mentioning it wasn't his cat. From the mischievous glint in Evie's eyes, he suspected she was exerting some subtle pressure of her own. "Your mother is a very good person."

The little girl nodded her head and placed a plastic slice of cake on each plate. "My mom helps doggies and kitties."

"That's her job as a grown-up."

"I wanna job." She placed a saucer under each teacup then poured from the toy pitcher that made a *glub, glub, glub* sound.

"Your job is to learn your letters, to eat your vegetables and play."

"We are playing. Is the tea good?"

"Oh ...." He pretended to sip from the cup that was smaller than a shot glass. "Very good."

She fished around in her pocket and pulled out two dollar bills and a quarter. "Mommy gave me this to buy treats when I go back to school. But I'm buying shoes for the kids that lost their shoes in the tora-na-do."

Whit set the tiny cup down carefully, his heart squeezing inside his chest at the weight this little girl was carrying on those small shoulders. Megan's words about having to be cautious for her daughter's sake rumbled around inside him.

"Kiddo, I think that's a very good idea."

She hung her head and poured more pretend refills. He couldn't stop thinking about that tiara and those costumes she always wore. He felt so damn helpless.

He'd been doing some nosing around on the internet about kids and trauma and had stumbled on an article about therapy dogs being used at schools. He wondered if he should run that idea by Megan now rather than later. Or would she think he was intruding?

As he looked into Evie's green eyes that carried far too many burdens and fears for one so young, he could understand Megan's need to protect her daughter.

Evie's nose scrunched, making her look so much like a mini-Megan. "I can't drive. And if I tell my mommy what I wanna do it will ruin the surprise."

"Are you asking for my help to surprise your mother?"

"Would you?" Her eyes went wide and hopeful. "Please?"

"Can do. In fact, I have an idea." He held out his hand. "If you pass me your iPad we can order shoes online now. Together we can buy lots of shoes."

"You're gonna buy some too? I like that." She sprinted to the sofa and jumped up beside him.

Was she going to hug him? He braced himself.

She rocked back on her heels, her forehead furrowed and worried. "I had two more coins but I bought a sucker. My mommy wouldn't have bought herself a sucker. I should have gotten somethin' for her instead."

He tugged one of her crooked pigtails. "Maybe we could get something for your mommy while we buy those shoes."

"Like flowers or candy. Mommy likes chocolate—and recycling." She grabbed her iPad off the end table.

He reached for the tablet. "Chocolate and a new recycling bin for your mom."

"Yay!" She wrapped her arms around his neck and squeezed tight. "You're a good boy, Mr. Whit."

God, the little minx was well on her way to wrapping him around her little finger.

On her way?

Too late.

The sense of being watched drew his gaze across the room. Megan stood in the archway between the living room and dining area, holding Tallulah in her arms. Her green eyes glinted with tears. She'd told him she was wary and she had every reason to be given her past. He needed to prove to her he could change, that he was a man worthy of a chance. He didn't know where they were going yet, but he damn well knew he couldn't walk away without digging deeper. Trying harder.

He patted Evie's back and looked at her mom. "Megan, I have an important question to ask."

She blinked in surprise while Evie spun around in her angel dress, humming a tune from the show that had just been on TV.

Megan sniffed and nodded. "Okay. What is it?"

"Can I take my cat home today or do I need to fill out an adoption application at the shelter when you open on Monday?"

Nine

Megan was so stunned by Whit's request to adopt Tallulah, she almost dropped the cat. She adjusted her hold on the calico and stepped closer to the man who continued to turn her world upside down. "Excuse me? You want to do what?"

"You said Tallulah's better now." He stepped closer to stroke the cat, his knuckles grazing Megan's breasts. "So I thought I could take her home, like you asked me."

She eyed him suspiciously. "Are you doing this just to impress me? Because if so, that's the wrong reason to adopt an animal. A pet is a lifelong commitment. If we…break up," the words lodged in her throat for an instant, "you still need to be committed to keeping and loving Tallulah."

He nodded solemnly. "I understand that. We may disagree on a lot of things, but I would never walk out on a commitment. That's why I didn't keep her the first day. I wasn't sure I could care for her the way she deserves. I'm certain now that I can."

Was he talking in some kind of code? Adding layers to his words? Talk of the future made her jittery when she was barely hanging on in the present. "Okay then. When would you like to take Tallulah?"

"I'll need to get supplies for her." He scratched his head. "I'll stop by the pet store on my way home. They'll let me bring her inside, right? I know I'm not supposed to leave an animal in the car."

She stifled a smile. He really was trying. "How about this, Whit? Let me gather some supplies to get you through the night and then you can shop at your leisure tomorrow for the things she'll need. I've got a flyer on file I can email you. We give it to all adopters."

"Thanks. I appreciate that." He leaned in and whispered in her ear, the warm rumble of his voice so close that it incited a nice kind of shiver. "Will Evie be upset to see Tallulah go?"

Megan rested a hand on her daughter's hair, no easy feat as she maneuvered around the halo and tiara. "She understands Tallulah isn't ours. Don't you, sweetie?"

Evie nodded. "Me and Mommy are rescuers. We find good homes for kitties and puppies. Tallulah is Mr. Whit's cat. I'll go get her bed and stuff." She looked up at Whit. "You won't forget about the shoes?"

He knelt down to look Evie in the eyes. "I won't forget. I promise." He tugged a pigtail. "And I always keep my promises."

"Good deal. Thanks." Evie kissed him on the cheek then sprinted to the laundry room where the kitty supplies were kept.

Megan drew in a shaky breath. Seeing flashes of

how good life could be with Whit around was tougher than she thought.

He looked at the tiny pink cup in his hand and shrugged sheepishly before setting it down on the coffee table. "About Tallulah—you're not going to call me out on all the BS reasons I gave you about why I couldn't keep a cat in the first place?"

She had questions, but not so much about the cat and certainly not right now with Evie a room away. "I don't believe in saying 'I told you so.'"

"Good to know. I hope there's a lot of information on that list. I've never taken care of an animal on my own before." His eyebrows pinched together and he stuffed his hands in his pockets as if having second thoughts. "I wouldn't want to screw this up."

"I'll be happy to give you our adoption briefing." She held back a smile since she didn't want to hurt his feelings. She truly was touched by his concern. If only more people were this careful. "The most important thing for her now is to get lots of TLC while she bonds with you. So, are you cool with letting her sleep in your lap while you watch ball games?"

"I think I can handle that." He rocked back on his boot heels.

"Sounds good." She rubbed her cheek against Tallulah's dark furry head before passing over the cat. "Let me go dig up an extra scratching post for her to use at your house."

"Would you like to come to dinner at my house tomorrow night?" Whit secured the cat in one arm so he could scratch her under the neck with his other hand. "You can give me that briefing and check on Tallulah."

He was asking her to take a big step. Another meal together. Spending time in his home and in his life. But no matter how nervous those ideas made her—and they still did—she couldn't deny the warm hopefulness that sparked to life insider her either.

Despite the risk, she wanted to try.

The next evening, Whit stepped into his house with Megan and it felt so damn right to have her here it shook the ground under him. She was becoming more and more a part of his life with each day that passed.

Last night's hot dogs with mac and cheese had tasted a helluva lot better than any of his catered dinners. But then he knew that was due to the people at the table with him. Then he'd taken his cat home. And holy hell, it still surprised him that he'd decided to get a pet. Except it felt right. Still did. His house didn't feel so damn empty with the cat checking out his furniture and deciding which places were worthy of her. Tallulah had sniffed out every corner and seemed to approve of his leather ottoman in the living room. His bed had gotten cat props too; Tallulah had curled up on the pillow next to his head as if she'd been sleeping at his place every night.

He'd actually had a good time using his lunch break to pick up cat gear and drop it off at his house. The calico had leaped off the ottoman in full attack mode when he tossed her a feather squeak toy and before he knew it, he'd spent an extra twenty minutes watching her chase a catnip ball and wrestle a fur mouse.

But by the time dinner rolled around he'd been damn near starving. He and Megan had decided to have supper at her house again, then her neighbor would watch Evie after the child went to sleep.

He'd asked Megan to come to his house for dessert.

He hadn't wanted to leave his cat alone any longer. Megan's smile told him he'd said the right thing.

She kicked off her shoes and lined them up by the door. "I can't believe you really ordered all those shoes with Evie."

"She's got her mother's entrepreneurial spirit. You've done a good job with her." He slipped an arm around her waist.

"Motherhood is the most important job I've ever had."

"Your commitment shows." His parents had vowed they loved him but they hadn't been big on teaching moral responsibility.

"How's Tallulah?"

"Come say hello to her and see for yourself." He guided her to his study where he'd closed Tallulah in for the evening. The space had a sunroom too, where he'd set up her litter box and food. "I put her in here for the day while she gets acclimated. I thought she would enjoy the sunshine through all the windows. I did some reading on the internet last night on cat care."

He pushed open the double mahogany doors and Megan gasped. She pointed at the six-foot scratching post he'd bought, complete with different levels and cubbies for climbing and snoozing.

"Oh, my God, Whit." She walked to the carpeted and tiered post he'd parked between two leather wingback chairs and reached into a cubby to pet Tallulah. "You obviously went shopping too."

He hefted his cat out and leaned back on the dark wood desk, scratching Tallulah's ears the way she liked. "I just stopped by the pet store on my lunch break and picked up a few essentials."

"A scratching post the size of an oak tree is an essential?"

"It looked cool? What can I say?" He was planning to talk to his contractor buddy Aaron about ordering mini solarium windows for Tallulah to hang out in.

"I wish all our animals could land this well." She dusted cat hair off his suit jacket.

"She needs something to keep her occupied while I'm at work." Tallulah purred like a freight train in his ear. "And I read online that if I want to save my furniture from her claws, she has to have an appropriate outlet for scratching at home."

Megan had perched on the arm of a wingback. The warmth in her eyes told him he was saying all the right things.

"I also read—" He stopped when the realization hit him. "You already know all of this."

"But it's nice hearing you're excited about having her. Not just in your house but in your life."

And he had to admit, it surprised him too. "I always thought I would be a dog person."

"It doesn't make you any less macho."

"Thanks. I'm not concerned with proving my masculinity."

"Hmm, I have to admit, your confidence about being tender with the cat is very appealing." She trailed a lone finger down his arm in a touch as enticing as any full-on stroke. "If you want a dog though, I'm more than happy to help you find the perfect one for your lifestyle."

One step at a time. "Tallulah needs time to adjust to her new home first."

"Spoken like a natural pet owner. That's really nice to hear." She flicked a cat toy dangling from one of the levels of the scratching post. "Although if you bought Tallulah this, I wonder what you would buy for a dog."

His mind churned with possibilities, like one of those agility courses the Cattleman's Club was working on for the shelter. "I bought one of those climbing trees for Safe Haven too."

"Truly?" she squealed, giving him an enthusiastic kiss with the cat squirming between them. "You do know me better than I gave you credit for."

He tucked Tallulah back into one of the cubbies attached to the climbing post. "You'll even find bottles and paper in the recycling. Will that get me another kiss?"

She laughed and looped her arms around his neck, kissing him again, nothing standing between them now but too many clothes. Her mouth on his felt familiar and new all at once. He knew so much about her, yet there was still so much more of her to explore. And he had a plan in mind for the next few hours to discover more about what pleased her.

Ending the kiss, he angled away while unfastening the clasp holding back her hair. "I'm learning fast that the way to your heart is less traditional than a bouquet of flowers."

She shook her hair free in a silky, wavy cloud around her shoulders and his hands. "Oh, I should share some of the catnip you gave me with Tallulah."

"I have some of my own." He slid an arm around her waist. All day, he'd been fantasizing about showing her his favorite part of the house. "Come with me. There's a part of my home you haven't seen yet."

She eyed him curiously. "I'm intrigued. Lead on."

He steered her into the hall again, toward the back of the house. "This way."

She tucked herself against his side. "Thank you again for helping Evie with the shoe donation drive."

"We shopped for some new video games too."

She stiffened and her footsteps slowed. "I have to approve all of her new games."

"Uh, sure," he said, wishing he'd thought of that himself. But he didn't have nieces or nephews. "Kids are new territory to me too, like the pets. Except I can't exactly shut a kid in a room with a climbing tree and a bowl of food."

"Not unless you want to end up in jail," she said with a laugh in her voice that let him know she wasn't angry with him. "I know you meant well. I just need for you to consult me on anything having to do with Evie."

"Sure, of course." He pushed open the back door into his landscaped yard. "For what it's worth, they were all labeled for her age group and I know the video game developer."

Walking beside him along the flagstone path, she glanced up at him, a hint of frustration in her eyes. "Not all video games are educational."

"You're right, and I do hear you." He guided her toward the left, under an ivy-covered arch. That led to a cluster of trees in the very back of his property. "I'll be more careful about consulting you when it comes to anything with Evie."

"I'm sorry for being prickly." She slid her arm under his suit coat and around his waist. "This is new territory for me too."

"You haven't dated anyone since you had Evie?" Where the hell had that question come from and why was her answer so important?

"In case you haven't noticed, there isn't much spare time in my life between my job and my daughter."

"No one at all?" He stopped at the concrete steps leading into his greenhouse, tucked away in the privacy of a circle of trees.

She took his lapels in her hands. "You're my first venture back into dating since Evie was born."

"I don't want to be your rebound guy." And he meant that. He'd already accepted that he wanted more than a short-term affair with her.

"It's been nearly five years since Evie's biological father walked out of our lives. I'm far past the rebound zone, don't you think?"

Five years? The bastard had walked out before Evie was even born? Whit had heard the jerk wasn't a part of Megan's life, but this was even worse than he'd thought. He let that information roll over him again now that he had a better feel for how much commitment and effort it took to raise a child. He knew logically, of course. But his admiration for how hard Megan had worked grew even more. For that matter, he understood a little better just how tough it must have been for her to let go of that control.

She smoothed his lapels back in place and turned to the greenhouse. "What do we have here?"

He thought about pushing the discussion further, then reconsidered. Better to take his time so he didn't spook her. And luckily for both of them, taking their time had deliciously sensual implications tonight. "Through this door, we have our dessert."

More than a little intrigued, Megan opened the greenhouse door and peered inside the dimly lit building. Warmth and humidity wafted out, carrying a verdant scent of lush life. She stepped inside, expecting some fancy garden typical of the rich and famous. But instead, she found a more practical space, filled with tomato plants and tiered racks of marked herbs, potted trees lining the center of the aisle to give room for their branches to spread. Curiosity drew her in deeper and deeper.

She reached up to tap lemons, limes and even an orange. "This is incredible."

"Glad you like it. The catnip is a recent addition, over that way." He pointed toward the back right corner.

She came around a tree and found a two-seat wrought-iron table set up with plates, water glasses and in the center…a fondue pot? Whit reached past her to turn up the flame.

"Chocolate sauce?" she asked.

"There's a pear tree that's producing, thanks to the climate control in here. When Evie told me you like chocolate, it all came together." He plucked a pear from a branch. "Why the suspicious look?"

"I'm trying to figure out why you're going to so much trouble to win me over?"

"You're worth it." He set the pear on a stone pottery plate and sliced through it with a paring knife.

"I'm appreciative, but why me when you could expend far less effort for any number of women around here?"

"I don't want them." He swirled the piece of fruit through the chocolate. "Just you." He offered her the dripping slice.

She bit into the end, the sweet fresh pear and gooey chocolate sending her taste buds into a flavor orgasm. She sank into the chair. "Okay, totally amazing," she said, reaching for another slice. "And I'm totally surprised."

"How so?" he sat across from her, their knees bumping under the small table.

"Well," she said, swirling the slice in the chocolate and stroking her toes along his ankle. "I wouldn't have expected you to be so…thrifty."

"I think I was just insulted."

"You're wealthy. Filthy-rich wealthy."

He resisted the impulse to get defensive and forced himself to answer logically. "That doesn't mean I'm wasteful. I've worked damn hard to get to where I am, but there are plenty of people who work just as hard for a lot less, like my mom did. I recognize that there was luck that partnered up with my work ethic."

"Well, your gardener has really outdone himself here." She picked up one of the heavy silver spoons laid out in the fondue display and swirled it through the sauce.

"The hits just keep coming." He laughed. "I don't have a gardener." He popped a slice of fruit in his mouth.

She dropped the spoon in surprise. "You tend all of this yourself?"

Her gaze roamed the neat rows of tomato plants again. The bins of gardening tools and the bags full of potting soil tucked under the plant shelves affirmed that all this work had been done right here. He hadn't just grabbed a bunch of plants from a nursery to decorate his greenhouse. What a lot of work. And patience. She remembered all the times she'd mentally accused him of not caring about the environment and felt a pang of guilt.

"Having money doesn't mean I should stop taking care of things myself." He held up a hand. "The catering service is a survival thing. I may have a green thumb, but my skills in the kitchen suck. It was less expensive to hire out than to continue throwing away food. Makes economic sense."

"But you don't have to pinch pennies." So much about this man was different than what she'd assumed for the past three years. She hadn't expected him to be so generous and thoughtful, and now to find this "green" side to him? Her head was reeling.

"I grew up in a feast-or-famine kind of childhood. When my dad had a job, we lived well, really well." He tugged an orange from a low-hanging branch and began peeling the ripe fruit. "And then he inevitably got fired and we skipped town, chasing a fresh start. At one point we lived in an RV for about eight months. Even at ten years old, I knew if we'd lived more frugally at the place prior, we would have had enough to carry us through the lean times."

Her heart ached for that little boy with so much upheaval in his life. "How is it that's never shown up in your official bio—or at least the grapevine gossip?"

"My life story is no one's business," he said with the brash confidence she'd seen so often in the past.

Now she saw that confidence with new eyes, saw the man who'd taken adversity and let it drive him to success. She couldn't help but respect that.

She scooped the peels into her hand. "A thrifty woman like myself would recycle this into potpourri."

"Hmm, I'm beginning to see merits in your recycling drive." He brought an orange slice to her mouth.

She held it in her teeth, tugging his tie until he leaned across the table to share the bite with her. The fruit burst in her mouth just as their lips met. His eyes held hers as they both ate and watched each other. He kissed a dribble of juice off her chin.

She loosened his tie. "You're a naughty man."

"Lady, I haven't even gotten started yet." He sank back in his seat again, yanking his tie the rest of the way off.

The night outside and the steamed windows inside provided more than enough privacy. It also helped that the greenhouse was tucked away in a cluster of pine trees. They were alone. Truly alone.

Megan's body came alive with anticipation and possibility.

This humid greenhouse was like a tropical retreat in the middle of their everyday small town. What a gift to have such a lush hideaway from the world nestled right here in Whit's backyard.

Standing, he draped his tie over a branch and shrugged out of his coat. She couldn't look away, wondering how far he would go. He flung his coat over the back of his chair and the swoosh of it landing snapped something inside her.

Without taking her eyes off him, she tugged her polo shirt from work over her head. His eyes widened in appreciation and then she lost track of who got undressed faster. She just knew somehow her bra had landed alongside his tie on the orange tree.

She would never again be able to eat an orange without tingling all over.

Whit reached behind a stack of bags full of soil and pulled out a quilt. He'd clearly thought this through and prepared. He shook it on the ground beside the table and took her hand in his. She stepped into his arms and savored the feel of masculine skin against her bare flesh. The rasp of bristle and muscle. A hum of pleasure buzzed through her, melting her as he lowered her onto the blanket.

She trailed her fingers along his shoulders. "This is the most perfect night. You're an ingenious man."

"You inspire me." He pulled an orange slice from the table and held the piece of fruit over her stomach with slow deliberation.

Delicious anticipation shivered through her a second before he squeezed the juice onto her one sweetly torturous drip a time.

"Whit," she gasped just as he dipped his head to sip away each drop.

He glanced up the length of her. "Should I stop?" he asked, kissing his way upward.

Her elbows gave way and she sank back. He snagged the rest of the orange from the iron table and drizzled more juice along one breast, his mouth soon following. She arched up into his caress and gave her hands free rein to enjoy this intriguing, sexy man who'd found his way into her life.

She let herself be swept away in sensations and desire. He was an intuitive lover, lingering when she sighed, in tune to the cues of her least sound or movement. His mouth skimmed lower and lower still until her knees parted and...yes...he sipped and licked, nuzzling at the bundle of nerves drawing tighter. He coaxed her pleasure closer and closer to the edge of completion.

For so long she'd been alone, and while she'd told herself she didn't need more in her life, right now she knew that was a lie. She needed this. This man.

The thought sent a bolt of ecstasy through her. Her fingers gripped his shoulders and dug in to let him know just how much she needed him to stay with her for every wave of pleasure. And he did, as each wave rippled through her.

Her arms fell to her sides as she breathed in ragged

gasps, her mind still in a fog. But even in her afterglow haze, need already built inside her again.

Soon, the goal of having Whit reach those heights with her had her reaching for another orange.

Ten

Tucking Megan to his side, Whit trailed his fingers up and down her arm, making the most of their last minutes together tonight. He understood she had to be home soon to relieve the sitter, but he wanted more time with Megan. He'd never dated a single mother before.

More importantly, he'd never been with anyone who captivated him the way she did, dressed or undressed. Although right now he was enjoying the hell out of the undressed Megan. Her silky hair teased along his arm in a fan of red. He'd explored every inch of her soft, pale skin.

He kissed a smudge of chocolate off her nose. Chocolate and oranges would long be his favorite flavors. He'd discovered a lot about her this evening, and intended to make the most of the time they had left before she sent the sitter home at midnight. "Penny for your thoughts."

Megan rubbed her foot along his calf. "Why do you

have a greenhouse full of fruits and vegetables if you order your food catered?"

He propped up on one elbow and gestured at the plants on either side. "There's a theme here, if you look closer," he said, surprised at her question but glad to have a chance to extend the evening. "Fresh fruits and vegetables for a salad or salsa. I may not be able to cook, but I can chop. Plus, free tomatoes are a great way to make friends with your neighbors."

"Just being neighborly?" she pressed. "I think there's more to your answer than that."

"Believe it or not, I like roots." If he wanted more from her, he would need to give more of himself. "I moved around so much as a kid, this place reminds me I'm here to stay."

One of those happy-sad smiles played on her lips, which were still plump from kissing. "You break my heart sometimes."

"How so?" He tensed. He didn't want her pity. Part of him wanted to pull back, but that would mean letting her go. And with her hands sketching lazy circles all over him, staying put seemed a better option.

"With those images of you as a kid longing for a home." One of her hands slid up to cradle his face.

"You're a nurturer." He kissed her palm.

"You're a builder and tender too, you know." She gestured to the greenhouse. "You just have to learn to see that in yourself."

Okay, enough of this kind of talk. It was one thing to share parts of their past. It was another altogether to submit to a cranial root canal. "This conversation is getting entirely too serious."

"Then why did you bring me out here and show me this part of your life?"

Why had he? Every time he got close to that answer, he mentally flinched away as if he were getting too close to a flame. He settled on the easy answer. "Because I had been fantasizing about making love to you out here, about tasting the fruit on your skin."

She paused and he could see in her eyes she wasn't buying into his dismissal of her assessment. Then she nodded as if conceding to give him space on the issue and arched up to nibble his bottom lip. "You taste mighty delicious yourself."

"I've developed a new appreciation for fondue."

She flicked her tongue along his chin before pressing her mouth to his collar bone, then settling back into his arms. "I appreciate the dessert and the thought that went into arranging such an amazing evening, and all you've done for Evie and for the shelter as well."

"I would like to pamper you every day if you would let me." He massaged along one of her narrow shoulders, then down her back, skimming along her curves and around her hip where he knew her tattoo trailed across her skin. He could get so used to this. "The way I see it, you don't get much time to relax between work and being a mom."

"I love my daughter and my job. That's always been enough." Yet as she said that, her eyes fluttered closed and she melted against him.

"That doesn't mean you can't have recreation."

"Is that what you are?" She tipped her face to look at him. "My recreation?"

"I'm just trying to be a help. We all need a break every now and again, right?" He couldn't hold back the burning question any longer. "Where does Evie's father live?"

Her body went rigid under his touch and she rolled

away, sitting up and gathering her clothes. "Not here. He's not a part of her life and chances are he never will be."

"But he knows about her."

"Of course," she answered indignantly, tugging on her panties, then her bra. "I would never keep that a secret. The minute he found out, he cut ties and ran."

The bastard. Whit wanted to find the guy and pummel him for the pain he'd caused Megan and her amazing daughter.

"He doesn't pay child support, does he?" Whit tugged on his suit pants.

She shrugged and pulled on her shirt. "He snowed me. Completely. Last I heard he was in the Keys heading for the Bahamas."

"Hey." Whit cradled her face in his hands. "It's not your fault he's a loser. He missed out on an amazing family." Whit's own father may not have been much of a provider but at least he'd been there.

"My fault or not," she gripped his wrists and stared straight into his eyes, "Evie will grow up knowing her father didn't want her and there's nothing I can do to change that."

She pulled away to slip on her khakis, her rigid back telling him she was holding on by a thread while rebuilding defenses he'd apparently blasted with one simple question.

Whit could see he didn't just need to be careful for Evie's sake. Megan was every bit as wounded by the past as her daughter. She just didn't wear the costumes.

And now he prayed like hell his idea to help with Evie wouldn't backfire.

"What's the matter with you?"

Beth's question cut through Megan's fog as she

picked at her lunch salad the next day. Evie had taken her lunch box and joined Miss Abigail at the front desk.

Megan sagged back in her office chair, the squeak in the old seat mixing with the muffled sound of a couple of dogs in the play yard. The kennel runs were quieter today than usual thanks to some new calming CDs brought in by one of the volunteers. If only that music could help calm her spinning thoughts.

Even the salad reminded her of Whit's greenhouse and how hard he was trying on her behalf. Yet she couldn't shake the jittery feeling that things would fall apart, and the closer she let herself get to him, the worse the breakup would hurt.

Tossing aside her fork, Megan reached for her water instead, staring at the photo on her desk of beach day in Galveston when Evie was two. She'd scrimped and saved for that trip, convinced she needed to start making special memories with her toddler. "I'm just pre-occupied."

"Because of Whit?" Beth unpacked her navy blue lunch sack that could have passed for a purse. "How did it go last night?"

"Did you know he has this massive greenhouse where he grows fresh fruits and veggies?"

Beth's eyebrows shot up. "No, I didn't know. And you think he would have told me since I have an organic farm. We could have shared clippings—" She stopped. "Wait. This is about you."

Megan tapped the catnip plant. "He brought this for the kitties. And he's rolling out all the stops romancing me and I have to admit, he seems so sincere."

"Seems?" Beth absently thumbed her engagement ring, spinning it around on her finger.

Admitting her insecurities, even to her close friend,

was tough for Megan. But God, if she didn't work through this and she blew it with Whit without even trying… "I don't trust my instincts when it comes to men. And he's known for being ruthless."

"In the work world," Beth pointed out. "That's different."

"Is it?"

"He adores Evie. He's not faking that. Evie would sense that a mile off." The natural blonde beauty smiled. "Remember that banker guy who pretended to be in the market for a dog so he could hit on you about six months ago? Evie made a point of getting peanut butter and jelly on his ties so you would see him freak out over kid germs."

Megan laughed at the memory. "She's a great little bodyguard." But even that thought was sobering in light of her daughter's fears since the storm. "Can I afford to let Evie grow any more attached to Whit when I'm not sure where the relationship is headed?"

"Unless you intend to spend your life alone, at some point you have to trust again," Beth said with undeniable reason.

"I could wait until Evie's eighteen." Except after last night's sex, fourteen years felt like an eternity.

Her friend stayed diplomatically silent and bit into an apple.

The noise level in the lobby grew. New voices and a squeal from Evie drew Megan's attention away from her pity party, thank heaven, because talking was just making her feel worse today.

She rolled back her chair and stood. "Beth, I should see what's going on out there."

She stepped into the lobby, her eyes drawn immediately to Whit. What was he doing here in the middle of

the workday? Then she noticed Evie petting a golden retriever. Megan's instincts went on alert at the thought of
her daughter petting a possible stray with an unknown
vaccination history. Except then she saw the dog was
wearing a "service dog" vest. What did all of this have
to do with Whit's arrival?

He turned to face her—and he wasn't alone. A
sleekly pretty woman with dark hair stood at his side.
Jealousy nipped. Hard.

Megan smiled tightly and knelt beside her daughter.
"Sweetie, that vest means this is a working dog. We
don't touch dogs with this special vest."

Her daughter—dressed as a Ninja Turtle today—
grinned. "I asked. She said it was okay and Mr. Whit
said it was okay. He brought the dog for my preschool
class."

Megan glanced up at him, confused. "What's going
on?"

Whit set his Stetson on the receptionist's desk. "I
talked to the day-care director about bringing in a therapy dog for the kids given all they went through with the
tornado. The local school psychologist recommended
this group in Dallas and contacted the other parents
to clear it. I said I would check with you to save her a
call, and well, here we are. The dog handler said she's
even interested in evaluating the dogs here for training."

Introductions were made in a blur and the next thing
she knew her wonderfully intuitive friend Beth was offering to walk the dog handler—Zoe Baker—back to
the play yard.

Megan's head was spinning in surprise. Of course
it was a great idea, but having someone take over decisions for her daughter so totally felt…alien. But there
wasn't much she could say since he'd gone straight to

the school and she didn't want to cause a scene that would upset Evie.

Still, she ducked her head and said, "Could we talk for a minute. Alone."

Miss Abigail knelt beside Evie. "Would you like to come with me to play with the cats? Your mom told me a new litter of kittens was just brought in."

Evie skipped alongside Abigail with a new spring in her step Megan hadn't seen in a month.

Whit swept his hat off the desk and followed Megan to her office. "I meant this to be a surprise, to show you I care about you and Evie, that I respect your work with animals."

"Okay," she said cautiously, "but why not consult me? This is my child. And animals are my area of expertise."

He scratched his head, wincing. "You're right. I should have. I was thinking about Evie's fear of going back to school and then I saw this article about the group in Dallas and I got caught up in the moment wanting to surprise you. Like with the catnip."

"This is a much bigger deal than catnip."

She couldn't help but feel defensive. "I don't want to push her before she's ready."

"Hey," he took her shoulders in his hands, "I'm not questioning your parenting. Thinking of her made me wonder the other kids. So I spoke with some of the dads at the Cattleman's Club and asked if their kids were having trouble this past month. This is for all of them. Not just Evie."

"You talked to the other parents…about their children?" Her lips went tight, anger nipping all over again.

But she couldn't help but remember how carefully he'd studied the instructions for taking care of Tallulah. Thinking about that kind of thoughtfulness applied to her daughter touched her. "Which other children?"

"Sheriff Battle said every time his son hears a train he thinks the tornado's coming back." He turned his hat around and around in his hands. "When I saw that article about therapy dogs going into nursing homes and schools, it got me thinking. Ms. Baker uses shelter dogs, which I knew would be appealing to you. I even learned there's a difference between service dogs, therapy dogs and emotional support dogs. Anyhow, what do you think? Aside from the fact I've been pushy, when I should have consulted you."

"I actually think that's a great idea. I'm kicking myself for not thinking of it." She sagged back against the edge of her desk. "You sure acted on this quickly."

"You've had your hands full. And I figured why wait. The day-care staff is expecting us this afternoon. I'm hoping Evie will be excited to take the dog to show off to her friends."

"I still wish you'd consulted me. We talked about this yesterday."

He flinched. "Guilty as charged and I truly am sorry. It seemed like a good surprise in my head. Would you have said no if I told you?"

Sighing, she conceded, "Of course not."

But that wasn't the point.

He scratched the back of his neck. "My buddies thought it was funny as hell that I was asking about kid stuff so word got around fast. The press is involved now too, planning to cover it. I figured it would be a good chance to talk about shelter dogs and how full your rescue is."

And he'd done all this for her when she'd given so little of herself in return. She'd just held back and questioned and worried. "You're really going all out to win me over."

"Busted." He slid his arms around her waist. "I want to be with you."

She toyed with his tie and knew he wouldn't give a damn if Evie painted it with jelly. "I'm still the same pain-in-the-butt person who's fighting with you over what parts of Royal you choose to develop."

"And I'm still the same guy who's going to argue there's a way around things."

"We're going to argue," she said with certainty.

"At least you'll be talking to me rather than ignoring me."

"Hey," she tugged his tie, "you ignored me too."

He tugged her loose ponytail in return. "I gave you space when it looked like you were going to cause a scene."

Before she could launch a retort, he kissed her silent, and this man knew how to kiss. Her arms slid around his neck and she knew without question he was a good man who would try like hell for her.

Which was going to make this hurt so much worse if it didn't work out.

Whit was mighty damn pleased with how the therapy dog issue had shaken down.

He stood in the back of the Little Tots Daycare classroom with Megan while all the kids sat in a circle on a rug. The town had done an amazing job at getting the facility functional quickly so the children could get back into a regular routine, the kind of reassurance they needed after such a frightening event.

Their teacher was reading them a book about tornadoes. The golden retriever was calm, but alert, carefully moving from child to child as if knowing which one was most in need of comfort, whether with a simple touch of his paw or resting his head on a knee, or just letting a dozen little hands burrow in his fur.

As the teacher closed the book, she looked up at her students. "What do you think about the story we just read?"

Beside Evie, a little girl with glasses admitted, "I was scared."

"Not me," said the boy in tiny cowboy boots sitting on the other side of Evie.

"Yes, you were," the girl with glasses retorted. "You were crying. I saw you wipe boogers on your sleeve."

Evie raised her hand until the teacher called on her. "I was scared," Evie said. "I told my mom I held Caitlyn's hand 'cause she was scared. But it was really me. I was the fraidy cat."

The retriever belly crawled over to Evie and rested his head on her leg. Evie rubbed the dog's ears, her eyes wide and watery.

The teacher leaned forward in her rocking chair. "We were all afraid that day. That's why we have the drills. So we know what to do in an emergency."

Evie kept stroking the dog and talking. "What if another tora-na-do comes to our school? What if it hurts Mommy's car again, 'cept it gets Mommy too?"

Megan started to move forward, but Whit rested a hand on her arm. It was hard as hell for him to hear the little imp's fears too, but she was talking. Thank God, she was talking. Megan's hand slid into his and held on.

The teacher angled forward, giving all the right grown-up answers that Evie took in with wide eyes, both her hands buried in the dog's fur.

Evie kept talking, but she smiled periodically. Something that didn't happen often.

Megan's chin trembled. "This is so incredible to watch," she whispered.

"I wouldn't have even thought twice about the article if not for you." He ducked his head to keep their voices low so as not to disturb the class. "You do a good job educating about your work at the shelter."

"Thank you." Her cheeks flushed a pretty pink.

"I knew about service dogs for the disabled and I'd heard there were studies showing that owning a pet lowers blood pressure." He scanned the group of little ones up front with the dog. "But this is a whole new world." In more ways than one.

"I think of it all as the balance of nature."

"That makes sense."

"Taking care of our resources." She looked up at him pointedly.

"Hey, I've started recycling water bottles and cans because of you."

She clapped a hand to her chest. "Be still my heart."

"Are you making fun of me?" He raised an eyebrow. "I happen to think that was a very romantic gesture on my part."

"It is sweet. But you would be wise to remember, sometimes I don't have much of a sense of humor when it comes to things like this. You just caught me on a good day."

"Fair enough." He had a feeling there was a lot more to learn about Megan before he could banish the wary look that still lurked in her green eyes. "I will keep that in mind."

He glanced at his watch, and damn, he was running late. When he woke up this morning, he hadn't thought there was a chance in hell he could get through the day of Craig's memorial service without a bottle by his side. But Megan and Evie had given him a welcome distraction. They were good for him.

"Do you have a meeting?" she asked.

"I need to go home to change and get some things together for Craig's memorial service."

She pressed a trembling hand to her mouth. "Oh God, Whit, I'm so sorry. How selfish of me not to think about how difficult today is for you." She touched his shoulder lightly. "What can I do?"

"This helped keep my mind off things."

"I'll meet you at the church."

"You don't have to—"

"I want to be there for you."

He brushed his hand along her back, which was as much contact as would be appropriate here in a classroom full of kids. But he knew how tough it was for Megan to spend time away from her daughter and appreciated her being there for him. "I'll see you tonight."

This wasn't a day when he could feel joyful by any means, but suddenly the weight didn't seem as heavy.

Since her parents' death, Megan had avoided funerals and memorial services, but she'd wanted to be here for Whit. As she stood in the church vestibule with Whit after the service, she was relieved it was over, and certain that attending had been absolutely the right decision.

It had been emotional experience for everyone. Not just mourning their friend, but also remembering that fateful day all their lives had been forever changed so quickly. Paige Richardson's husband was taken from her in an instant…. A thought that had Megan reaching for Whit's hand.

Whit's words about his friend had brought tears to her eyes, reaffirming how important it was to be here for him. He was trying so hard and there was danger in a relationship that was too one-sided. It wasn't fair to him.

At least the service had been in the evening so she wouldn't be spending as much time away from Evie. Her daughter had been excited talking about going to preschool tomorrow. She'd chattered about her friends and all the fun activities coming up for December.

Megan stood silently at Whit's side while he gave his condolences to Craig Richardson's widow Paige and his twin brother Colby, who'd returned to town from his home in Dallas.

Everyone was making small talk, doing their best to hold it together. Then Whit took her elbow and guided her outside, shouldering through the crowd and into the chilly night full of stars. In the dark, the scars from the storm didn't show. It was almost if it never happened. Except tonight reminded her too well it had.

She tucked her arm in his. "Are you okay?"

"Hanging in there. It's hard to believe he's been gone for over a month." Whit sighed, cricking his neck to the side as they walked to his truck.

"Did I hear right that R&N Builders is helping out with the reconstruction?" Colby Richardson and Whit's friend Aaron Nichols were partners in the business.

"You did. Colby has offered all the services of his very successful company to help," Whit confirmed, although his forehead was still furrowed over what should have been a good piece of news.

"I'm sure you'll be glad to have more time with your friends, especially now."

"Hmm."

She squeezed his arm as they walked. "Something's bothering you?"

"The whole evening is just surreal. Especially seeing Colby with Paige."

"Because Colby is Craig's twin?"

He shook his head. "Because Colby and Craig each went out with Paige in high school. There is still a lot of tension between Colby and Paige."

"It must be difficult for her to have him around reminding her of her dead husband."

"Maybe so." He nodded, stopping beside his truck and opening the door for her. "Tonight sure makes a person think hard about what's important."

"That's an understatement." She climbed inside, thinking back to the first time she'd sat inside this vehicle, terrified for her daughter.

He settled behind the wheel without starting the truck. "It meant a lot to me to have you here."

"Of course I was here for you."

He stretched his arm along the seat, his fingers toying with her hair. "I think we both know what we have going is about more than sex."

His words stirred up a flurry of nerves in her belly. "Are you saying you're thinking about happily ever after and white picket fences?"

"I'm saying you mean something to me." He angled toward her, his eyes intense in the darkness. "And yeah, that scares the hell out of me, but this isn't casual. Not for me."

"Well, it scares the hell out of me to think about letting a man in my life again." As terrified as she was to say the words out loud, tonight had reminded her there were no guarantees in life. She linked her fingers with his. "But it scares me more to think about not trying at all."

Eleven

Whit couldn't remember being this nervous—and genuinely pumped up—about a Friday night date.

But then he'd never proposed to a woman before.

The diamond solitaire damn near burning a hole in his suit coat pocket, he shifted gears on his Porsche as he drove through Royal with Megan at his side. They weren't hiding out in some tucked away place. He'd chosen a restaurant near his Pine Valley home, where the odds of running into friends were high. Megan had agreed. The whole town knew they were dating. Evie had accepted him into their routine this past week.

And soon, everyone would see the ring on her finger.

Things were moving fast, sure, but during the week since Craig's memorial service, Whit had felt as if he and Megan had lived two lifetimes together. Their lives fit together. More than fit. They were good together and he didn't want to lose that. He'd been searching his whole life for a steady home life to build a family. Megan was the perfect woman for him.

Steering through the night streets, he noted the Christmas lights just beginning to crop up in windows and could see the efforts to rebuild the town starting to bear fruit. There was still a lot of work to be done, but then couldn't that be said about life overall? Everything was a work in progress. And he looked forward to meeting the challenge with Megan at his side.

God, she was gorgeous in a green lace dress, her thick hair swept up into one of those loose kinds of topknots that somehow stayed in place but begged his fingers to set free. She was such an intriguing mix of contrasts. On the one hand, a no-nonsense kind of woman not afraid to get her hands dirty whether she was working with animals or building a compost heap. On the other hand, an elegant woman as comfortable curled up reading her daughter a book as she was dressing up for a five-star evening out. Megan's confidence didn't come from a sense of entitlement or wealth. It came from within. From having tackled life head on and made her way in the world.

He respected that.

Megan trailed her fingers along the window as they drove past the Royal Diner, still closed due to damages from the storm. "Evie and I used to have supper there on days I would work late."

"Amanda will reopen," he said. "It's just going to take a while. I hear she and Nathan took out good insurance on the place. With luck the diner will be even better than ever."

"Like the hospital?" She smoothed a hand over her green lace dress. "I almost feel guilty getting all dressed up to have fun when there are still people dealing with the chaos of the aftermath."

"There's nothing wrong with enjoying yourself. You work hard and deserve a break. I think even the people who are struggling take comfort from seeing life returning to normal around them. It's good to do regular things. Support local businesses." He rested his hand on top of the steering wheel. "I know a perfect diner Evie will love when you two move in with me—I guess I should say, 'What if you and Megan moved in with me?'"

Wait, that wasn't what he'd meant to say. He was going to propose, then ask her to move in while they were engaged. But damn it, the words were already out there, so he held his peace as he stopped at a red light and waited for her response.

"What did you say?" she asked carefully.

"I have plenty of space." The light changed and he accelerated, weighing his words. "It's a gated community, so you two would have more security. And Evie would enjoy the Pine Valley community stables and pool. I'm thinking she could use some jodhpurs. Maybe for Christmas?"

"Maybe," Megan said noncommittally. To the riding clothes or moving in?

He needed to shift into damage control ASAP.

"Is that a no to moving in?" If so, that didn't bode well for his plans to propose.

"You've sprung this on me rather quickly. Can we talk more about it, please?" Her fingers clenched and tangled together in her lap. "I have a lot to consider with Evie. She's only just stopped wearing costumes—thank you again for bringing the therapy dog to her school. You were right about that."

Did that mean she trusted him more? "I did it for all the kids. And for the animals too. I'm glad Ms. Baker was able to take two off your hands."

"You and me both." She twisted in the seat toward him. "I didn't mean to be short about moving in together. You just caught me unaware."

He glanced at her beautiful face, full of worry. "It's okay. Like you said, we can talk more later. We have time."

They had time and he had plans. He knew the right opportunity would present itself for the proposal. And he'd even chosen a gift for her he thought would let her know just how much he cared about her as a person and accepted their differences.

She smiled, and it damn near took his breath away. "Taking our time. I like the sound of that."

Megan had barely tasted a bite of the appetizer, soup, salad or main course. Her mind was still on Whit's surprise suggestion that they live together. Things were moving so fast, she felt as if she was still stuck in the tornado sometimes.

But with each minute that passed, she found herself considering the possibility more seriously.

They were all but spending every waking hour outside of work together. Evie didn't even question his presence. If anything, her daughter questioned when he would arrive. She'd even asked if he could pick her up from day care. He was everything Megan could have hoped for in a man, on so many levels. So much so, it scared her sometimes how well things were going. Maybe that's why she was nervous about moving in together. It was like tempting fate.

The waiter cleared away their dinner plates and brought dessert. "Mr. Daltry," the waiter said, "just as you ordered, our chef made this especially for your celebration. A dark chocolate and orange tart with toasted almonds. I hope it is to your satisfaction."

Orange and chocolate? Surely not a coincidence?

The twinkle in Whit's eyes confirmed he'd intended the treat as a reminder of their time together in the greenhouse.

"I'm sure it will be perfect," Whit answered smoothly. "Please pass along my thanks."

Megan pressed a hand to her mouth to stop a laugh as the waiter left them alone again. "You're wicked."

"Just reminding you of all the wonderful times we can have together in the future." His hand gravitated to his suit coat, smoothing his lapel as he'd done a number of times throughout the dinner.

Was he as nervous as she over this? In a strange way she found it comforting, more of a sign he took this big step seriously.

"About what you said in the car regarding moving in together, I'm still not ready to say yes outright, but I want to think about it. And for me that's huge."

His hand fell away from his jacket and she linked fingers with him.

"Whit, we have something wonderful started. Let's not rush."

"Sure, of course," he agreed, but the tight lines of his mouth indicated that she'd let him down.

Couldn't he see how hard she was trying by letting herself be swept into his world so fast? She thought they'd really made progress. And it wasn't as if she just had herself to consider. A move would be a lot of upheaval for Evie at a time when she was just settling back into school and enjoying herself.

Megan tried to think of a better way to help Whit understand—to ease that tense expression on his face—when a cleared throat from behind him drew her attention upward.

Colby Richardson stood there with his hands shoved in his pockets. His resemblance to his late brother Craig was shocking. The man had a closed-off air emotionally, but that was understandable given what he must be going through. "Sorry to interrupt your dinner, but I wanted to congratulate you."

Megan looked up in confusion. Whit couldn't have already told people of his plans to move in together, could he? Whit stood, as if to quiet the man, which only fueled her concerns—and confusion.

"Thanks, Colby. I appreciate that. Could I treat your table to another round of drinks?" Whit asked, clearly trying to divert him.

"Of course. I see you have a bottle of champagne on its way over. I should leave you both to celebrate your big purchase."

Megan frowned. "Big purchase?"

"Yes," Colby said. "Whit managed quite a coup this week in scooping up the stretch of wetlands on the edge of town."

Her insides chilled faster than that bottle of bubbly in the ice bucket. "You bought up the wetlands?"

"Yes," Whit shuffled his feet, "but it's not exactly what you're thinking."

Colby backed away. "Sorry to have spilled the beans prematurely. I'll just leave the two of you to talk. Good evening."

The clean-cut real estate mogul turned and made a beeline to his table, leaving Megan alone with Whit again.

She restrained the urge to snap at Whit. He was a businessman, first and foremost. She knew that. She shouldn't be surprised that he'd proceeded as planned. He'd never misled her about who he was.

Still, she couldn't stem the deep well of disappointment pooling in her stomach.

"Megan? Do you want to hear what I have to say?"

She shook her head. "It doesn't matter." She folded her napkin in her lap, wishing she could sweep this disagreement away along with the breadcrumbs. "I understand we're different people. I'm not angry."

It cost her, but she would make peace. Try harder. Damn it, she was trying harder.

"But you're upset with me." Tension threaded through his shoulders, his jaw flexing.

She met his eyes and answered honestly. "Disappointed."

"Megan, our careers are separate. I respect your professionalism and I expect you to respect mine."

"Okay," she answered carefully, "but that doesn't mean I'm going to compromise my principles."

"You're calling me unprincipled?"

She struggled for a way to wind back out of this discussion that was playing out like too many confrontations they'd had over the years. Had the past couple of weeks just been a fluke, with reality now intruding once again? "We've had this disagreement for years. Did you think I was magically going to change because we…"

She couldn't even push the last words free without her voice cracking. She snatched up her water glass, her hand trembling with emotion.

He held her eyes without speaking for what felt like an eternity. Dishes and silverware clanked. The candles flickered between them, the dim chandelier above casting more shadows than light.

Finally, he shook his head. "You've already made up your mind about me. It's clear we have nothing left to say to each other."

How dare he act disillusioned with her? In the span of a couple of weeks, she'd done an about-face on so many of her stances to be with him. She was even willing to overlook this land purchase, as much as it galled her, and accept that they were different.

But now she suspected in spite of all his words to the contrary, he didn't want to be with her after all. Because it wasn't good enough for him that she would compromise on this issue. He needed her to be on his side. Think like him. Cheer on his plan to destroy wetlands she felt passionately about.

Why couldn't they just leave it be? Like so many men she'd seen in the past, he was okay to let their relationship self-destruct. He'd found an out and taken it. The knowledge burned all the way down her throat. She shot up from her chair before she did something humiliating like burst into tears.

Or worse yet, accept anything he said as truth just to stay with him.

Anger and frustration making his blood boil, Whit strode through the restaurant after Megan. He angled past the Richardson family at one table, the sheriff and his wife at another, and barely registered that they spoke to him because his focus was fully on Megan.

He charged past a Christmas tree covered in golden lone stars and white twinkling lights. Whit pushed through the door and stopped beside Megan, who was standing under the restaurant awning. "Megan—"

"The doorman is calling a cab for me." Her arms were crossed tight over her chest as her teeth chattered, her face every bit as chilly as her body language.

He held up a hand to stop the doorman from hailing

a taxi. "Damn it, that's not necessary. I brought you here. I'll drive you home."

"That would be awkward." She squeezed her eyes closed and then nodded to the doorman, silently signaling him to flag down a ride. "Please, just let me go. You already made it clear we have nothing left to say to one another."

Her struggle to hold back tears tugged at him. Damn it all, the last thing he wanted was to hurt her. But pride held him back from telling her the truth about that land. He needed her to believe in him. "You're upset. I get that." He took her arm and gently guided her away from the restaurant's main entrance. "But this isn't the place."

She let him steer her a few steps to the side. "The facts won't change if we're in your car."

"The facts?" He bit back a weary sigh. "You don't understand—"

"How about this for facts?" Her arms slid to her side, her hands clenched in tight fists. "You've been buying up land since the tornado. Taking advantage of people's pain. So fine. Tell me how I'm wrong," she finished defiantly.

"Taking advantage?" He searched for the words to make her understand, for the words to keep her in his life. "I've been buying property from people who needed to cut their losses. If I wasn't there to buy from them, they would lose everything rather than walking away with the money to start over. We've discussed this before."

He'd spent his childhood seeing his family's life repossessed. He wasn't lying when he told her he tried to help people in his town as best he could. He swallowed back the past and focused on the present, on Megan.

She shook her head. "And destroying the wetlands?

How is that 'helping' people? Sounds like you're making excuses. You can justify it however you want, but I don't see it the same way."

The sound system hummed with a symphonic version of "Have Yourself a Merry Little Christmas," as if mocking him with memories of a holiday spent in a homeless shelter until his dad landed on his feet again. Granted, they had all gotten gifts that year, courtesy of a local church group.

Even if he told her his real reason for buying the wetlands, that wouldn't change who he was. "You're employed by a non-profit organization and get paid a salary. I own a business where people only get paid if I make a profit. That's how life works."

She held up a finger, her hand shaking with restrained emotion. "Don't speak to me like I'm a child. There are plenty of people who make a profit without compromising their values."

"I follow the letter of the law in my business practices." He wasn't like his father, damn it.

"Just because something is legal doesn't mean it's morally right."

Okay, now she was stepping over the line.

"And what makes you the authority on right and wrong? There can be a middle ground if you'll stop being judgmental and—"

Gasping, she backed up a step. "Is that what you think of me? That I'm uptight and judgmental just because I live my life by a moral code that isn't identical to yours?"

He looked into her eyes and didn't see any room for changing her mind. She'd dug in her heels deeply. He recognized the look from the three years he'd known her. These past few weeks had been an anomaly. She wasn't interested in a real relationship with him.

"I think you're just looking for a reason to break it off with me. I think you're so locked onto the past that you're convinced every man is like your dad or Evie's dad. So much so, that you never really gave me a chance. Not three and a half years ago and not now."

"That's not fair," she whispered.

"None of this is." His hand gravitated to the ring box in his pocket again by habit, but he left it inside. He met her gaze and willed her to see the love in his eyes, to understand how he felt. To trust him.

To trust *in* him.

For an instant, he could have sworn he saw her stance softening and he reached to caress her arm.

The taxi rolled to a stop at the front entrance.

She pulled her hands in tight again, closing herself off from him, from what they could have had together. "Goodnight, Whit. I just…I can't do this."

Looking so damn beautiful that she took his breath away and broke his heart, Megan rushed past him and slid into the cab.

The taxi's taillights disappeared into the night like fading Christmas lights. His big night with Megan was over and he'd botched it from the start. He'd been so busy making plans for them, looking for angles to persuade her and win her over. All the while missing the most important thing of all.

This wasn't about winning a deal like some business merger. This was about having Megan in his life forever. This was about being in love with her. Somehow, he'd never once used that all-important word and because of that, he'd lost her.

Twelve

After a sleepless night, Megan took out her frustration by trying to restore order to some part of her world. She grabbed the bottle of disinfectant and moved on to spritz the next cat kennel. Her gloved hands scrubbed with a vengeance.

She'd spent most of the night crying and second-guessing herself. Today was supposed to be a day off. She should have been spending it with Whit. Evie had even asked to go to a friend's house to play, her costumes and fears fading. Which left Megan alone in her too quiet house. So she'd come to the shelter to get her mind off things, but it wasn't working.

Somehow she and Whit had shifted from considering moving in together to broken up in the span of one dinner, and all because of a land purchase.

A land purchase they had been at odds over for months. She should have seen the signs, but she'd been so blinded by how much she enjoyed being with him. Her eyes watered again. She sniffled and rubbed her wrist under her nose.

Footsteps echoed in the corridor and she blinked faster to clear her eyes—as if that would make any difference given how puffy they were. God, she hoped whoever it was wouldn't stop and talk. She just wanted to clean and clean until she dropped into an exhausted sleep and didn't have to think.

The footsteps stopped right outside the doorway.

"Soooo?" Beth's voice called. "How did your big date with Whit go last night?"

Megan could have diverted an employee or regular volunteer. But there would be no escaping Beth.

Eyes stinging from the sharp scent of bleach, she spoke over her shoulder, keeping her face averted. "The meal was five-star quality."

"Everyone knows the place is great." Beth pulled up alongside her. "It's one of those restaurants where guys take women to propose. Megan? Sweetie? Are you okay?" Beth dipped her head to make eye contact.

Megan flinched and scrubbed harder. "Would you like to help me here? I'm expecting a call from a grant writer any minute." Her words tumbled over each other as she sought to distract. "The guy's going to donate his services to help us put in a proposal to help fund a voucher spay/neuter program."

Beth grabbed a second bottle of antiseptic spray and tore off some paper towels. "Abigail and I can finish up here. On one condition."

She tucked her head into the steel kennel. "What's that?"

Her friend rested a hand on her shoulder. "Can you take off the glove so I can see the ring?"

Is that what her friend thought? This day just got worse.

Megan knew the moment had come. She couldn't hide anymore. "There's no ring."

She couldn't even begin to think about all that didn't happen between them last night. All her hopes...up in flames.

"Oh. Really? I could have sworn that he planned to..." Genuine confusion was stamped on Beth's face. "I mean..."

Seeing her friend's certainty was bittersweet. "Just because he takes me out to eat doesn't mean he planned to propose."

Beth took Megan by the shoulders gently and turned her. "Those are dark circles under your puffy eyes. Were you crying? Honey, what's wrong?"

Megan sagged back against the empty kennels they used for new cats to get acclimated before going into the free roaming facility. "We had a...really bad argument, and, well, it's over between us."

"No," Beth whispered, "that's not possible."

But it was. She knew that all too well. "I heard about his land grab...the wetlands."

Beth's eyes narrowed. "Who told you that?"

"Colby Richardson. We crossed paths at the restaurant last night."

"What did Whit say when you asked him for his side of things?"

"I said I...I mean, we talked about it." She chewed her bottom lip, thinking back over their argument and trying to remember when things really went off the rails. "He didn't deny it."

Beth nodded, but stayed silent.

Alarms jangled in Megan's mind. "You're trying to say there was a good reason for what he did?"

She thought back over the evening. It had been the perfect setup for a proposal. He'd even asked her to move in on the drive over. He was clearly serious.

Reflecting on how quickly things had spiraled out of control, she started to question why she hadn't asked rather than just assume. At the time it had seemed as if asking would have given him a chance to lie. But now she wondered if she had subliminally sabotaged the evening because deep down, she was afraid to trust any man again. Just as Whit had accused her of doing.

She looked at Beth, guilt stinging over the way she'd jumped to conclusions when Whit had done nothing but try to see and meet her needs. Her eyes watered again and she didn't bother hiding the emotion from her friend. "I should have asked him about the land purchases."

Beth hugged her close. "Sweetie, it's hard to push aside a lifetime of insecurities. I understand that well." She angled back and smiled. "But the risk is so very much worth it."

Megan eyed her friend suspiciously. "You wouldn't happen to know why he bought the wetlands?"

Beth shrugged. "You should be asking him."

"I'm asking you, because I think you know the answer."

"And if I did?" Beth replied enigmatically, "I think it would be wrong for me to tell you. A relationship needs to be built on trust and if I give you the easy answer, then you will have missed an amazing chance to make things right between you."

Beth's words sunk in. Deep. As Megan looked back

over her time with Whit, once she'd gotten to know him, he'd been honest, thoughtful, generous. Loving.

The way she'd assumed the worst and walked away had to have hurt him. He had plenty of friends, but no family that had ever come through for him. His father had let him down time and time again.

Even skipping out on bills.

And God, she'd accused Whit of being dishonest. She squeezed her eyes shut and rested her head against the cool steel kennel. At every turn since the tornado, she'd seen his quietly philanthropic spirit. He wasn't the type to shout his good deeds from the rooftops. He didn't seek thanks or accolades.

He was a good man.

And she'd messed up, big-time.

She'd been so afraid of getting hurt, she'd turned her back on the love of a lifetime. As she peeled off her gloves, she made up her mind—she owed Whit an apology. She was done being scared.

In his greenhouse, Whit dug his hands into the dirt and pulled the catnip from its original pot. The plant had taken off, outgrowing the small container. He'd come out here today to get his thoughts together. About half-way through the night he'd gotten past his pride. Sure, he'd hoped for more trust from Megan. But he'd pushed too much too fast. He needed to back up and regroup.

He wasn't a quitter. He'd worked to build a better life for himself and now he realized how narrow his view of success had been. It wasn't about the house. It was about the people. He just had to figure out the right way to win her back.

He dropped the catnip into a larger container and scooped more potting soil around the exposed roots.

He'd made a lot more headway with Megan when he'd given her simpler gifts. But damn it, he'd thought buying the wetlands for her and leaving them untouched was the right decision.

Damn it, he still did. He just needed to find the right time to try again.

The greenhouse door opened and he called out for the deliveryman, "You can leave the crate of plants by the door."

"I don't have any plants to offer." Megan's voice carried down the long walkway. "Can I stay anyway?"

The sound of her, here, where they'd shared such an amazing night, was like water poured on parched soil. Incredible relief. Hope for new life. But he needed to tread carefully rather than steamrolling her as he'd done too often in the past.

Whit pulled his hands out of the dirt and grabbed a rag. "Did you leave something here last week?"

She walked toward him, every bit as gorgeous in jeans and a T-shirt as she'd been in her lace gown last night. "I did, actually."

Damn, disappointment kicked through him. "What did you leave? I'll keep an eye out for it."

"You already have it in your hands, Whit." She stopped in front of him and pressed her palms to his chest. "I left my heart here with you."

Had he heard her right? "Megan, about last night and the wetlands—"

"Wait." She tapped his lips. "Let me finish. It's important. I brought something for you, but I need to say some things first. I want you to know that I trust you. I know you have an answer and a reason for whatever you've done. We may not agree, but I do respect your right to do as you see fit. We are different, you and I. And that's a good thing too."

"You really mean that."

He was stunned to *his* roots that she gave him her trust so fully. He'd been so used to working like hell for everything in his life. He'd never expected something so perfect, so incredible to land so smoothly in his arms.

"Absolutely." She sounded so sure of herself. Of him. The constant worry in her green eyes was nowhere in sight.

"God, Megan, I l—"

She tapped his mouth again. "I'm still not finished. I need for you to listen. I know I said some unforgivable things last night and I'm sorry. I should have asked for your side of the story rather than assuming."

He held her with his eyes. "I haven't given you a lot of time to trust me. I realize trust has to be earned."

"And you've done that. More times than most people in this town know and probably far more than I've realized." She stroked his face. "I looked back and realized that you use your money and influence to help so many people without ever taking credit."

He shrugged off those words. "It's easy for me to help. Doesn't put a dent in my bank balance. That's not a sacrifice."

She shook her head. "I think for a kid who was homeless a few times, it probably is a lot tougher to let go of the security of extra money in the bank than you let on."

God, she humbled him and amazed him and made him fall in love with her all over again. "You see me through far nicer eyes than I deserve."

"And you see yourself through a much harsher lens than you should."

Relief shuddered through him as he began to accept

that she'd given him a second chance. He wrapped his arms around her waist, hauled her to his chest and just held her, a simple pleasure he would never take for granted again.

He nuzzled her hair, her cinnamon scent tempting his nose and giving him ideas for something new to add to his garden. "What made you change your mind? Who told you about my plans for the wetlands?"

"No one told me about your plans." She angled back to look at him. "I meant it when I said I'm here because I trust you."

"Megan," he said hoarsely. "I bought the tract of land to give to you. It will stay just as it is as a tribute to how damn lucky I am to have you in my life."

Her eyes went misty and then bright with tears. "Are you kidding? Oh my God, Whit." She hugged his neck, kissed him, hugged him again, then dabbed her eyes. "I'm so sorry for doubting you. Can you forgive me?"

"There's nothing to forgive. You're here." He stroked along her back, loving the way she felt in his arms. Loving her, period. "You said you'd brought something for me. What is it?"

"Oh, right." Her tears vanished and she smiled mysteriously. "A couple of things actually for your—our?— house." She reached into her purse and passed him two silver picture frames. The first had a photo taken at the ice rink in Colorado of him with Megan and Evie. The second picture was of Evie on the sofa holding Tallulah, with Truffles, Pixie and Scooter sleeping along the back, while Piper and Cosmo stood by the coffee table set for a tea party.

A lump rose in his throat.

He hauled her close with a ragged sigh. "God,

Megan, I love you so damn much. The thought of spending another night wondering if I'd lost you forever…"

"You'll never have to wonder again." She arched up on her toes and brought her lips close to his. "I love you, too, Whit Daltry. Today, tomorrow and forever. Me, you, Evie and our menagerie of animals—we're a family."

"I like the sound of that." A lot. Deciding to leave his heart very much in *her* hands, he knelt on one knee in front of her. "Megan Maguire, will you do me the honor of being my wife, my lover, my love for the rest of our lives? Will you allow me the honor of being a father to Evie and any brothers or sisters we might give her in the years to come? Because there is nothing more that I want than to build a life with you by my side. I love you, Megan. I have a ring too, inside—"

"Yes, yes, with or without a ring, yes." She sank to her knees and took his hands in hers. "Of course, I'll marry you, live with you, love you, for the rest of our lives."

He reached for that quilt he'd never gotten around to putting away and snapped it out onto the floor, then remembered what a mess he was. "We should shower. Together. In the interest of conserving water, you know."

She whispered against his lips. "Oh, we will. But first I have some plans for you and those oranges."

He had some plans for her too. And a lifetime to fulfill them right here in Royal, Texas, where finally he'd put down real roots, thanks to Megan's love.

* * * * *

PREGNANT BY
THE TEXAN

BY
SARA ORWIG

Sara Orwig lives in Oklahoma. She has a patient husband who will take her on research trips anywhere, from big cities to old forts. She is an avid collector of Western history books. With a master's degree in English, Sara has written historical romance, mainstream fiction and contemporary romance. Books are beloved treasures that take Sara to magical worlds, and she loves both reading and writing them.

With a big thank-you to Stacy Boyd, Harlequin Desire
Senior Editor, and Charles Griemsman,
Harlequin Desire Series Editorial.

Also, with love to my family.

One

Early in December as the private jet came in for a landing, Aaron Nichols looked below. Even though the tornado had hit two months earlier, the west side of Royal, Texas, still looked unrecognizable.

No matter how many times he had gone back and forth between Dallas and Royal, he was shocked by the destruction when he returned to Royal. The cleanup had commenced shortly after the storm, but the devastation had been too massive to get the land cleared yet. Hopefully, he and his partner, Cole Richardson, could find additional ways for R&N Builders to help in the restoration. As he looked at the debris—the broken lumber, bits and pieces of wood and metal, a crumpled car with the front half torn away—he thought of the lives wrecked and changed forever. It was a reminder of his own loss over seven years ago that had hit as suddenly as a storm: a car accident, and then Paula and seventeen-month-old Blake were gone. With time the pain had dulled, but it never went away and in moments like this when he had a sharp reminder, the hurt and memories hit him with a force that sometimes made him afraid his knees would buckle.

Realizing his fists were doubled, his knuckles white, he tried to relax, to shift his thoughts elsewhere. He remembered the day in October when he had met Stella Daniels during the cleanup effort. He thought of their one night together and his desire became a steady flame.

He hoped he would see her on this trip, although since their encounter, he had followed her wishes and refrained from calling her to go out again. The agreement to avoid further contact hadn't stopped him from thinking about her.

At the time he and Stella parted ways, he expected it to be easy. In the seven years since he lost his wife and baby son, women had come and gone in his life, but he had never been close to any of them. Stella had been different because he hadn't been able to walk away and forget her.

He settled in the seat as the plane approached the small Royal airport. Royal was a West Texas town of very wealthy people—yet their wealth hadn't been enough to help them escape the whirlwind.

Almost an hour later he walked into the dining room at the Cozy Inn, his gaze going over the quiet room that was almost empty because of the afternoon hour. He saw the familiar face of Cole Richardson, whose twin, Craig, was one of the storm's fatalities. A woman was seated near Cole. Aaron's heart missed a beat when he saw the brown hair pulled back severely into a bun. He could remember taking down that knot of hair and watching it fall across her bare shoulders, transforming her looks. Stella Daniels was with Cole. Aaron almost whispered "My lucky day" to himself.

Eagerness to see her again quickened his step even though it would get him nowhere with her. He suspected when she decided something, she stuck by her decision and no one could sway her until she was ready to change. Her outfit—white cotton blouse buttoned to her throat and khaki slacks with practical loafers—was as severe and plain as her hairdo. She wore almost no makeup. Few men would look twice at her and he wondered whether she really cared. Watching her, a woman who appeared straitlaced and plain, Aaron couldn't help thinking that the passionate night they'd had almost seemed a figment of his imagination.

As Aaron approached them, Cole stood and Stella glanced over her shoulder. Her gaze met Aaron's and her big blue eyes widened slightly, a look of surprise forming on her face, followed by a slight frown that was gone in a flash.

He reached Cole and held out his hand. "Hi, Cole. Have a seat."

"Aaron, good to see you," Cole said. Looking ready for construction work, he wore one of his T-shirts with the red, white and blue R&N Builders logo printed across the front. "You know Stella Daniels."

Bright, luminous eyes gazed at him as he took her hand in his. Her hand was slender, warm, soft, instantly stirring memories of holding her in his arms.

"Oh, yes," he answered. "Hi, Stella," he said, his voice changing slightly. "We've met, but if we hadn't, anyone who watches television news would recognize you. You're still doing a great job for Royal," he said, and she smiled.

One of the administrative assistants at town hall, Stella had stepped in, taking charge after the storm and trying to help wherever she could. It hadn't taken long for reporters to notice her and start getting her on camera.

Aaron shed his leather jacket and sat across from Cole, aware of Stella to his left. He caught a whiff of the rose-scented perfume she wore, something old-fashioned, but it was uniquely Stella and made him remember holding her close, catching that same scent then.

"I'm glad to have you back in Royal," Cole said. He looked thinner, more solemn, and Aaron was saddened by Cole's loss as well as the losses of so many others in town. He knew from experience how badly it could hurt.

"I know help is needed here, so I'm glad to be back."

"Thanks," Cole said. "I mean it when I say I appreciate

that. When you can, drop by the Texas Cattleman's Club. They're rebuilding now and moving along. They'll be glad to have you here, too."

"Our club friends in Dallas said to tell you and the others hello."

Cole nodded as he glanced at Stella. "Getting to the business at hand, Stella and I were talking about areas where more lumber is needed—all over the west side of town, it seems."

"Each time I see Royal, I can't believe the destruction. It still looks incredible. I've made arrangements to get another couple of our work crews here."

"R&N Builders have helped tremendously," Stella said.

"I'm sure everyone in town thanks you for doing such a great job right from the start, Stella—acquiring generators, getting help to people and directing some of the rescue efforts. When disaster happens unexpectedly like that, usually all hell breaks loose and it takes a calm head to help the recovery," Aaron stated.

"Thanks. I just did what I could. So many people pitched in and we appreciate what R&N Builders, plus you and Cole individually, have donated and done to aid Royal."

"We're glad to. Everyone in the company wanted to help," Cole replied. "So we're adding two more work crews. Stella, you can help coordinate where they should go. I asked men to volunteer for the assignment. They'll be paid by us the same as if they were working on a job at home, but R&N is donating their services to help Royal rebuild."

"That would be a tremendous help," Stella said. "Local companies are booked solid for the next few months. There's so much to be done that it's overwhelming."

"Also, we might be able to get one of the wrecking companies we work with to come in here and pick up debris. I doubt you have enough help now when there's so much to clean up," Aaron said.

"We need that desperately. We have some companies from nearby towns, but we can use more help. There is an incredible amount of debris and it keeps growing as they get the downed trees cut up."

Cole made a note on a legal pad in front of him.

"Right now I wonder if we'll ever get all the debris cleared. It would be great to have more trucks here to help haul things away."

Stella made notes as they discussed possibilities for the next hour. Even as he concentrated on the conversation, Aaron could not keep from having a sharp awareness of Stella so nearby. He wished she had not asked him to back off and forget their night of passion.

He'd done so, but now that he was back in her presence, he found it difficult to keep memories from surfacing and wished he could take her out again, dance with her and kiss her, because it had been an exciting, fun night.

Her long slender fingers thumbed through the notebook she held as she turned to a page of figures. He recalled her soft hands trailing across his bare chest, and looked up to meet her blue-eyed gaze.

She drew a deep breath and her cheeks flushed as she looked down and bent over her open binder. Startled, he realized she had memories, too. The idea that she had been recalling that night stirred him and ignited desire. He wondered how many men paid no attention to her because of her buttoned-up blouses and austere appearance. Her actions that night hadn't been austere. Aware he should get his thinking elsewhere, he tried to focus on what Cole was saying.

At half past three Cole leaned back in his chair. "Sorry to have to break this up. You two can continue and, Aaron, you can fill me in later. I'm going out to a long-time friend Henry Markham's ranch to stay five or six days. He invited me out. He also lost his brother in the storm and he's had a lot of damage, so I'm going to help him. I'll see you both next week and we can continue this."

"Don't forget," Stella said, "I have to leave town for part of the day tomorrow. I'll be back in the afternoon." As Cole nodded, she looked at Aaron. "I'm flying to Austin where my sister lives."

"If you need to stay longer, you should," Cole said.

"I don't think I'll need to stay. Just a short time with her and then I'll be back."

Cole glanced at Aaron. "I'm glad you're here, Aaron. We've got good people running the place in Dallas while we're gone, so everything should be all right."

"It'll be fine. George Wandle is in charge. And if anything comes up he promised he would call one of us."

"Good deal." Cole stood, pulled on a black Western-cut jacket and picked up his broad-brimmed Resistol hat. "Thanks, Stella, for meeting with me."

"All the thanks go to you and Aaron for the help you and your company are giving to Royal. You've been terrific."

"We're glad to help where we can. Aaron, if you need me for anything, I have my phone with me."

"Sure, Cole."

Aaron watched his partner walk through the restaurant and then he turned back to Stella. "It's nice to see you again."

"Thank you. It's nice to see you, too. I really mean it. Your company has done so much to help."

"There's still so much more to do. How's the mayor?"

A slight frown creased her brow as she shook her head at him. "Since the mayor was in the town hall when it sustained a direct hit, he was hurt badly. He was on the critical list a very long time. He's hurt badly with broken bones, internal ruptures and complications after several surgeries. He was in the ICU for so long. With all the problems he's had, he's still a long way from healed."

"That's tough. Tough for him, for you, for all who work for him and for the town. The deputy mayor's death complicated things even more. No one's really in charge. You've sort of stepped into that void, Stella."

"I'm just doing what I can. There are so many things—from destroyed buildings to lost records and displaced pets. Megan Maguire, the animal shelter director, has worked around the clock a lot of the time. It just takes everybody pulling together and it's nice you're back to help."

He smiled at her. "Maybe, sometime, you need a night out to forget about Royal for a few minutes."

"Frankly, that sounds like paradise, but I don't have time right now. Someone texts or calls every other minute. This has been one of the quietest afternoons, but this morning was a stream of calls."

"Royal could manage without you for a couple of hours."

"Don't tempt me, Aaron," she said, smiling at him. "And I won't be here tomorrow."

"I have the feeling that you're working late into the night, too."

"You're right, but every once in a while now, there'll be a lull in the calls or appointments or hospital visits. Lately, I've had some nights to myself. While you're here, let me show you which projects Cole has finished and where we need the work crews next."

She spread a map on the table and he pulled his chair closer to her. Aware of her only inches away now, he once again inhaled a faint scent of her rose perfume. He helped her smooth the map out and leaned close, trying to focus on what she told him but finding it difficult to keep his attention from wandering to her so close beside him.

She showed him where they had repaired houses and finished building a new house. Stella told him about different areas on the west side of town, which had taken the brunt of the storm, the problems, the shortages of supplies, the people in the hospital. The problems seemed staggering, yet she was quietly helping, as were so many others she told him about.

He wondered if she had suffered some deep loss herself and understood their pain. He wouldn't ask, because she probably wouldn't want to talk about it. He didn't want anyone to ask him about his loss and he hadn't reached a point where he could talk about it with others. He didn't think he ever would. The hurt was deep and personal.

"Aaron?"

Startled, he looked at her. "Sorry, I was thinking about some of these people and their terrible losses. Some things you can't ever get back."

"No," she answered, studying him with a solemn expression. "Houses can be rebuilt, but lives lost are gone. Even some material possessions that hold sentimental value or are antiques—there's no replacing them. You can't replace sixty-year-old or older trees—not until you've planted new ones and let them grow sixty or seventy years. It tears you up sometimes." She smiled at him. "Anyway, I'm glad you're here."

"We'll just help where we can. To have a bed and a roof over your head is good and we need to work toward that for everyone."

"Very good. You and Cole are a godsend," she said, smiling at him and patting his hand.

He placed his hand on hers. Her hand was soft, warm,

smooth. He longed to draw her into his arms and his gaze lowered to her mouth as he remembered kissing her before.

She slipped her hand out from under his. "I think they're beginning to set up the dining room for tonight. I wonder if they want us to leave," she said. Her words were slightly breathless and her reaction to him reinforced his determination to spend time with her again.

"We're not in anyone's way and I doubt they want us to leave."

"I didn't realize how long we've talked," she said.

"Have dinner with me. Then I'll give you a ride home tonight."

"I'm still staying here at the inn until the repairs are done on my town house," she said.

"I'm staying here, too, so I'll see you often," he said. She had a faint smile, but he had the feeling that she had put up a barrier. Was she trying to avoid the attraction that had boiled between them the last time they were together? Whatever it was, he wanted to be with her tonight for a time. "Unless you have other plans, since we're both staying here, then, by all means, have dinner with me."

There was a slight hesitation before she nodded. "Thank you," she replied. Even though she accepted his invitation, she had a touch of reluctance in her reply and he had the feeling she was not eager to eat with him.

"Is this headquarters for you?" he asked, his thoughts more on her actions than her words.

"Not at all. I'm not in charge—just another administrative assistant from town hall helping like the others."

"Not quite just another administrative assistant," he said, looking at her big blue eyes and remembering her passionate responses. For one night she had made him forget loss and loneliness. "Should your town house be on our list of places to help with reconstruction?" he asked her.

"Thank you, no. The damage wasn't that extensive, but I was pretty far down on the priorities list. I finally have the work scheduled and some of it has already started. I'm supposed to be back in my place in about a week. Thank goodness. I want to be there before Christmas."

"Good, although I'm glad you're staying here in the hotel because that means we can see each other easily," he said, deciding he would get his suite moved to whatever floor she was on. "They're setting up for tonight and I need to wash up before dinner. Want to meet again in an hour?" he asked her.

"That's a good idea. I've been busy since seven this morning and I'd welcome a chance to freshen up."

As they walked out of the restaurant, he turned to her. "What floor are you on?"

"The sixth floor. I have a suite."

"The same floor I'm on," he said, smiling at her.

"That's quite a coincidence," she said in a skeptical voice.

"It will be when I get my suite moved to the sixth floor, after seeing you to your suite."

She laughed. "I can find my own way to my suite. You go try to finagle a suite on the sixth floor. I don't think you can. It's hopeless. Every available space has been taken because of so many homeless folks having their houses repaired after the storm. People reserved every nook and cranny available in Royal and all the surrounding little towns. Some had to go to Midland, Amarillo and Lubbock. We're packed, so I don't think I'll see you on my floor."

"So you approve if I can get a suite," he said.

"I figure it won't happen," she answered, looking at him intently.

"Not if you don't approve," he said.

"I don't want more complications in my life and you're

a wicked influence, Aaron," she said mischievously, for the first time sounding as if she had let down her guard with him.

"Wicked is more fun and you know you agree," he said softly, standing close in front of her. "I'll show you tonight when we're together."

"Oh, no, you won't. I don't need you to show me one thing. We'll have dinner, talk a little and say good-night. That's the agenda. Got it?"

"Oh, I have an agenda. I had it the moment I walked through the door and saw you sitting there with Cole. One of the goals on my agenda is to get you to take down your hair."

"Amazing. One of my goals is to keep my hair pinned up, so one of us is going to fail completely," she said, her blue eyes twinkling.

Eager to be with her for the whole evening, to flirt and dance and hopefully kiss, he leaned a bit closer. "If I placed my hand on your throat, I'll bet I'd feel your pulse is racing. You want the same thing I do. I'm looking forward to dinner and spending the evening together."

"I'm looking forward to the evening, too, so I can talk to you more about how you and your company can continue to help with the restoration of Royal. You're doing a wonderful job so far, and it's heartwarming to know you're willing to continue to help."

"We'll help, but tonight is a time for you to relax and catch your breath. It's a time for fun and friendship and maybe a kiss or two to take your mind off all the problems, so don't bring them with you. C'mon, I'll walk you to your door," he said, taking her arm and heading to the elevators.

She laughed. "Well now, don't *you* have a take-charge personality."

"It gets things done," he answered lightly as they entered

the elevator and rode to the sixth floor. When they got off, she walked down the hall and put her key card in a slot. As she opened the door, she held the handle and turned to him.

"Thanks, Aaron. I'll meet you in the lobby."

"How's seven?" he asked, placing one hand on the door frame over her head and leaning close. "It's good to see you again. I'm looking forward to the evening."

Her eyes flickered and he saw the change as if she had mentally closed a door between them. "Since I'm leaving town tomorrow, let's make it an early evening, because I have to get up at the crack of dawn. My life has changed since you first met me. I have responsibilities now that I didn't have then."

"Sure, whatever you want," he said, wondering what bothered her. For a few minutes downstairs she had let down that guard. He intended to find out why she was now being distant with him. "See you at seven."

"Bye, Aaron," she said, and stepped inside her suite, closing the door.

As he rode down in the elevator, his thoughts were on her. He knew she had regretted their night of lovemaking. It was uncustomary for her and in the cool light of day, it upset her that she had allowed herself to succumb to passion. Was she still suffering guilt about that night?

He didn't think that was what had brought on the cool demeanor at the door of her suite. Maybe partially, but it had to be more than that. But what else could it be? He intended to find out.

He took the elevator back down and crossed the lobby, determined to get a suite on the sixth floor even if he had to pay far more to do so.

It turned out to be easier than he had thought because someone had just moved out.

My lucky day.

Two

Stella Daniels walked through the living room of the suite in the Cozy Inn without seeing her surroundings. Visions came of Aaron when he had strolled to the table where she sat with Cole. Looking even better than she had remembered, Aaron exuded energy. His short dark blond hair in a neat cut added to his authoritative impression. The warmth in his light brown eyes had caused her heart to miss a beat.

She had a mixture of reactions to seeing him—excitement, desire, dread, regret. She hoped she'd managed to hide her tangled opposing emotions as she smiled and greeted him. Her first thought was how handsome he was. Her second was happiness to see him again, immediately followed by wishing he had stayed in Dallas where the company he shared with Cole was headquartered. His presence complicated her busy life more than he knew.

She'd offered her hand in a business handshake, but the moment his fingers had closed over hers, her heartbeat had jumped and awareness of the physical contact had set every nerve quivering. Memories taunted and tempted, memories that she had tried to forget since the one night she had spent with Aaron in October.

It had been a night she yielded to passion—which was so unlike her. Never before had she done such a thing or even been tempted to, but Aaron had swept her away. He had made her forget worries, principles, consequences, all her usual levelheaded caution, and she had rushed into a blissful night of love with him.

Now she was going to pay a price. As time passed after their encounter, she suspected she might have gotten pregnant. Finally she had purchased a pregnancy kit and the results confirmed her suspicions. The next step would be a doctor. Tomorrow she had an appointment in Austin. Her friends thought she was going there to visit her sister; Stella hadn't actually said as much, but people had jumped to that conclusion and she had not corrected anyone. She did not want to see a doctor in Royal who would know her. She didn't want to see one anywhere in the vicinity who would recognize her from her appearances on television since the storm. If a doctor confirmed her pregnancy, she wanted some time to make decisions and deal with the situation herself before everyone in Royal had the news, particularly Aaron.

Tomorrow she would have an expert opinion. Most of the time she still felt she wasn't pregnant, that something else was going on. It had only been one night, and they'd used protection—pregnancy shouldn't have resulted, regardless of test results or a missed period.

She studied herself in the mirror—her figure hadn't changed. She hoped the pregnancy test was wrong, even though common sense said the test was accurate.

Given all that was going on, she should have turned Aaron down tonight, but she just couldn't do it.

She looked at her hair and thought about what he had said. She would keep it up in a bun as a reminder to stop herself from another night of making love with him. In the meantime, she was going to have dinner with him, work with him and even have fun with him. Harmless fun that would allow them each to say goodbye without emotional ties—just two people who had a good time working together. What harm could there be in that?

Unless it turned out that she was pregnant. Then she couldn't say goodbye.

She showered, took down her hair to redo it and selected a plain pale beige long-sleeved cotton blouse and a dark brown straight wool skirt with practical low-heeled shoes. She brushed, twisted and secured her hair into a bun at the back of her head. She didn't wear makeup. Men usually didn't notice her and she didn't think makeup would make much difference. The times she had worn makeup in high school, boys still hadn't noticed her or wanted to ask her out except when they were looking for help in some course they were taking.

An evening with Aaron. In spite of her promises to herself and her good intentions, the excitement tingled and added to her eagerness.

When it was time to go meet Aaron, she picked up a small purse that only held necessities, including her card key, wallet and a list of temporary numbers that people were using because of the storm. She wouldn't need a coat because they wouldn't be leaving the Cozy Inn.

When she stepped off the elevator, she saw him. She tried to ignore the faster thump of her heart. In an open-neck pale blue shirt and navy slacks, he looked handsome, neat and important. She thought he stood out in the crowd in the lobby with his dark blond hair, his broad shoulders and his air of authority.

Why did she have such an intense response to him? She had from the first moment she met him. He took her breath away and dazzled her without really doing anything except being himself.

He spotted her and her excitement jumped a notch. She felt locked into gazing into his eyes, eyes the color of caramel. She could barely get her breath; realizing how intensely she reacted to him, she made an effort to break the eye contact.

When she looked again, he was still watching her as he approached.

"You look great. No one would ever guess you've been working since before dawn this morning."

"Thank you," she answered, thinking he was just being polite. Nobody ever told her she looked great or gorgeous, or said things she heard guys say to women. She was accustomed to not catching men's attention so she didn't give it much thought.

"I have a table in the dining room," he said, taking her arm. The room had been transformed since they'd left it. Lights had been turned low, the tables covered in white linen tablecloths. Tiny pots wrapped in red foil and tied with bright green satin bows held dwarf red poinsettias sprinkled with glitter, adding to the festive Christmas atmosphere.

A piano player played softly at one end of the room in front of a tiny dance floor where three couples danced to a familiar Christmas song. Near the piano was a fully decorated Christmas tree with twinkling lights.

Aaron held her chair and then sat across from her, moving the poinsettia to one side even though they could both see over it.

"I haven't seen many Christmas trees this season," she said. "It's easy to even forget the holiday season is here when so many are hurting and so much is damaged."

"Will you be with your family for Christmas?"

"No. My parents don't pay any attention to Christmas. They're divorced and Christmas was never a fun time at our house because of the anger between them. It was a relief when they finally ended their marriage."

"Sorry. I know we talked about families before. Earlier today you said you are going to see your sister in Austin tomorrow. Do you see her at Christmas?"

"Some years I spend Christmas at her house. Some years I go back and forth between my parents and my sister. Mom has moved to Fort Worth. She's a high school principal there. After the divorce my dad moved his insurance business to Dallas because he had so many customers in the area. I see him some, but not as much as my mom. My grandmother lives with her and my grandfather is deceased."

"So this year what will you do at Christmastime?"

"I plan to stay here and keep trying to help where I can until the afternoon of Christmas Eve. Then I'll fly to Austin to be at my sister's. I have a feeling the holidays will be extremely difficult here for some people. I'm coming back Christmas afternoon and I've asked people here who are alone to come over that evening—just a casual dinner. So far there are about five people coming."

"That's nice, Stella," Aaron said, sounding sincere with a warmth in his gaze that wrapped her in its glow.

"What about you, Aaron? Where will you spend Christmas? You know more about my family than I do about yours."

For an instant he had a shuttered look that made her feel as if she had intruded with her question. Then he shrugged and looked at her. "My parents moved to Paris and I usually go see them during the holidays. My brother is in Dallas and I'll be with him part of the time, although he's going to Paris this year. I like to ski, and some years I ski. This year I'll see if I can help out around here. You're right. A holiday can hurt badly if someone has lost his home or a loved one. After losing his brother, Cole will need my support. So I'm going to spend the holidays in Royal."

As he spoke quietly, there was a glacial look in his eyes that made her feel shut out. She wondered about his past. More and more she realized how little she knew about him.

Their waiter appeared to take their drink order, and Aaron looked at her, his brown eyes warm and friendly again. "The last time we were together you preferred a glass of red wine. Is that what you'd like now?"

She shook her head. "No, thank you. I would prefer a glass of ice water. Maybe later I'll have something else," she said, surprised that he remembered what she had ordered before. She didn't want to drink anything alcoholic and she also didn't care to do anything to cause him to talk about the last time they were together.

"Very well. Water for the lady, please, and I'll have a beer," he said to the waiter.

As soon as they were alone, Aaron turned to her. "Let's dance at least one time and then we'll come back to place our order. Do you already know what you want? I remember last time it was grilled trout, which is also on this menu here."

"I don't know what I want and I need to read the menu. I'll select something and then we'll dance," she said, trying to postpone being in his arms. If she could gracefully skip dancing, she would, but he knew from the last time that she loved to dance. He was remembering that last time together with surprising clarity. She figured he had other women in his life and had forgotten all about her.

"Let's see what we want. When he brings drinks, we can order dinner. I remember how much you like to dance."

"You have a good memory."

"For what interests me," he said, studying her.

"What?" she asked, curious about the intent way he looked at her.

"You're different from last time. Far more serious."

Her breath caught in her throat. "You notice too much, Aaron. It's the storm and all the problems. There are so many things to do. How can I look or feel or even be the same person after the event that has touched each person who lives here," she said, realizing she needed to lighten the situation a bit so he would stop studying her and trying to guess what had changed and what was wrong.

"C'mon. One dance. You need to get your mind off Royal for just a few minutes at least. We can order dinner after a dance. You're not going to faint on the dance floor from hunger. Let it go for a minute, Stella. You've got the burden of the world on your shoulders."

She laughed and shook her head. "I don't think it's that bad. Very well, you win," she said. By trying to stay remote and all-business, she was drawing more attention instead of less, which wasn't what she wanted.

"That's more like it," he said, smiling. "What time do you leave in the morning?" he asked.

"I'll fly the eight-o'clock commuter plane from here to Dallas and change planes for Austin."

They reached the dance floor as the music changed to an old-time fast beat. She was caught in Aaron's direct look as they danced, and his brown eyes had darkened slightly. Desire was evident in his expression. Her insides clenched while memories of making love with him bombarded her.

His hot gaze raked over her and she could barely get her breath. How could she resist him? He was going to interfere in her work in Royal, interfere in her life, stir up trouble and make her want him. The last part scared her. She didn't want Aaron involved too soon because he was a man who was accustomed to taking charge and to having things his way.

Watching him, she gave herself to dancing around the floor with him, to looking into brown eyes that held desire and a promise of kisses, to doing what he said—having fun and forgetting the problems for just a few minutes. The problems wouldn't go away, but she could close her mind to them long enough to dance with Aaron and have a relaxing evening.

As they danced the beat quickened. Smiling, she shut her mind to everything except dancing and music and a drumming beat that seemed to match her heartbeat. The problems would be waiting, but for a few minutes, she pushed them aside.

Her gaze lowered to Aaron's mouth and her own lips parted. Having him close at hand stirred up memories she had been trying to forget. If only she could go back and undo that night with him, to stop short at kissing him.

The dance ended and when a ballad began he held her hand to draw her closer.

"Aaron, I thought we were going to have one dance and then go order dinner," she said, catching her breath.

"I can't resist this. I've been wanting to dance with you and hold you close."

The words thrilled her, scared her and tormented her. They danced together and she was aware of pressing lightly against him and moving in step with him. Memories of being in his arms became more vivid. His aftershave was faint but she recalled it from before. Too many things about him were etched clearly in her memory, which hadn't faded any in spite of her efforts to try to avoid thinking about him.

The minute the song ended, she stepped away and smiled. "Now, we've danced. Let's go order so we get dinner tonight."

"There, that's good to see you relax a little and laugh and smile. That's more the way I remember you."

"I think you just wanted to get your way."

"No. If I just wanted to get my way, we wouldn't be here right now. We'd be upstairs in my room."

She laughed and shook her head, trying to make light of his flirting and pay no attention to it.

At their table she looked over the menu. She selected grilled salmon this time and sipped her cold water while Aaron drank a beer.

"See, it's good to let go of the problems for at least a brief time. You'll be more help to others if you can view things with a fresh perspective."

"I haven't done much of this. The calls for help have been steady although it's not like it was at first. We've had some really good moments when families found each other. That's a triumph and joy everyone can celebrate. And it's touching when pets and owners are reunited. Those are the good moments. Frankly, I'll be ready to have my peace and quiet back."

Her phone dinged and she took it out. "Excuse me," she said as she read the text message and answered it.

Their dinner came and they talked about the houses that were being rebuilt by his company and the families who would eventually occupy them. With Aaron she had a bubbling excitement that took away her appetite. She didn't want him to notice, so she kept eating small bites slowly. Before she was half-through, she got a call on her phone.

"Aaron—" She shrugged.

"Take the call. I don't mind."

She talked briefly and then ended the call. "That's Mildred Payne. She's elderly and lives alone. Her family lives in Waco. Her best friend was one of the casualties of the storm. She just called me because her little dog got out and is lost. Mildred's crying and phoned me because I've helped her before. I'm sorry, Aaron, but I have to go help her find her dog."

He smiled. "Come on. I'll get the waiter and then I'll take you and we'll find the dog."

"You don't have to."

"I know I don't have to. I want to be with you and maybe I can help."

"I need to run to my suite and get my coat."

"I'll meet you in the lobby near the front door in five minutes."

"Thanks."

"Wouldn't miss a dog hunt with you for anything," he said as they parted.

She laughed and rushed to get her coat. When she came back to the lobby, Aaron was standing by the door. He had on a black leather bomber jacket and once again just the sight of him made her breathless.

His car was waiting outside and a doorman held the door for her as Aaron went around to slide behind the wheel. She told him the address and gave him directions. "You're turning out to be a reliable guy," she said. "I appreciate this."

"You don't know the half about me," he said in an exaggerated drawl, and she smiled.

"To be truthful, I'm glad I don't have to hunt for the dog by myself. I do know the dog. It's a Jack Russell terrier named Dobbin. If you'll stop at a grocery I'll run in and get a bag of treats because he'll come for a doggie treat."

"I'll stop, but if we were home and I was in my own car, we wouldn't have to. My brother has a dog and I keep a bag of treats in the trunk of my car. That dog loves me."

"Well, so do I," she said playfully. "You're willing to hunt for Dobbin."

"When we find Dobbin, we'll go back to the Cozy Inn and I'll show you treats for someone with big blue eyes and long brown hair—"

"Whoa. You just find Dobbin and we'll all be happy,"

she said, laughing. "Seriously, Aaron, I appreciate you volunteering to help. It's cold and it's dark out. I don't relish hunting for a dog, and Dobbin is playful."

"So am I if you'll give me half a chance," he said. She shook her head.

"I'm not giving you a chance at all. Just concentrate on Dobbin."

"I'll only be a minute," he said, pulling into the brightly lit parking lot of a convenience store. He left the engine running with the heater on while he hurried inside. She watched him come out with a bag of treats.

"Thanks again," she said.

"Hopefully, Dobbin will be back home before we get there. You must get calls for all kinds of problems."

"I'm glad to help when I can. I'm lucky that my house didn't have a lot of damage and I wasn't hurt. Mildred had damage to her house. She's already had a new roof put on and windows replaced. She has a back room that has to be rebuilt, but she was one of the fortunate ones who got help from her insurance company and had a construction company she'd worked with on other jobs, so she called them right after the storm."

"That's the best way. Make the insurance call as soon as possible."

"It worked for Mildred." They drove into a neighborhood that had damage but not the massive destruction that had occurred in the western part of Royal. Houses were older, smaller, set back on tree-filled lots. Stella saw the bright beacon of a porch light. "There's her house where the porch light is on. Mildred is in a block where power got restored within days after the storm. Another help. There she is, waiting for us and probably calling Dobbin."

"He could be miles away. It's a cold night and she's elderly. Get her in where it's warm and I'll drive around looking for Dobbin. Hopefully, he loves treats."

When they reached the house, Aaron turned up the narrow drive. A tall, thin woman with a winter coat pulled around her stood on the porch. She held a sack of dog treats in her hand.

"Thanks again, Aaron. You didn't know what you were in for when you asked me to eat dinner with you. I'll get her settled inside and then I'll probably walk around the block and look. She said he hadn't been gone long when she called."

"That's good because a dog can cover a lot of ground. I have my phone with me. My number is 555-4378."

"And mine—"

"Is 555-6294," he said, startling her. "I started to call you a couple of times, but you said you wanted to say goodbye, so I didn't call," he said.

That gave her a bigger surprise. She figured he had all but forgotten the night they were together. It was amazing to learn that not only had he thought about calling her, he even knew her phone number from memory. He had wanted to see her again. The discovery made her heart beat faster.

"Stella—"

Startled, she looked around. He had parked and was letting the motor idle. She was so lost in her thoughts, for a moment she had forgotten her surroundings or why they were there. "I'll see about Mildred," she said, stepping out and hurrying to the porch as Aaron backed out of the drive.

"Hi, Mildred. I came as quickly as I could."

"Thank you, Stella. I just knew you would be willing to help."

"I'm with Aaron Nichols, who is Cole Richardson's partner. They own one of the companies that has helped so much in rebuilding Royal. Aaron will drive around to search for Dobbin."

"I appreciate this. He's little and not accustomed to being out at night."

"Don't worry. We'll find him," Stella said, trying to sound positive and cheerful and hoping they could live up to what she promised. "Let's go inside where it's warm and I'll go look, too. You should get in out of the cold."

"You're such a help to everyone and I didn't know who else to turn to. There was George, my neighbor, but their house is gone now and he and his family are living with his sister."

They went inside a warm living room with lights turned on.

"You get comfortable and let us look for Dobbin. Just stay in where it's warm. May I take the bag of treats with me?"

"Of course. Here it is." Mildred wiped her eyes. "It's cold for him to be out." Gray hair framed her long face. She hung her coat in the hall closet and stepped back into the living room.

"I'm going to walk around the block and see if I can find him. Aaron is looking now. We'll be back in a little while."

Mildred nodded and followed Stella to the door.

"This is nice of you, Stella. Dobbin is such company for me. I don't want to lose him."

"Don't worry." She left, closing the door and hurrying down the porch steps. "Dobbin. Here, Dobbin," she called, rattling the treat sack and feeling silly, thinking Dobbin could be out of Royal by now. She prayed he was close and would come home. No one in Royal needed another loss at a time like this.

"Dobbin?" she called, and whistled, walking past Mildred's and the lot next door where a damaged house stood dark and empty. The roof was half-gone and a large elm had fallen on the front porch. Away from the lights the area was grim and cold. She made a mental note to check tomorrow about Mildred's block because she thought this section of town had already had the fallen trees cleared away.

"Dobbin," she called again, her voice sounding eerie in the silent darkness.

A car came around the corner, headlights bright as it drove toward her. The car slowed when it pulled alongside her and she recognized Aaron's rental car. He held up a terrier. Thrilled, she ran toward the car. "You have Dobbin?"

"Dobbin is my buddy now. He's waiting for another treat."

"Hi, Dobbin," she said, petting the dog. "Aaron, you're a miracle man. I'll meet you on Mildred's porch."

"Get in and ride up the drive with me. I'll hold Dobbin so he doesn't escape."

She laughed, thinking it was becoming more and more difficult to try to keep a wall up between them. All afternoon and this evening he had done things to make her appreciate and like him more.

She climbed into the warm car. "I'll hold Dobbin," she said. When Aaron released the terrier, he jumped into her lap. Aaron drove up the drive and parked.

"Come in and meet Mildred because she'll want to thank you."

"Here, you might as well give Mildred the bag of treats. I'll carry Dobbin until we get to the door," Aaron said, taking the dog from her.

On the porch Aaron rang the bell. In seconds the door opened and Mildred smiled. "You found him. Thank you, thank you." She took the dog from Aaron and the bags of treats from Stella. "Please come in. I'm going to put him in my room and I'll be right back. Please have a seat."

When she came back, Stella introduced everyone. "Mildred, this is Aaron Nichols. Aaron, meet Mildred Payne."

"Nice to meet you, ma'am. Dobbin was in the next block, sitting on a porch of a darkened, vacant home as if waiting for a ride home. I had a bag of treats, so he came right to me."

"Good. He doesn't like everybody."

"Mildred, we're going back. It's been a long day and I still have some things to do."

"I wish you could stay. I have cookies and milk."

"Thanks, but we should go," Stella said. Mildred followed them onto the porch, thanking them as they left and still thanking them when they got into the car.

"Now you've done your good deed for today," Stella said when he backed down the drive. "It was appreciated."

"It was easy. I think you've become essential to this town."

"No. I'm just happy to help where help is needed. And I'm just one of many helping out. The Texas Cattleman's Club has been particularly helpful, and you and Cole have certainly done more than your fair share."

"Your life may have changed forever because of the storm. I'm surprised you haven't had job offers from people who saw you on television."

"Actually, I have from two places. The attorney general's office in San Angelo has an opening for an administrative assistant and another was a mayor's office in Tyler that has a position that would have the title of office manager."

"Are you interested in either one?"

"No, I thanked them and turned them down. My friends are in Royal and I've grown up here so I want to stay. Besides, they need me here now."

"Amen to that. I'm glad you're staying here because

we'll be working together and maybe seeing each other a little more since we're both at the Cozy Inn."

"Did you get your suite changed to the sixth floor?"

"Indeed, I did," he said. "I'll show you."

"I'll take a rain check."

"Oh, well, it's still early. Let's go have a drink and a dance or two."

She hesitated for just a moment, torn between what she should do and what she wanted to do.

"You're having some kind of internal debate, so I'll solve it. You'll come with me and we'll have a drink. There—problem solved. You think you'll be back in Royal tomorrow night?"

"Yes," she said, smiling at him.

When they got back to the hotel, Aaron headed for a booth in the bar. The room was darker and cozier than the dining room. There was a small band playing and a smattering of dancers.

Over a chocolate milk shake, she talked to Aaron. They became enveloped in conversation, first about the town and the storm and then a variety of topics. When he asked her to dance, she put him off until later, relieved that it did not come up again.

"Our Texas Cattleman's Club friends want an update on the progress here. Cole is good about keeping in touch with both groups."

"I think you'll be surprised by how much they have rebuilt and repaired," she replied.

"Good. I'm anxious to see for myself what's been done."

"You'll be surprised by changes all over town."

Later, she glanced at her watch and saw it was almost one, she picked up her purse. "Aaron, I have to fly out early in the morning. I didn't know it was so late. I never intended to stay this late."

"But you were having such a good time you just couldn't tear yourself away," he teased, and she smiled at him.

"Actually, it has been a good time and the first evening in a while that has had nothing to do with the storm."

They headed out to the elevator and rode to the sixth floor. The hallway was empty and quiet as Aaron walked her to her door.

"Let me take you to the airport in the morning and we can get breakfast there."

"No, thank you. It's way too early."

"I'll be up early. It'll save you trouble and we can talk some more. All good reasons—okay?"

She stopped at her door, getting her card from her purse. "I know you'll get your way in this conversation, too, Aaron. See you in the lobby at six o'clock. Thanks for dinner tonight and a million thanks for finding Dobbin. That made Mildred happy."

"It was fun. Mostly it was fun to be with you and see you again. Before we say good-night, there's something I've been wanting to do since the last time we were together."

"Do I dare ask—what have you been wanting to do?"

"Actually, maybe two or three things," he said softly. "First, I want to kiss you again," he said, moving close and slipping his arm around her waist. Her heart thudded as she looked up at him. She should step back, say no, stop him now, but what harm was there in a kiss? She gazed into his light brown eyes and there was no way to stop. Her heartbeat raced and her lips tingled. She leaned closer and then his mouth covered hers. His arms tightened around her and he pulled her against him.

She wrapped her arms around him to return his kiss, wanting more than kisses. She felt on fire, memories of being in his arms and making love tugging at her.

He leaned over her while he kissed her, his tongue going

deep, touching, stroking, building desire. She barely felt his fingers in her hair, but in minutes her hair fell over her shoulders.

She had to stop, to say no. She couldn't have another night like the last one with him.

"Aaron, wait," she whispered.

He looked down at her. His brown eyes had darkened with passion. "I've dreamed of you in my arms, Stella," he whispered. "I want to kiss you and make love."

"Aaron, that night was so unlike me."

"That night was fantastic." He held long strands of her hair in his fingers. "Your hair is pretty."

She shook her head. "I have to go in," she whispered. "Thank you for dinner, and especially for finding the dog."

She opened her door with her card.

"Stella," he said. His voice was hoarse. She paused to look at him.

"I'll meet you in the lobby at six in the morning. I'll take you to the airport."

She nodded. "Thanks," she said, and stepped into her entryway and closed the door. The lock clicked in place. She rested her forehead against the door and took a deep breath. She didn't intend to get entangled with him at this point in time. Not until she had a definite answer about whether she was pregnant.

At six the next morning Aaron stood waiting. He saw her step off the elevator. She wore a gray coat and a knitted gray scarf around her neck. Her hair was back in a bun. She was plain—men didn't turn to look at her as she walked past, yet she stirred desire in him. She was responsive, quick-witted, kind, helpful, reliable. She was bright and capable and—he knew from firsthand experience—sexy.

He drew a deep breath and tried to focus on other things.

But he was already thinking about how long she would be gone and when he would see her again. He hoped that would happen as soon as she returned to Royal. Maybe she would let him pick her up at the airport.

He needed to step back and get a grip. If anyone would be serious in a relationship, it would be Stella. She would want wedding bells, which was reason enough that he should leave her alone. He didn't want a long-term relationship. But she might be one of those women who couldn't deal with a casual affair.

"Good morning," he said as she walked up.

"I'm ready to catch a plane," she said, smiling at him and looking fresh. Beneath the coat he saw a white tailored blouse, tan slacks and brown loafers. Always practical and neat, so what was it about her that made his pulse jump when he saw her?

"You look as if you don't have a care in the world and as if you had a good night's sleep."

"Well, I'm glad I look that way. By the end of some of the days I've spent dealing with all the storm problems, I feel bedraggled."

"I think we can do something about that," he said, flirting with her and wanting to touch her if only just to hold her hand.

"I pass on hearing your suggestions. Let's concentrate on getting to the plane."

"The car is waiting."

As soon as they were headed to the Royal airport, Aaron settled back to drive. "Cole left a list of what we're working on and I have the list we made yesterday of more places where we can help. I'll spend the day visiting the sites, including the Cattleman's Club. When Cole gets back, I want to be able to talk to him about what I can do to help."

"If you have any questions, I'll have my phone, although some of the time it may be turned off."

"I'll manage," he said.

She chuckled. "I'm sure you will."

"You should be able to get away a day without a barrage of phone calls from Royal. Maybe we should think about a weekend away and really give you a break."

She laughed again. "No weekend getaways, Aaron. For more than one reason. You can forget that one. I'll manage without a weekend break."

"Can't blame me for trying," he said, giving her a quick grin. "I'll miss you today," he said.

"No, you won't. You'll be busy. Once people find out who you are and that you're here in Royal, you'll be busy all day long with questions and requests and just listening to problems. I can promise you—get ready to be in high demand."

"Is that the way it's been for Cole? If it has, it probably is good for him because it takes his mind off his loss."

"I'm sure it's what he deals with constantly. We've come a long way, but we still have so far to go to ever recover from all the devastation."

He turned into the small airport and let her out, then parked and came back to join her for breakfast. All too soon she was called to board. He stood watching until she disappeared from sight and then he headed back to town. At least she had agreed to let him pick her up when she returned later today. He was already looking forward to being with her again, something that surprised him. Since losing Paula and Blake, he hadn't been this excited about any woman. Far from it. He felt better staying home by himself than trying to go out with someone and fake having a good time.

That had all changed with Stella—which surprised and puzzled him, because she was so unlike anyone who had ever attracted him before.

Three

Stella left the doctor's office in a daze. The home pregnancy test had been accurate. She was carrying Aaron's baby. Why, oh, why had she gotten into this predicament?

She climbed inside her rental car and locked the doors, relieved to be shut away from everyone else while she tried to adjust to the news.

To make matters worse, now Aaron was not only in Royal, but staying in the neighboring sixth floor suite at the Cozy Inn. He wanted to be with her, to dance with her. She did not want him to know yet. She wished he would go back to Dallas to R&N headquarters and give her time to think things through. She had to decide how much and when she would tell him.

She groaned aloud and put her forehead against the steering wheel. Aaron was a good guy. He had military training, was caring and family oriented, from what little she knew. She could guess his reaction right now. He would instantly propose.

She groaned again and rubbed her temples with her fingertips. "Oh, my," she whispered to the empty car.

She couldn't let Aaron know yet. She would have to get so busy she couldn't go out with him. Her spirits sank lower. He had a suite next to hers—there wasn't going to be any way to avoid him.

He was a take-charge guy and he would definitely want to take charge of her situation.

He would want to marry her. She was as certain of that as she was that she was breathing air and sitting in Austin.

Glancing at her watch, she saw she would be late meeting her sister for lunch. Trying to focus, she started the car and drove to the restaurant they'd agreed on earlier.

At the restaurant, she saw that her sister was already seated. When Stella sat down at the table, her sister's smile faded. "You've had bad news."

"Linda, I just can't believe the truth," Stella said, tears threatening, which was totally unlike her. "I'm pregnant. The test was correct."

"Oh, my, of all people. Stella, I can't believe it. I'll tell you something right now. I know you—you're a wonderful aunt to my children. You're going to love this baby beyond your wildest imaginings. You'll see. I know I'm right."

"That will come, but at the moment this is going to complicate my life. This shouldn't have happened."

"Here comes the waiter."

"I've lost my appetite. There's no way I can eat now."

"Eat something. You'll be sorry later if you don't."

Linda ordered a salad and Stella ordered chicken soup.

As soon as they were alone, Linda turned to Stella. "Look, I'll help any way I can, anytime. When the baby is due, you can stay here and I'll be with you."

"Thank you," Stella said, smiling at her sister. "I can't believe this is happening."

"You've said the dad is a nice guy. Tell him."

"I'll have to think about what I'm going to do first and make some decisions. I know I have to tell him eventually, but not yet. The minute he finds out, I'm sure he'll propose."

"That may solve your problem. Marry him. Accept his

proposal. You've already been attracted to each other or you wouldn't be pregnant. There's your solution."

"It's not that simple. Aaron and I are not in love. Look at our parents. That's marriage without love and it was horrible for them and for us. I don't want that. And I feel like there are moments Aaron shuts himself off. He doesn't share much of himself."

"You may be imagining that. Marry him and if he's nice and you've been attracted to each other, you'll probably begin to love him."

"I'm not falling into that trap. Linda, when you married, you and Zane were so in love. That's the way I want it to be if I marry. I couldn't bear to do it otherwise. And it will be a sense of duty for Aaron. He won't give it one second's thought. I'm just sure."

"I'm telling you—if he proposes, marry him. You'll fall in love later."

"Think back to our childhood and the fights that our parents had—the yelling and Mom throwing things and Dad swearing and storming around slamming doors. Oh, no. You can forget the marriage thing. I'll work this out. It's just takes some getting used to and careful planning."

"At least consider what I'm saying. If this man is such a nice guy, that's different from Mom and Dad."

"You know Dad can be a nice guy when he wants to. Mom just goads him. And vice versa. Here comes lunch."

"Try to eat a little. You'll need it."

"It helps to have someone to talk to about it."

"Do you have anyone in Royal?"

"Of course. You should remember Edie. We're close enough that I can talk to her about it. She'll understand, too. Actually, I can probably talk to Lark Taylor."

"I know Lark, but not as well as you do since you're

both the same age. She's not the friendliest person until you get to know her."

"In this storm, believe me, we got to know each other. She and the other nurses from the hospital were out there every day trying to help. So were others that I feel are lifelong friends now. Megan Maguire, the shelter director. I feel much closer to some of the people I've worked with since the tornado. I can talk to them if I want."

"Is he good-looking?"

"I think so."

"Well, then you'll have a good-looking baby."

"Frankly, I hope this baby doesn't look *exactly* like him." Stella smiled. "I'm teasing. I'll think about what you've said. Actually, Aaron is in Royal. I'm having dinner with him tonight."

"There," Linda said, sounding satisfied, as if the whole problem was solved. "Go out with him some before you tell him. Give love a chance to happen. You're obviously attracted to each other."

"I might try, Linda. It's a possibility. But that's enough about me. How are the kids?"

They talked about Linda's three children, their parents, progress in rebuilding Royal and finished their lunch.

As they stood in the sunshine on the sidewalk saying their goodbyes, Linda asked, "You're coming for Christmas, aren't you?"

"Yes. I'll fly in late afternoon Christmas Eve and then back home Christmas afternoon."

"Think about what I've said about marrying the dad. That might turn out a lot better than it did for Mom and Dad."

"I'll think about that one. You take care. See you next time." She turned and hurried to the rental car.

She paused to do a search on her phone and located the

nearest bookshop, which was only two blocks away. She drove over and went inside. It took a few minutes to find a book on pregnancy and what to expect with a first baby but before she knew it, she was back in the car, headed to the airport.

All the way to Dallas on the plane she read her new book. She would have to find a doctor in Royal. She was certain Lark could help her there. She knew of two who were popular with women her age.

When she changed planes for Royal, she tucked her new book into her purse and tossed away the shopping bag in the airport.

As she flew to Royal her dread increased by the minute. She felt as if she had gained ten pounds and her waist had expanded on this trip. She felt uncomfortable in her own skin.

When she stepped off the plane, Aaron was waiting. He had on jeans and a navy sweatshirt. There was no way to stop the warmth that flowed over her at the sight of him and his big smile. She had mixed reactions just as she always had with him.

"Hi," he said, walking up and draping his arm across her shoulders to give her a slight hug as they headed for the main door leading to the parking lot. His brown-eyed gaze swept over her. He saw too much all the time. How long did she have before he could tell she was expecting?

"How's your sister?"

"She's fine. I enjoyed seeing her and all is well."

"Good. I hope you had a restful day."

"I did. How was it here?"

"I imagine if you'd been here, you would answer, 'The usual.' I saw a great deal of the construction and talked to a lot of people. I've been at the Texas Cattleman's Club most of the day. Repairs have begun on the clubhouse.

They didn't have total destruction, so it should be done before too long. Actually, I helped some with the work there today." They reached his car and he held the door for her. She watched him walk around the car and slide behind the wheel.

As soon as they were on the freeway, he said, "Let me take you to dinner again. We'll eat at the Cozy Inn if you prefer."

"Thanks, Aaron, I would like that. There's still time for me to go by the hospital this afternoon. By the end of the day, all I'll be up for is the Cozy Inn for dinner. Right now I want to go back to my suite and catch up on emails."

"You may regret doing that. What if you have over a hundred emails waiting? You might have to go look for another lost dog."

She smiled, feeling better.

"I'll tell you one thing," he said, "people are really grateful to you for all you've done. I've had a lot of people out of the blue mention your name. I guess they assume everyone knows who you are and they'll just start talking about 'Stella did this' or 'Stella did that.'"

"I'm always happy to help."

"A lot of people are also talking about Royal needing an acting mayor because it's obvious now that the mayor can't return to work anytime soon. And people I talked to are mentioning your name in the same breath they talk about needing an acting mayor."

"Aaron, I'm an administrative assistant. A lot of us are helping others."

"You've been a big help to lots of people and they appreciate it."

She shook her head and didn't answer him as he pulled to a stop at the front door of the Cozy Inn.

"I'm letting you out here and heading back to the club. I'll see you at seven."

"Let's just meet in the lobby in case I get delayed."

"Sure," he said as a doorman opened her door and she stepped out. She walked into the inn without looking back.

In her room she went straight to her mirror to study her figure. She didn't look one bit different from when she had checked earlier, but she felt different. For one minute she gave herself over to thinking *if only*—if she were married to Aaron this would be one of the most joyous occasions for her.

With a long sigh, she stopped thinking about being married to Aaron and faced the reality that Aaron was in his thirties and still single. She thought back to the night she had met him after the storm. She had been comforting Paige Richardson whose husband, Craig, had died in the tornado. Others had come to call on Paige and someone introduced Stella to Aaron. He was staying in a motel on the edge of Royal, but he offered to take Stella back to the Cozy Inn. They had talked and one thing had led to another until they were in bed together—a rare event to her.

The next morning, when she told Aaron the night was totally uncharacteristic of her and she wanted to avoid further contact, he had agreed to do whatever she wanted and also told her he wasn't in for long-term relationships. She really didn't know much about him. That night they had had fun and lots of laughter, lots of talking, but she was beginning to realize that none of their conversation was about anything serious or important. Last night with him could be described the same way. She knew almost nothing about him and he hadn't questioned her very much about her background. Aaron Nichols would be the father of her child, and it was time she found out more about him. Whether he hated or loved becoming a dad, that was what had happened and they both would have to adjust to the reality of parenthood.

She went to her laptop to read her emails, answering what she needed to, and then left for Royal Memorial Hospital.

The west side of town had taken the brunt of the F4 tornado. Town hall where she had worked was mostly reduced to debris. Almost all three stories of the building had been leveled. The only thing left standing was part of the clock tower—the clock stuck at 4:14 p.m., a permanent reminder of the storm. She couldn't pass it without shivering and getting goose bumps as she recalled the first terrifying moments.

Approaching the hospital, she saw the ripped and shattered west wing. As far as she could tell, rebuilding had not yet begun.

As soon as she went inside the building, outside sounds of traffic and people were shut out. She stepped into an elevator. A nurse had already boarded and Stella realized it was Lark Taylor. They had known each other since childhood, but had become closer in the weeks after the storm. Some accused the ICU nurse of being unfriendly, but Stella couldn't imagine how anyone could feel that way.

"Here to see the mayor's family?" Lark asked.

"Yes. I try to stop by every few days. The changes are slow, but I want to keep up with how he's doing. How's Skye?" As she asked about Lark's sister, Stella gazed into Lark's green eyes and saw her solemn look.

"No change, but thank you for asking about her." Skye had sustained head injuries during the tornado and had been in a medically induced coma ever since. Stella knew Lark was worried about her sister and the baby and it hadn't helped that no one knew who the baby's father was.

"And how's her baby?"

"She's doing well," Lark answered, her voice filling with relief. "I'm so thankful to work here so I can be closer to them."

"I'm glad Skye is doing well," Stella said, happy to hear good news about Skye's tiny baby, who came into the world two months prematurely after her mother was injured during the storm. "Every storm survivor is wonderful," Stella said.

"Right now, we're looking for Jacob Holt." Stella remembered the gossip four years earlier when Jacob had run away with Skye.

"You think he's in Royal?"

"No. If he was here in Royal, I think, in a town this size someone would know. But they're trying to find him. His brother is looking."

"If Keaton doesn't know where Jacob is, I doubt if anyone else does."

"You know so many people—have you heard anything about him?"

"No, nothing. If I do, I'll let you know."

When the elevator stopped on Lark's floor, she stepped into the doorway and turned back.

"If you do hear about him, please let me know. Skye can't tell us anything, and her baby certainly can't. We need to talk to Jacob. With him missing and Skye in a coma, Keaton wants to test the baby's DNA to see if she's a Holt." Lark shook her head. "If you hear anything at all about Jacob, please call me. You have my cell number. Just call or text."

Stella nodded. "I will."

The doors closed and Stella thought about Skye. So many people had been hurt by the storm. But Stella was happy to hear the joy in Lark's voice when she said the little preemie was doing well.

The elevator stopped on Mayor Richard Vance's floor. When she went to the nurse's station, she was told the mayor's wife was in the waiting room.

It was an hour later when Stella left the hospital and hurried to her car. Before she left downtown she stopped at a drugstore to pick up a few things she needed at the Cozy Inn. When she went inside, she recognized the tall, auburn-haired woman she had known for so long because their families were friends. She walked over to say hello to Paige Richardson.

At her greeting Paige turned and briefly smiled. Stella gazed into her friend's gray eyes.

"How are you? How's the Double R, Paige?" she asked about Paige's ranch, which she now had to run without her husband.

"Still picking up the pieces," Paige said. "I heard Aaron Nichols is here again to help. Are you working with Cole and Aaron?"

"A little. A lot of their paperwork comes through the mayor's office. Cole is out at a friend's ranch now—Henry Markham, who lost his brother, too, in the storm."

"His ranch was badly damaged. Cole's probably helping him."

"The storm was hard on everybody. I'm sure you keep busy with the Double R."

"Some days I'm too busy to think about anything else. Is Cole staying very long with Henry?"

"It should be four or five more days."

"How's the mayor?" Paige asked. "I'm sure you're keeping up with his condition."

"It's a slow healing process, but each time I check, he's holding his own or getting better."

"It's been nice to talk to you because you have some

good news. Sometimes I dread coming to town because of more bad news," Paige said.

"This week I've gotten some hopeful reports. It's been great to see you, and you take care of yourself."

"Thanks," Paige replied with another faint smile. "You take care of yourself."

Stella left Paige and greeted other people in the store while she got the things she needed, paid for them and left. Outside she ran into two more people she hadn't seen for a few weeks. They talked briefly and she finally started back to the hotel. Her thoughts shifted from the people she had seen to being with Aaron shortly.

At the Cozy Inn, she walked through to her bedroom and went straight to a mirror to study herself and how she looked. So far, she didn't think she showed no matter which way she stood. She felt fine. The baby should be due next summer. Her baby and Aaron's. She felt weak in the knees whenever she thought about having his baby.

Did she want to go out with him, keep quiet and hope they both fell in love before she had to confess that she was pregnant?

She didn't think that was the way it would work out. She pulled out a navy skirt and a white cotton blouse from the dresser, then put on a navy sweater over the blouse. Once again she brushed and pinned up her hair. She saw she just had a few minutes to get to the lobby to meet Aaron.

If anything, when she spotted him standing near the door of the main restaurant, her excited response resonated deeper than it had the night before. At the same time, she had a curl of apprehension. How would she tell him? When would she? How long could she wait until she did?

Wearing a navy sweater, navy slacks and black cowboy boots, he stood near a potted palm while he waited. She crossed the lobby with its ranch-style plank floor scattered with area rugs. Hotel guests sat in clusters and chatted with each other. The piano music from the restaurant drifted into the lobby. So many local hotels had become temporary homes for the folks displaced by the tornado; whole families were staying and becoming friends.

When she approached, she saw a look in Aaron's brown eyes that made her tingle inside. "I've been looking forward to this all day," he said in greeting.

"So have I," she said. "I haven't had many leisurely dinners with a friend since the storm hit and I hope we can have one tonight."

"We're going to try. You know you can turn that phone off."

She shook her head. "This from the man who would never turn down helping someone. There are too many real emergencies. Later, when everyone calms down and is back on an even keel, I'll think about turning it off, but not yet."

Once they had settled at their table and their drinks arrived—water for her and beer for Aaron—she listened to him describe his work at the Cattleman's Club that day.

"How's your sister?" Aaron asked when he was done.

"She's fine. We had a nice time and had lunch together before I left. We don't see each other much, just the two of us."

"Any change with Mayor Vance?"

She shook her head. "No. But his wife told me he's stable. He's had a very rough time. I talked to Lark Taylor briefly. Her sister Skye is still in a medically induced coma, which sounds terrible to me, but I know it's necessary sometimes. I didn't ask further and, of course, she can't tell me details."

"How is Skye's baby? Still in NICU?"

"Yes, but Lark said Skye's baby is doing well."

"That's good," he said. He tilted his head to look at her. "What?" he asked. "You look puzzled."

"Most single men don't have much to say about a pree-mie baby in NICU."

He gave her that shuttered look he got occasionally. She seemed to have hit a nerve, but she didn't know why. She didn't pry into other's lives. If Aaron wanted to share something with her, he would.

Their dinners came, and once again her appetite fled even though the baked chicken looked delicious.

About halfway through dinner, Aaron noticed. "No appetite?"

"We had a big lunch just before I went to the airport."

She didn't like looking into his probing brown eyes that saw too much. Aaron was perceptive and an excellent listener, so between the two qualities, he guessed or understood things sooner than some people she had known better and longer.

"One thing I didn't mention," she said, to get his attention off her. "Lark said they were searching for Jacob Holt."

"Cole told me something about that. I imagine they are, with Skye in a coma and a new baby no one knows anything about. It's tough. The Holts must be anxious to know if the child is Jacob's."

"You can't blame him. Most people who've lived here long know about the Holt-Taylor feud."

"From what Cole told me, that feud goes back at least fifty years. What I've always heard is that it was over a land dispute."

"There are other things, too. A creek runs across both ranches, so they've fought over water rights," Stella said.

"There's been enough publicity, even nationally, over the tornado, I'd think Jacob Holt would have heard."

"I can't imagine he's anywhere on earth where he wouldn't hear something about it," she said.

"If the baby is Jacob's, she will be both a Taylor and a Holt and it might diminish the feud."

"High time that old feud died. I wonder if Jacob will ever come back to Royal."

"One more of those mysteries raised by the storm." He smiled at her. "Now speaking of the storm—I have a surprise for you."

Startled, she focused intently on him, unable to imagine what kind of surprise he had.

"I have made arrangements for you to speak to a men's group in Lubbock to raise funds for Royal to help in the rebuilding."

Her surprise increased, along with her dread. "Aaron, thank you for setting up an opportunity to raise funds, but I'm not the one to do it. You didn't even ask me. I'm not a public speaker or the type to talk a group of people into giving money for a cause," she said, feeling a momentary panic.

"You've done this countless times since the storm—you've been the town hall spokesperson really. With Mayor Vance critically ill and Deputy Mayor Rothschild killed in the storm, someone had to step forward and you did. You've done a fantastic job getting people to help out and donate. That's all you've been doing since the storm hit," he said, looking at her intently.

"That's so different," she said, wondering why he couldn't see it. "I did those things in an emergency situation. I was talking to people I knew and it was necessary. Someone had to step in. I was helping, not trying to persuade total strangers to donate to a cause. I'm not the person for that job. I'm not a public speaker and I'm not persuasive. I'm no salesperson or entertainer. A group like that will want to be entertained." Her panic grew because what Aaron expected was something she had never done. "Aaron, I can't persuade people to give money."

"I'm not sure I'm hearing right," he said. "You've persuaded, ordered and convinced people to do all sorts of things since the afternoon the storm hit."

"What I've been doing is so different. I told you, I stepped in when someone had to and the mayor couldn't. Of course people listened to me. They were hurt, desperate—what you've set me up to do is to entertain a group of businessmen in a club that meets once a month with a guest speaker. They're used to a fun speaker and then they go back to work. If I'm to walk in and convince them they should contribute money to Royal, I can't do it." Her old fears of public speaking, of having to try to deal with an audience—those qualms came rushing back.

"When you get there, you'll be fine," he said, as if dismissing her concerns as foolish. "When you meet and talk to them, you'll see they're just like people here. I'll go with you. I think once you start, it'll be just like it is when you're here. Relax, Stella, and be yourself. You've done a great job on national television and state and local news." He smiled at her and she could tell he didn't have any idea about her limitations.

"When I had interviews that first afternoon and the day after the tornado, I didn't have time to think about being on national television. I just answered questions and went right back to wherever I was needed."

"This isn't going to be different, Stella. You'll see. You'll be great."

"You may be surprised," she said, feeling glum and scared. "Really, Aaron, I don't know why you think I can do this. So when is this taking place?"

"Day after tomorrow. They have a program that day, so

you're not the only one to talk to them if that makes you feel better."

"It makes me feel infinitely better. Day after tomorrow. Next time run this past me, please, before you commit me to going."

"Sure. Stella, it never occurred to me that you wouldn't want to do this. It'll be so easy for you. I have great faith in you. This will help raise funds for Royal. People will know you're sincere in what you say, which will help."

She shook her head in exasperation. "That's what keeps me from flat-out telling you I refuse. I know it will help Royal. I just think someone else might make a better pitch. Thanks, Aaron, but you just don't get it," she said.

"Sure I do and I'm certain it will be easy for you. But all that is in the future. Right now, in our immediate future, I think it's time to dance," he said, holding out his hand.

She went to the dance floor with him, but her thoughts were on the group in Lubbock. She wanted to ask how many people would be in the audience, but she had already made a big issue of it and she couldn't back out now. It was a chance to raise funds and awareness for Royal, so she had to get over her fears and help. She wanted to help her town so maybe she should start planning what to say.

They danced three fast numbers that relaxed her and made her forget the rest of the week. Next, the piano player began an old ballad and Aaron drew her into his arms.

For a moment she relished just being held so close and dancing with him.

They danced one more song and then sat down and talked. Later, he ordered hot cocoa and they talked longer until she looked at her watch and saw it was after one in the morning.

"Aaron, I lost track of time. I do that too much with

you. I need to go to my suite. It's been a long day. I'm exhausted," she said as she stood up.

"I'm glad you lost track of time," he said, standing and draping his arm across her shoulders to draw her close to him.

When she reached for her purse, it fell out of her hands. As the purse hit the floor, Aaron bent down instantly to pick it up for her. A coin purse, a small box of business cards and a book fell out.

Horrified, she realized she had not taken the book she had bought earlier out of her purse. She tried to grab it, but Aaron had it in his hand and was staring at the cover with its picture of a smiling baby. For a moment her head spun and she felt as if she would faint, because in his hands that tiny book was about to change their future.

Four

Your Pregnancy and Your First Baby. The title jumped out at Aaron. Stella grabbed the book and dropped it into her purse.

When he looked up at her, all color had drained from her face. She stared, round eyed, looking as if disaster had befallen her.

He felt as if a fist slammed into his chest. Was she pregnant from their night together? She couldn't be, because he'd used protection. Gazing into her eyes, he had his answer that the impossible had happened—apparently the protection they'd used wasn't foolproof after all. Her wide blue eyes looked stricken. Shivering, she clutched her purse in both hands.

"I need to go to my suite," she said in almost a whisper. "We can talk tomorrow."

She brushed past him and for one stunned moment he let her go. Then he realized she would be gone in another minute and went after her. He caught up with her at the elevators and stepped on with her. Another couple joined them and they couldn't talk, so they rode in silence to the fourth floor, where the couple got off.

Aaron looked at her profile. Color had come back into her flushed cheeks. She looked panicked. It had to be because she was carrying his child.

Stunned, he couldn't believe what had happened. She might as well shout at him that he had gotten her pregnant. Her stiff demeanor, terrified expression and averted eyes were solid proof.

He felt as cold as ice, chilled to the bone, while his gaze raked over her. Her sweater hid her waist, but he had seen her waist yesterday and she was as tiny as ever, her stomach as flat as when they had met.

He took a deep breath and followed her out of the elevator.

At her door she turned to face him. "Thank you for dinner. Can we talk tomorrow?"

"Are you really going to go into your suite, get in bed and go to sleep right now?" he asked. His own head spun with the discovery, which explained why she had been so cool the other day when she had first seen him again. Shock hit him in waves and just wouldn't stop. She was pregnant with his baby. He would be a father. He had no choice now in the situation. He had made his choice the night he seduced her and he couldn't undo it now. "You're not going in there and going to sleep."

She met his gaze. "No, I guess I'm not," she replied in a whisper. "Come in."

There was only one thing for him to do. She carried his baby. He had gotten her pregnant. He had taken precautions and both of them thought they had been safe when in reality they had not been. It was done and could not be undone. As far as he could see there was no question about what he needed to do.

She unlocked her door and he closed and locked it behind them, following her into a spacious living area with beige-and-white decor that was similar to the suite he had. The entire inn had a homey appearance with maple furniture, old-fashioned pictures, needlepoint-covered throw pillows, rocking chairs in the living areas and fireplaces with gas logs.

"Have a seat, please. Do you want anything to drink?" she asked.

"Oh, yeah. Have any whiskey?"

"No. There's a bottle of wine," she replied, her voice cold and grim.

"That's okay. I'll pass. Have you been to a doctor yet?"

"Yes. That's where I went today," she said, her voice barely above a whisper. "I couldn't go to a doctor here in Royal where I know everybody and they know me. If they don't know me, a lot of people recognize me now from seeing me on television."

She sat perched on the edge of a wing chair that seemed to dwarf her. He studied her in silence and she gazed back. Her hands were knotted together, her knuckles white; once again she had lost her color. He suspected if he touched her she would be ice-cold.

He was in such shock he couldn't even think. This was the last possible thing he thought would happen to him. Actually, he'd thought it was impossible.

"You're certain you're pregnant?"

"Yes, Aaron, I am. There isn't really much to talk about right now. It's probably best you think about it before you start talking to me. I know this is a shock."

He stared at her. She was right in that he needed to think, to adjust to what had happened. It was a huge upheaval, bigger even than the storm, where he had merely come in afterward to try to help. Now he had his own storm in his life and he wondered if he could ever pick up the pieces.

She looked determined. Her chin was tilted up and she had a defiant gleam in her eyes. He realized he had been entirely focused on himself and the shock of discovering that he would be a father. He needed to consider Stella.

He crossed the room and pulled her to her feet, wrapping his arms around her. She stood stiffly in his embrace and gazed up at him.

"Stella, one thing I don't have to think about—I'm here for you. I know it's going to be hard, but let's try to reason this out and avoid worry. First, you're not alone. I want—"

She placed her finger on his lips. "Do not make any kind of commitment tonight. Not even a tiny one. You've had a shock, just as I had, and it takes a bit of time to adjust to this. Don't do something foolish on the spur of the moment. Don't do something foolish because of honor. I know you're a man of honor—Cole has said that and he knows you well. It shows, too, in things you've done to help the people here."

"You've had a head start on thinking about this and the future," he said, listening to her speech. "Stella, I don't have to think about this all night. It seems pretty simple and straightforward. We were drawn to each other enough for a baby to happen."

He took her cold hands in his. Her icy hands indicated her feelings and he wanted to reassure her. He saw no choice here.

"Stella, this is my responsibility. I want to marry you."

She closed her eyes for a moment as if he had given her terrible news. When she opened them to look up at him, she shook her head.

"Thank you, but no, we will not get married. I didn't want you to know until I decided what I would do. I knew you would propose the minute you learned about my pregnancy."

"I don't see anything wrong with that. Some women would be happy to get a proposal," he said, wondering if she was thinking this through. "I'm not exactly repulsive to you or poor husband material, am I?"

"Don't be absurd. There's something huge that's wrong with proposing tonight—within the hour you've discovered you'll be a father. We're not in love, Aaron. Neither one of us has ever said 'I love you' to the other."

"That doesn't mean we can't fall in love."

She frowned and her lips firmed as she stared at him and shook her head. "There was no love between my parents. I don't think there ever was," she said. "They had the most miserable, awful marriage. There was no physical abuse or anything like that. There were just tantrums, constant bickering, tearing each other down verbally. My sister and I grew up in a tense, unhappy household. I don't ever want to be in that situation. I'll have to be wildly in love to marry someone. My sister and her husband are, and it's a joy to be around them. They love each other and have a happy family. I couldn't bear a marriage without love and I don't want you to be in that situation, either. We're not in love. We barely know each other. We'll work this out, but marriage isn't the way."

He pulled her close against him to hold her while they stood there quietly. "Look, Stella, we're not your parents. I can't imagine either one of us treating the other person in such a manner."

She stood stiffly in his arms and he felt he couldn't reach her. He'd had his second shock when she turned down his offer of marriage. It didn't occur to him that she wouldn't marry him. Now there were two shocks tonight that hit him and left him reeling.

"You got pregnant when we were together in October," he said.

"Yes," she whispered.

He tilted her face up to look into her eyes. He caressed her throat, letting his fingers drift down her cheek and around to her nape. He felt the moment she relaxed against him. The stiffness left her and he heard her soft sigh.

"I didn't want you to know yet," she whispered.

"Maybe it's best I do. We'll work through this together," he said.

As he looked into her wide blue eyes, he became more aware of her soft curves pressed against him. His gaze lowered to her lips and his heart beat faster as desire kindled.

"Stella," he whispered, leaning closer. When his lips brushed hers, she closed her eyes.

He wrapped his arms more tightly around her, pulling her closer against him as he kissed her. It started as a tender kiss of reassurance. But then his mouth pressed more firmly against hers as his kiss became passionate. He wound his fingers in the bun at the back of her head and combed it out, letting the pins fall.

He wanted her. As far as he was concerned, their problem had a solution and it would only be a matter of time until she would see it. The moment that thought came to him, he remembered her strength in tough situations. If she said no to him, she might mean it and stick by it no matter what else happened.

She opened her eyes, stepping back. "Aaron, when we make love, I want it to be out of joy, not because of worry and concerns. Tonight's not the night."

Her hair had partially spilled over her shoulders and hung halfway down her back. A few strands were still caught up behind her head. Her lips had reddened from his kisses. Her disheveled appearance appealed to him and he wanted to draw her back into his embrace. Instead, he rested his hands lightly on her shoulders.

"You don't have to be burdened with worry and concerns tonight," he said. "We're in this together."

"Aaron, has anything ever set you back in your life?"

Her question was like a blow to his heart. She still hadn't heard about Paula and Blake, and he still didn't want to talk about them or his loss. Over the years, the pain had dulled, but it would never go away. Everyone had setbacks in life. Why would she think he had never had any? "All right, Stella. You want to be alone. I'll leave you alone," he said, turning to go. He had tried to do the right thing and been rebuffed for it.

"Aaron," she said, catching up with him, "I know you're trying to help me. I appreciate it. A lot of men would not have proposed. You're one of the good guys."

Realizing she needed time to think things through, he gazed at her. "I'm the dad. I'm not proposing just for your sake. It's for mine, too. Stella, this baby coming into my life is a gift, not an obligation," he said.

Her eyes widened with a startled expression and he realized she hadn't looked at it from his perspective, other than to expect him to propose.

"We can do better than this," he said, pulling her into his arms to kiss her again, passionately determined to get past her worries and fears.

For only a few seconds she stood stiffly in his arms and then she wrapped her arms around him, pressing against him and kissing him back until he felt she was more herself again and their problems were falling into a better perspective.

As their kiss deepened, his temperature jumped. He forgot everything except Stella in his arms while desire blazed hotly.

Leaning back slightly, he caressed her throat, his hands sliding down over her cotton blouse. He didn't think she could even feel his touch through the blouse, but she took a deep breath and her eyes closed as she held his forearms. Her reaction made him want to peel away the blouse, but he was certain she would stop him. He slipped his hand to the top button while he caressed her with his other hand. As he twisted the button free, she clutched his wrist.

"Wait, Aaron," she whispered.

He kissed away her protest, which had sounded faint and halfhearted anyway. He ran his fingers through her hair, combing it out, feeling more pins falling as the locks tumbled down her back.

"You look pretty with your hair down," he whispered.

She turned, maybe to answer. Instead, he kissed her and stopped any conversation.

"I want to love you all night. I will soon, Stella. I want to kiss and hold you," he whispered when the kiss subsided.

She moaned softly as he twisted free another button, his hand sliding beneath her blouse to cup her breast.

She gasped, kissing him, clinging to him. He wanted to pick her up, carry her to bed, but he suspected she would end their kisses and tell him good-night.

She finally stepped back. "We were headed to the door."

He combed long strands of brown hair from her face. "I'll go, but sometime soon, you'll want me to stay. I'll see you in the morning." He started out the door and turned back. "Don't worry. If you can't sleep, call me and we'll talk."

She smiled. "Thanks, Aaron. Thanks for being you."

He studied her, wondering about her feelings, wondering where they were headed, because he could imagine her sticking to the decisions she had already made involving their future. "Just don't forget I'm half the parent equation."

"I couldn't possibly forget," she said, standing in the open doorway with him.

"Good night," he said, brushing a light kiss on her lips and going to his suite.

When he got there, he went straight to the kitchen and

poured himself a glass of whiskey. Setting the bottle and his drink on the kitchen table, he pulled out his billfold. As he sat, he took a long drink. He opened the wallet and looked at a picture of Paula holding Blake. Aaron's insides knotted.

"I love you," he whispered. "I miss you. I'm going to be a dad again. I never thought that would happen. It doesn't take away one bit of love from either of you. That's the thing about love—there's always more."

He felt the dull pain that had been a part of him since losing Paula and Blake. "This isn't the way it was supposed to be. I know, if you were here, you'd tell me to snap out of it, to marry her and be the best dad possible." He paused a moment and stared at the photo. "Paula, Blake, I love you both. I miss you."

He dropped his billfold and put his head in his hands, closing his eyes tightly against the hurt. He got a grip on his emotions, wiped his eyes and took a deep breath. He was going to be a dad again. In spite of all the tangled emotions and Stella's rejection of his proposal, he felt a kernel of excitement. He would be a dad—it was a small miracle. A second baby of his own. How would he ever persuade Stella to marry him? She wanted love and marriage.

He could give her marriage. He would have to try to persuade her to settle for that. Just marriage. A lot of women would jump at such a chance. One corner of his mouth lifted in a grin and he held up his drink in a toast to an imaginary companion. "Here's to you, Stella, on sticking to your convictions and placing a premium on old-fashioned love. You'll be a good mother for our child."

So far, in working with her, Stella had proved to be levelheaded, practical and very intelligent. That gave him hope.

He finished his drink and poured one more, capping the bottle. Then he stood up and put it away. He started to pocket his billfold, but he paused to open it and look once more at the picture of his baby son. As always, he felt a hollow emptiness, as if his insides had been ripped out. Now he was going to have another baby—another little child, his child. It was a miracle to him, thrilling.

Stella had to let him be a part of his child's life. It was a chance to be a dad again, to have a little one, a son or daughter to raise. In that moment, he cared. He wanted Stella to marry him or let him into the life of his child in some way. He wasn't giving up a second child of his. One loss was too many. He sure as hell didn't plan to lose the second baby. He would have to court Stella until she just couldn't say no. He had to try to win her love.

As much as he hurt, he still had to smile. Stella wouldn't go for any insincere attempt to fake love or conjure it up where it didn't exist.

He had to make her fall in love with him and that might not be so easy when he didn't know whether he could ever really love her in return.

The next morning Stella was supposed to have breakfast with Aaron, but he called and told her to go ahead because he'd be late. A few minutes after she'd settled in and ordered, she watched him cross the dining room to her table. He was dressed for a day of helping the cleanup effort in jeans, an R&N sweatshirt and cowboy boots. Even in the ordinary clothes, he looked handsome and her heart began racing at her first glimpse of him. The father of her baby. She was beginning to adjust to the idea of being pregnant even though she had slept little last night.

"Sorry. You shouldn't have waited. Did you order from the menu or are you going with the buffet?"

"I've ordered from the menu and I didn't wait," she said, smiling.

"I'll get the buffet and be right back."

While they ate, Aaron sipped his coffee. "So, did you sleep well last night?" he asked.

"Fine," she replied, taking a dainty bite of yellow pineapple.

"Shall I try again? Did you get any sleep last night?"

She stared at him. "How do you know I didn't?"

"You're a scrupulously honest person so prevarication isn't like you. You were a little too upset to sleep well."

"If you must know, I didn't sleep well. Did you?"

"Actually, pretty good after I thought things through."

"I'm glad. By the way, today after work, I'll try to get something together for the presentation in Lubbock tomorrow. Please tell me this is a small group."

"This is a small group," he said, echoing her words.

She wasn't convinced. "Aaron, is this a large or small group?"

"It's what I'd call in-between."

"That's a real help," she said. He grinned and took her hand in his to squeeze it lightly.

"All you need is an opening line and a closing line. You know the stuff in between. You'll be fine. I know what I'm talking about. And so will you, so just relax," he said, his eyes warm and friendly. She would be glad to have his support for the afternoon.

When they finished breakfast and stood to go, she caught him studying her waist. She wore a tan skirt and matching blouse that was tucked in. She knew from looking intently in her mirror before she came down for breakfast, that her pregnancy still didn't show in her waist and that her stomach was as flat as ever.

His gaze flew up to meet hers. "You don't look it," he said quietly.

"Not yet. I will," she replied, and he nodded.

They walked out together and climbed into Aaron's car. He dropped her off at the temporary headquarters for town hall and drove away to go to the Cattleman's Club. Today she would be overseeing the effort to sort records that had been scattered by the storm. She wondered how many months—or worse, years—of vital records they would find. She hoped no one's life changed for the worse because of these lost records.

Stella entered the makeshift office that had been set up for recovered documents. The room held long tables covered with boxes labeled for various types of documents. As Stella put her purse away, Polly Hadley appeared with a box filled with papers that she placed on a cleared space on a desk.

"Good morning, Stella. You're just in time," her fellow administrative assistant said. "Here's another box of papers to sort through. I glanced at a few of these when I found them. What I saw was important," Polly said.

"I'm thankful for each record we find."

"Most of these papers were beneath part of a stockade fence."

"Heaven knows where the fence came from," Stella said.

"I don't want to think about how long we'll be searching for files, papers, records. Some of these were never stored electronically."

"Some records that were stored electronically are destroyed now," Stella stated as she pulled the box closer. "We'll just do the best we can. Thank goodness so many people are helping us."

"I'll be back with more." Polly smiled as she left the makeshift office.

Stella picked up a smudged stack of stapled papers from the top of the pile and looked at them, sighing when she saw they were adoption papers. A chill slithered down her spine as she thought again of important documents they might not ever find. She smoothed the wrinkled papers and placed them in a box of other papers relating to adoptions. She picked up the next set of papers and brushed away smudges of dirt as she read, her thoughts momentarily jumping back to breakfast with Aaron. In some ways it was a relief to have him know the truth. If only he would give her room to make decisions—that was a big worry. As for dinner with him tonight—she just hoped he didn't persist about marriage.

That evening as they ate, she made plans with Aaron to go to Lubbock the next day. She tried to be positive about it, but she had butterflies in her stomach just thinking about it.

She had finished eating and sat talking to Aaron while he sipped a beer when her phone rang. She listened to the caller, then stood up and gave instructions. When she hung up, she turned to Aaron.

"I heard some of that call. Your part," he said.

"We can talk as we walk to the car. That was Leonard Sherman. He's fallen and his daughter is out of town. He can't get up and he needs someone to help him. He hit his head. I told him that I would call an ambulance."

Aaron waited quietly while she made the call. As soon as she finished, she turned to him. "I need to go to his house to lock up for him when the ambulance picks him up. He lives alone near his daughter. He said his neighbor isn't home, either."

"Does everyone in town call you when they have an emergency?"

Smiling, she shook her head. "Of course not, but some of these people have gotten so they feel we're friends and

I'll help, which I'm glad to do. It's nice they feel that way. I'm happy to help when I can."

"I'll take you."

A valet brought Aaron's car to the door of the inn. As they drove away, she finished making her calls.

"You don't need to speed," she said. "I don't think he's hurt badly."

"You wanted to get there before they took him in the ambulance, so we will."

In minutes Aaron pulled into Leonard Sherman's driveway. She stepped out of the car and hurried inside while Aaron locked up and followed.

The ambulance arrived only minutes later and soon they had their patient loaded into the back and ready to go to the hospital. As the paramedics carefully pulled away from the curb, Stella locked up Leonard's house, pocketed the key and walked back to the car with Aaron.

"You don't have to go to the hospital with me. I'll call his daughter and she'll probably want to talk to the doctor. He said she's coming back tonight, so hopefully, she'll be home soon."

"I'll go with you. These evenings are getting interesting."

She laughed. "I told you that you don't have to come."

"You amaze me," Aaron said. "I've never told you any news I get about anyone in Royal that you don't already know. People tell you everything. I'll bet you know all sorts of secrets."

"I'm just friendly and interested."

"People trust you and you're a good listener. They call you for help. Mayor Vance doesn't do all this."

Stella watched him drive, thinking he was one person who didn't tell her everything. She always had a feeling that Aaron held personal things back. There were parts of his life closed to her. A lot of parts. She still knew little about him. She suspected Cole knew much more.

She called Leonard's daughter and, to her relief, heard her answer.

When Stella was done with the call, she turned to Aaron. "I'll go to Memorial Hospital to give her the key to his house, but his daughter is back and she'll be at the hospital, so we don't need to stay."

"Good. You said you wanted to get ready for tomorrow, so now you'll have a chance unless calamity befalls someone else in this town tonight."

"It's not that bad," she said.

"I had other plans for us this evening. We're incredibly off the mark."

"That's probably for the better, Aaron," she said.

"You don't have to do everything for everyone. Learn to delegate, Stella."

"Some things are too personal to delegate. People are frightened and hurting still. I'm happy to help however I can if it makes things even the smallest bit better."

He squeezed her hand. "Remind me to keep you around for emergencies," he said lightly, but she again wondered about what he kept bottled up and how he had been hurt. He might want them to be alone tonight, but she had to respond when someone called.

And she stuck to her guns. When they got back to the hotel, she told Aaron good-night early in the evening so she could get ready to leave for Lubbock with him the next morning.

As soon as she was alone in her suite, she went over her notes for the next day, but her thoughts kept jumping to Aaron. Every hour they spent together bound her a little more to him, making his friendship a bit more important to her. Now she was counting on him for moral support tomorrow.

The next morning, when she went to the lobby to meet Aaron and head for Lubbock, she saw him the minute she emerged from the elevator. The sight of him in a flawless navy suit with a red tie took her breath away and made her forget her worries about speaking. He looked incredibly handsome, so handsome, she wondered what he saw in her. She was plain from head to toe. Plain clothes, plain hair, no makeup. This handsome man wanted to marry her and she had turned him down. Her insides fluttered and a cold fear gripped her. Was she willing to let him go and marry someone else? The answer still came up the same. She couldn't marry without love. Yet Aaron was special, so she hoped she wasn't making a big mistake

This baby coming into my life is a gift, not an obligation. She remembered his words from the night before last. How many single men who had just been surprised to learn they would be a dad would have that attitude? Was she rejecting a very special man?

He saw her and she smiled, resisting the temptation to raise her hand to smooth her hair.

She was aware of her plain brown suit, her skirt ending midcalf. She wore a tan blouse with a round neck beneath her jacket. Her low-heeled brown pumps were practical and her hair was in its usual bun. When she crossed the lobby, no heads would turn, but she didn't mind because it had been that way all her life.

When she walked up to him, he took her arm. "The car is waiting," he said. "You look pretty."

"Thank you. Sometimes I wonder if you need to get your eyes checked."

He smiled. "The last time I was tested in the air force, I had excellent eyesight," he remarked. "You sell yourself short, Stella. Both on giving this talk and on how you look."

She didn't tell him that men rarely told her she was pretty. They thanked her for her help or asked her about their problems, just as boys had in school, but they didn't tell her how pretty she looked.

In minutes they were on the highway. She pulled out a notebook and a small stack of cards wrapped with a rubber band. "These are my notes. I have a slide presentation. I think the pictures may speak for themselves. People are stunned when they see these."

When she walked into the private meeting room in a country club, her knees felt weak and the butterflies in her stomach changed to ice. The room was filled with men and women in business suits—mostly men. It was a business club and she couldn't imagine talking to them. She glanced at Aaron.

"Aaron, I can't do this."

"Of course you can. Here comes Boyce Johnson, my friend who is president," he said, and she saw a smiling, brown-haired man approaching them. He extended his hand to Aaron, who made introductions that she didn't even hear as she smiled and went through the motions.

All too soon, Boyce called the group to order and someone made an introduction that Aaron must have written, telling about how she had helped after the storm hit Royal. And then she was left facing the forty or so people who filled the room, all looking at her and waiting for her to begin.

Smiling and hoping his presence would reassure her, Aaron sat listening to Stella make her presentation, showing pictures of the devastation in the first few hours after the storm hit Royal. That alone would make people want to contribute. After her slide presentation, Stella talked. She was nervous and it showed. He realized that right after the storm, adrenaline—and the sheer necessity for someone to take charge with Mayor Vance critically injured and the deputy mayor killed—had kept her going. Now that life in Royal was beginning to settle back into a routine, she could do it again, but she had to have faith in herself.

He thought of contacts he had and realized he could help her raise funds for the town. Her slide presentation had been excellent, touching, awesome in showing the storm's fury and giving the facts about the F4 tornado.

He sat looking at her as she talked and realized she might like a makeover in a Dallas salon. She could catch people's attention more. The men today were polite and attentive and she was giving facts that would hold their interest, but if she had a makeover, she might do even better. It should bolster her self-confidence.

She had done interviews and brief appearances almost since the day of the storm. Maybe it was time she had some help. He had statewide contacts, people in Dallas who were good about contributing to worthwhile causes. While she talked, he sent a text to a Dallas Texas Cattleman's Club member. In minutes he got a reply.

He sent a text to a Dallas salon, and shortly after, had an appointment for her.

He hoped she wouldn't balk at changing her hair. She clung to having it up in a bun almost as if she wanted to fade into the background, but hopefully, the makeover in the salon might cause her to be willing to change.

When she finished her speech and opened up the floor to questions, she seemed more poised and relaxed. She gave accurate facts and figures and did a good job of conveying the situation in Royal. Finally, there were no more questions. Boyce thanked her and Aaron for coming. He asked if anyone would like to make a motion to give a check to Stella to take back to Royal now because they seemed to need help as soon as they could possibly get it.

Boyce turned to ask their treasurer how much they had available in their treasury at present and was told there was $6,000.

One of the women made a motion immediately to donate $5,000. It was seconded and passed. A man stood and said he would like to contribute $1,000 in addition to the money from the treasury.

Aaron felt a flash of satisfaction, happy that they could take these donations back to Royal and happy that he had proved to Stella she could get out and lead the recovery effort now, just as she had right after the storm.

By the time the meeting was over, they had several checks totaling $12,000. Stella's cheeks were once again rosy and a sparkle was back in her blue eyes and he felt a warm glow inside because she was happy over the results.

With the help he planned to give her, he expected her to do even better. As he waited while people still talked to her, he received a text from the TCC member he had contacted. Smiling, he read the text swiftly and saw that his friend had made some contacts and it looked hopeful for an interview on a Fort Worth television station. Aaron sent a quick thank-you, hoping if it worked out Stella would accept.

It was almost four when they finally said goodbye and went to his car. When he sat behind the wheel, he turned to her, taking her into his arms. His mouth came down on hers as he kissed her thoroughly. Finally he leaned away a fraction to look at her.

"You did a great job. See, you can do this. You've raised $12,000 for Royal. That's fantastic, Stella."

She smiled. "My knees were shaking. Thank heavens you were there and I could look at your smiling face. They were nice and generous. I couldn't believe they would take all that out of their treasury and donate it at Christmastime."

"It's a Christmas present for Royal, thanks to you. That's what that club does. It's usually to help Lubbock, but Royal is a Texas town that is in desperate need of help. You did a great job and I think I can help you do an even bigger and better one," he said.

She laughed. "Aaron, please don't set me up to talk to another group of businesspeople. I'm an administrative assistant, not the mayor."

"You did fine today and I promise you, I think I can help you do a bit better if you'll let me."

"Of course, I'll let you, but I keep telling you, this is not my deal."

"You're taking $12,000 back to Royal. I think you can make a lot more and help people so much."

"When you put it that way—what do you have in mind?"

"I have lots of contacts in Dallas and across the state. Let me set up some meetings. Not necessarily a group thing like today—what I have in mind is meeting one-on-one or with just two or three company heads who might make some big donations. You can also make presentations to agencies that would be good contacts and can help even more."

"All right."

"Good. After your talk today I went ahead and contacted a close friend in Dallas. Through him you may get a brief interview on a local TV show in Fort Worth. Can I say you'll do it?"

"Yes," she answered, laughing. "You're taking charge again, Aaron."

"Also, if you'll let me contact them, I think I can get meetings in Dallas with oil and gas and TV executives, as well as some storm recovery experts. The television people will help get out the message that Royal needs help. The oil and gas people may actually make monetary donations. How's that sound?"

"Terrifying," she said, and smiled. "Well, maybe not so bad."

"So I can try to set up the meetings with the various executives?"

She stared at him a moment while she seemed to give thought to his question. "Yes. We need all the help we can get for the people at home."

"Good," he said, kissing her lightly.

"Let's take some time and talk about dealing with the press and interviews. We can talk over dinner. The press is important."

"I'll be happy to talk about interviews, but I don't think that I'll be giving many more."

"It's better to be ready just in case," he said, gazing into her wide blue eyes.

"Also I sent a text and asked for a salon makeover in Dallas for you. It's a very nice salon that will really pamper you. Would you object to that?" he asked, thinking he had never known a woman before that would have had to be given a sales pitch to get her to consent to a day at an exclusive Dallas salon.

She laughed. "Aaron, that seems ridiculous. I'm not going into show business. Mercy me. I don't think I need to go to Dallas to have a makeover and then return to Royal to help clean up debris and hunt through rubble for lost documents at town hall. That seems ridiculous."

"Stella, we can raise some money for Royal. A lot more than you did today. Trust me on this," he said, holding back a grin. "I told you that it's a very nice salon."

Shaking her head, she laughed again. "All right, Aaron. I can arrange to get away to go to Dallas. When is this makeover?"

"Someone canceled and they have an opening next Wednesday and I told them to hold it. Or they can take you in January. With the holidays coming, they're booked."

"How long does this take? I'll have to get to Dallas," she said, sounding as if he had asked her to do a task she really didn't relish.

"Cole and I have a company plane. We can fly to Dallas early Tuesday morning and be there in time for you to spend the day. I'll get you to the Fort Worth interview and I'll try to set up a dinner in Dallas that night. Afterward, we can stay at my house. I have lots of room and you can have your own suite there."

She smiled at him. "Very well. I can go to the salon Wednesday and get this over with. Thank you, Aaron," she said politely.

"Good deal," he said, amused at the reluctance clearly in her voice. "Take a dress along to go out to dinner. The next convenient stop, I'm pulling over to text the salon about Wednesday."

"I think this is going to be expensive for you and a waste of your money. People can't change in a few hours with a makeover. I really don't expect to do many more appearances or interviews."

"Just wait and see," he said.

"While we're on the subject of doing something for Royal, I've been thinking about Christmas. There are so many people who lost everything. We've talked about Christmas being tough for some of them. I want to organize a Christmas drive to get gifts for those who lost their homes or have no income because of their business losses. I want to make sure all the little children in those families have presents."

"That's a great idea, Stella. I'll help any way I can."

"I'm sure others will help. I'll call some of the women I

know and get this started. It's late—we should have started before now, but it's not too late to do this."

"Not at all. I think everyone will pitch in on this one. You're doing a great job for Royal."

"Thanks, Aaron. I'd feel better knowing that everyone has presents. We have a list now of all those who were hurt in some way by the storm. It's fairly detailed, so we know who lost homes and who is in the hospital and who lost loved ones or pets—all that sort of thing, and I can use it to compile a list for the Christmas gifts."

With a quick glance he reached over to take her hand. As he looked back at the highway, he squeezed her hand lightly. "Royal is lucky to have you," he said.

She laughed. "And you. And Cole and Lark and Megan and so many other people who are helping." He signaled a turn. "There's a farm road. We're stopping so I can send the text."

As soon as he stopped he unbuckled his seat belt and reached over to wrap his arms around her and pull her toward him.

"Aaron, what are you doing?"

"Kissing you. I think you're great, Stella," he said. As she started to reply, his mouth covered hers. It was as if he had waited years to kiss her. Startled, she didn't move for a second. Then she wrapped her arm around his neck to hold him while she kissed him in return.

What started out fun and rewarding changed as their desire blossomed. She wound her fingers in his hair, suddenly wanting to be in his arms and have all the constraints out of her way. She wanted Aaron with a need that overwhelmed her. The kiss deepened, became more passionate. She wanted to be in his arms, in his bed, making love. Would it give them a chance to fall in love?

She moaned softly, losing herself in their kiss, running

one hand over his muscled shoulder, holding him with her other arm.

She realized how intense this had become and finally leaned away a fraction. Her breathing was ragged. His light brown eyes had darkened with his passion. Desire was blatant in their depths, a hungry look that fanned the fires of her own longing.

"You did well today. You're taking back another check to help people," he said, his gaze drifting over her face. "When we get back we'll go to dinner and celebrate."

"I'm glad you went with me."

He moved away and she watched as he sent a text. He lowered his phone. "I want to wait a minute in case they answer right away."

His phone beeped and he scanned the message. "You're set for Wednesday," he said, putting away his phone. "We'll go home now."

She had a tingling excitement. Part of it was relief that the talk was over and she had been able to raise some money for Royal. Part of it was wanting Aaron and knowing they would be together longer.

They met again for dinner in the dining room at the inn. Both had changed to sweaters and slacks. Throughout dinner Stella still felt bubbly excitement and when Aaron finally escorted her back to her suite, she paused at her door to put her arms around him and kiss him.

For one startled moment he stood still, but then his arm circled her waist and he kissed her in return. Without breaking the kiss, he took her key card from her, unlocked her door and stepped inside. He picked her up and let the door swing shut while she reached out to hit the light switch.

Relishing being in his arms, she let go of all the problems for a few minutes while they kissed. Their kisses were becoming more passionate, demanding. He set her on her feet and then his hands were in her hair. The long locks tumbled down as the pins dropped away. As he kissed her, his hand slipped beneath her sweater to cup her breast and then lightly caress her.

She moaned, clinging to him, on fire with wanting him. He stepped back, pulling her blue sweater over her head and tossing it aside. He unfastened her bra and cupped her full breasts lightly in his hands. "You're soft," he whispered, leaning down to kiss her and stroke her with his tongue.

She gasped with pleasure, clinging to him, wanting him with her whole being but finally stopping him and picking up her sweater to slip it over her head again.

"Aaron, I need to sort things out before we get more deeply involved, and if we make love, I'll be more involved emotionally."

"I think we're in about as deep as it gets without marriage or a permanent commitment," he said solemnly. His voice was hoarse with passion. "You can 'sort' things out. I want you, Stella. I want you in my arms, in my bed. I want to make love all night."

Every word he said made her want to walk back into his arms, but she stood still, trying to take her time the way she should have when she first met him, before she made a physical commitment. Could they fall in love if she just let go and agreed to marry him? Or would she be the only one to fall in love while Aaron still stayed coolly removed from emotional involvement or commitment?

"Aaron, we really don't know a lot about each other," she said, and that shuttered look came over his expression. A muscle worked in his jaw as he stared at her in silence.

"What would you like to know?" he asked stiffly.

"I don't know enough to ask. I just think we should get to really know each other."

He nodded. "All right, Stella. Whatever you want. Let's eat breakfast together. The more we're together, the better we'll know each other."

"I'll see you at breakfast. Thanks again for today. It was nice to raise the money for people here and to have your moral support in Lubbock today."

"Good. See you at seven in the morning."

"Sure," she said, following him to the door. He turned to look at her and she gazed into his eyes, her heart beginning to drum again as her gaze lowered to his mouth. She wanted his kisses, wanted to stop being cautious, but that's how she had gotten pregnant. Now if she let go, she might fall in love when he wouldn't. Yet, was she going to lose a chance on winning his love because of her caution? She couldn't see any future for them the way things were.

Five

The next morning after breakfast with Stella, Aaron sent text messages to three more Texas Cattleman's Club members in Dallas. Stella had given him permission to plan two meetings, so he wanted to get them arranged as soon as possible.

Next, he drove to the temporary office R&N Builders had set up in Royal. It was a flimsy, hastily built building on a back street. He saw Cole's truck already there and was surprised his partner had returned a little earlier than he had planned.

Seated at one of the small tables that served as a desk, Cole was in his usual boots, jeans and R&N Builders T-shirt. His broad-brimmed black Resistol hung on the hat rack along with his jacket.

"How's Henry?" Aaron asked in greeting.

"He's getting along, but he needs help and he still has a lot of repairs to make. He had appointments with insurance people and an attorney about his brother's estate, so I came back here."

"I'm sorry to hear he still has a lot to do. That's tough. In the best of times there's no end to the work on a ranch."

"You got that right. And he's having a tough time about losing his brother. I figure I'm a good one to stay and give him a hand."

"I'm sure he'll appreciate it. I think a lot of people are glad to have you back in Royal. You didn't go home much before the storm."

"I've avoided being here with Craig and Paige since their marriage. I've gone home occasionally for holidays, but never was real comfortable about it since Craig and I both dated Paige in high school," Cole said, gazing into space. Aaron wondered if Cole still had feelings for Paige or if he had been in love with her when she'd married Craig.

"When the folks died, I came even less often." He turned to look at Aaron. "I'm ready to leave for the TCC. Want to ride with me?"

"I'll drive one of the trucks because I'm going to see Stella for lunch. She raised $12,000 from people in Lubbock yesterday afternoon."

"That's good news. Royal needs whatever we can get. There's still so much to be done."

"Cole, she has an idea—she's worried about Christmas and the people who lost everything, the people with little kids who are having a hard time. She wants to have a Christmas drive to get presents."

"She's right. Those people need help. Christmas is going to be tough."

"She's getting some women together to organize it. Meanwhile TCC has its Christmas festival coming up. Sure, you and I are members of the Dallas TCC, so I don't want to come in and start asking for favors, but I'm going to this time. I thought about talking to Gil and Nathan and a few other members. It might be nice to tie this Christmas present drive to the festival and invite all those people and let them pick up their presents then. What do you think?"

"I think that's a great idea. I'd say do it."

"Also, I think we should ask the Dallas TCC to make a

Christmas contribution to Royal. We could invite Dallas members to the Royal TCC Christmas Festival."

"Another good idea. We know some guys who would be willing to help and are usually generous when it's a good cause. I hope the whole town is invited this year. Everyone needs a party."

"I agree. We can talk to Gil."

"I'd be glad to," Cole replied, standing to get his jacket and hat. "I'll see you at the Cattleman's Club."

Aaron waved as he put his phone to his ear to make a call. When he was done, he stuffed some notes into his jacket pocket and locked up to go to the TCC.

When he arrived at the club, he glanced at the damage to the rambling stone and dark wood structure. Part of the slate roof of the main building had been torn off, but that had already been replaced. Trees had fallen on outbuildings, and many windows had to be replaced. A lot of the water damage had been taken care of early while the outbuildings were still in need of repair.

Aaron knew that repairs had started right away. The sound of hammers and chainsaws had become a fixture in Royal as much as the sight of wrecking trucks hauling away debris. As Aaron parked the R&N truck and climbed out, he saw Cole talking to Nathan Battle. Cole motioned to Aaron to join them.

The tall, brown-haired sheriff shook hands with Aaron. "Glad you're here. Work keeps progressing. We have the windows replaced now and that's a relief. You get tired of looking through plastic and hearing it flap in the wind."

"I told Nathan about Stella's idea for the Christmas drive and how it might be nice to combine it with the TCC Christmas festival," Cole said.

"I think it would be great. It'll add to the festivities. The holidays can be hard enough, as both of you know too well," Nathan said. "This will be a nice way to cheer people up."

"When will Gil be here?" Aaron asked.

"He's inside now," Nathan replied. "Let's go find him. We need the president's approval before you take it to a meeting."

Aaron worked through the morning, sitting in one of the empty meeting rooms. He did take time to make some calls to set up more appointments for Stella. He grinned to himself. She might not like all the appointments he planned to get for her, but he was certain she would rise to the occasion and he would help her.

Hopefully, the makeover might help her self-confidence a little. He would talk to her about dealing with the press and interviews and then see what kind of meetings he could help her get with people who would be willing to contribute to rebuilding Royal.

He had heard people mention her for the role of acting mayor if Mayor Vance didn't recover and someone was needed to step in. He wondered whether she had heard those remarks. He suspected if she had, Stella would dismiss them as ridiculous. She had been too busy to take time to realize that she was already fulfilling the position of acting mayor.

He had to admire her in so many ways. And in private— she was about to become a lot more important to him.

He leaned back in his chair, stretching his legs. Stella was going to have his baby. The thought still shocked him. He wanted this baby to be part of his life. He had lost one child. He didn't want to lose this one. And Stella was the mother of his child. He needed to forget shock and do something nice for her right now. Neither of them were in love, but they liked being together. As he thought about it, he was startled to realize she was the first woman he had truly enjoyed being with since his wife.

That was good enough to build a relationship as far as he was concerned, and Stella was a solid, super person who was appealing and intelligent. She deserved better from him. He glanced at his watch, told Cole he was going to run an errand and left the club to head to the shops in town. He intended to do something for Stella soon. Even if he couldn't give her love, he could help her and be there for her.

Stella decided to start with Paige. They agreed to meet briefly in the small café in the Cozy Inn midmorning over coffee. Stella arrived first and waved when she saw Paige step into the wide doorway. Dressed in jeans, a navy sweater, Western boots and a denim jacket, she crossed the room and sat at the small table across from Stella.

"What's up?"

"Thanks for taking time out of your busy day. I want to ask you a favor. I'm concerned about how hard Christmas will be on the people who lost so much in the storm," she said. "Christmas—any holiday—is a tough time when you've lost loved ones, your home, everything. I know you suffered a devastating loss, so if it upsets you to deal with this, Paige, say so and bow out. I'll understand."

"No. The holiday is going to be hard for a lot of people."

"Well, there are some people here who can't afford to have any kind of Christmas after all they lost. It's another hurt on top of a hurt. This is about the people who can't afford to get presents for their kids, for their families, who'll be alone and don't have much, that sort of thing."

"They should have help. What did you have in mind?"

"A Christmas drive with gifts and maybe monetary donations for them so they can buy things."

"Stella, I think that's grand. Thank goodness we can afford to do things at Christmas. But you're right about some of these people who have been hurt in every sort of way including financially. I think a Christmas drive to get presents would be wonderful. I'm so glad you thought about that."

"Well, what I really want— I need a cochair and you would be perfect if you'd do it. I know you're busy—"

Shaking her auburn hair away from her face, Paige smiled. "Stop there. I think it's a good cause so, yes, I'll cochair this project."

"That's so awesome," Stella said, smiling at her friend. "I can always count on you. I'm going to call some others to be on our committee."

"If you need my help, I can ask some friends for you."

"Here's my list. I've already sent a text to Lark and I left a message. I'll call Megan and my friend Edie."

"I can talk to Beth and Julie. I know Amanda Battle and I think she would help."

"I have my lists. We'll have a Christmas tree in the temporary town hall or I can get some of the merchants to take tags and hang them in their windows. We can make little paper ornaments and hang them on merchant's Christmas trees. Each ornament will match up with a person who will receive a gift. The recipients can choose an ornament and take it home. They'll match up with our master list, so we can tell who gets what present and we won't have to use names. So, for instance, the ornament could read, 'Boy—eight years old' plus a number to match our list and suggested gift ideas. We'll need to have gifts for the adults, too."

"Sounds good to me. We'll need to set up a Christmas-drive fund at one of the banks, so people can get tax credit for their donations," Paige said.

"I can deal with that because I'll be going by the bank anyway," Stella said.

"Fine. You take care of setting up the bank account."

"Paige, I appreciate this so much. I talked to Aaron about it and he'll run it past Cole and the TCC guys. I have a list of people who will probably participate in the drive. I'll email it to you."

"Good. I better run."

"Thanks again. I'll walk out with you. I'm going to the office—our temporary one. I think town hall will be one of the last places to get back to normal."

"There are so many places that still need to get fixed, including the Double R," she said.

"How're you doing running that ranch by yourself?"

"I run it in Craig's place, but not by myself. Our hands have been wonderful. They've really pitched in and gone the extra mile."

"I'm glad. See you soon."

They parted and Stella drove to town hall, trying to focus on work there and stop thinking about Aaron.

It was seven when she went down to meet Aaron in the Cozy Inn dining room, which had gotten to be a daily occurrence. She thought about how much she looked forward to being with him as she glanced once more at her reflection in the mirror in the elevator. Her hair was in a neat bun, every hair in place. She wore a thick pale yellow sweater and dark brown slacks with her practical shoes. The night air was chilly, although it was warm in the inn.

She stepped off the elevator and saw him only a few yards away.

Tonight he was in slacks, a thick navy sweater and Western boots. He looked sexy and appealing and she hoped he asked her to dance.

"You're not in your usual spot tonight. I thought maybe you decided not to come," she said.

"Never. And if something ever does interfere with my

meeting you when I said I would, believe me I'll call and let you know unless I've been knocked unconscious."

She laughed. "I hope not. I had a productive day, did you?"

"Oh, yes, I did. Let's get a table and I'll tell you all about it, because a lot of it concerns you. I'll bet they were pleased at town hall with the checks you got yesterday."

"Oh, my, yes. We have three families that are in a desperate situation and need money for a place to stay. Then some of it will go to buy more supplies where needed. Do you want me to keep going down the list?"

"No need." He paused to talk to the maître d', who led them to a table near the fireplace. Mesquite logs had been tossed in with the other logs and the pungent smell was inviting.

Stella ordered ice water again. When they were alone, she smiled at him. "I saw Paige Richardson today. She agreed to cochair my Christmas-drive committee."

"You didn't waste time getting that going."

"No, we need to as soon as possible. Actually, I kept $2,000 of the check from Lubbock to open a fund at the bank for the Christmas drive. She is recruiting some more members for the committee and I have Megan's and Julie's help."

"I talked to Cole about it and then we talked to Gil Addison and Nathan Battle and the TCC is willing to tie the Christmas drive in with their Christmas festival. They'll invite all the families and children to receive their gifts during the festival."

"That's wonderful, Aaron. Thank you. Paige was going to contact Amanda Battle and see if she will be on our committee."

"That's a good person to contact. So you're off to a roaring start there."

"Now tell me more about the Dallas trip."

"Here comes our waiter and then we'll talk."

They ordered and she waited expectantly. "Next week you have one little fifteen-minute spot on the noon news in Fort Worth. This will be your chance to kick off the Christmas drive and maybe get some donations for it."

"I'm looking forward to getting news out about the Christmas drive."

"Good. That night I have the oil and gas executives lined up. We will meet them for dinner and you can talk to them about the storm and what people need. I know you'll reach them emotionally because you have so many touching stories."

"Thank you. I'll be happy to do all of these things but I still say I wasn't meant to be a fund-raiser," she said, suspecting she wasn't changing his mind at all.

"You'll be great. You'll be fine. You've been doing this sort of thing since the storm. I've seen your interviews. I even taped one. You're a natural."

"Aaron, every cell in your body is filled with self-assurance. You can't possibly understand having butterflies or qualms."

"I have to admit, I'm not burdened with being afraid to talk to others about subjects I know."

Smiling, she shook her head. "I don't know everything about my subject."

"You know as much as anybody else in Royal and more about the storm than about ninety-eight percent of the population. You went through it, for heaven's sake. You were at town hall. You were there for all the nightmarish first hours after the storm and you've been there constantly ever since. I heard you crawled under debris and rescued someone. Is that right?"

"Yes. I could hear the cries. She was under a big slab of

concrete that was held up by rubble. Not fun, but we got her out. It was a twenty-year-old woman."

"That's impressive," he said, studying her as if he hadn't ever seen her before. "If you did that, you can talk to people in an interview. After we eat let's go up to your room or mine and go over ways you can handle the interview."

When their tossed green salads came, Aaron continued to talk. She realized he was giving her good advice on things to do and she soaked up every word, feeling she would do better the next appearance she made.

Aaron kept up his advice and encouragement throughout the meal, and when they were through dinner, Stella didn't want him to stop. "Aaron, why don't we go to my room now and you can continue coaching me?"

"Sure, but a couple of dances first," he said, standing and taking her hand. In minutes she was in his arms, moving with him on the dance floor, relishing dancing, being in his arms.

Aaron was becoming important to her. She was falling in love with him, but would he ever let go and fall in love with her? She felt he always held himself back and she still had that feeling with him. There couldn't be any real love between them until all barriers were gone.

Was she making a mistake by rejecting intimacy when Aaron obviously wanted it, as well as wanted to marry her? The question still constantly plagued her.

In the slow dances, their steps were in perfect unison as if they had danced together for years. Sometimes she felt she had known him well and for a long time. Other times she realized what strangers they were to each other. Sometimes when he got that shuttered look and she could feel him withdrawing, she was certain she should tell him goodbye and get him out of her life now. Yet with a baby between them, breaking off from seeing Aaron was impossible.

When the music ended they left and went to her suite. He got the tape of her interview.

"Want something to drink while we watch?" she asked. "Hot chocolate? Beer?"

"Hot chocolate sounds good. Go easy on the chocolate. I'll help."

They sat on the sofa and he put on the tape. While they watched, Aaron gave her pointers and when the tape ended, he talked about dealing with the press. Removing pins from her hair, he talked about doing interviews. As the first locks fell, she looked up at him.

"You don't need to keep your hair up all the time. You surely don't sleep all night this way."

"Of course not. It wouldn't stay thirty minutes."

"So, we'll just take it down a little early tonight," he said. "Now back to the press. Get their cards and get their names, learn their names when you meet them. They have all sorts of contacts and can open doors for you."

As she listened to him talk, she paid attention, but she was also aware of her hair falling over her back and shoulders, of Aaron's warm breath on her nape and his fingers brushing lightly against her. Every touch added a flame to the fires burning inside. Desire was hot, growing more intense the longer she sat with him. She wanted his kiss.

She should learn what he was telling her, but Aaron's kisses seemed more important. When the bun was completely undone, he placed the pins on a nearby table. He parted her hair, placing thick strands of it over each shoulder as he leaned closer to brush light kisses across her nape.

Catching her breath, she inhaled deeply. Desire built, a hungry need to turn and wrap her arms around him, to kiss him.

She felt his tongue on her nape, his kisses trailing on her skin. He picked her up, lifting her to his lap. She gazed into his brown eyes while her heart raced and she could barely get her breath.

"I want you, Aaron. You make me want you," she whispered. She leaned closer to kiss him, her tongue going deep. Her heartbeat raced as she wrapped her arms around his neck.

His hands slipped lightly beneath her sweater, sliding up to cup her breasts. In minutes he cupped each breast in his hands, caressing her. She moaned with pleasure and need, wanting more of him. She wanted to be alone with him. To make love and shut out the world and the future and just know tonight.

Would that bring him closer to her? Her to him? She couldn't marry him without love, but intimacy might be a way to love.

She tightened her arms, pressing against his solid warmth, holding him as they kissed. His fingers moved over her, touching lightly, caressing her, unfastening snaps, unfastening her bra.

His fingers trailed down over her ribs, down to her slacks. While they kissed, she felt his fingers twisting free buttons. Without breaking their kiss, he picked her up and carried her into her bedroom. Light spilled through the doorway from the front room, providing enough illumination to see. He stood her on her feet by the bed and continued to kiss her, leaning over her, holding her against him as his hand slipped down to take off her slacks.

She stepped out of them and kicked off her shoes, looking up at him for a moment as she gasped for breath.

Combing his fingers into her hair on either side of her face, he looked down at her. "I want you. I want to make love to you all night long."

"Aaron—"

He kissed her again, stopping any protest she might have made, but she wasn't protesting. She wanted him, this strong man who had been at her side for so much now, who was willing to do the honorable thing and marry her. She wanted his love. She wanted him with her, loving her. That might not ever happen if she kept pushing him away.

He tugged her sweater up, pulling it over her head and tossing it aside. Her unfastened bra slipped down and she let it fall to the floor. Cupping her breasts again, he trailed light kisses over her while she clung to him and gasped with pleasure. When he tossed away his sweater, she ran her hands across his chest, stroking his hard muscles, caressing him lightly.

Wanting to steal his heart, she kissed him.

It was an impossible, unreasonable fantasy. Yet she could love him until he found it difficult to resist her and impossible to walk away. Would she ensnare her own heart in trying to win his?

He placed his hands on her waist, stepping back to look at her, his gaze a burning brand. "You're beautiful, so soft," he whispered, and leaned forward to trail kisses over her breasts.

Desire continued to build, to be a fire she couldn't control. She wanted him now and there were no arguments about whether she should or shouldn't make love with him. She unfastened his slacks, letting them fall, and then removed his briefs. He pulled her close, their bare bodies pressed together, and even that wasn't enough. Again, he picked her up and turned to place her on the bed, kneeling and then stretching beside her to kiss her while his hands roamed over her to caress her.

She moaned softly, a sound taken by his kisses. Now union seemed necessary, urgent. Her hands drifted over him, down his smooth back, over his hard butt and along a muscled thigh.

He moved, kneeling beside her, looking at her as his hands played over her and then he trailed kisses over her knees, up the inside of her thighs, parting her legs, kissing and stroking her.

Arching beneath his touch, she wanted more of him. Her eyes were shut as he toyed with her, building need. One of his hands was between her thighs, the other tracing her breasts, light touches that drove her wild until she rose to her knees to kiss and stroke him.

His eyes were stormy, dark with desire. Need shook her because of his intensity. His groan was deep in his throat while his fingers locked in her hair and she held and kissed him, her tongue stroking him slowly. He gasped and slipped his hands beneath her arm to raise her.

He kissed her hard, one arm circling her waist, holding her close against him, his other hand running over her, caressing her and building need to a fever pitch.

She clung to him as she kissed him. "Aaron," she whispered. "Let's make love—"

They fell on the bed and he moved over her as she spread her legs for him and arched to meet him, wanting him physically as much as she wanted his love.

He entered her slowly, filling her, taking his time while he lowered himself, moving close to kiss her.

When he partially withdrew, she raised her hips, clinging to him to draw him back.

"Aaron, I want you," she whispered.

He slowly entered her again, and she gasped with pleasure, thrashing beneath him and running her hands over his back. He loved her with slow deliberation, maintaining control, trying to increase her pleasure as she moved beneath him and her need and desire built. Her pulse roared in her ears as his mouth covered hers again in another hungry kiss that increased her need.

Caught in a compelling desire that drove her beyond thought to just react to every stroke and touch and kiss from him, she tugged him closer, moving faster beneath him.

Beaded in sweat, he rocked with her until she reached a pinnacle and burst over it, rapture pouring over her while she moved wildly. When his control ended, he thrust deeply and fast.

Arching against him, she shuddered with another climax. Letting go, she slowed as ecstasy enveloped her.

"Aaron, love," she cried, without realizing what she had said.

Aaron groaned and finally slowed, his weight coming down partially on her. He turned his head to kiss her lightly.

While each gasped for breath, they lay wrapped in each other's arms. Gradually, their breathing slowed until it was deep and regular. He rolled to his side, keeping her with him.

She opened her eyes to look at him and he kissed her lightly again.

"I don't want to let go of you," he whispered.

"I don't want you to," she answered, trailing her fingers over his chest, feeling rock-solid muscles. She kept her mind closed to everything except the present moment and enjoying being in his arms and having made love with him.

"Stella, if you would marry me, we could have this all the time," he whispered, toying with a lock of her long hair.

She didn't feel like talking and she didn't care to argue, so she kept quiet, still stroking him.

They held each other in a silence that was comfortable for her. She suspected it was for him, too. She knew he wasn't asleep because he continued to play with strands of her hair. He had to know she was awake, because she still ran her fingers lightly over him, touching, caressing, loving him.

"Before I commit to marriage, I will have to be deeply in love and so will you. If that happens, we'll both know it and the rest of the world will know it. We're not at that point. We're not in love with each other," she said, the words sounding bleak to her.

"I still say it could come in marriage."

"I don't want to take that chance," she whispered, hoping she wasn't throwing away her future and her baby's future in a few glib sentences that were easy to say when she was being held close to his heart.

"Think about it. We're good together, Stella."

She raised herself slightly on her elbow, propping her head on her hand, and looked down at him. "You think about it. Do you want a marriage without love?"

Again, she got that look from him as if he had closed a door between them. She felt as if he had just gone away from her, almost as if he had left the room even though he was still right here beside her. An ache came to her heart. Aaron had closed himself off. There was a part of his life he wouldn't share, and with time it could become a wedge between them.

She thought about asking him what made him withdraw into a shell, but she suspected that would only make him do so more and make things worse.

"No, I suppose you're right. I don't want that," he answered, and she heard a note of steel in his voice.

"Maybe things will change if we keep seeing each other."

"I want to be in my child's life, so someday we'll have to work out how we're going to share our baby," he said in a different tone of voice. Why had he changed? Only minutes ago he hadn't been this way. She wondered whether they would ever be truly close, much less truly in love.

She lay down beside him again, her hair spreading on his shoulder as he pulled her close against him, leg against leg, thigh against thigh, her head on the indention between his chest and shoulder. He had proposed. He'd helped her. He wanted to be with her and take her out. What had happened in his life to cause him to let it get between him and someone else he would otherwise be close to in a relationship?

Would he ever feel close enough to her to share whatever he held back from her now?

Six

"Hey, why so solemn?" he asked, nuzzling her neck and making her giggle.

"That's better. Let's go shower and see what happens."

"Evidently you have plans," she said, amused and forgetting the serious life-changing decisions that loomed for her.

He stepped out of bed, scooped her up and carried her to the large bathroom, to stand her on her feet in the roomy tiled shower.

They played and splashed beneath the warm water until he looked at her and his smile faded, desire surfacing in his eyes. He reached out to caress her breasts and she inhaled, placing her hands on his hips and closing her eyes.

He was aroused, ready to love again, and she wanted him. She stroked him, stepping closer to kiss him and hold him. His lips were wet, his face wet, his body warm and wet against hers.

He turned off the water and moved from the shower, taking her hand as she stepped out. Aaron picked up a thick towel, shaking it out and lightly drying her in sensuous strokes that heightened desire. She picked up another fresh towel to dry him, excited by the look in his eyes that clearly revealed desire.

She rubbed the thick white towel over sculpted muscles, down over his flat belly, lightly drawing it across his thick staff.

He groaned, dropping his towel and grabbing hers to toss it away. He scooped her into his arms and carried her back to bed as he kissed her. Their legs were still wet, but she barely noticed and didn't care as she clung to him and kissed him.

He shifted between her legs and then rose up slightly, watching her as he entered her again. She cried out, arching to meet him, reaching for him to pull him back down into her embrace.

They made love frantically as if they never had before and she cried out with her climax.

He climaxed soon after, holding her as he pumped, finally lowering his weight and then rolling on his side to hold her against him.

"Fantastic, Aaron," she whispered, floating in euphoria. "Hot kisses and sexy loving."

"I'll have to agree," he said. "I want to hold you all night."

"No arguments from me on that one."

Once again they were silent and she ran her hand over him, thinking she would never tire of touching him. Aaron brought joy, help, fun, excitement, sex into her life. He was giving her his baby. If only he could give her his love.

"This has cut short all your help with giving interviews and dealing with the press."

"I'm still here and we'll continue. Besides, you're a fast learner."

"You don't really know that, but I'm trying. Aaron, when we fly to Dallas on Tuesday, I want to visit with my mom in Fort Worth. I called her and we made plans to have lunch. She's meeting me on her lunch hour and my grandmother has gone to Abilene to stay a week with my aunt. You're welcome to join us for lunch if you want, but you don't have to do that."

"I'll pass because you don't see her real often, so she may want to talk to you alone. I've got a limo for you—"

"A limo? Aaron, that's ridiculous. I can rent a car at the airport."

"No need. Cole and I have a limo service we use and two men who regularly drive for us. Sid will drive you Tuesday. He'll take you to Fort Worth for lunch and the interview and then he'll drive you back to a shop I recommend in Dallas where you can buy some new dresses. He'll either wait or give you a number and you can call him when you're ready to be picked up."

"I'm beginning to feel like your mistress."

Aaron laughed. "This is for Royal. I expect you to get a lot of donations for the town. Just keep thinking about the good we can do. Now if you would like to be my mistress—"

"Forget that one," she said, and he chuckled.

"We'll get back to talking about business tomorrow. Tonight I have other things on my mind. You don't have any morning sickness, do you?"

"Not a bit so far. I just can't eat as much and sometimes I get sleepy about two in the afternoon."

"Why don't you catch a few winks. The world won't stop spinning if you do. You're vital to Royal, Stella. You've done a superb job, but the world will go on without you for the time it takes you to get a good night's sleep."

"Thank you, Dr. Nichols. How much do I owe you for that advice?"

"About two dozen kisses," he said, and she laughed, pushing him on his back and rolling over on top of him.

"I'm going to pay you now."

"Best collection I'll ever make," he said, wrapping his arms around her.

Aaron stirred and rolled over to look at Stella. She lay on her back, one arm flung out, her hair spread over the pillow. She was covered to her chin by the sheet. Even in her sleep she stayed all covered, which amused him.

She continued to fill in for the mayor. It amazed him how people turned to her for help, everyone from the city treasurer to ordinary citizens. He didn't think Stella was even aware of the scope of what she was doing for the citizens of Royal. She was one of the key people in restoring the town and securing assistance for people. She was willing to accept his help and he could introduce her to so many people who would contribute to rebuilding Royal. He liked being with her. He liked making love with her. She excited him, and the more he got to know her, the more he enjoyed her. If she would agree to marriage, he thought, with time they would come to really love each other.

He thought of Paula and Blake, and the dull pain came as it always did.

Along with it came second thoughts. Maybe he was wrong about never being able to love someone else again. And maybe Stella was right—the only time to marry someone would be if he was as wildly in love as he had been with Paula. If he only married to give his baby a father, and wasn't really in love, that wouldn't be fair to Stella and might not ever be a happy arrangement.

He thought the fact that they got along well now and he liked being with her would be enough. The sex was fantastic. But there was more to life than that.

He sighed. He wanted to know this baby of his. He

wanted to be a dad for his child, to watch him or her grow up. Aaron wanted to be a part of that.

If he didn't marry her, she could marry someone else who would take her far away where Aaron wouldn't get to see his son or daughter often. Maybe he needed to contact one of his lawyers and get some advice. The one thing he was certain about—he did not want to lose his second child.

He lifted a strand of Stella's hair. She excited him and he liked being with her. She was levelheaded, practical. If he gave it a little more time and attention, maybe they could fall in love.

He had been a widower for seven years now. How likely was he to change?

If anyone could work a change, it would be Stella. She had already done some miracles in Royal. If Mayor Vance recovered, someone should tell him exactly how much Stella had stepped in and taken over.

Desire stirred. There might not be love, but there was a growing fiery attraction for both of them. He wanted to be with her and he was going to miss her when he returned to Dallas. Right now that wasn't going to happen—without her being beside him—until after the holidays. He would worry about that when it came time for them to part.

He leaned down to brush a kiss on her temple as he pushed the sheet lower to bare her breasts so he could caress her. Then he shifted to reach her so he could trail light kisses over her full breasts. Beneath those buttoned-up blouses she wore, there were some luscious curves.

She stirred, opened her eyes and blinked. Then she smiled and wrapped her arms around his neck, pulling him down so she could kiss him.

Forgetting his worries, Aaron wrapped his arms around her, drawing her close as he kissed her passionately.

* * *

It was Saturday, but still like a workday for her with all that needed to be done in Royal. She glanced at the clock and sat up, yanking the sheet beneath her arms. Alarmed, she glanced at Aaron. "Aaron, it's nine in the morning," she said, horrified how late they had slept. "Aaron."

He opened his eyes and reached up to pull her down. She wriggled away. "Oh, no, you don't. We've got to get out of this bed."

Looking amused, he drew her to him. "No, we don't. It's Saturday. Come here and let me show you the best possible way to start our weekend."

"Aaron, I work on Saturday. Royal needs all sorts of things. I have a list of things to do."

"Any appointments with people?"

"I don't think so, just things to do."

"Like finding Dobbin and locking up Mr. Sherman's house?"

"Maybe so, but I spend Saturdays doing those things. I don't lollygag in bed."

"Let me show you my way of lollygagging in bed." He pulled her closer.

"Aaron, look—"

He kissed away her words, his hand lightly fondling her, caressing her breast while he kissed her thoroughly. He raised up to roll over so he was above her as he kissed her.

She was stiff in his arms for about ten seconds and then she melted against him, knowing she was lost.

It was two hours later when she grabbed the sheet and stepped out of bed. "Aaron, I'm going to shower alone," she said emphatically. "There are things I think I should do today and if someone came looking for either one of us, I would be mortified."

He grinned. "You shouldn't be. First, it's none of anyone

else's business. Second—and most important—you're passing up a chance to spend a day in bed with me."

She had to laugh. "You do tempt me beyond belief, but I know there are things I can get done and sooner or later someone will ask me to help in some manner. I'm going to shower."

She heard him chuckle as she left the room. When she came out of the shower, he was nowhere around. As she looked through the suite, she realized he must have left.

She found a note and picked it up. In scrawling writing, she read, "Meet me in the dining room in twenty minutes."

"Twenty minutes from when?" she said aloud to no one. She shook her head and went to get dressed to go to the dining room and eat with him.

She spent the day running the errands on her list, making calls, going by the hospital again. At dinner she ate with Aaron, and for a short time after he talked to her more about dealing with the press, until she was in his lap, his kisses ending the coaching session on how to deal with the press.

They had grown more intimate, spent more time together, yet he still shut himself and his past off from her.

She could ask someone else about Aaron, but she wanted him to get close enough to her to stop keeping part of himself shut away. Moments still came when she could sense him emotionally withdrawing and at those times, she thought they would never really be close or deeply in love with each other. Not in love enough to marry.

Why was true intimacy so difficult for Aaron when he was so open about other aspects of his life?

The days leading up to the Dallas trip flew by.

Sunday morning Aaron went to church with her. After the service he stood to one side waiting as people greeted her and stopped to talk briefly.

When she finally joined him to go eat Sunday dinner, he smiled at her.

"What are you smiling about?"

"You. How can you lack one degree of confidence about talking to crowds? You had as long a line of people waiting to speak to you as the preacher did."

She laughed. "You're exaggerating. They were just saying good morning."

"Uh-huh. It looked like an earnest conversation three or four times."

"Maybe one or two had problems."

"Sure, Stella. Sometime today or tomorrow I'll bet you do something about those problems."

"Okay, you win. I still say helping people one-on-one is different from talking to a group of people I don't know and trying to get them to donate to the relief effort in Royal."

He grinned and squeezed her arm lightly. "Let's go eat. We missed breakfast."

By midafternoon she was in bed again with Aaron. She felt giddy, happy, and knew she was in love with him. She might have huge regrets later, but right now, she was having the time of her life with him.

Sunday night while she was in his arms in bed, she turned to look at him. "You should either go home now or plan to get up very early because Monday will be a busy day."

"I'll opt for the get-up-early choice," he drawled, toying with locks of her hair. "The more time with you, the better life is."

"I hope you mean that," she said, suddenly serious.

He shifted to hold her closer. "I mean it or I wouldn't have said it." He kissed her and their conversation ended.

Monday, after breakfast with Aaron, she got back on track with appointments and meetings. Later that afternoon, she had another brief meeting with Paige at the Cozy Inn café.

"Paige, we need to have a meeting with everyone who wants to be on this committee. I've talked to Megan Maguire, Gloria Holt, Keaton's mom, Lark Taylor, Edith Simms—they all volunteered to help us. I told Lark that Keaton's mom had volunteered and Lark said she still wanted to be a volunteer. I think it will all be harmonious."

"Great. I have Beth, Amanda Battle and Julie Kingston. This is such a good idea, Stella. It would have been dreadful if we'd ignored these people at this time of year."

"Someone would have thought of it if we hadn't. But it's especially nice to do this in conjunction with the TCC Christmas festival. Also, I intend to raise some money beyond what we'll need for getting presents. It'll be wonderful to have people bring presents for those who lost so much, but I also want them to get cash to spend as they want to. Everyone wants to give their children something they've selected. Donated presents are wonderful, but giving these families a chance to buy and wrap their own gifts is important, too."

"Another good idea, Stella. You're filled with them."

"'Tis the season. I'll be in Dallas tomorrow and gone for the rest of the week. Aaron has made appointments for me to meet people he thinks will be willing and able to help Royal."

"That's good. I'll take care of the Christmas drive while you're gone. You see if you can get some more donations."

"Thanks for all your help," Stella said, giving Paige's hand a squeeze, always sorry for Paige's losses.

After they parted, Stella went to the hospital. Mayor Vance was improving and now he could have visitors. She knocked lightly on the door and his wife called to come in. The mayor was propped up in bed. His legs were in casts and he was connected to machines with tubes on both sides of the bed.

"He's sitting up now and he's on the mend," his wife said.

"Mayor Vance, I am so happy to see you," Stella said, walking closer. He had always been thin, but now he was far thinner and pale, his dark brown hair a bigger contrast with his pale complexion. His brown eyes were lively and she was glad he was improving.

"Stella, it's good of you to come by. I've heard you've been a regular and I've heard so many good things about you. I could always count on you at the office."

"Thank you. The whole town has pulled together. Support for Royal has poured in—it amazes me and the donations to the Royal storm recovery fund grow steadily."

"That's so good to hear. It doesn't seem possible the tornado happened more than two months ago. It's almost mid-December and here I am still in the hospital."

"At least you're getting better," she said, smiling at him and his wife.

"I've talked with members of the town council. We need an acting mayor and I hope you'll be willing to do it."

"Mayor Vance, thank you for the vote of confidence, but I think there are more qualified people. I'm sure the town council has others in mind."

"I've heard all the things you've been doing and what you did the first twenty-four hours after the storm hit. You're the one, Stella. I'm pushing for you so don't let me down. From the sound of it, you're already doing the job."

"Well, I'll think about it," she said politely, wanting to avoid arguing with him in her first visit with him since the storm. "We've had so much help from other places that it's really wonderful."

She sat and visited a few more minutes and then left. His wife followed her into the hall.

"Stella, thanks again for coming. You've been good to check on him through all this."

"I'm glad to see he's getting better steadily."

"We're grateful. Come again. Think about what he said about filling in for him. He can't go back for a long time."

"I will," Stella said, maintaining a pleasant expression as she left and promptly dismissing the conversation.

Tuesday morning she flew to Dallas with Aaron. He picked up his car at an agency near the airport and they headed to his house in a gated suburb north of the city.

"We'll leave our things at my house. I've got the limo for you, and Sid will drive you to Fort Worth for lunch with your mother and next, to your interview at the Fort Worth TV station. After that he'll drive you back to Dallas to a dress shop while I go to the office. If you're having a makeover, you should have some new clothes. Get four or five dresses and a couple of suits."

"Seriously?" she asked, laughing. "Have you lost it, Aaron? I don't need one new thing, much less a bunch."

"Yes, you do for the people I'll introduce you to."

"When you tell me things like that, I get butterflies again."

"Ignore them and they'll vanish. Buy some new duds and shoes—the whole thing. This is an investment in Royal. Get something elegant, Stella."

She laughed again. "Aaron, you're talking to me, Stella. I don't need to look elegant to climb over debris in Royal."

"You need to look elegant to raise money so we can get rid of the debris in Royal."

She studied his profile, wondering what he was getting her into and if she could do what he wanted. Would it really help Royal? She thought about the money she had raised in Lubbock and took a deep breath. She would give it a try. "You're changing me," she said, thinking about how that was true in every way possible.

He picked up her hand to brush a kiss across her knuckles while he kept his attention on the highway. "Maybe you're changing me, too," he said.

Startled, she focused more intently on him. How had she made even the tiniest change in his life?

He remained focused on his driving, but he had sounded serious when he spoke. Was she really causing any changes in his life? Continually, ordinary things popped up that reminded her how little she really knew about him, and his last remark was just another one of them.

"Aaron, you and I don't really know each other. You don't talk about yourself much," she said, wondering how many times she had told him the same thing before.

"I think you should be grateful for that one. Also, I think we're getting to know each other rather well. We can work on that when we're home alone tonight."

"I didn't mean physically."

"Whoa—that's a letdown. You got me all excited there," he teased.

"Stop. Your imagination is running away with you," she said, and he grinned.

They finally arrived at his neighborhood and went through the security gate. Tall oaks lined the curving drive and she glimpsed an occasional mansion set back on landscaped lawns through the trees.

"This isn't where I pictured you living."

"I'm not sure I want to ask what you pictured."

"Just not this big." She looked at the immaculate lawns with multicolored flowerbeds. In many ways Aaron's everyday life was far removed from her own. Even so, he was doing so much for her, including all he had set up for today.

"Aaron, thanks for doing all this for me. The appointments, the opportunities to help Royal, the salon visit. I appreciate everything."

With a quick glance, he smiled at her. "I'm happy to help because you've been doing a great job."

"The mayor seemed happy with reports he's had of what's been happening and I'm glad. It would be terrible if he felt pressured to get out of the hospital and back to work."

"I'm sure he's getting good reports. I think he'll get more good reports from what you do today."

"You're an optimist, Aaron."

"It's easy where you're concerned," he said, and she smiled at him. "Earlier, I talked to Cecelia at the dress shop and she'll help you. We're friends and I've known her a long time. Pick several things so you have a choice. It'll go on my bill. You don't even have to take my credit card. If you don't choose something, I will, and I promise you, you won't like that."

She shook her head. "Very well, I won't argue with you, because you won't give up. Don't forget, I'm meeting my mom at half past eleven. You're welcome to join us."

"Thanks, but I have a lot of catching up to do at the office and you and your mom will enjoy being by yourselves. What I will do, if you want me to be there, is meet you at the television station for the interview."

"You don't need to drive to Fort Worth to hold my hand through an interview," she said, smiling. "I can do this one alone. Now tonight, you better join me."

"I'll be with you tonight."

"Buying more clothes and going to a salon will be a

whole new experience," she said. "Aaron, I think I can raise just as much money looking the way I already look."

"Humor me. We'll see. I think you can raise more and you'll be more at ease on television for interviews."

"I don't think clothes will make a bit of difference."

He grinned. "Clothes will make all kinds of difference. You go on television without any and you'll get so much money—"

"Aaron, you know what I mean," she interrupted, and they both laughed. She had fun with him and he was helpful to her. She gazed at him and wished she didn't still feel some kind of barrier between them, because he was growing more important to her daily. And she was falling more in love with him daily while she didn't think his feelings toward her had changed at all.

They passed through another set of iron gates after Aaron entered a code. When he drove up a winding drive to a sprawling three-story house, she was shocked at the size and obvious wealth it represented. "You have a magnificent home."

"I'm in the construction business, remember?"

She rode in silence, looking at the mansion that was far too big for one person. It was just another reminder of how little she knew about Aaron and how closed off he was about himself.

When he parked at the back of the house and came around the car to open the door for her, she stepped out. Stella stood quietly staring at him and he paused.

"What?" he asked. "Something's worrying you."

"I don't even know you."

He studied her a moment and then stepped forward, his arm going around her waist as he pulled her against him and kissed her. For a startled moment she was still and then she wrapped her arms around him to return the kiss.

"I'd say you know me," he said to her when he released her.

As she stepped back, she waved her hand at the house. "This is not what I envisioned."

"You'll get accustomed to it. C'mon, let me show you your room," he said, retrieving their bags from the back.

"We'll take a tour later," he said, walking through a kitchen that was big enough to hold her entire suite at the Cozy Inn. It had dark oak walls and some of the state-of-the-art appliances had a dark wood finish.

She walked beside him down a wide hallway, turning as hallways branched off in opposite directions. He stepped into the first open doorway. "How's this?" he asked, placing her bag on a suitcase stand.

She looked around a spacious, beautiful room with Queen Anne furniture, dark and light blue decor and thick area rugs.

"I'll get my mail and you can meet me in the kitchen. As soon as you're ready, we'll go to town. It'll give you more time to shop and I need to get to the office." He stepped closer, placing his hands on her shoulders and lowering his voice. "There are other things I'd rather do this morning, but with your appointments we better stick to business."

"I agree. You check your mail and I'll meet you."

He nodded and left.

Twenty minutes later, he stood waiting in the kitchen when she returned. "The limo's here. C'mon and I'll introduce you to Sid."

When they stepped outside, a brown-haired man who looked to be in his twenties waited by a white limo. He smiled as they walked up.

"Hi, Sid," Aaron said. "Stella, meet Sid Fryer. Sid, this is Ms. Daniels."

"Glad to meet you, Sid," she said.

"She's going to Cecelia's shop later and you can hang

around or give her a number and she'll call you. She'll be there two hours minimum," Aaron instructed.

Stella was surprised. She couldn't imagine spending that much time picking out dresses.

Sid held the limo door for her and she climbed inside, turning to the window as Aaron stepped away and waved.

Sid climbed behind the wheel and they left. When she glanced back, Aaron was already in his car.

"Sid—?"

He glanced at her in the rearview mirror. "Yes, ma'am?"

"Just call me Stella. Everyone does in my hometown of Royal. I just can't be that formal—we'll be together off and on all day."

She could see him grin in the rearview mirror. "Yes, ma'am. Whatever you say."

When Sid turned out of the gated area where Aaron lived, Stella looked behind them and saw Aaron turning the opposite way.

She met her mother in a coffee shop near the high school where her mother was principal. As Stella approached the booth where her mother sat looking at papers on the table, she realized where she got her plain way of dressing and living. Her mother's hair was in a roll, fastened on the back of her head. She wore a brown blouse and skirt, practical low-heel shoes and no makeup. Stella hadn't told her mother about the pregnancy yet and intended to today, but as she looked at her mother bent over her papers, she decided to wait a bit longer, until she had made more definite plans for raising the child. Her mother would probably want to step in and take charge, although she was deeply wrapped up in her job and, in the past few years, had interacted very little with either Stella or her sister.

Stella greeted her mother, gave her a slight hug and a

light kiss on the cheek and slid into the booth across from her. "How are you?" Stella asked.

"So busy with the end of the semester coming. I can only stay an hour because I have a stack of papers on my desk I have to deal with and three appointments with parents this afternoon. How are things in Royal?"

"Slowly improving."

"I've seen you in television clips. It looks as if you're busy. When will the mayor take over again so you won't have to do his job for him?"

"Mom, he was hurt badly and was on the critical list for a long time. The deputy mayor was killed."

"I'm glad I moved out of Royal. You should give it thought."

"I'll do that," she said, reminded again of why she was so much closer to her sister than her mother.

They talked over salads and then her mother gathered up papers and said she had to get back to her office. Stella kissed her goodbye and waited a few minutes before calling Sid for the limo—something she did not want to have to explain to her mother.

Sid drove her to the television station. Everyone she dealt with welcomed her and was so friendly that she was at ease immediately. A smiling receptionist let the host know Stella had arrived and in minutes a smiling blonde appeared and extended her hand.

"Welcome. I'm Natalia Higgens and we're delighted to have you on the show."

"Thank you," Stella said, shaking the woman's hand and relaxing. "I hope this does some good for my hometown."

"We're happy to have you and sorry about Royal. The tornado was dreadful. I think our viewers will be interested and I think you'll get some support. We'll show a short video one of our reporters made after the storm. I'll have some questions for you. People are responsive when someone has been hurt and you have a town filled with people who have been hurt."

"I really appreciate this opportunity to try to get help for Royal."

"We're glad to air your story. If you'll come with me."

Fifteen minutes later, Natalia Higgens made her brief introduction, looking at the camera. "The F4 tornado struck at 4:14 p.m. on October 6th, a Monday." The camera cut to the video the studio had taken after the storm. As soon as the video ended, Natalia turned to ask Stella about Royal.

From the beginning of the interview, Natalia's friendliness put Stella at ease. She answered questions about the storm and the people in Royal, listing places that were badly damaged, giving facts and figures of families hit, the people who died in the storm and the enormous cost of the cleanup.

"If people would like to help, do you have an address?" Natalia asked.

"Yes," Stella replied, giving the address of the bank in Royal where the account had been set up for donations. "Also, the Texas Cattleman's Club of Royal will have a Christmas festival and we hope to be able to provide toys for all the children of families who were so badly hurt by the storm. Some families lost everything—their homes, their livestock, their livelihoods—and we want to help them have a happy holiday," Stella said, smiling into the camera before turning to Natalia.

Before Stella knew it, her fifteen-minute segment was finished.

When the show ended, Natalia turned to Stella. "Thank you. You gave a wonderful presentation today that should get a big response."

"I enjoyed having a chance to do the show and to tell

about our Christmas festival. I'm very excited about that
and the joy it will bring."

"Maybe we can have someone from the Royal and the
Dallas TCC be on our show soon to mention it again."

"That would be wonderful," Stella said.

Natalia got a text, which she scanned quickly. "We're
getting donations. Your bank will be able to total them up
and let you know. Congratulations on getting more help
for Royal."

Stella smiled broadly, happy that the interview went
well, hoping they did get a big response.

After thanking them, telling them goodbye and making arrangements to get a video of the interview, she was
ready to go back to Dallas.

As she left the station, people who worked there stopped
to greet her and wish her success in helping her town.

Exhilarated, she saw Sid holding the door of the limo
as she emerged from the building.

"I watched your interview in the bar down the block
and two guys there said they would send some money to
Royal. Way to go," he said, and she laughed, giving Sid a
high five, which after one startled moment, he returned.

Sid drove to an upscale shopping area in that city. He
parked in front of a redbrick shop with an ornate dark wood
front door flanked by two huge white pots of red hibiscus
and green sweet potato vines that trailed over the sides of
the pots. To one side of the door a large window revealed
an interior of subdued lighting and white and red furniture. The only identifying sign was on the window near the
door. Small gold letters spelled out the name, Chez Cecilia.

Sid hopped out to open her door. "Here's my number.
Just give me a call a few minutes before you want to be
picked up and I'll be right here."

"Thanks, Sid," she said, wondering what Aaron had gotten her into. She went inside the shop—which had soft music playing in the background, thick area rugs, contemporary oil paintings on the walls and ornately framed floor-to-ceiling mirrors—and asked for Cecelia.

A tall, slender brunette appeared, smiling and extending her hand. "You must be Stella. I'm happy to meet you. Let me take your coat," she said, taking Stella's jacket and hanging it up. "Aaron has told me about you."

"That surprises me," Stella said, curious how Aaron knew Cecelia and the dress shop but not wanting to pry. She'd rather Aaron would tell her the things he wanted her to know.

"Surprised me, too. Aaron keeps his world to himself. From what he told me, I think I know what we should show you. Let's get you comfortable. I have a few things picked out. He said you have a dinner date tonight with some people who want to hear about Royal and the storm and how they can help."

"You're right."

"Now make yourself comfortable. Can I get you a soft drink? Coffee or tea? Ice water?"

"Ice water please," she said, thinking this whole excursion was ridiculous, a feeling that changed to dismay when Cecelia began to bring clothes out to show her.

"Just tell me what appeals to you and we'll set it aside for you to try on if you'd like."

Within minutes Stella felt in a daze. Nothing Cecelia brought out looked like anything Stella had ever worn. Necklines were lower; hemlines were higher. Skirts were tighter and material was softer. "Cecelia, I can't imagine myself in these," she said, looking at a green dress of clinging material that had a low-cut cowl neckline and a tight, straight skirt with a slit on one side. "These are so unlike me."

"You may be surprised how nice they'll look on you. These are comfortable dresses, too."

Her dazed feeling increased when she tried on the dresses she selected, yet when she looked in the mirror, she couldn't keep from liking them.

When she tried to stop shopping, Cecilia shook her head. "You need to select an elegant dress for evening. You need two suits. You should have a business dress. Aaron made this very clear and he'll come down and pick something out himself if you don't. You will not want him to do that. Aaron is not into shopping for dresses. Our clothing is tasteful and lovely, but he doesn't select what's appropriate for business unless I help him. Fortunately, he'll listen."

Even as Stella laughed, she was surprised and wondered how Cecelia knew this about Aaron. It hinted at more mysteries in his life before she knew him.

Stella tried on a red silk wool sleeveless dress with a low V-neck that she would have to grow accustomed to because she hadn't worn a dress like this one ever. "Cecilia, this isn't me."

"That's the point, Stella. Aaron wants you to have dresses that will help you present a certain image. From what Aaron has said, you're trying to get help for your town. Believe me, that dress will help you get people's attention. It's beautiful on you."

Stella laughed and shook her head. "Thank you. I feel as if I'm only half-dressed."

"Not at all. You look wonderful."

Stella shook her head and studied her image, which she barely recognized.

"Try it," Cecilia urged. "You don't want Aaron shopping for you."

"No, I don't." She sighed. "I'll take this one."

The next two were far too revealing and she refused. "I

would never feel comfortable even though these are beautiful dresses."

The next was a black dress that had a high neck in front, but was backless as well as sleeveless.

She had to agree with Cecilia that she looked pretty in the dress, but she wondered whether she would ever really wear it.

"You should have this. It's lovely on you," Cecilia said. "I know Aaron would definitely like this one."

She felt like telling Cecilia that she was not buying the dresses to please Aaron, but she wondered if she would be fooling herself in saying that. She finally nodded and agreed to take it, because she had to agree that she looked nice in it.

Not until the business suits was she comfortable in the clothes she tried on. The tailored dark blue and black suits were plain and her type of clothing. Until she tried on blouses to go with them. Once again, it was low necklines, soft, clinging material—so different from her usual button-down collars and cotton shirts.

Finally she was finished and had all her purchases bagged and boxed. She was shocked to look at her watch and see that it was almost four.

Sid came in to pick her purchases up and load them into the limo as Stella thanked Cecelia and the two other women who worked in the shop. Finally she climbed into the limo to return to Aaron's to get ready for dinner with the oil and gas executives who were potential donors.

When she arrived, Aaron was waiting on the drive. After she stepped out of the limo, Aaron and Sid carried her purchases into the house.

When Sid left them, Aaron closed the back door and turned to take her into his arms. "We're supposed to meet the people we're having dinner with in less than two hours. These are the oil and gas executives I told you about."

"Thanks, for setting this up, Aaron."

"I'm glad to, and Cole has made some appointments with potential donors, as well. How was your mother?"

"Busy with her own life."

"Have you told her about your pregnancy?"

"No. She was very unhappy to learn she was going to be a grandmother when my sister had her first baby. I think Mom thought it aged her to suddenly become a grandmother. She's not close to her grandchildren and doesn't really like children in general. My mother is in her own world. To her, my news will not be good news."

"Thank heavens you don't take after her. She's missing out on one of the best parts of life," he said, surprising her that a single guy would express it that way.

"It'll take over half an hour to drive to the restaurant," he continued after a pause. "We better start getting ready. I need to shower and shave."

"In other words, I need to start getting ready now," she said, "because I want to shower."

"We can shower together."

"If we don't leave the house tonight," she said.

He smiled. "We can't afford to stand these people up so we'll get ready and shower separately. Maybe tomorrow we can be together. Cecelia said she thinks I'll like what you bought."

"I don't know myself when I look in the mirror. In those dresses the reflection doesn't look like me, but hopefully, we'll achieve the effect you expect. If not, you wasted a lot of money."

"I think it'll be worth every penny."

"So you better run along and let me get ready."

He nodded, his eyes focused intently on her as he looked

at her mouth. She stepped away. "Bye, Aaron. See you shortly."

"Come here," he said, taking her hand and leading her out to the central hall. "See that first open door on the left? When you're ready, meet me there. I'll wait for you in the library."

"The library. Fine," she said.

"See you soon," he said, brushing a light kiss on her lips and leaving her. She went back to shower and dress in the tailored black suit she had bought earlier with an old blouse that had a high collar—an outfit that she could relax in and be comfortable.

When she was ready, she went to the library to meet Aaron, who was already there waiting. Dressed in a brown suit and dark brown tie, he looked as handsome as he always did. His gaze raked over her and he smiled.

"You look pretty," he said, crossing the room to her. "We have to go, but I know what I'd prefer doing."

"I definitely feel the same, but you're right about having to go."

"Before we do, there's something I want you to have," he said, turning to walk to a chair and pick up a gift that she hadn't noticed before. Wrapped in silver paper, it had a blue silk ribbon tied around it and a big silk bow on top. "This is for you."

Surprised, she looked up at him. "It's not my birthday," she said quietly, startled he was giving her a present.

"You're carrying my baby. That's very special and I want to give you something that you'll always have to celebrate the occasion."

"Aaron, that is so sweet," she said, hugging and kissing him. She wondered about the depth of his feelings for her. He had to care to give her such gifts and do so much for her. As quickly as that thought came and went, another occurred to her—that the makeover and clothes benefited Royal. Was she just a means to an end with him? She looked at the present in her hands. This one was purely for her because of the baby—a sweet gesture, but it still didn't mean he had special feelings for her beyond her motherhood.

Finally she raised her head. "Thank you," she whispered.

"Look at your present," he said. "You don't even know what I'm giving you."

Smiling, she untied the bow and carefully peeled away the paper. She raised the lid to find a black velvet box. She removed it from the gift box, opened it and gasped. "Aaron!" she exclaimed as she looked at a necklace made of gold in the shape of small delicate oak leaves, each with a small diamond for a stem. There was a golden leaf and diamond bracelet to match. "These are beautiful." She looked up at him. "These are so gorgeous. Thank you." She stepped forward to kiss him. He held her in one strong arm and kissed her. In seconds the other arm circled her waist and he leaned over her, still kissing her.

"Want to wear them tonight?"

She looked at her suit. "Yes, I'd love to."

"I tried to get something that you can wear whether it's day or night—in other words, all the time."

"I love this necklace and bracelet. I love that you thought of me and wanted to do this," she said, smiling at him.

"Let me put it on you," he said, and she nodded.

In seconds he stepped back. "Hold out your wrist." When she did, he fastened the bracelet on her slender wrist and kissed her lightly. "We'll celebrate more tonight when we get back home. Stella, a baby is precious. It is a celebration and this is just a tiny token."

"It's more than a token and I'll treasure it always, Aaron. It's absolutely beautiful," she said, thrilled that he was that happy about the baby.

"I'm glad you feel that way."

She nodded. Touched, wishing things were different, she felt her emotions getting out of hand. Tears stung her eyes.

"Ready? Sid's waiting."

"Yes," she answered, turning toward the door. She wanted to wipe her eyes but didn't want Aaron to know she was crying. If only he loved her—then his gift would hold a deeper meaning for her.

Seven

That evening, Stella really wowed her dinner companions. She gave a talk similar to the one in Lubbock, showing pictures of the devastation in Royal, which she had on her iPad. By the time the evening was over, it looked promising that the oil and gas executives were going to publicize Royal's need for financial help and make a large donation. As she and Aaron left the restaurant, she breathed a sigh of relief that her efforts for the town were paying off.

Then they went back to Aaron's house to make love through the night. They were in the big bed in the guest bedroom where she was staying. She wore her necklace and bracelet through the night, but in the morning as Aaron held her in his arms, he touched the necklace lightly. "Put your necklace and bracelet away today. Just leave them here instead of taking them to the salon."

"Sure," she answered, smiling at him.

"Sid has the limo waiting," Aaron said. "Tonight, we're meeting television executives from here in Dallas. These people can do a lot, Stella. Tomorrow we'll fly to Austin. You have a lunch, an interview and a dinner there and then we fly back to Dallas for one more interview at noon on Friday."

"Don't say another word. You'll just stir up my nerves more than ever."

"You're doing great. I'll tell you again, relax and enjoy your day at the salon. You better go now. I'm going to the office and I'll see you tonight. It'll take all day at the salon and, afterward, Sid will take you to the restaurant. Just call me when you're on the way. I'll try to get there before you do. That way we'll be ahead of the people we're meeting, so we can just sit and talk until they get there."

"You're getting me into more things," she said, holding a bag with her new dress and clothes that she would wear to dinner. Aaron grinned.

"You'll look back on all of this and be glad. I promise." He took her arm and they left, pausing while he locked up.

When they greeted her at the salon, she couldn't believe her day was turning out this way. It commenced with a massage. As she relaxed, she thought of the contrast with her life the first night after the tornado and how she had fallen into bed about four in the morning and slept two hours to get up and go back to work helping people.

She had her first manicure and first pedicure, which both seemed unnecessary. In the afternoon she had a facial. Following the facial, a salon attendant washed her hair and passed her over to the stylist to cut and blow-dry her hair. By the time she was done, Stella felt like a different woman. Instead of straight brown hair that fell halfway down her back, her hair was now just inches above shoulder length. It fell in a silky curtain that curled under, with slight bangs that were brushed to one side.

Next, a professional did her makeup and took time to show Stella how to apply it herself.

By late afternoon when she looked in the mirror, Stella couldn't recognize herself. She realized that she had so rarely ever tried makeup and then only lipstick that it gave her an entirely different appearance, although the biggest change was her hair.

The salon women gushed over the transformation that was amazing to her. Finally, she dressed for the evening.

"I really don't even know myself," she told the tall blonde named Gretchen at the reception desk.

"You look gorgeous. Perfect. The dress you brought is also perfect. We hope you love everything—your makeup, your hair and your nails."

She smiled at Gretchen. "I'll admit that I do," she said, pleased by the result and wondering what Aaron would think. "I've had the same hairdo since I was in college. It became a habit and it was easy. It's amazing how different I look," she said, turning slightly to look at herself in the mirror. The red silk dress fit her changing waistline; her old clothes were beginning to feel slightly tight in the waist because of her pregnancy.

She still wore her black wool coat and couldn't see any reason for a new coat. When she thanked them and left, Sid smiled at her as he held the limo door.

"You look great," he said appreciatively. "Mr. Nichols isn't going to know you."

"Thanks, Sid. I don't feel quite like me."

"Might as well make the most of it," he said, and grinned. "You'll turn heads tonight."

"You think? Sid, that would be a first," she admitted, laughing as she climbed into the limo and he closed the door.

Midafternoon Aaron went home to shower and change into a charcoal suit, a custom-made white dress shirt and a red tie. He returned to the office to spend the rest of the day catching up on paperwork. Just as he was ready to leave, he was delayed by a phone call. It only took a few minutes, but he guessed he might not get to the restaurant ahead of Stella, so he sent her a text.

He had received a call from the businessmen who'd had dinner with them last night, and they wanted to donate $20,000 to Royal's relief efforts, which he thought would be another boost to Stella's self-confidence. Aaron knew Stella hadn't faced the fact that she was filling in for the mayor as Royal's representative to the outside world even if it wasn't official. She was filling in and getting better at it all the time.

When he arrived at the restaurant, Aaron parked and hurried across the lot. He wanted to see what transformations they had made at the salon. Whatever they had done, he hoped the bun had disappeared for the evening.

The only people in the lobby besides restaurant employees in black uniforms were a couple standing, looking at a picture of a celebrity who had eaten at the restaurant. He didn't see any sign of Stella. The couple consisted of a tall, black-haired man and a beautiful woman half-turned toward him as she looked at the photograph.

He saw the maître d' and motioned to him to ask him about Stella. As the maître d' approached, Aaron glanced again at the woman. The man had walked away, and she was now standing alone. She was stunning in a red dress that ended at her knees, showing shapely long legs and trim ankles in high-heeled red pumps.

"Sir?" the maître d' asked.

"I'm supposed to meet someone here," he said. "Ms. Daniels."

"Aaron?"

He heard Stella's voice and looked up. The woman in red had turned to face him and he almost looked past her before he realized it was Stella. "She's here," he heard himself say to the maître d'. Aaron had expected a change, but not such a transformation that he didn't recognize her. Desire burst with white heat inside him as he walked over to her.

"I didn't even recognize you," he said, astounded and unable to stop staring at her. The temperature around him climbed. He tried to absorb the fact that this was Stella, because she had changed drastically. He was now looking at a stunning beauty.

"I told you long ago you might need to get your eyes checked," she said, smiling at him and making him feel weak in the knees. "Aaron, it's still me."

"You're going to knock them dead with your looks," he said without even thinking about it.

"I hope not," she said, laughing. "Aaron, you're staring."

"Damn straight, I'm staring. I can't recognize you."

"Get used to it. I'm really no different. I take it you like what you see," she prompted.

"Like? I'm bowled over. Stella, do you recognize yourself?"

"I'll admit it's quite a change. I have to get accustomed to my hair."

"You look fantastic. Wait right here," Aaron said and walked back to the maître d' to talk to him. After a moment, Aaron came back to take her arm. "Come with me," he said. The maître d' smiled at them and turned to lead the way.

"Aaron?" she asked, glancing at him.

"Just a moment, you'll see," he answered her unasked question.

The maître d' stopped to motion them through an open door. They entered an office with a desk covered by papers. The maître d' closed the door behind them.

"I asked where I could be alone with you for a few minutes. He's right outside the door should anyone want in this office."

"What on earth are we doing here?"

"I gave you a necklace and bracelet as a token of a celebration because you're carrying my baby, Stella. It's a relatively simple gold necklace and bracelet that you can wear in the daytime and wear often, which is what I wanted. To celebrate our baby, I also want you to have something very special, because this is a unique time in your life and mine. This present you can't wear as often, but you can wear it tonight," he said, handing her a flat package tied in another blue ribbon.

"You've given me a beautiful present. You didn't need to do this." Her blue eyes were wide as she studied him and then accepted the box. She untied the ribbon and opened the velvet box and gasped. "Aaron. Oh, my heavens. This is beautiful. It's magnificent."

He picked up a diamond necklace that sparkled in the light. "Turn around and I'll put it on," he said.

"I've never had anything like this. I feel as if I need a bodyguard to wear it." She turned and he fastened it around her slender throat, brushing a kiss on her nape, catching a scent that was exotic and new for Stella.

"You've got one—me. There," he said after a moment, turning her to face him, his gaze going over her features. Her blue eyes looked bigger than ever with thick lashes framing them. She didn't have on heavy makeup, just enough to alter her looks, but her hair was what had thrown him off.

And now her figure showed in the red dress, which fit a waistline that still was tiny. The diamonds glittered on her slender throat.

"You're beautiful, and that's an inadequate description. *Stunning* is more like it."

"Thank you. I'm glad you're pleased and thank you for doing this for me."

"Do you like the change?"

"After your reaction, yes, I do. It takes some getting used to. I sort of don't recognize myself, either."

They looked at each other and smiled. "I'd kiss you, but it would mess up that makeup."

"Wait until later."

"We better give the guy back his office. I just wanted a private moment to give the necklace to you."

"It's dazzling. I've never had anything like it."

He took her arm and they stepped out. "Thanks," Aaron said, slipping some folded bills to the maître d'. Then he turned to Stella and said, "Let's go meet your public. You'll wow them and get a bundle for Royal."

"Don't make me jittery," she said, but she sounded far more sure of herself than she had on that first drive to Lubbock.

"Also, I didn't tell you. I got a text from the guys last night. They're sending a check to the Royal storm recovery fund for $20,000."

She turned to gaze at him with wide eyes. "Mercy, Aaron. That's a big amount."

"You just wait and see what you can do for your hometown." He glanced at the maître d'. "We're ready for our table now and you can show the others in when they arrive."

Aaron introduced her to two men and a woman, all executives of a television station. Through salads and dinner Stella told them stories of people affected by the storm. Over dessert, and after-dinner drinks for everyone except Stella, she showed them her presentation on her iPad.

"Stella has suggested a Christmas drive," Aaron said, "to get presents for those who lost everything, for families with children and people still in the hospital."

"That's a wonderful idea," the woman, Molly Vandergrift, said. "I think that would be a great general-interest story. Would you like to appear on our news show and talk about this?"

"I'd love to," Stella replied, meaning it, realizing she was losing the butterflies in her stomach. Along with the change in her appearance and the money that she had already raised, she was gaining more confidence in her ability to talk to people about Royal. And tonight, the three television executives were so friendly, enthusiastic and receptive that she felt even better.

"We're going to try to tie it into the Texas Cattleman's Club Christmas festival in Royal this year," she added.

"That'll be good to have on a show. I know Lars West with the Dallas TCC. We could get him to come on, too, with Stella. Are the TCC here doing anything?"

"They will," Aaron replied. "I've just started talking to them."

"I'm sure the sooner you can do this, the better. I'll send a text now," Molly said, "and see if we can get you on the Friday show."

"That would be grand," Stella answered. "Everyone in Royal will appreciate what you're doing to help." She was aware Aaron had been quieter all evening than he had been in Lubbock, letting her do most of the talking. When she glanced at him, he looked pleased.

Excitement hummed in her because she was going to get so much support for Royal. As the evening wore on, she was even more pleased with her makeover, relieved that she could begin to relax talking to people and enjoy meeting them.

They didn't break up until after ten o'clock. She and Aaron told them goodbye outside as valets brought the cars to the door.

Finally she was alone in Aaron's car with him. He drove out of the lot, but on the drive back, he pulled off the road slightly, put the car in Park and turned to kiss and hug her.

Then he leaned away. "You were fantastic tonight. No butterflies either—right?"

"I think they're gone," she said.

"They'll never come back, either. Awesome evening. You did a whiz-bang job. Watch. The television show will be wonderful for Royal."

"I think so, too," she said, feeling bubbly and excited. "Thanks, Aaron, for all you've done for me. And thank you again for this fabulous necklace that I was aware of all evening."

"You're welcome. Stella, you'll be able to do more and more for Royal."

"I hope so." As he drove home they discussed the evening and what they would do Friday.

The minute they were in the kitchen of his house, Aaron turned her. "You take my breath away," he said.

Her heart skipped a beat as she gazed at him. "Thank you again for the diamonds. They're beautiful."

"That's why I didn't want you to take your gold necklace for tonight. I had something else in mind." He slipped his arms around her and kissed her, his tongue thrusting deeply as he held her. After a while he raised his head. "Go with me to the TCC Christmas festival. Will you?"

"I'd be delighted, thank you," she replied.

He kissed her again, picking her up to carry her to the guest bedroom where she was staying. Still kissing her, he stood her on her feet by the bed. "I can't stop looking at you," he whispered. He drew her to him to kiss her. When he released her, he slid the zipper down the back of her dress and pushed it off her shoulders. As it fell around her feet, he leaned back to look at her. "You changed everything," he said.

"I bought the underwear when I purchased the dress," she said as he unfastened the clasp of the lacy red bra that was a wisp of material and so different from her usual practical cotton underwear.

He placed his hands on her hips and inhaled deeply. "You're gorgeous," he whispered, his eyes raking over her lacy panties down to her thigh-high stockings. She was still in her red pumps.

As he looked at her she unfastened the buttons of his shirt and pushed it off his shoulders. Her hands worked to loosen his belt and then his suit trousers and finally they fell away and she pushed down his briefs to free him.

She stroked him lightly and he inhaled, picking her up. She kicked off her pumps, and he placed her on the bed, switching on a small bedside light before kneeling beside her to shower her with kisses.

As she wound her arms around his neck, she rose up slightly, pulling him to her to kiss him. "Aaron, this is so good," she whispered.

He moved over her, kissing her passionately while she clung to him.

Later, she lay in his arms, held closely against him. "Aaron, you're changing my life."

He shifted on his side to face her, toying with locks of her hair. "You're changing mine, too, you know."

"I suppose," she said, gazing solemnly into his eyes. "I hadn't thought about that, but I guess a baby will change both of us. Even just knowing we'll have a baby will bring changes. I was talking about this week and my makeover, my new clothes, meeting so many people and persuading them to help. Of course, I have the pictures and figures to persuade them."

"You're the cause, more than pictures and numbers. The mayor couldn't have had anyone do a better job." Aaron wound his fingers in her hair.

"It's a long time from now, but do you think you'll be present when our baby is born?"

"I want to be and I hope you want me to be there," he said.

"Yes, I do," she answered, hurting, wishing she had his love. "I want you to be there very much."

He hugged her again. "Then that's decided. I'll be there." They became silent and she wondered if he would still feel the same way when their baby came into the world.

"You're beautiful, Stella," Aaron said hoarsely. He drew her closer against him. "I don't want to let you go," he whispered as his arms tightened around her.

Her face was pressed against his chest and she hugged him in return. "I don't want you to let me go ever," she whispered, certain it was so soft, he couldn't hear her. "Tonight we have each other," she said. "Tomorrow we go home and back to the problems."

When they flew back to Royal on Saturday afternoon, she had eight more big checks to deposit in the Royal storm recovery fund. As they sat in the plane, she was aware of Aaron studying her. "What?" she asked. "You're staring."

"I'm thinking about all the changes in you. Now you'll be the talk of Royal with your makeover, plus the money you're bringing in to help everyone."

She laughed. "I'll be the talk of Royal maybe for five minutes. But the checks will last for quite a while. Aaron, I'm so thrilled over the money. People have been really generous. Thank for your introductions."

"Thanks, Stella, for talking to all of them. You're doing a fantastic job. As for the talk of the town—it'll be longer than five minutes. I suspect some guys are going to ask you out. I think I should make my presence known."

She was tempted to fling *What do you care?* at him.

How much did he care? He acted as if he wanted to be with her. He had done so much for her—in the long run, the results had been for Royal, so she didn't know how much of his motivation came from feelings for her or if it was for the town. Even the jewelry had been for her because she was having his baby—not necessarily because he loved her for herself.

She didn't know any more about what he felt now than she had after their first night together.

The sex was fabulous, but did it mean deeper feelings were taking root with Aaron or was it still simply lust and a good time?.

Aaron would talk to Cole Saturday or Sunday and then she would know if the TCC had made any more decisions about the Christmas festival. It could be so much fun for everyone if they opened it up for all to attend.

She hoped to get into her town house soon and have her own little Christmas tree. Each day she was in Royal, she noticed more trees going up in various places in town. Some Christmases they had had a decorated tree on the lawn of the town hall. She wanted to ask about putting up a Christmas tree on the town-hall lawn this year because she hated for the storm to destroy any customs they had.

"You have appointments for us starting Monday with a lunch in Austin and dinner that night. The next day we go to Houston and Wednesday, we have a noon meeting in Dallas. We won't be back to Royal until after lunch Wednesday. No more until after Christmas, Aaron. I need to be in Royal so I can focus on the Christmas gift drive."

"You'll be back Wednesday afternoon. Then you can start catching up."

After landing she ate with Aaron at the Cozy Inn, sitting and talking until after ten. At the door to her suite, she glanced at him as she inserted the card in the slot. "Want to come in?"

"I thought you'd never ask," he said. He held the door for her and she entered.

She turned to face him. "Want something to drink?"

He walked up to her and pulled her close. "No, thank you. I want you in my arms."

She kissed him, wrapping her arms around his narrow waist, holding him, wondering if they were forging any kind of lasting bond at all.

After appearing in Austin for a TV interview on Monday, they flew to Houston on Tuesday. During the flight, Stella turned to Aaron. He was dressed to meet people as soon as they landed. He had shed his navy suit jacket and loosened his matching tie. He sat across from her with his long legs stretched out in the roomy private jet.

She was comfortable in her new navy suit and matching silk blouse. She, too, had shed her suit jacket.

"Still no morning sickness?" he asked.

"Not at all," she said. "Aaron, I've had three job offers this week."

His eyebrows arched. "Oh? Who wants to hire you?"

"The Barlow Group in Houston. They want me for vice president of public relations. It's a prestigious Texas foundation that raises money for good causes."

"I know who you're talking about. I have a friend on their board. Who else has made an offer?" he asked, frowning slightly as he waited.

"A Dallas charity—Thompkins Charities, Ltd. They also want me for director of public relations."

"Another prestigious group that does a lot of good. That's old oil money. I have several friends there."

"The third one is No Hungry Children in Dallas who

want me for a coordinator-of-services position. The only one I'm considering is the Barlow Group in Houston. I'm seriously thinking about taking that job. It pays more than I make now. It would be in Houston, which would be nice. I can help a lot of people—that would be my dream career."

"Congratulations on the offers. Frankly, you're needed in Royal, though."

"Royal is beginning to mend. They can get along without me."

"People have talked to me and I think the whole town wants you to step in and become acting mayor."

"I definitely don't think it's the whole town. The town council would be the ones to select someone and they haven't said a word to me. I can't imagine the town really wanting me for that role."

"Wednesday we're going back to Royal. Are you moving out of the Cozy Inn Friday?"

"Yes. My town house is all fixed up, so I'm going home. Friday or Saturday I'm getting a Christmas tree and decorating it."

"I have appointments Thursday in Royal and Friday I have to go to Dallas. I hate to leave now, but this is a deal I've worked on since before the storm hit. A wealthy family from back east wants to move to Dallas and build a new home. He was a college buddy, so there is a personal interest. I made a bid for R&N on building it. Now they've finally decided to go with R&N Builders. It's a five-million-dollar house, so I have to see them and be there to sign the contract. Cole could, but that would take him away from Royal and this is really something I've dealt with and I know the family."

"Aaron, go to Dallas," she said, smiling. "That's simple enough."

"That's what I have to do. I just wanted you to know

why. I still can move you in early Friday morning before I go to Dallas. Also, I'll help you get a tree on Saturday if you'd like."

"I'd like your help on the tree," she said, smiling at him. "I don't have a lot to move, so I can move home all by myself. Will you stay in Royal through Christmas and New Year's?"

"Yes. Probably about January 3, I'll go back to Dallas for a little while. I'll still be back and forth."

That thought hurt. She would miss him, but she had known that day was inevitable.

Sadness gripped her and she tightened her fist in her lap. "Next week is the TCC Christmas festival. It should be so much fun, Aaron. We're getting lots of presents and I haven't been there this week, but I've had texts from Lark, from Paige and from Megan Maguire."

"You're right—it will be fun. You'll be shocked by the number of presents that are coming into the TCC. That doesn't count the ones dropped off at businesses, fire stations, all over town."

"We have envelopes with checks for individuals and families that are on our list. I'm so grateful we've been able to do this."

"The Christmas drive is a great idea," he said.

She smiled. "Right now I'm excited over the Christmas festival," she said, thinking it would be another chance for her to spend time with Aaron. When January came and he returned to Dallas, it was going to be hard on her without him. She knew that, but she pushed aside her fears. Friday she would move out of the Cozy Inn. She would never again see it without thinking of Aaron.

Their pilot announced they were approaching the Houston area.

"This is exciting, Aaron. I hope we can raise a lot of money and get more help for Royal," she said, slipping into her suit jacket.

By Wednesday afternoon they had finished the interviews, the dinners, the talks to groups, and were flying back to Royal. Aaron knew some money had been sent directly to Royal, some checks had been given to Stella and some to him. He sat with a pen and pad in hand figuring out a rough total. She remained quiet.

When he raised his head, he smiled. "You've done a wonderful job, Stella. As far as the money, the checks that have been promised and the ones we're taking back with us total approximately a quarter of a million dollars. That's tremendous. I don't think the mayor himself could have done any better."

"I'm just astounded by the help we've received. Some of it was from out-of-state people seeing interviews that got picked up and broadcast nationally. I can't believe I've had three more offers to go on television news and local interest shows after the first of the year."

"You look good on camera."

She laughed. "Don't be ridiculous. That isn't why I'm asked."

"I think that's a big part of it."

"I'm sure that it's much more because Royal has some touching stories."

"They do, but it helps to have a pretty lady tell them."

Shaking her head at him, she changed the topic. "I'm hungry and ready to get my feet on the ground in Royal and have dinner."

"That's easy. Where would you like to eat? I'll take you wherever you'd like to go?"

"After being gone this week, I'm happy to eat at the inn."

"That suits me."

"Good," she answered, certain their lives would change and wondering if Aaron would leave hers.

"We'll be on the ground now in about thirty minutes," he said, and she looked out the window, glad to get back to Royal and home.

"It'll be my last two nights in the Cozy Inn," she said, thinking how soon Aaron would be leaving the hotel, too.

"Stella, would you like for me to go with you to a doctor's appointment?"

"I've got to find a doctor in Royal. I went to Houston to my sister's doctor, but I want a doctor here."

"Definitely. I'd like to go with you and meet the doctor."

"I think that would be nice. I'll ask about a pediatrician here, too. I don't want to drive to Dallas each time I need to see the doctor."

"No, you shouldn't. I'll make arrangements for our plane to take you to Dallas when you need to go, but I think you should have a doctor here."

"Thanks, Aaron. I'm glad you're interested."

"Stella, you'd be surprised if you knew how deep my interest runs. You and this baby are important to me," he said in a serious tone and with a somber look in his brown eyes. Her heart skipped. How much did he really mean that? He had included her with the baby. She figured that he had an interest in his child, but she had no idea of the depth of his feelings for her.

How important was she to him?

Stella went by the hospital Thursday. A doctor was with Mayor Vance, so she couldn't see him. She talked briefly with his wife and found out he was still improving, so Stella said she would come back in a few days. She called on others and talked to Lark briefly about the Christmas drive.

Lark smiled at her. "Stella, I really didn't recognize you at first. Your hair is so different and it changes your whole appearance. I saw you on a Dallas TV show. You were great and you took our case to a big audience. It's wonderful for people here to find out about these agencies and how to access them."

"Some of those agencies were new to me. I didn't know all that help was available."

"The shows should do a lot for us. You got in a plug for the Christmas drive also, which was nice. Speaking of the drive, I think there will be some big presents for people this Christmas."

"I hope so. Some of the stores are donating new TV sets for each family on our list. That'll be a fun present. Other stores are sending enough iPads for each family to have one. It makes me feel good to be able to help. I hope Skye and the baby are getting along."

"We just take everything one day at a time for both of them. There's still no word on Jacob Holt. If you hear anything, please call."

"I will, I promise. I'm home to stay now until Christmas Eve day when I'll go to my sister's."

"You just look beautiful. I love your hair."

"Thanks. You're nice."

"I have a feeling your quiet nights at home that you talk about are over," Lark said, smiling at her.

Stella laughed. "I'll keep in touch on the Christmas drive."

As she left the hospital, outside on the sidewalk, she heard someone call her name. She turned to see Cole headed her way.

"Hey, you look great."

"Thanks, Cole." To her surprise, he smiled at her. Since the storm she had rarely seen Cole smile.

"You're doing a bang-up job for the town. Aaron has let me know. Excellent job."

"Thanks. I'm glad to and I'm thrilled by people's generosity and finding specific agencies that can meet people's needs."

"I just wanted to thank you. See you around."

"That's nice, Cole."

He headed toward the hospital entrance and she wondered whom he was going to see. There were still too many in the hospital because of the storm over two months later.

"Stella, wait up."

She turned to see Lance Higgens, a rancher from the next county and someone she had known most of her life. She smiled at him, feeling kindly because the afternoon of the tornado he had come to Royal to help and that night he had made a $1,000 donation to the relief effort.

"I saw you on television yesterday."

"Good. I guess a lot of people caught that show around here."

"I didn't recognize you until they introduced you. You look great and you did a great job getting attention for Royal. I'd guess you'll get some donations."

"We did, Lance," she said. "We received one right away."

"Good. Listen, there's a barn dance at our town center next Saturday night. Would you like to go with me?"

Startled, she smiled at him. "I'm sorry, I'm going to a dinner that night, but thanks for asking me, Lance. That's very nice."

"Sure. Maybe some other time," he said. "Better go. Good to see you, Stella."

"Good to see you, too," she said, wanting to laugh. He had never looked at her twice before, never asked her to anything even though they had gone through high school together.

Her next stop was the drugstore where she ran into Paige. "Stella!" Paige called, and caught up with her.

"You never come to town. What are you doing here again?" Stella asked, smiling at her friend.

"I didn't plan well for anything this week. I saw you on television yesterday. Word went around that you'd be on—probably thanks to Aaron. You look fantastic and you did a great job. I love your makeover except I hardly know you."

"Thanks. It's the same me."

"Actually, I didn't even recognize you at first glimpse."

"Frankly, I barely recognize myself. The makeover has been fun and brought a bit of attention."

Paige's eyes narrowed. "I'll bet you're getting asked out by guys who never have asked you before."

Stella could feel her cheeks grow hot. "A little," she admitted. "I suppose looks are important to guys."

"Stella, most girls come to that conclusion before they're five years old," Paige remarked, and they both laughed. "We need a brief meeting soon for our Christmas drive to figure out how to coordinate the last-minute details. It's almost here."

"If you have a few minutes," Stella said, "we can go across the street to the café and talk about the drive now."

"Sure. Now's as good a time as any," Paige said. "We're running out of time. Christmas is one week away and the TCC festival is next Tuesday."

They walked to Stella's car, where she picked up her notebook. Then they crossed the street to a new café that had opened since the storm. As soon as they were seated, Stella opened the binder with notes and lists.

"Presents and donations are pouring in and I can add to them with checks I brought back from my talks this week."

"That's fantastic. I'll be there that night and I'll check with the others so we can help pass out envelopes with checks and help people get their presents. I'm sure some of the TCC guys will pitch in."

"I really appreciate all you're doing. I think we've contacted everyone we should and there's been enough publicity that no one will be overlooked. We'll have money or gifts for all the people who've lost so much and lost a loved one— I'm sorry, Paige, to bring that up with you," Stella said.

"It's the reality of life. So many of us live with loss. Lark's sister in a coma, Cole's lost his brother, Henry Markham lost a brother—you know the list. Holidays are tough for people with any big loss—that doesn't have to be because of the tornado—people like Aaron. I suppose that's why he's so sympathetic toward Cole."

"Aaron?"

Paige's gray eyes widened. "Aaron's wife and child."

Stella stared at Paige. "Aaron lost a wife and child?" she repeated, not thinking about how shocked she sounded.

"Aaron hasn't told you? You didn't know that?" Paige asked, frowning. "I thought that was general knowledge. It happened years ago. Maybe I know more about Aaron because of his connection to Cole and Craig."

Stella stared into space, stunned by Paige's revelation. "He's never told me," she said, talking more to herself than Paige. She realized Paige had asked her a question and looked at her. "I'm sorry. What did you say?"

"I'm surprised he hasn't told you. I've always known— Cole and I went to the service. A lot of people in Royal knew. I think his baby was a little over a year old. The little boy and Aaron's wife were killed in a traffic accident. It was sudden—one of those really bad things. He's been single since then. It was six or seven years ago. A long time. I don't think he's dated much since, but I know the two of you have been together. I figured that's because of the storm."

"He doesn't talk about his private life or his past and I don't ask. I figure he'll tell me what he wants me to know."

"Men don't talk about private things as much. Aaron may be one of those who doesn't talk at all. I know at one point Craig said Aaron was having a tough time dealing with his loss."

"Paige, I just stayed at his house in Dallas this week. I didn't see any pictures of a wife and child."

"He may not have any. That wouldn't occur to some men."

"Maybe. I also wasn't all over the house. I was just in the back part and the guest bedroom. We didn't even eat there."

"Well, then, it would be easy to not see any pictures. Especially if he has a big house like Cole. Sorry if finding out about his wife and child upset you."

"Oh, don't be silly. It's common knowledge as you said. I'm glad to know. He's just never talked to me about it. It does explain some things about him. Well, back to this Christmas drive—" Stella said, trying for now to put Aaron and his past out of her thoughts and concentrate on working out last-minute details of the event with Paige.

They worked another fifteen minutes before saying goodbye. Stella watched Paige walk away, a slender, willowy figure with sunlight glinting on her auburn hair, highlighting red strands.

Stella sat in the car, still stunned over Aaron's never mentioning his loss. Now she had the explanation for the barrier he kept between himself and others, the door he closed off when conversations or situations became too personal.

No wonder he held back about personal relationships— he was still in love with his late wife. And he'd lost his baby son. That's why babies were so special to him. Stella was unaware of the tears running down her cheeks. She had to stop seeing so much of Aaron. She couldn't cut him out of her life completely because of their baby, but she saw no future in going out with him. She didn't want to keep dating, because she was falling more deeply in love with him all the time while his emotions, love and loyalties were still back with the wife and child he had lost. She was glad he loved them, but he should have leveled with her.

Tears fell on the back of her hand and she realized she was crying. "Aaron, why didn't you tell me?" she whispered. If he really loved her, he would have shared this hurt with her, shared that very private bit of himself. Love didn't cut someone off and shut them out.

She wiped her hand and got a tissue to dry her eyes and her cheeks. Knowing she would have to pay attention to her driving, she focused on the car lot as she turned the key in the ignition.

She drove to the Cozy Inn and stepped out of the car, gathering packages to take inside. She hoped she didn't see Aaron before she reached her suite. She wanted to compose herself, think about what she would say.

She would have to make some decisions about her life with Aaron.

She would see him tonight at dinner. Once again her life was about to change. The sad part was that she would have to start to cut Aaron out of it and see far less of him.

Stella was tempted to confront him with the information she'd learned and ask why he hadn't told her, but instead she wanted him to tell her voluntarily without her asking about it. There was no way she would accept his marriage proposal when he didn't even trust her enough to tell her something that vital. And if he still loved his first wife with all his heart, Stella didn't want to marry him.

Sadly, he wasn't ready to marry again—at least not for love. He had to love his late wife and child enormously still, maybe to the point of being unable to let go and face that they had gone out of his life forever.

Deep inside, her feelings for him crashed and shattered.

Eight

For their dinner tonight, Stella wore one of her new sweaters—a pale blue V-neck—and black slacks. She wore his gold-leaf necklace and bracelet but fought tears when she put the jewelry on.

She went to meet him, her body tingling at the sight of him while eagerness tinged with sadness gripped her as she crossed the Cozy Inn lobby. Aaron was in a black sweater, jeans and boots. She really just wanted to walk into his embrace, but she had to get over even wanting to do so.

"You're gorgeous, Stella. I've missed seeing you all day."

She smiled at him as he took her arm. As soon as they were seated, she picked up a menu.

After they ordered and were alone, he looked at her intently, his gaze slowly traveling over her. "I can't get used to the change in you. I've seen women change hairdos, men shave their heads and grow mustaches, a lot of things that transform appearances, but yours is the biggest change I've ever seen. I never expected you to change this much. It's fabulous."

"Thank you," she said, beginning to wonder if he would lose interest if she returned to looking the way she always had. The minute she thought about it, she remembered that it wouldn't matter because she was going to see him less often.

"Several people have called to thank me for getting you on television because they've found the agency they need for help."

"Good," she said. It was the first bright bit of news since she had sat down to dinner with him.

"Club members have been getting word out that the entire town is invited to the TCC Christmas festival, so I think we will have a big turnout."

"That is wonderful," she said. "It should be a happy time for people," she said. "For a little while that evening, maybe they can all forget their losses and celebrate the season. I know it's fleeting, but it's better than nothing."

"It's a lot better than nothing. It will help people so much and kids will have a great time. Some of the women are beginning to plan games and things they can do for the kids. It'll be an evening to look back on when we all pulled together and had a great time."

"That's good," she said, and then thought of his loss, sorry that Christmas was probably a bad time for Aaron.

She felt responsible for him staying in Royal for the holidays. She didn't think he would be if she hadn't talked about how it would help others if he would stay and do things for people who needed something at holiday time.

She didn't want to deliberately hurt him. But it had ended between them as far as she was concerned. She had to get over him even though she had fallen in love with him.

How long would it take her to get over Aaron?

"Did you buy a dress for the Christmas festival?" he asked.

"Aaron, I already had a dress," she said, beginning to wonder if he was wound up in her new persona and really didn't have that much interest in the former plain Jane that she was. It was a little annoying. Was he not going to like her if she reverted to her former self? She suspected it didn't matter, because after the Christmas festival she didn't expect to continue the intimate relationship they had. She would see him because of their baby, but it would be a parental relationship and not what they had now. She might be with him a lot where their child was concerned, but they wouldn't be having an affair and she wasn't going to marry a man who was still in love with his deceased wife. Aaron couldn't even talk to her about his wife and baby, so he hadn't let go at all.

"I think you should have something new and special," he said, breaking into her thoughts.

"Don't go shopping for a dress for me," she said. "I have a new dress for the festival I got at Cecilia's shop."

Three people stopped by their table to talk to her and tell her what a great job she had done on television Saturday. As the third one walked away, Aaron smiled at her. "I can see the butterflies are completely gone to another home."

"Yes, they are. Thanks to you."

"No, Stella. You did that yourself. You're the one who's developed poise to deal with people. You're the one who's talking to people, telling them what happened, telling people here how to get help. Oh, no. This isn't me. It's you. You have more confidence now and you're handling things with more certainty. You've brought about the changes in yourself. Maybe not hair and makeup, but confidence and self-assurance, making some of the tough decisions that have to be made about who gets help first. No, this is something you've done yourself."

"Thanks for the vote of confidence."

"I've had several people ask me if I would talk to you about stepping in as acting mayor. They're going to have to find someone soon."

"Now *that* position I'm not qualified for," she said firmly.

"Of course, you are. You're already doing the job. Take

a long look at yourself," he said, and his expression was serious, not the cocky friendliness that he usually exhibited.

"I see an administrative assistant."

"Look again, Stella. The administrative assistant disappeared the afternoon of the storm. You're all but doing Mayor Vance's job now. And I checked. The role will end before you have your baby next summer, so that won't be a problem."

She was thinking half about the job and half about Aaron, who looked incredible. How was she going to break things off with him?

All she had to do was remember than he had not recovered from his loss enough to even talk about it. He could not love anyone else and she hadn't changed her views of marrying without love. She wasn't going to do it.

They ate quietly. She listened to him talk about Royal and the things that had happened in the past few days. Finally, he leaned back in his chair, setting down his glass of water while he gazed at her.

"You're quiet. You've hardly said two words through dinner."

"Part of it was simply listening to you and learning what happened while we were in Dallas. I'm worn-out from the whirlwind week coming on top of everything else I've been doing."

"I think it's more than that. You weren't this quiet yesterday."

They stared at each other and she then looked down at her lap. "Aaron, tomorrow I move back to my town house. We have the festival coming up and we're going together. I want to get through that without any big upsets in my life."

"Why do I feel I'm part of what might be a big upset in your life? I don't see how I can be, but I don't think you'd be so quiet with me if I wasn't."

"I think it would be better if we talk when we're upstairs. This really isn't the place."

"I'd say that's incentive to get going," he said. "Are you ready?"

"Yes," she said. When she stood up, he held her arm lightly and led her from the dining room, stopping to say something to the maître d' and then rejoining her.

At her door to her suite, she invited him inside. When they were in the living room, she turned to face him. "What would you like to drink?"

He shook his head as he closed the space between them. He drew her close to kiss her. She melted into his arms, her heart thudding as she kissed him. She wound her arms around him to hold him close, kissing him in return, her resolutions nagging while she ignored them to kiss him.

She ran her fingers in his short, thick hair at the back of his head. She didn't want to stop kissing. She wanted him in her bed all night long. She thought about his loss and knew she couldn't keep spending days and nights with him or she would be so hopelessly in love she would be unable to say no to him.

Finally she stepped back. Both of them were breathing hard. She felt a tight pang and wanted him badly. Just one more night—the thought taunted her. It was tempting to give in, to step back into his arms and kiss him and forget all the problems.

In the long run, it would be better to break it off right now. She wouldn't be hurt as much. She didn't think he would ever love anyone except the first wife. It had been long enough for him to adjust to his loss better than he had. No one ever got over it, they just learned to deal with it and go on with life.

She could imagine how desperately he wanted this baby after losing his first one. She suspected before long he would start showering her with more presents and pressuring her to marry him—and it would be because of their baby.

She would be glad to have him in their baby's life, but that was where it would have to stop. She couldn't go into a loveless marriage just to please Aaron.

She stared at him, making sure she had his attention and he wasn't thinking about kissing her again. "I can't do this, Aaron. We're not wildly in love. I think this is a purely physical relationship. Frankly, it's lust. If we keep it up, I might fall in love with you."

"So what's wrong with that picture," he said, frowning and placing one hand on his hip.

"Because I don't think you're going to fall in love. This is a physically satisfying relationship that you can walk away from at any point in time. Emotionally, you're not in it. I don't want that. I don't want to be in love with a man who isn't in love with me in return."

"I might fall in love and I think we've been good together, and I think I've been good with you and to you, Stella."

"You've been fantastic and so very good to me. I don't want to stop seeing you, I just want to back off and take a breather from the heavy sex. That isn't like me and I can't do that without my emotions getting all entangled."

His frown disappeared and he stepped closer to place one hand lightly on her hip. "I can back off. Are you going to still let me kiss you?"

His question made her feel ridiculous. "As if I could stop you."

"I don't use force," he said as he leaned forward to brush a light kiss on her lips. "Okay, so we don't go to bed together. You'll set the parameters and send me home when you want me to go. In the meantime, kisses are good. Don't cut me off to the point where we don't even have a chance to fall in love," he whispered as he brushed kisses on her throat, her ear, the corner of her mouth.

She should have been more firm with him, but when he started talking, standing so close, his eyes filled with desire, his voice lowering, coaxing—she couldn't say no or tell him to leave. She would have to sometime during the night, but not for a few minutes. There wasn't any point in ending seeing him before Christmas, because they were going to be thrown together constantly and she didn't want a pall hanging over them.

And she couldn't ever end it entirely because of their baby.

His kiss deepened as his arms tightened around her, holding her against him. He was aroused, kissing her passionately, and she stopped thinking and kissed him in return.

Finally he picked her up. She was about to protest when he sat in the closest chair and held her on his lap, but ended up forgetting her protest and wrapping her arms around his neck to continue kissing him. How was she going to protect her heart?

His hand went beneath her sweater to caress her and in minutes he had both hands on her. When he slipped her sweater over her head, she caught his wrists, taking her sweater from him to pull it on again and slide off his lap.

"Aaron, let's say good-night," she said, facing him as she straightened her sweater.

"This is really what you want?" he asked.

"Tonight, it is. I need some space to think and sort out things."

He nodded. "Sure. Maybe you just need some time off. It's been a great week, Stella. You've done so much. You've been a great representative for Royal."

"Thanks. Thanks for everything," she whispered, scared she would cry or tell him to stay for the night or, worse, walk back into his arms, which was what she wanted.

"See you in the morning, hon," he said, brushing a kiss on her cheek and leaving.

She closed the door behind him and touched her cheek with her hand while tears spilled over. She loved him and this was going to be hard. After Christmas she would break up with him. But she wasn't ruining Christmas for either one of them. Suppose she had a little boy who looked like Aaron and was a reminder of his daddy every day of his life?

She had expected Christmas to be so wonderful. Instead, she was beginning to wonder how she would get through it

"Aaron," she whispered, knowing she was in love. He had been so good to her, helping her in multiple ways, changing her life, really. He was a good guy, honorable, loyal, fun to be with, sexy, loving. Was she making a mistake sending him away? Should she live with him and hope that someday he would love her? Was not telling her about his family an oversight—did he think she already knew because so many did?

She doubted it. She thought it was what gave him the shuttered look, what caused him to throw up an invisible barrier. He still had his heart shut away in memories and loss and she couldn't reach it, much less ever have his love.

Aaron lay in bed in the dark, tossing and turning, his thoughts stormy. He missed Stella. He wanted to make love to her, wanted just to be with her. It was obvious something was bothering her. Why wouldn't she just tell him and let them work it out?

Had it been the gifts? Did she want an engagement ring, instead?

He had proposed that first night he learned she was pregnant, but she had turned him down and she would until he declared he loved her and made a commitment to her with his whole heart. Without talking about it, he knew she was bothered and scared she was falling in love and he wouldn't love her in return.

He liked her and maybe there was love up to a point, but he wasn't into making a total commitment to her. He couldn't tell her he loved her with his whole heart and that was what she wanted to hear. They hadn't talked about it, but he felt he was right.

He enjoyed being with her more than any other woman since Paula. It surprised him to realize he wasn't thinking as often of Paula. He would always love her and Blake and always miss them. He knew every time February 5 came around that it would have been Blake's birthday. It always hurt and it always would.

All the more reason he wanted Stella in his life—because this baby was his and he wasn't losing his second child. All he had to do was tell Stella he loved her with his whole heart. But he couldn't; he had to be truthful about it. He was trying to back off and give her room, let her think things through. Why wouldn't she settle for what they had, which was very good. They might fall in love in time and he might be able to handle his loss better. But that wasn't good enough for Stella, because she wouldn't take a chance on falling in love later.

Stella had some strong beliefs and held to them firmly.

Tossing back the covers, he got out of bed. This was his first night away from her for a little while, and he was miserable. What would he feel like in January when they parted for maybe months at a time?

Aaron felt caged in the small suite at the Cozy Inn. At home he would just go to his gym and work out hard enough that he had to concentrate on what he was doing until he was so exhausted he would welcome bed and sleep. Even without her. He couldn't do that here. Knowledge that she was sleeping nearby disturbed him. He could go to her easily, but she would just say no.

Stella was intelligent. He figured at some point she would see they were compatible, the sex was fantastic and she surely would see that, hands down, it would be best for her baby to have a daddy—a daddy who would love him or her and be able to provide well for all of them.

Then he thought about Stella's makeover. He had heard enough talk—guys in Royal had asked her out since she had been back in town after their first trip to Dallas. Trey Kramer had even asked Aaron if they were dating because he wanted to ask her out if she wasn't committed. That didn't thrill him. He had told Trey that he was dating Stella, but when he returned to work in Dallas in January, Aaron expected her to be asked out often by several men.

The thought annoyed him. He didn't want to think about her with other men and he didn't want the mother of his child marrying another man. He realized on the latter point, he was being selfish. If he couldn't make a real commitment to her, he needed to let her go.

He suspected she was going to walk out of his life if he didn't do something. The notion hurt and depressed him.

He paced the suite, hoping he didn't disturb people on the floor below. He tried to do some paperwork, but he couldn't stop thinking about Stella.

It was after four in the morning when he fell asleep. He woke at six when he heard his phone ring, indicating he'd received a text. Instantly awake, Aaron picked up his phone to read the message, which was from Stella.

I have very little to move. Mostly clothes. I've loaded my car and checked out. I won't need any help, but thanks anyway. I'll keep in touch and see you Tuesday evening when we go to the TCC Christmas festival.

She didn't want to see him until Tuesday evening for the party. He had a feeling that she was breaking up with him. The day after the festival would be Christmas Eve when she would fly out of Royal to go to her sister's in Austin. Aaron stared at her message. In effect, she was saying goodbye.

At least as much as she could say goodbye when she was pregnant with his baby. One thing was clear: she had moved on from spending nights with him. No more passion and lovemaking, maybe not even kisses.

He was hurt, but he could understand why she was acting this way. He should accept what she wanted. He needed to go on with his life and adjust to Stella not being a part of it.

He did some additional paperwork, then after a while picked up his phone again to make calls. Soon he had moved his Dallas appointment until later in the day so he didn't have to leave Royal as early. He showered, shaved and dressed, ordering room service for a quick breakfast while he made more calls.

He may have to tell Stella goodbye this week, but before that happened, there was one last thing he could do for her. Hurting, he picked up the phone to make another call.

As soon as the hospital allowed visitors that morning, Aaron went to see Mayor Vance.

After he finished his business in Dallas later that afternoon, Aaron went home to gather some things to take back to Royal with him. He paused to call Stella. He had tried several times during the day, but she had never answered and she didn't now.

He suspected she didn't want to talk to him, because

she kept her phone available constantly in case someone in Royal needed help.

Certain he wouldn't even see her, he decided to stay at home in Dallas Friday night and go back Saturday. He wouldn't have even gone then except he had appointments in Royal all day Saturday to talk to people about the upcoming appointment of an acting mayor.

He already missed Stella and felt as if he had been away from her for a long time when it really wasn't even twenty-four hours yet.

He wondered whether she was thinking seriously about taking the Houston job offer. It would be a good job, but Aaron knew so many people in Royal wanted her to take the acting mayor position—including the mayor, who had now talked to the town council about it.

That night Aaron couldn't get her on her phone. When she didn't answer at one in the morning, he gave up, but he wondered where she was and who she was with. He missed her. She had filled an empty place in his life. He sat thinking about her—beautiful, intelligent, fun to be with, sexy—she was all that he wanted in a woman. Had he fallen in love with her without realizing it?

The idea shook him. He went to his kitchen and got a beer and then walked back to the guest bedroom downstairs where she had stayed when she had been at his house. He thought about being in bed with her, holding her in his arms.

He missed her terribly and he didn't want to tell her goodbye. It shocked him to think about it, and decided that he was in love with her. Why hadn't he seen it before now? He'd wanted to be with her day and night.

When he recognized that he loved Stella, he also saw he might be on the verge of losing her. She was a strong woman with her own standards and views and so far she had turned him down on marriage. Plus, she was considering accepting a very good position in Houston, which was a long way from Dallas.

He was in love with her and she was going to have his baby. He didn't want to lose her. He ran his hand over his short hair while he thought about what he could do to win her love. She'd accused him of proposing out of a sense of duty instead of love, which was exactly what he had done at the time. But he had spent a lot of time with her since then. There had been intimacy between them, hours together. They had worked together regarding Royal, had fun being together.

Why hadn't he seen that his feelings for her were growing stronger? He admired her; he respected and desired her. She was all the things he wanted in a woman. He had to win her love.

While he had never heard a declaration of love from Stella, she had to feel something for him. She acted as if she did. He was certain she would never have gone to bed with him with only casual feelings about him. That would be totally unlike her. Was she in love, too?

Had he already tossed away his chance with her?

He stood and moved impatiently to a window to gaze out at the lit grounds of his estate. If nothing else he would see her Tuesday night when he took her to the TCC Christmas festival. He wished he could move things up or go back to last week, but he couldn't.

He walked down the hall to his office. Crossing the room, he switched on a desk lamp and picked up a picture of his wife and child. "Paula, I've fallen in love. I think you'd approve. You'd like Stella and she would like you."

He realized that the pain of his loss had dulled slightly and he could look at Paula's picture and know that he loved

Stella also. He set the picture on the desk, picked up his beer and walked out of the room, switching off the light.

He wanted to see Stella, to kiss her, to tell her he loved her. This time when he proposed, he would try to do it right. Was she going to turn him down a second time?

Next Tuesday was the TCC Christmas festival, a special time. The town was getting ready to appoint an acting mayor and they wanted Stella, but she just didn't realize how many wanted her and how sincere they were about it.

If he had lost her love, there still was something good that he could do for her.

Saturday morning Stella selected a Christmas tree, getting one slightly taller than usual. As soon as she had set it up on a table by the window across the room from her fireplace, she got out her decorations. Her phone chimed and she glanced at it to see a call from Aaron. She didn't take it. She would talk to him soon enough Tuesday night; right now she still felt on a rocky edge. Aaron could get to her too easily. She wanted to be firm when she was with him. After Tuesday night, she really didn't expect to go out with him again except in the new year when she had to talk to him about their baby.

She placed her hand on her tummy, which was still flat. Her clothes had gotten just the slightest bit tighter in the waist, but otherwise, she was having an easy pregnancy so far.

She was excited about the Christmas drive, which was going even better than she had expected. The presents were piling up at the TCC. Paige had told her that each day now, TCC members picked up presents from drop-off points around town and took them to the club to place around the big Christmas tree.

She tried to avoid thinking about Aaron, but that was

impossible. She wasn't sleeping well, which wasn't good since she was pregnant. After Tuesday, maybe it would be easier to adjust because they wouldn't be in each other's lives as much.

She talked to her sister and learned their mother would be in Austin Christmas Eve, too. Stella checked again on her flight, scheduled to leave Christmas Eve and come back Christmas afternoon.

Aaron finally stopped calling on Monday and she heard nothing from him Tuesday. He must have caught on that she didn't want contact with him. She assumed he would still pick her up, but if he didn't show by six-thirty, she would go on her own. According to their earlier plans, he would come by for her at 6:15 p.m., which was early because the celebration did not begin until six-thirty. Her anticipation had dropped since she had parted with Aaron. She just wanted to get through the evening, leave the next day for Austin and try to pick up her life without Aaron.

For the first time in her life, Stella had her hair done at the Saint Tropez Salon. The salon was on the east side of town, which had escaped most of the storm damage.

As she dressed, a glimmer of the enthusiasm she had originally experienced for the night returned. It was exciting to have a party and to know it would be so good for so many people who had been hurt in the storm. It cheered her to know that all the families would have presents and money and hope for a nice Christmas.

On a personal level, she hoped things weren't tense all evening with Aaron, but she thought both of them would have enough friends around that they could set their worries aside and enjoy the party. And Aaron might not care as much as she did that they would be saying goodbye.

She guessed Aaron would ask about her job offers. She

still had not accepted the job offer in Houston. Every time she reached for the phone to talk to them, she pulled back.

Getting ready, she paused in front of the full-length mirror to look at herself. She wore the red dress she had worn before. One other new dress still hung in the closet, but the red dress was a Christmas color and it should be fine for the evening. When she put it on, the waist felt tighter. It was still comfortable, but she thought this was the last time she would wear the red dress until next winter.

Thinking it would be more appropriate for this party and also draw less attention, she wore the gold and diamond necklace. Once again, she wondered if Aaron was more interested in the person she had become after the makeover and all that had happened since, or the plain person she really was.

She made up her face as they had taught her at the salon, but when she started to put something on her lips, she stared at herself and put away the makeup, leaving her lips without any. She studied herself and was satisfied with her appearance.

She heard the buzzer and went to the door to meet Aaron. When sadness threatened to overwhelm her, she took a deep breath, thought of all the gifts people would be receiving tonight and opened the door with the certainty that this was the last time she would go out with Aaron Nichols.

Nine

Looking every inch the military man in civilian clothes, ready for a semiformal party, Aaron stood straight, handsome and neat with his short dark blond hair. Wearing a flawless navy suit and tie and a white shirt with gold cuff links, he made her heart beat faster.

"I've missed you," he said.

Her lips firmed and she tried to hang on to her emotions. "This is a night we've both looked forward to for a long time. Come in and I'll get my purse and coat."

"You're stunning, Stella," he said as he stepped inside and closed the door behind him. "I'm glad you wore your necklace."

"It's lovely, Aaron."

He studied her intently and she tilted her head, puzzled by his expression.

"So what are you thinking?"

"That you're the most gorgeous woman in the state of Texas."

His remark made her want to laugh and made her want to cry. It was a reminder of one of the reasons it was going to hurt so much to tell him goodbye. "A wee exaggeration, but thank you. I'm glad you think so."

"Tonight should be fun," he said. "Let's go enjoy the evening."

"We're early, but there may be things to do."

He pulled her close. "I don't want to mess up your makeup so I won't kiss you now, but I'm going to make up for it later."

She pulled his head down to kiss him for just a minute and then released him. "Nothing on my lips—see. I'm not messed up."

"No, you're hot, beautiful and I want you in my arms, Stella," he said in a husky voice with a solemn expression that might indicate he expected her to tell him goodbye tonight.

"C'mon, Aaron. We have a party to go to." He held her coat and then took her arm to go to his car.

When they arrived at the Texas Cattleman's Club, she was amazed to see the cars that had already filled the lot and were parked along the long drive all the way back down to the street.

"Aaron, it looks like most of the people in Royal are here. Wasn't this scheduled to start at six-thirty tonight?"

"It was. I can't believe they already have such a huge turnout."

"I never would have imagined it," she said. "I know the TCC invited everyone in Royal, but I never dreamed they would all come. Did you?"

"The town's pulled together since the storm—neighbor helping neighbor. I think everyone is interested."

"I'm surprised. This isn't what I expected."

"It's what I expected and hoped for." A valet opened the door for her and she stepped out. Aaron came around to take her arm. Once inside the clubhouse, she glanced around at the rich, dark wood, the animal heads that had been mounted long ago when it was strictly a men's club. Now women were members and there was a children's center that had a reputation for being one of the finest in Texas. They paused by a coatroom where Aaron checked their coats and then he turned to take her arm again.

They headed for the great room that served for parties, events, dances and other club-wide activities. The sound of voices grew louder as they walked down the hall.

When they stepped inside the great room, a cheer went up, followed by thunderous applause. Stunned, Stella froze, staring at the smiling crowd. Everywhere she looked, people held signs that read, Stella for Acting Mayor, We Want Stella, and Thanks, Stella.

The TCC president, Gil Addison, appeared at her side. "Welcome, Stella."

Dazed, she tried to fathom what this was all about. She looked at Gil.

"This little surprise is to show you the support you have from the entire town of Royal. We all want you to accept the position of acting mayor until an election can be held and a new mayor chosen."

"I'm speechless," she said, smiling and waving at people.

"Stella, I have a letter from the mayor that I want to read to you and to all," Gil said. "Let's go up to the front."

"Did you know about this?" she asked, turning to Aaron. He grinned and gave her a hug.

"A little," he said, and she realized that Aaron might have been behind organizing this gathering of townspeople.

Gil smiled. "Aaron, you come with us," Gil said, and led the way. There was an aisle cleared to the stage at the front of the room.

As she approached the stage, people greeted her and shook her hand and she smiled, thanking them. Dazed, she couldn't quell her surprise.

At the front as she climbed the three steps to the stage,

more people greeted her. She shook hands with the town council and other city dignitaries. The sheriff greeted her, and the heads of different agencies in town crowded around to say hello.

"Stella, Stella, Stella," several people in the audience began chanting and in seconds, the entire room was chanting her name. She saw her friends Paige and Edie in the front row, smiling and waving.

"Mercy, Aaron, what is all this?" Dazed, embarrassed, she turned to Gil. "Gil—" She gave up trying to talk with all the chanting. Smiling, she waved at everyone.

Gil stepped forward and held up his hands for quiet. "Thanks to all of you for coming out tonight. The Texas Cattleman's Club is happy to have nearly everyone in Royal come celebrate the Christmas season and the holidays. We have a bit of business we wanted to discuss before the partying begins."

The crowd had become silent and Gil had a lapel mike so it was easy to hear him. "We have some people onstage—I imagine everyone here knows them, but in case they don't, I want to briefly tell you who is here. Please save your applause until I finish. I'll start with our sheriff, Nathan Battle." Gil ran through the list, reeling off the names of the town council members and heads of various agencies, and when he was done, the audience applauded.

"Now as you know, Mayor Vance was critically injured by the tornado. He is off the critical list—" Gil paused while people clapped. "He is still in the hospital and unable to join us tonight, but he has sent a letter for me to read, which I will do now.

'To the residents of Royal,
I am still recovering from the storm and most deeply

grateful to be alive and that my family survived. My deepest sympathy goes out to those who lost their loved ones, their homes, their herds or crops. We were hurt in so many ways, but from the first moment after the storm, people have helped each other.

It was with deep regret that I learned that Deputy Mayor Max Rothschild was also killed by the tornado. Since I will not be able to return to this job for a few more months, Royal will temporarily need an acting mayor. I have talked to our city officials, agency heads and concerned citizens, and one name comes up often and we are all in agreement. I hope we can persuade Ms. Stella Daniels to accept this position.'"

Gil paused to let people applaud and cheer. The noise was making her ears ring. Just then, Aaron leaned close to whisper in her ear, "I told you everyone wants you."

She smiled and threw kisses and waved, then put her hand down, hoping Gil could calm the crowd. She was stunned by the turnout and the crowd's enthusiastic support—for the first time in her life, she felt accepted by everyone. She glanced at Aaron, who smiled and winked at her, and she was certain he was the one behind this crowd that had gathered.

Gil raised his hand for quiet. "Folks, there's more from Mayor Vance.

'Please persuade Ms. Stella Daniels to accept this position. Since the first moments after the storm Stella has been doing my job. Now that I have recovered enough to read the mail I receive, I have had texts, emails, letters and cards that mention Stella and all she is doing for Royal and its citizens. I urge

Stella to accept this position and I am heartily supported by the town council, other officials of Royal and by its citizens.

Merry Christmas. Best wishes for your holiday,

The Honorable Richard Vance, Mayor of Royal, Texas.'"

There was another round of cheers and applause and Gil motioned for quiet. "At this point, I'm turning the meeting over to Nathan Battle."

Nathan received applause and motioned for quiet. "Thanks. I volunteered to do this part of the program. Royal needs an acting mayor." Nathan turned to Stella. "Stella, I think you can see that Mayor Vance, the town council and the whole town of Royal would like you to accept this position that will end in a few months when Mayor Vance can return to work. Will you be acting mayor of Royal?"

Feeling even more dazed, she looked up at Nathan Battle's dark brown eyes. Taking a deep breath, she smiled at him. "Yes, I'll accept the job of acting mayor until Mayor Vance gets back to work."

Her last words were drowned out by cheers and applause. Nathan shook her hand as he smiled. "Congratulations," he shouted. He stepped back and applauded as she turned and Aaron gave her a brief hug.

Everyone onstage shook her hand and tried to say a few words to her. The audience still cheered so she waved her hands for quiet.

"I want to thank all of you for this show of support. I'm stunned and amazed. I'll try my best to do what I can for Royal, as so many of you are doing. Let's all work together and, hopefully, we can get this town back in shape far sooner than anyone expected. Thank you so very much."

As the crowd applauded, Gil stepped forward and motioned for quiet again. "One more thing at this time. We can go from here to the dining hall. There's a buffet with lots of tables of food. Everyone can eat and during dessert we'll have Stella perform her first task as acting mayor and make presentations of gifts. There will be singing of Christmas carols in the dining room and then dancing back in this room, games in other rooms and the children's center will be open for the little ones. We have staff to take care of the babies. Now let's adjourn to the dining hall."

They applauded and Stella started down the steps to shake hands with people and talk to them. She lost track of Aaron until he showed up at her side and handed her a glass of ice water.

Gratefully, she sipped it and continued moving through the crowd toward the dining room. "You did this," she said to him.

"All I did was tell people we would do this tonight. No one would have come tonight if they hadn't wanted you for acting mayor and hadn't wanted to thank and support you."

"Aaron, I don't know what to say. I'm still reeling in shock."

"Congratulations. Now you'll get paid a little more for what you've been doing anyway. That's the thing, Stella. You're already doing this job and you have been for the past two months."

"If people know I'm pregnant, they might not want me for the job."

"It's most likely only for a couple more months and you're doing great so far."

"How many more surprises do you have in store tonight, Aaron?"

"I'm working on that one," he said, and she rolled her

eyes. "The band is coming in now. Let's head to the dining room and nibble on something while they set up."

"I don't know how long I'm going to feel dazed."

"It'll wear off and life will go right back to normal. You'll see."

Cole suddenly appeared in front of her. "Congratulations, Stella. You deserve to have the official title since you're doing all the work that goes with it."

"Thank you for coming tonight, Cole. I appreciate everyone showing their support. I had no idea."

"Well, Aaron organized this and I'm glad to be here because you should have this position. Just keep up what you're doing," he said, smiling at her.

"Thanks so much," she said.

"I'm touched you came tonight, Cole. I'm really amazed."

"I wouldn't have missed this."

As they moved on, she leaned closer to Aaron. "I'll remember this night all my life. I'll go see Mayor Vance tomorrow and thank him. But I suppose my biggest thanks goes to you. You must have been really busy talking to everyone."

"It didn't take any persuasion on my part. Everyone thought you'd be the best person for the job."

"Well, I'm amazed and touched by that, too. I just did what needed to be done, like hundreds of other people in Royal."

Gil Addison appeared again. "Stella. As acting mayor you should take charge of the next event on tonight's schedule. We'd like to tell people to pick up their envelopes and their presents whenever they want. Some families have little children and they won't want to stay long. Also, as acting mayor, you really should be at the head of the food line."

"I don't want to cut in front of people," she said, laughing and shaking her head. "I'll just get in line."

"Enjoy the few little perks you get with this job," Gil said. "There won't be many."

As they headed toward the dining room, people continued to stop and congratulate her. Paige walked up while the Battles talked to Aaron.

"You look gorgeous," she said. "Your necklace and bracelet are beautiful."

"Thank you. Aaron gave them to me."

"Aaron? I'm surprised, but glad Aaron is coming out of his shell. All our lives are changing, some in major ways, some in tiny ones, but the storm was a major upheaval for all of us. At least it looks as if we're all pulling together."

"I'm astounded, but oh, so thrilled. Thanks, Paige, for your part in this evening."

"Whatever I can do, I'm glad to. After I eat, I'll be at the table with the envelopes we're giving out. Members of the TCC will help us and we're doing this in shifts."

"Great, thanks."

Paige moved on and Aaron took Stella's arm to walk to the dining room. Enticing smells of hot bread, turkey and ham filled the air, and the dining room had three lines of long tables laden with food. The rest of the room was filled with tables covered in red or green paper where people could sit. At the back of the room was a huge decorated Christmas tree. Presents surrounded it, spilling out in front of it, lining the wall behind it. There appeared to be hundreds of wrapped presents. Paige, Lark, Edie, Megan and four TCC members sat at two tables to hand out envelopes of money some families would be receiving.

Gil appeared again. "Stella, you're the guest of honor—you get to go to the head of the line."

"I feel ridiculous doing that."

"We need you to go anyway so you can make the announcement about the gifts. Aaron, you go with her. Everyone's waiting for you to start."

Aaron took her arm as they followed Gil to the head of a line.

She had little appetite, but she ate some of the catered food that was there in abundance—turkey, dressing, mashed potatoes and cream gravy, ham, roasts, barbecued ribs, hot biscuits, thick golden corn bread, pickled peaches, an endless variety.

When they finished, Gil excused himself and left the table. He was back in minutes to sit and lean closer to talk to Stella. "We're ready to start matching people up with their gifts. People can pick up their things all evening long until eleven-thirty. The volunteers will change shifts at regular intervals so no one has to spend the whole evening handing out presents. If you're ready, I'll announce you. Aaron, go onstage. You'll be next about the Dallas TCC."

"Sure," she said. "Excuse me," she said to Nathan Battle, who sat beside her.

At the front of the room, Gil called for everyone's attention. "As I think all of you know, some people in Royal lost everything in the storm. A good number of Royal residents have been badly hit. So many of us wanted to do something about that. This was Stella's idea and I'll let her tell you more about it—" He handed a mike to Stella.

"As you all know," Stella began, "we decided to do a Christmas drive to provide presents and support for the people who need it most. All the Texas Cattleman Club's members, along with the ladies from the Christmas-drive committee volunteered to help. Those who could do so, both from Royal and other parts of Texas have contributed generously so everyone in Royal can have a wonderful holiday.

"Each family receiving gifts tonight has been assigned a number. First, go over to the table where the volunteers are seated near the west wall and pick up the envelope that matches your number. That envelope is for you and your family. Also, there are gifts that correspond to those numbers under the Christmas tree and along the back wall. Just go see a volunteer, who will help you. You get both an envelope plus the wrapped gifts that correspond to your number.

"We want to give a huge thanks to all who contributed money, time and effort to this drive to make sure everyone has a merry Christmas. Thank you."

People applauded and Stella started to sit, but Gil appeared and motioned her to wait. He took the mike. "I have one more important announcement—some really good news for us. Aaron Nichols and Cole Richardson are members of the Dallas, Texas, Cattleman's Club, but they are spending so much time and money in Royal trying to help us rebuild the town that the Texas Cattleman's Club of Royal invited them to join, which they did. Aaron Nichols and Cole will tell you about the rest. Aaron," Gil said, and handed the mike to Aaron while everyone applauded.

"Thanks. We're glad to help. This is Cole's hometown and I feel like it's mine now, too, because I've been here so much and everyone is so friendly. We've talked to some of our TCC friends in Dallas. I'll let Cole finish this." Aaron handed the mike to Cole, who received applause.

"It's good to be home again." He received more applause and waved his hand for quiet as he smiled. "We have friends here tonight from the Dallas TCC. They told us today that they wanted to make a presentation tonight. I want to introduce Lars West, Sam Thompkins and Rod

Jenkins. C'mon, guys," he said as each man waved and smiled at the audience.

Tall with thick brown hair, Lars West stepped forward. "Thanks, Cole. We know the TCC suffered damage along with so much of Royal. We talked to our Dallas TCC and we want to present a check to the TCC here in Royal," he said, turning to Gil Addison. "We'd like the Royal TCC to have a check for two million dollars to use for Royal storm aid however the TCC here sees fit."

The last of his words were drowned out by applause as the audience came to their feet and gave him a standing ovation.

Aaron motioned to Stella to join him and he introduced her to the men from Dallas. "Thank you," she said. "That's an incredibly generous gift and will do so much good for Royal."

"We hope so. We wanted to do something," Sam said.

They talked a few more minutes and then left the stage while Cole lingered and turned to Stella.

"I was about to go home," Cole said. "I thought Aaron could do this by himself, but he talked me into staying for the presentation. There are other Dallas TCC members here for a fun night. These three guys insist on going back to Dallas tonight, so we're all leaving now," Cole told them as Gil shook hands and thanked the Dallas TCC members.

"Cole, again, thanks so much for coming out," Stella said.

"I want to thank you, too," Aaron added.

"I hope all of this tonight brightened everybody's Christmas," Cole said. He left the stage to join the TCC Dallas members, moving through the crowd. He passed near Paige Richardson, speaking to her, and she smiled, speaking in return, both of them looking cordial as they passed each other.

Gil left to put the check in a safe place. Aaron took Stella's arm to go back to the great room where a band played and people danced. People stopped to congratulate Stella, to thank her. Some thanked Aaron for the TCC Dallas contribution.

"I'm going to dance with you before we leave here," Aaron said.

"I just hope we didn't miss anyone tonight in terms of the presents and money we're giving to families."

"Everyone could sign up who felt the need and some people signed up friends who wouldn't come in and sign up themselves. I don't think anyone got overlooked, but there's no way to really know," he said. "And with that, let's close this chapter on Royal's recovery for tonight and concentrate on you and me."

Startled, Stella looked up at him.

"Let's dance," he said, taking her into his arms. "We can't leave early, Stella. All these people came for you and they'll expect you to stay and have a good time. They'll want to speak to you."

"Aaron, in some ways," she said as she danced with him, "all my life I've felt sort of like an outsider. I've always been plain—I grew up that way and my mother is that way. For the first time tonight, I feel really accepted by everyone."

"You're accepted, believe me. Stella, people are so grateful to you. I've talked to them, and they're grateful for all you've done. And as for plain—just look in the mirror."

"You did that for me," she said solemnly, thinking the evening would have been so wonderful if she'd had Aaron's love. It was a subject she had shut out of her mind over and over since their arrival at the club tonight. Tears threatened again and she no longer felt like dancing.

"Aaron, I need a moment," she said, stepping away from him. She knew the clubhouse from being there with members for various events and she hurried off the dance floor and out of the room, heading for one of the small clubrooms that would be empty on a night like this. Tears stung her eyes and she tried to control them, wiping them off her cheeks.

A hand closed on her arm and Aaron stopped her. He saw her tears and frowned.

"C'mon," he said, holding her arm and walking down the hall to enter a darkened meeting room. Hanging a sign, Meeting in Progress, on the outside knob and switching on a small lamp, he closed the door.

She wiped her eyes frantically and took deep breaths.

He turned to face her, walking to her and placing his hands on his hips. "I was going to wait until we went home tonight to talk to you, but I think we better talk right now. What started out to be a great, fun evening for you has turned sour in a big way."

"Aaron, we can't talk here."

"Yes, we can." He stepped close and slipped one arm around her waist. His other hand tilted her chin up as he gazed into her eyes. "This is long overdue, but as the old saying goes, sometimes you can't see the forest for the trees. I've missed you and I've been miserable without you. I love you, Stella."

Startled, she frowned as she stared at him. "You're saying that—I don't think you mean it. It's one of those nice and honorable things you do."

"No. I'm not saying it to be nice and not out of honor. It's out of love. After I lost Paula and Blake, I didn't think I would ever love again. I didn't think I could. I was wrong, because there's always room in the heart for love. I just couldn't even see that I had fallen in love with you."

Shocked, she stared at him. "Aaron, I didn't know about your wife and son until this past week."

He frowned. "I thought everyone around here knew that. I just didn't talk about it."

"That's been a barrier between us, hasn't it?"

"It was, but it's not now. I'm in love with you. I want to marry you and if you'd found out today that you're not really pregnant, I would still tell you the same thing. I love you. When I lost Paula and Blake, I didn't want to live, either. I hurt every minute of every day for so long. When I finally did go out with a woman, I think it was three or four years later and after the date, I just wanted to go home and be alone."

She hurt for him, but she remained silent because Aaron was opening himself up completely to her and gone was the shuttered look and the feeling that a wall had come between them.

"I finally began to socialize, but I just never got close to anyone until you came along. I soon realized that you were the first woman I'd enjoyed being around since Paula. I also noticed I didn't hurt as much and I didn't think about her as much.

"Stella, I will always love Paula and Blake. There's room in my heart for more love—for you, for our baby. I love you and I have been miserable without you and it's my own fault for shutting you out, but I just didn't even realize I was falling in love with you."

"Aaron," she said, her happiness spilling over.

He pulled her close, leaning down to kiss her, a hungry, passionate kiss as if he had been waiting years to do this.

Joyously she clung to him and kissed him. "I love you, Aaron. I missed you, but I want your love. I just want you to be able to share the good and the bad, the hurts, the happiness, everything in your life with me and me with you. That's love, Aaron."

He held her so tightly she could barely breathe. "You mean everything to me. I just couldn't even recognize what I felt until I saw I was losing you. Thank goodness I haven't."

"No, you haven't. You have my heart. I love you, Aaron. I've loved you almost from the very first."

"Stella, wait." He knelt on one knee and held her hand. "Stella Daniels, will you marry me?" he asked, pulling a box from his jacket pocket and holding it out to her.

"Aaron." She laughed, feeling giddy and bubbly. "Yes, I'll marry you, Aaron Nichols. For goodness' sake, get up," she said, taking the box from him. "What is this, Aaron?"

She opened the box and gasped. Aaron took out the ten-carat-diamond-and-emerald ring he had bought. He held her hand and slipped the ring onto her finger. "Perfect," he said, looking into her eyes. "Everything is perfect, Stella. I will tell you I love you so many times each day you'll grow tired of hearing it."

"Impossible," she said, looking at the dazzling ring. "Oh, Aaron, I'm overwhelmed. This is the most beautiful ring. I can't believe it's mine."

"It is definitely yours. Stella, I love you. Also, I'm going to love our baby so very much. This child is a gift and a blessing for me. The loss of my first child—I can't tell you how badly that hurt and I never dreamed I'd marry and have another baby."

"We'll both be blessed by this child. I'm so glad. From the first moment, I thought this would be the biggest thrill in my life if I had your love when I found out we would have a baby."

"You have my love," he said, hugging her and then kissing her. After a few minutes, he leaned away. "C'mon. I think it's time for an announcement."

She laughed again. "Aaron, I'm used to staying in the background, being quiet and unnoticed. My life is undergoing every kind of transformation. I don't even know myself anymore in so many ways.

"I'm announcing this engagement to keep the guys away from you. I've even had them ask me if I cared if they asked you out. Yes, I cared. I wanted to punch one of them."

She laughed, shaking her head as he took her hand.

"C'mon. I'm making an announcement and then all those guys will stay away from my fiancée."

When he said *my fiancée*, joy bubbled in her as she hurried beside him.

"Stella, let's get married soon."

"You need to meet my family. I should meet yours."

"You will. I'll take you to Paris soon to meet them. Either before or after the wedding, whichever you want."

"You're changing my life in every way."

In the great room, when the band stopped between pieces, Aaron found Gil. Stella couldn't believe what was happening, but Gil motioned to the band and hurried to talk to them.

He turned to the dancers and people seated at small tables around the edge of the room. There was a roll from the drummer and people became quiet. "Ladies and gentlemen," Gil said. "May I have your attention? We have a brief announcement."

Stella shook her head. "Aaron, you started this," she said, and he grinned.

Aaron stepped forward, but Stella moved quickly to take the mike from a surprised Gil. "Folks," she said, smiling at Aaron as he took her hand. "I'd like to make my first announcement as acting mayor. I'd like to announce my engagement to Aaron Nichols," she proclaimed, laughing and looking at Aaron.

As everyone applauded and cheered, Aaron turned to slip his arm around her and kiss her briefly, causing more applause and whistles.

When he released her, he took the mike. "Now we can all go back to partying! Merry Christmas, everybody!"

There was another round of applause as the band began to play.

"Thanks, Gil," Aaron said, handing back the mike. "Let's go dance," he said to Stella. "Two dances and then we start calling family."

It was a fast piece and she danced with Aaron, having a wonderful time. She wanted him and was certain they would go home and make love. When the number ended, people crowded around them to congratulate her and look at her ring. She left the dance floor to let them and remained talking to friends until Aaron rescued her a whole number later.

"Instead of dancing some more, how about going to your place?"

"I'll beat you to the door," she said, teasing him, and he laughed. "I have to get my purse and start thanking people."

"Everybody is partying. Save the thank-you for one you can write on a Christmas card or wedding announcement or something."

"You're right about everyone partying," she said. "You win. Let's go."

He took her hand and she got her purse. They stopped

to get their coats and then at the door they waited while a valet brought Aaron's car.

Everybody who passed them congratulated her on becoming acting mayor and on her engagement.

When they drove away from the club, she turned toward him slightly. It was quiet and cozy in his car. "Aaron, this has been the most wonderful night of my life," she said. "Thanks to you."

"I'm glad. Let's have this wedding soon."

"That's what I'd like."

"I don't care whether we have a large or small one."

"My parents will want no part of a large wedding. I got my plain way of life from my mother."

"If you prefer a large wedding, have it. I'll pay for it and help you."

She squeezed his knee lightly. "Thank you. That's very nice. What about you?"

"I don't care. Mom and Dad will do whatever we want. So will my brother."

"Probably a small wedding and maybe a large reception. After tonight, I feel I have to invite the entire town of Royal to the reception."

"I agree. That was nice of everyone. All the people I talked to were enthused, everybody wanted you to be acting mayor. Stella, I didn't find anyone who didn't want you. Mayor Vance definitely wanted you."

"That makes me feel so good. I can't tell you. In high school I was sort of left out of things socially. I guess I always have been."

"Not now. You'll never be left out of anything with me."

"I think you're speeding. I'd hate for the new acting mayor to get pulled over the first few hours I have the job."

"I want to get home to be alone with you," he said as he slowed.

In minutes they reached her town house. "My trunk is filled with Christmas gifts. I'm not carrying them in tonight. I'll get them in the morning," he said.

"I have to go shopping tomorrow. I've been so busy I haven't gotten all my presents and I don't have any for you yet. I really didn't expect to be with you Christmas."

"But now you will be if I can talk you into it. How disappointed will your sister be if you don't come this year and we spend Christmas here, just the two of us?"

"With three kids, she won't care. We can go sometime during the holidays. We can call her."

"We sure can, but later. I have other plans when I close the door."

"Do you really?" she teased.

He parked where she directed him to and came around to open her door. As soon as they stepped into her entryway, Aaron closed the door behind him and turned to pull her into his embrace, giving a kiss that was filled with love and longing.

Later Stella lay in his arms while he toyed with her hair. The covers were pulled up under her arms.

Aaron stretched out his arm to pick up his phone and get a calendar. "Let's set a date now."

"Aaron," she said, trailing her fingers along his jaw, "since I just accepted the job of acting mayor, I feel a responsibility for Royal. I'll have to live here until I'm no longer acting mayor."

"I'm here all the time anyway. I'll work from here and go to Dallas when I feel I need to. We can build a house here if you want. Remember, that is my business."

"Whatever you'd like. When my job ends, I don't mind moving to Dallas."

"We'll work it all out. I just want to be with you."

"Our honeymoon may have to come after baby is here," she said.

"Baby is here," he echoed. "Stella, I've told you before and I'll tell you again—I'm overjoyed about the baby. I lost Blake and he was one of the big loves of my life. I have a second chance here to be a dad. I'm thrilled and I hope you are."

"I am. Do you particularly want another little boy?"

"No, I don't care," he said, and she smiled, relieved and happy that he didn't have his heart set on having a boy.

"Just a baby. I can't tell you." His voice had gotten deep and she realized he was emotional about the baby he'd lost. She hugged him and rose up to kiss him, tasting a salty tear. His hurt caused her heart to ache. "Aaron, I'm so glad about this baby. And we can have more."

He pulled her down to kiss her hard. When he released her, she saw he had a better grip on his emotions. "For a tough, military-type guy, you're very tenderhearted," she said.

"I am thrilled beyond words to be a dad. That's why I got those necklaces for you. I love you, Stella."

"I love you," she responded.

"Now let's set a date for a wedding. How about a wedding between Christmas and New Year's? That's a quiet time. January won't be."

"You're right. I'd say a very quiet wedding after Christmas. Can you do that, Mr. Nichols?"

"I can. Want to fly to Dallas next week to get a wedding dress from Cecilia? That'll be a Christmas present to you."

She smiled. "Your love is my Christmas present. Your

love, your baby, this fabulous ring. Aaron, I love you with all my heart. I give you my love for Christmas." Joy filled her while she looked into his brown eyes.

"Merry, merry Christmas, darling," he said as he wrapped his arms around her and pulled her close to kiss her.

Happiness filled her heart and after a moment she looked up at him. "Your love is the best Christmas gift possible." She felt joyous to be in Aaron's strong arms and to know she had his love always.

* * * * *

TEXAS CATTLEMAN'S CLUB:
AFTER THE STORM
Don't miss a single story!

STRANDED WITH THE RANCHER
by Janice Maynard
SHELTERED BY THE MILLIONAIRE
by Catherine Mann
PREGNANT BY THE TEXAN
by Sara Orwig
BECAUSE OF THE BABY...
by Cat Schield
HIS LOST AND FOUND FAMILY
by Sarah M. Anderson
MORE THAN A CONVENIENT BRIDE
by Michelle Celmer
FOR HIS BROTHER'S WIFE
by Kathie DeNosky

MILLS & BOON®
By Request

RELIVE THE ROMANCE WITH THE BEST OF THE BEST

A sneak peek at next month's titles...

In stores from 15th December 2016:

- **Unbiddable Attraction** – Kathie DeNosky, Robyn Grady & Barbara Dunlop

In stores from 29th December 2016:

- **Matched to Mr Right** – Kat Cantrell

- **His Ultimate Demand** – Maya Blake, Dani Collins & Victoria Parker

- **Capturing Her Heart** – Leanne Banks & Cindy Kirk

Just can't wait?
Buy our books online a month before they hit the shops!
www.millsandboon.co.uk

Also available as eBooks.

Give a 12 month subscription
to a friend today!

Call Customer Services
0844 844 1358*

or visit
millsandboon.co.uk/subscriptions

*** This call will cost you 7 pence per minute plus your
phone company's price per minute access charge.**

MILLS & BOON®

Why shop at millsandboon.co.uk?

Each year, thousands of romance readers find their perfect read at millsandboon.co.uk. That's because we're passionate about bringing you the very best romantic fiction. Here are some of the advantages of shopping at www.millsandboon.co.uk:

* **Get new books first**—you'll be able to buy your favourite books one month before they hit the shops

* **Get exclusive discounts**—you'll also be able to buy our specially created monthly collections, with up to 50% off the RRP

* **Find your favourite authors**—latest news, interviews and new releases for all your favourite authors and series on our website, plus ideas for what to try next

* **Join in**—once you've bought your favourite books, don't forget to register with us to rate, review and join in the discussions

Visit **www.millsandboon.co.uk**
for all this and more today!

MILLS_WEB